By Birth a Lady

by

George Manville Fenn

By Birth a Lady
by George Manville Fenn

ISBN: 978-93-59959-25-2

Published by

DOUBLE 9 BOOKS

2/13-B, Ansari Road
Daryaganj, New Delhi – 110002
info@double9books.com
www.double9books.com
Tel. 011-40042856

ABOUT THE AUTHOR

George Manville Fenn was a very productive author of novels, a writer, an editor, and an educator from England. He was born on January 3, 1831, in Pimlico, London. He mostly learned on his own; he taught himself Italian, French, and German. During the years 1851-1854, he went to Battersea Training College for Teachers and then became the head of a state school in Alford, Lincolnshire. In the early 1850s, Fenn started to write short stories and pieces for newspapers and magazines. The Old Forest Ranger, his first book, came out in 1856. Afterward, he wrote more than 100 books, many of them for teenagers and young adults. He was one of the most famous writers of his time, and his books were well-liked and read by many people. I also worked as a reporter and writer for Fenn. Among the newspapers and magazines, he worked for was The Boy's Own Paper, which he ran from 1866 to 1874. He worked hard to make children's books better and was a strong supporter of education and reading. The Englishman Fenn passed away on August 26, 1909, in Isleworth.

CONTENTS

Volume Two

Volume Three

VOLUME ONE

Chapter One
Something about a Letter

"He mustn't have so much corn, Joseph," said Mr Tiddson, parish doctor of Croppley Magna, addressing a grinning boy of sixteen, who, with his smock-frock rolled up and twisted round his waist, was holding the bridle of a very thin, dejected-looking pony, whose mane and tail seemed to have gone to the cushion-maker's, leaving in their places a few strands that had missed the shears. The pony's eyes were half shut, and his nose hung low; but, as if attending to his master's words, one ear was twitched back, while the other pointed forward; and no sooner had his owner finished speaking than the poor little beast whinnied softly and shook its evidently remonstrating head. "He mustn't have so much corn, Joseph," said Mr Tiddson importantly. "He's growing wild and vicious, and it was as much as I could do this morning to hold him."

"What did he do, *zir?*" said the boy, grinning a wider grin.

"Do, Joseph? He wanted to go after the hounds, and took the bit in his teeth, and kicked when they crossed the road. I shall have to diet him. Give him some water, Joseph, but no corn."

The poor pony might well shake his head, for it was a standing joke in Croppley that the doctor tried experiments on that pony: feeding him with chaff kept in an oaty bag, and keeping him low and grey hound-like of rib, for the sake of speed when a union patient was ill.

But the pony had to be fetched out again before Joseph had removed his saddle; for just as Mr Tiddson was taking off his gloves and overcoat, a man came running up to the door, and tore at the bell, panting the while with his exertions.

"Well, what now? Is Betty Starger worse?"

"No," —puff— "no, sir;" —puff— "it's—it's—"

"Well? Why don't you speak, man?"

"Breath, sir!" —puff. "Run—all way!—puff."

"Yes, yes," said Mr Tiddson. "And now what is it?"

"Hax—haxiden, sir," puffed the messenger.

"Bless my soul, my good man! Where?" exclaimed the doctor, rubbing his hands.

"Down by Crossroads, sir; and they war takin' a gate off the hinges to lay him on, and carry him to the Seven Bells, when I run for you, sir."

"And how was it?—and who is it?" said the doctor.

"Gent, sir; along o' the hounds."

"Here, stop a minute," exclaimed the doctor, ringing furiously till a servant came. "Jane, tell Joseph to bring Peter round directly; I'm wanted.— Now go on, my good man," he continued.

"See him comin' myself, sir. Dogs had gone over the fallows, givin' mouth bea-u-u-tiful, when he comes—this gent, you know—full tear, lifts his horse, clears the hedge, and drops into the lane—Rugley-lane, you know, sir, where the cutting is, with the sand-martins' nestes in the bank. Well, sir, he comes down nice as could be, and then put his horse at t'other bank, as it couldn't be expected to get up, though it did try; and then, before you know'd it, down it come back'ards, right on to the poor gent, and rolled over him, so that when three or four on us got up he was as white and still as your 'ankychy, sir, that he war; and so I come off arter you. And you ain't got sech a thing as a drop o' beer in the house, have you, sir?"

"No, my man, I have not," said Mr Tiddson, mounting his steed, which had just been brought round to the front; "but if you will call at my surgery when I return, I daresay I can find you a glass of something. —Go on, Peter."

But Peter did not seem disposed to go on; and it was not until his bare ribs had been drummed by the doctor's heels, and he had been smitten between the ears by the doctor's umbrella, that he condescended to shuffle off in a shambling trot—a pace that put the messenger to no inconvenience to keep alongside, since it was only about half the rate at which he had brought the news.

To have seen Mr, or, as he was generally called, *Dr* Tiddson ride, any one would have called to mind the printed form upon his medicine labels— "To be well shaken;" for he was well shaken in the process, and had at short intervals to push forward his hat, which made a point of getting down over his ears. But, though not effectively, Dr Tiddson and his pony Peter managed to shuffle over the ground, and arrived at the Seven Bells—a little roadside inn—just as four labouring men bore a gate to the door, and then, carefully lifting an insensible figure, carried it into the parlour, where a mattress had been prepared by the landlady.

Dr Tiddson did not have an accident to tend every day, while those he did have to do with were the mishaps of very ordinary people. This, then, was something to make him descend from his pony with the greatest of dignity, throwing the reins to the messenger, and entering the little parlour as if monarch of all he surveyed.

"Tut—tut—tut!" he exclaimed. "Clear the room directly; the man wants air. Mrs Pottles, send every one out, and lock that door."

The sympathising landlady obeyed, and then the examination commenced.

"Hum!" muttered the doctor. "Ribs crushed—two, four, certainly; probable laceration of the right lobe; concussion of the brain, evidently. And what have we here? Dear me! A sad case, Mrs Pottles; a fracture of the clavicle, I fear."

"Lawk a deary me! Poor gentleman! he 'ave got it bad," said the landlady, raising her hands.

"Yes, Mrs Pottles," said the doctor, compressing his lips, "it is, I fear, a serious case. But we must do what we can, Mrs Pottles—we must do what we can."

"Of course we must, sir!" exclaimed the landlady. "And what shall us do first?"

"Let me see; another pillow, I think, Mrs Pottles," said the doctor, not heeding the question. "He will not be able to leave here for some time to come."

Mrs Pottles sighed; and then from time to time supplied the doctor with bandages, water, sponge, and such necessaries as he needed; when, the patient presenting an appearance of recovering from his swoon, they watched him attentively.

"He won't die this time, Mrs Pottles," said the doctor, with authority.

"Lawk a deary me! no, sir, I hope not," said the landlady—"a fine, nice, handsome young fellow like he! He'll live and break some 'arts yet, I'll be bound. It's all very well for old folks like us, sir, to die; but I shouldn't like to see him go that-a-way—just when out taking his pleasure, too."

Mr Tiddson did not consider himself one of the "old folks," so did not reply.

"A poor dear!" said Mrs Pottles. "I wonder who he is? There'll be more 'n one pair o' bright eyes wet because of his misfortun', I know. You've no idee, sir, how like he is to my Tom—him as got into that bit of trouble with the squire, sir."

"Pooh, woman!—not a bit. Tchsh!"

The raised finger of the doctor accompanied his ejaculation, as the patient unclosed his eyes, muttered a little, and then, turning his head, seemed to sink into a state of half sleep, half stupor.

The doctor sat for some time before speaking, frowning severely at the landlady, and then impatiently pulling down the blind to get rid of half a dozen lads, who were spoiling the symmetry of their noses against the window.

"I s'pose you have no idea who he is?" said the doctor at last.

"Not the leastest bit in the world, sir. They do say they've had a tremenjus run to-day. But perhaps we shall have some of the gents coming back this way, and they may know him."

"Precisely so, Mrs Pottles; but you'd better feel in his pockets, and we may be able to find out where his friends are, and so send them word of his condition."

"Lawk a deary me, sir! But wouldn't it be wrong for me to be peeping and poking in his pockets? But how so be if *you* wish it, sir, I'll look."

"I *don't* wish it, Mrs Pottles; but it is our duty to acquaint his friends, so you had better search."

Now Mrs Pottles's fingers were itching to make an examination; and doubtless, had the doctor left, her first act would have been to "peep and poke," as she termed it; so, taking up garment after garment, she drew out a handsome gold watch and seal chain with an eagle crest; then a cigar-case bearing the same crest, and the letters "C.Y.;" and lastly a plain porte-monnaie, containing four sovereigns and some silver.

"No information there, Mrs Pottles. But I'll make a list of these, and leave them in your charge till the patient recovers."

"Lawk a deary me, no, sir, don't do that! We're as honest as the day is long here, sir, so don't put no temptation in our way. Make a list of the gentleman, if you like, and leave *him* in our charge, and we'll nurse him well again; but you'd better take the watch and things along of you."

"Very good, Mrs Pottles—ve-ery good," said the doctor, noting down the articles he placed in his pocket, and thinking that, even if called upon for no further attendance, through the coming of some family doctor, he was safe of the amount in the porte-monnaie, for he considered that no gentleman would dream of taking that back.

"And you think he'll get well, then, sir?" said Mrs Pottles.

"Ye-e-e-s—yes, with care, Mrs Pottles—with care. But I'll ride over to my surgery now, and obtain a little medicine. I shall be back in an hour."

Mrs Pottles curtsied him out, and then returned to seat herself by her injured visitor, looking with motherly admiration on his broad white forehead and thick golden beard, as she again compared him with her Tom, who got into that bit of trouble with the squire. But before the doctor had been gone an hour, the patient began to display sundry restless movements, ending by opening his eyes widely and fixing them upon the landlady.

"Who are you? and where am I?" he exclaimed. "Let me see, though—I recollect now: my horse came down with me. I don't think I'm much hurt, though."

"O, but you are, sir, and very badly, too. Mr Tiddson says you are to be very quiet."

"Who the deuce is Mr Tiddson?" said the patient, trying to rise, but sinking back with a groan.

"Lawk a deary me, sir! I thought everybody know'd Mr Tiddson: he's our doctor, and they do say as he's very clever; but he ain't in rheumatiz, for he never did me a bit o' good."

"Poor dad!" muttered the young man thoughtfully, and then aloud: "Give me a pen and ink and a sheet of paper."

"But sewerly, sir, you're not going to try to—"

"Get me the pen and ink, woman!" exclaimed the sufferer impatiently.

Mrs Pottles raised her hands, and then hurriedly placed a little dirty blotting-case before her guest, holding it and the rusty ink so that he was able to write a short note, which he signed, and then doubled hastily, for he was evidently in pain.

"Let some man take that to the King's Arms at Lexville, and ask for Mr Bray. If he is not there, let them send for him; but the note is to be given to no one else."

"Very good, sir," said the woman; "but it's a many miles there. How's he to go?"

"Ride—ride!" exclaimed the sufferer impatiently, and then he sank back deeper in his pillow.

"I didn't think, or I would have sent for some one else," he muttered, after a pause; "but I daresay he will come."

And then he lay thinking in a dreamy, semi-delirious fashion of the contents of that note—a note so short, and yet of itself containing matter that might bring to the writer a life of regret, and to another, loving, gentle, and true-hearted, the breaking of that true gentle heart, and the cold embrace of the bridegroom Death!

Chapter Two
"Bai Jove!"

Three months after the incidents recorded in the last chapter, Littleborough Station, on the Great Middleland and Conjunction Railway, woke into life; for it was nearly noon, and the mid-day up-train would soon run alongside of the platform, stay for the space of half a minute, and then proceed again on its hurrying, panting course towards the great metropolis; for though such a thing did sometimes happen, the taking up or setting down of passengers at Littleborough was not as a matter of course. Nobody ever wanted to come to Littleborough, which was three miles from the station, and very few people ever seemed to take tickets from Littleborough to proceed elsewhere: the consequence being that the station-master—a fair young man with budding whiskers, and a little cotton-woolly moustache—spent the greater part of his time in teaching a rough dog to stand upon his hind-legs, to walk, beg, smoke pipes, and perform various other highly interesting feats, while the one porter spent his in yawning and playing "push halfpenny," right hand against left—a species of gambling that left him neither richer nor poorer at the day's end. But his yawning was something frightful, being extensive enough to have startled a child into the belief that ogres really had an existence in the flesh, though the said porter was after all but a simple, lazy, ignorant boor, with as little of harm in his nature as there was of activity.

But, as before said, Littleborough Station now woke into life; for after crawling into the booking-office, and yawing frightfully at the clock, the porter went and turned a handle, altering the position of a signal, and then returned to find the station-master framed in the little doorway through which he issued tickets, and now pitching little bits of biscuit for the dog to catch.

"Here's summun a-coming!" said the porter, excitedly running to the door and checking a yawn half-way.

"No!—is there?" cried the station-master, running out, catching up the dog and carrying it in, to shut himself up once more behind his official screen and railway-clerk dignity.

"Swell in a dog-cart, with groom a-drivin'," said the porter aloud; and then, as the vehicle came nearer: "Portmanty and bag with him, and that there gum's all dried up, and won't stick on no labels. Blest if here ain't somebody else, too, in the 'Borough fly, and two boxes on the top."

The porter threw open the doors very widely, the station-master tried his ticket-stamper to see if it would work, and then peered excitedly out for the coming travellers.

He had not to wait long. The smart dog-cart was drawn up at the door; and as the horse stood champing its bit and throwing the white foam in all directions, a very languid, carefully-dressed gentleman descended, waved his hand towards his luggage and wrappers in answer to the porter's obsequious salute, and then sauntering, cigar in hand, to the station-master's pigeon-hole, he languidly drawled out:

"First cla-a-ass—London."

"Twenty-eight-and-six, sir," said the station-master, when the traveller slowly placed a sovereign and a half before him.

"Tha-a-anks. No! Give the change to the porter fellare." And the new arrival strolled on to the platform, leaving the porter grinning furiously, and carrying the portmanteau and bag about without there being the slightest necessity for such proceedings.

Meanwhile the fly had drawn up, the driver dismounted, and opened the door for a closely veiled young lady in black to alight, when she proceeded to pay the man.

"Suthin' for the driver, miss, please," said the fellow gruffly.

"I understood from your master that the charge would be five shillings to the station," said the new arrival, in a low tremulous voice.

"Yes, miss, but the driver's allus hextry. Harf-crown most people gives the driver."

There was no sound issued from beneath that veil, but the motion of the dress showed that something very much like a sigh must have been struggling for exit as a little soft white hand drew a florin from a scantily-furnished purse, and gave it to the man.

"Humph," growled the fellow, "things gets wuss and wuss," and climbing on to his box-seat, he gathered up reins and whip, and sat stolid and surly without moving.

"Will you be kind enough to lift down my trunks?" said the traveller gently.

"You must ast the porter for that 'ere," said the man: "we're drivers, we are, and 'tain't our business. Here, Joe, come and get these here trunks off the roof," and he accompanied his words with a meaning wink to the porter, which gentleman, in the full possession of an unlooked—for eighteenpence, felt so wealthy that he could afford to be supercilious.

"What class, miss?" he said, reaching his hand to a trunk.

"Third, if you please," was the reply.

"Ah! there'll be something extry to pay for luggidge: third-class passengers ain't allowed two big boxes like these here.—Why didn't you put 'em down, Dick?"

"Ain't got half paid for what I did do," said the driver gruffly. "People as can't afford to pay for flies oughter ride in carts. Mind that 'ere lamp!"

Certainly a lamp had a very narrow escape, as trunk number one was brought to the ground with a crash, the second one being treated almost as mercilessly, but without a word from their owner, who quietly raising her veil and displaying a sweet sad face, now went to the pigeon-hole, regardless of the leering stare bestowed upon her by the exquisite, who had sauntered back into the booking-office.

"Third-class—London," said the station-master aloud, repeating the fair young traveller's words. "Nine-and-nine;" and he too bestowed a not very respectful stare.

The threepence change was handed to the porter, with a request that he would see the boxes into the van, which request, and the money, that incorruptible gentleman received with a short nod and an "all right," pocketing the cash in defiance of all by-laws and ordinances of the company.

Turning to reach the platform, the young lady—for such her manners indicated her to be—became aware of the fixed insolent stare of the over-dressed gentleman at her side, when quietly and without ostentation the black fall was lowered, and she walked slowly to and fro for a few minutes, in expectation of the coming train—hardly noticing that she was met at every turn, and that the gentlemanly manoeuvres were being watched with great interest by station-master and porter.

"Nice day, deah!" was suddenly drawled out; and the traveller started to find that, in place of being met at every turn, her persecutor was now close by her side. Quickening her steps, she slightly bent her head and walked on; but in vain.

"Any one going to meet you?" was next drawled out; when turning shortly round, the young traveller looked the exquisite full in the face.

"I think you are making a mistake, sir," she said coldly.

"Mistake? No, not I, my deah," was the insolent reply. "Give me your ticket, and I'll change it;" and the speaker coolly held out a tightly-gloved hand.

The black veil hid the flush that rose to the pale face, as, glancing rapidly down the line for the train that seemed as if it would never come, the traveller once more quickened her steps and walked to the other end of the platform; for there was no waiting-room at the little wooden station, one but newly erected by way of experiment.

"Now, don't be awkward, my deah," drawled the exquisite, once more overtaking her. "Here we are both going to town together, and I can take care of you. Pretty gyurls like you have no business to travel alone. Now, let me change your ticket;" and again he stretched forth his hand. "I'll pay, you know."

"Are you a gentleman, sir?" was the sudden question in reply to his proposition.

"Bai Jove, ya-a-a-s!" was the drawled reply, accompanied by what was meant for a most killing leer.

"Then you will immediately cease this unmanly pursuit!" exclaimed the lady firmly; and once more turning, she paced along the platform.

"Now, how can you now," languidly whispered the self-styled gentleman, "when we might be so comfortable and chatty all this long ride? Look here, my deah—take my arm, and I'll see to your luggage."

As he spoke, with the greatest effrontery he caught the young traveller's hand in his, and drew it through his arm—the station-master and porter noting the performance, and nodding at one another; but the next moment the former official changed his aspect, for the hand was snatched away, and the young lady hurried in an agitated manner to the booking-office.

"Have you a room in which I could sit down until the train comes?" she exclaimed. "I am sorry to trouble you; but I am travelling alone, and—"

"To be sure you are, my deah," drawled the persecutor, who had laughingly followed, "when you have no business to do such a thing, and I won't allow it. It's all right, station-master—the train will be here directly. I'll see to the lady: friend of mine, in fact."

"Indeed! I assure you, sir," exclaimed the agitated girl, "I do not know this gentleman. I appeal to you for protection."

Here, in spite of her self-control, a sob burst from her breast.

"Here, this sort of thing won't do, sir," said the youth, shaking his head. "I can't allow it at my station. You mustn't annoy the lady, sir." And turning very pink in the face, he tried to look important; but without success.

"I think you have the care of this station, have you not, my good lad?" drawled the exquisite.

"Yes, I have, sir," was the reply, and this time rather in anger, for the young station-master hardly approved of being called a "good lad."

"Then mind your station, boy, and don't interfere."

"Boy yourself, you confounded puppy!" exclaimed the young fellow, firing up. "I never took any notice till the lady appealed to me; but if she was my sister, sir, I'd—I'd—I don't know what I wouldn't do to you!"

"But you see she is not your sister; and you are making a fool of yourself," drawled the other contemptuously.

"Am I?" exclaimed the young man, whose better nature was aroused. "I consider that every lady who is being insulted is the sister of an Englishman, and has a right to his help. And now be off out of this office, for I'm master here; and you may report me if you like, for I don't care who you are, nor yet if I lose my place."

Red in the face, and strutting like a turkey-cock, the young man made at the dandy so fiercely, that he backed out on to the platform, to have the door banged after him so energetically, that one of the panes of glass was shivered to atoms.

"Come in here, miss, and I'll see that he don't annoy you again. Why didn't you speak sooner? Only wish I was going up to London, I'd see you safe home, that I would, miss; only, you see, I should lose my berth if I was absent without leave; and that wouldn't do, would it? May p'r'aps now, for that chap's a regular swell: come down here last week, and been staying at old Sir Henry Warr's, at the Beeches; but I don't care; I only did what was right—did I, miss?"

"Indeed, I thank you very, very much!" exclaimed the protected one, holding out a little hand, which was eagerly seized. "It was very kind; and I do sincerely hope I may not have been the cause—"

Here a sob choked further utterance.

"Don't you mind about that," said the young man loftily, and feeling very exultant and self-satisfied. "I'd lose half a dozen berths to please you, miss—I would, 'pon my word. Don't you take on about that. I'm your humble servant to command; and let's see if he'll speak to you again on my platform, that's all!"

Here the young man—very young man—breathed hard, stared hard, and blushed; for his anger having somewhat evaporated, he now began to think that he had been very chivalrous, and that he had fallen in love with this beautiful girl, whom it was his duty to protect evermore: feelings, however, not at all shared by the lady, who, though very grateful, was most earnestly wishing herself safely at her destination. The embarrassing position was, however, ended by the young station-master, who suddenly exclaimed:

"Here she comes!"

Then he led the way, pulling up his collar and scowling very fiercely till they reached the platform, where the exquisite was languidly pacing up and down.

"Now, you take my advice, miss," said the protector: "you jump into the first cab as soon as you get into the terminus, and have yourself driven home: I'll see that you ain't interfered with going up. I wish I was going with you; and, 'pon my word, miss, I should like to see you again."

"Indeed, I thank you very much," said the stranger. "You have acted very nobly; and though you may never again be thanked by me, you will have the reward of knowing that you have protected a *sister* in distress."

She laid a stress upon the word "sister," as if referring to the young fellow's manly reply to the dandy. But now "she"—that is to say, the train—had glided up, when, turning smartly—

"See those boxes in, Joe!" exclaimed the station-master; and then catching the traveller's hand in his, he led her to the guard. "Put this young lady in a compartment where there's more ladies," he said. "She's going to London, and I want you to see that she's safely off in a cab when she gets there. She's my sister."

"All right, Mr Simpkin—all right," said the guard.

"Good-bye, miss—good-bye!" exclaimed the young man confusedly, shaking her hand. "Business, you know—I must go."

Just at that moment a thought seemed to have struck the dandy, who made as if to get to where the porter was thrusting the two canvas-covered trunks into the guard's van; but he was too late.

"Now, then, sir, if you're going on!" exclaimed the station-master. "Third-class?" he asked by way of a sneer.

"Confound you! I'll serve you out for this—bai Jove I will!" muttered the over-dressed one, jumping hastily into a first-class *coupé*, when, looking out, he had the satisfaction of seeing the young station-master spring on to the step of a third-class carriage, and ride far beyond the end of the platform, before he jumped down and waved him a triumphant salute as the train swept by.

The dandy made a point of going up to that carriage at every stopping—station where sufficient time was afforded; but the fair young traveller sat with her face studiously turned towards the opposite window.

"I've a good mind to ride third-class for once in a way," the gentleman muttered, as he passed the carriage during one stoppage.

Just then a child cried out loudly; and a soldier, smoking a dirty black pipe, thrust his head out of the next compartment with a "How are you, matey?"

"Bai Jove, no! Couldn't do it!" murmured the exquisite, with a shudder; and he returned to his seat, to look angry and scowling for the rest of the journey.

He had made up his mind, though, as to his proceedings when they reached London; but again he was doomed to disappointment; for on his approaching the object of his pursuit in the crowd, he found the stout guard a guard indeed in his care of his charge; when, angrily turning upon his heel, he made his way to the luggage-bar, where, singling out the particular trunks that he had seen at Littleborough, he pressed through the throng, and eagerly read one of the direction-labels.

"Bai Jove!" he exclaimed, with an air of the most utter astonishment overspreading his face; and then again he read the direction, but only again to give utterance to his former ejaculation—"Bai Jove!"

He seemed so utterly taken aback that he did not even turn angrily upon a porter who jostled him, or upon another who with one of the very boxes knocked his hat over his eyes. The cab was laden and driven off before his face so slowly that, once more alone, he could have easily spoken to the veiled occupant. But, no: he was so utterly astounded that when he hailed a hansom, and slowly stepped in, his reply to the driver as he peered down through the little trap was only—

"Bai Jove!"

"Where to, sir?" said the man, astonished in his turn.

"Anywhere, my good fellow."

"All right, sir."

"No, no—stop. Drive me to the Wyndgate Club, Saint James's-square."

"All right, sir."

And the cab drove off, with its occupant wondering and startled at the strange fashion in which every-day affairs will sometimes shape themselves, proving again and again how much more wild the truth can be than fiction, and musing upon what kind of an encounter his would be with the fair traveller when next he went home.

There was no record kept of the number of times the over-dressed gentleman gave utterance to that peculiarly-drawling exclamation; but it is certain that he startled his valet by jumping up suddenly at early morn from a dream of his encounter, to cry, as if disturbed by something almost painful:

"Who could have thought it? Bai Jove!"

Chapter Three
Blandfield Court

"Did you ring, sir?" said a footman.

"Yes, Thomas. Go to Mr Charles's room, and tell him that I should be glad of half an hour's conversation with him before he goes out, if he can make it convenient."

The library-door of Blandfield Court closed; and after taking a turn or two up and down the room, Sir Philip Vining—a fine, florid, grey-headed old gentleman—stood for a moment gazing from the window at the sweep of park extending down to a glittering stream, which wound its way amidst glorious glades of beech and chestnut, bright in the virgin green of spring. But anxious of mien, and ill at ease, the old gentleman stepped slowly to the handsome carved-oak chair in which he had been seated, and then, intently watching the door, he leaned back, playing with his double gold eyeglass.

Five minutes passed, and then a step was heard crossing the hall—a step which made Sir Philip's face lighten up, as, leaning forward, a pleasant smile appeared upon his lip. Then a heavy bold hand was laid upon the handle, and the patient of Dr Tiddson—fair, flushed, and open-countenanced—strode into the room, seeming as if he had brought with him the outer sunshine lingering in his bright brown hair and golden beard. He swung the door to with almost a bang; and then—free of gait, happy, and careless-looking, suffering from no broken rib, fractured clavicle, or concussed brain, as predicted three months before—he strode towards Sir Philip, who rose hurriedly with outstretched hands.

"My dear Charley, how are you this morning? You look flushed. Effects remaining of that unlucky fall, I'm afraid."

"Fall? Nonsense, dad! Never better in my life," laughed the young man, taking the outstretched hands and then subsiding into a chair. "Mere trifle, in spite of the doctor's long phiz."

"It is going back to old matters, but I'm very glad, my dear boy, that I saw Max Bray, and learned of your condition; and I've never said a word before, Charley, but why should you send for him in preference to your father?"

"Pooh!—nonsense, dad! First man I thought of. Did it to save you pain. Ought to have got up, and walked home. But there, let it pass. Mind my cigar?"

"No, no, my dear boy, of course not," said the old gentleman, coughing slightly. "If it troubles me, I'll open the window."

"But really, father," said the young man, laying his hand tenderly on Sir Philip's arm, "don't let me annoy you with my bad habit."

"My dear boy, I don't mind. You know we old fogies used to have our bad habits—two bottles of port after dinner, to run down into our legs and make gouty pains, eh, Charley—eh? And look here, my dear boy—look here!"

Charley Vining laughed, and, leaning back in his chair, began to send huge clouds of perfumed smoke from his cabana, as his father drew out a handsome gold-box, and took snuff *à la* courtier of George the Fourth's day.

"I don't like smoking, my boy; but it's better than our old drinking habits."

"Hear—hear! Cheers from the opposition!" laughed the son.

"Ah, my dear boy, why don't you give your mind to that sort of thing? Such a fine opening as there is in the county! Writtlum says they could get you in with a tremendous majority."

"Parliament, dad? Nonsense! Pretty muff I should be; get up to speak without half-a-dozen words to say."

"Nonsense, Charley—nonsense! The Vinings never yet disgraced their name."

"Unworthy scion of the house, my dear father."

"Now, my dear Charley!" exclaimed Sir Philip, as he looked with pride at the stalwart young fellow who was heir to his baronetcy and broad acres. "But, let me see, my dear boy; John Martingale called yesterday while you were out. He says he has as fine a hunter as ever crossed country: good fencer, well up to your weight—such a one as you would be proud of I told him to bring the horse on for you to see; for I should not like you to miss a really good hunter, Charley, and I might be able to screw out a cheque."

"My dear father," exclaimed the young man, throwing his cigar-end beneath the grate, "there really is no need. Martingale's a humbug, and only wants to palm upon us some old screw. The mare is in splendid order—

quite got over my reckless riding and the fall. I like her better every day, and she'll carry me as much as I shall want to hunt."

"I'm glad you like her, Charley. You don't think her to blame?"

"Blame? No! I threw her down. I like her better every day, I tell you. But you gave a cool hundred too much for her."

"Never mind that. By the way, Charley, Leathrum says they are hatching plenty of pheasants: the spinneys will be full this season; and I want you to have some good shooting. The last poacher, too, has gone from the village."

"Who's that?" said Charley carelessly.

"Diggles—John Diggles. They brought him before me for stealing pheasants' eggs, and I—and I—"

"Well, what did you do, dad? Fine him forty shillings?"

"Well, no, my boy. You see, he threw himself on my mercy—said he'd such a character no one would employ him, and that he wanted to get out of the country; and that if he stopped he should always be meddling with the game. And you see, my dear boy, it's true enough; so I promised to pay his passage to America."

"A pretty sort of a county magistrate!" laughed Charley. "What do you think the reverend rectors, Lingon and Braceby, will say to you? Why, they would have given John Diggles a month."

"Perhaps so, my dear boy; but the man has had no chance, and—No; sit still, Charley. I haven't done yet; I want to talk to you."

"All right, dad. I was only going to give the mare a spin. Let her wait." And he threw himself back in his chair.

"Yes, yes—let her wait this morning, my dear boy. But don't say 'All right!' I don't like you to grow slangy, either in your speech or dress." He glanced at the young man's easy tweed suit. "That was one thing in which the old school excelled, in spite of their wine-bibbing propensities—they were particular in their language, dressed well, and were courtly to the other sex."

"Yes," yawned Charley; "but they were dreadful prigs."

"Perhaps so—perhaps so, my dear boy," said the old gentleman, laying his hand upon his son's knee. "But do you know, Charley, I should like to see you a little more courtly and attentive to—to the ladies?"

"I adore that mare you gave me, dad."

"Don't be absurd. I want to see you more in ladies' society; so polishing— so improving!"

"Hate it!" said Charley laconically.

"Nonsense—nonsense! Now look here!"

"No, dad. Look here," said Charley, leaning towards his father and gazing full in his face with a half-serious, half-bantering smile lighting up his clear blue eye. "You're beating about the bush, dad, and the bird won't start. You did not send for me to say that Martingale had been about a horse, or Leathrum had hatched so many pheasants, or that Diggles was going to leave the country. Frankly, now, governor, what's in the wind?"

Sir Philip Vining looked puzzled; he threw himself back in his chair, took snuff hastily, spilling a few grains upon his cambric shirt-frill. Then, with his gold-box in his left hand, he bent forward and laid his right upon the young man's ample breast, gazing lovingly in his face, and said:

"Frankly, then, my dear Charley, I want to see you married!"

Chapter Four
Concerning Matrimony

Charles Vining gazed half laughingly in his father's earnest face; then throwing himself back, he burst into an uncontrolled fit of merriment.

"Ha, ha, ha! Me married! Why, my dear father, what next?" Then, seeing the look of pain in Sir Philip's countenance, he rose and stood by his side, resting one hand upon his shoulder. "Why, my dear father," he said, "what ever put that in your head? I never even thought of such a thing!"

"My dear boy, I know it—I know it; and that's why I speak. You see, you are now just twenty-seven, and a fine handsome young fellow—"

Charley made a grimace.

"While I am getting an old man, Charley, and the time cannot be so very far off before I must go to my sleep. You are my only child, and I want the Squire of Blandfield to keep up the dignity of the old family. Don't interrupt me, my boy, I have not done yet. I must soon go the way of all flesh—"

"Heaven forbid!" said Charley fervently.

"And it is the dearest wish of my heart to see you married to some lady of good birth—one who shall well do the honours of your table. Blandfield must not pass to a collateral branch, Charley; we must have an heir to these broad acres; for I hope the time will come, my boy, when in this very library you will be seated, grey and aged as I am, talking to some fine stalwart son, who, like you, shall possess his dear mother's eyes, ever to bring to remembrance happy days gone by, my boy—gone by never to return."

The old man's voice trembled as he spoke, and the next moment his son's hands were clasped in his, while as eye met eye there was a weak tear glistening in that of the elder, and the lines seemed more deeply cut in his son's fine open countenance.

"My dear father!" said the young man softly.

"My dear Charley!" said Sir Philip.

There was silence for a while as father and son thought of the days of sorrow ten years back, when Blandfield Court was darkened, and steps passed lightly about the fine old mansion, because its lady—loved of all for miles round—had been suddenly called away from the field of labour that she had blessed. And then they looked up to the portrait gazing down at them from the chimneypiece, seeming almost to smile sadly upon them as they watched the skilful limning of the beloved features.

A few moments after, a smile dawned upon the old man's quivering lip, as, still retaining his son's hand, he motioned him to take a seat by his side.

"My dear Charley," he said at last, "I think you understand my wishes."

"My dear father, yes."

"And you will try?"

"To gratify you?—Yes, yes, of course; but really, father—"

"My dear boy, I know—I know what you would say. But look here, Charley—there has always been complete confidence between us; is there—is there anything?"

"Any lady in the case? What, any tender *penchant*?" laughed Charley. "My dear father, no. I think I've hardly given a thought to anything but my horses and dogs."

"I'm glad of it, Charley, I'm glad of it! And now let's quietly chat it over. Do you know, my dear boy, that you are shutting yourself out from an Eden? Do you not believe in love?"

"Well, ye-e-es. I believe that you and my dear mother were most truly happy."

"We were, my dear boy, we were. And why should not you be as happy?"

"Hem!" ejaculated Charley; and then firmly: "because, sir, I believe that there is not such a woman as my dear mother upon earth."

The old gentleman shaded his eyes for a few moments with his disengaged hand.

"Frankly again, father," said the young man, "is there a lady in view?"

"Well, no, my dear boy, not exactly; but I certainly was talking with Bray over our port last week, when we perhaps did agree that you and Laura seemed cut out for one another; but, my dear boy, don't think I want to play the tyrant and choose for you. They do say, though, that the lady has a leaning your way; and no wonder, Charley, no wonder!"

"I don't know very much about Laura," said Charley musingly. "She's a fine girl certainly; looks rather Jewish, though, with those big red lips of hers and that hooked nose."

"My dear Charley!" remonstrated Sir Philip.

"But she rides well—sits that great rawboned mare of hers gloriously. I saw her take a leap on the last day I was out—one that I took too, about half an hour before that fall; but hang me if it wasn't to avoid being outdone by a woman! I really wanted to shirk it."

"Good, good!" laughed Sir Philip.

"But she's fast, and not feminine, to my way of thinking," said Charley, gazing up as he spoke at the picture above the mantelpiece, and comparing the lady in question with the truly gentle mother whom he had almost worshipped. "She burst out with a hoarse 'Bravo!' when she saw me safely landed, and then shouted, 'Well done, Charley!' and I felt so nettled, that I pulled out my cigar-case, and asked her to take one."

"But she did not?" exclaimed Sir Philip.

"Well, no," said Charley, "she did not, certainly—she only laughed; but she looked just as if she were half disposed. She's one of your Spanish style of women: scents, too, tremendously—bathes in Ihlang-Ihlang, I should think; perhaps because she delights in garlic and onions, and wants to smother the odour!"

"My dear boy—my dear boy!" laughed Sir Philip, "you do really want polish horribly! What a way to speak of a lady! It's terrible, you know! But there, don't judge harshly, and you are perfectly unfettered; only just bear this in mind: it would give me great pleasure if you were to lead Laura Bray in here some day and say—But there, you know—you know! Still I place no tie upon you, Charley: only bring me some fair sweet girl—by birth a lady, of whom I can be proud—and then all I want is that you shall give me a chair at your table and fireside. You might have the title if it were possible, but you shall have the Court and the income—everything. Only let me have my glass of wine and my bit of snuff, and play with your children. Heaven bless you, my dear boy! I'll go off the bench directly, and you shall be a county magistrate; but you must be married, Charley—you must be married!"

Charley Vining did not appear to be wonderfully elated by his future prospects, for, sighing, he said:

"Really, father, I could have been very happy to have gone on just as we are; but your wishes—"

"Yes, my dear boy, my wishes. And you will try? Only don't bother yourself; take time, and mix a little more with society—accept a few more invitations—go to a few of the archery and croquet parties."

"Heigho, dad!" sighed Charley. "Why, I should be sending arrows for fun in the stout old dowagers' backs, and breaking the slow curates' shins with my croquet mallet! There, leave me to my own devices, and I'll see what I can do!"

"To be sure—to be sure, Charley! And you do know Maximilian Bray?"

"Horrid snob!" laughed Charley, "such a languid swell! Do you know what our set call him? But there, of course you don't! 'Donkey Bray' or else 'Long-ears!'"

"There, there—never mind that! I don't want you to marry him, Charley. And there—there's Beauty at the door!" exclaimed the old gentleman, shaking his son's hand. "Go and have your ride, Charley! Good-bye! But you'll think of what I said?"

"I will, honestly," said the young man.

"And—stay a moment, Charley: Lexville flower-show is to-morrow. I can't go. Couldn't you, just to oblige me? I like to see these affairs patronised; and Pruner takes a good many of our things over. He generally carries off a few prizes. I see they've quite stripped the conservatory. You'll go for me, won't you?"

"Yes, father, if you wish it," sighed Charley.

"I do wish it, my dear boy; but don't sigh, pray!"

"All right, dad," said the young man, brightening, and shaking Sir Philip's hand, "I'll go; give away the prizes, too, if they ask me," he laughed. And the next moment the door closed upon his retreating form.

Sir Philip Vining listened to his son's departing step, and then muttering, "They will ask him too," he rose, and went to the window, from which he could just get a glimpse of the young man mounting at the hall-door. The next moment Charley cantered by upon a splendid roan mare, turning her on to the lawn-like sward, and disappearing behind a clump of beeches.

"He's a noble boy!" muttered the father proudly; and then as he walked thoughtfully back to his chair, "A fine dashing fellow!"

But of course these were merely the fond expressions of a weak parent.

Chapter Five
Charley's encounters

"Bai Jove, Vining! that you?" languidly exclaimed a little, thin, carefully-dressed man, ambling gently along on one of the most thoroughly-broken of ladies' mares, whose pace was so easy that not a curl of her master's jetty locks was disarranged, or a crease formed in his tightly-buttoned surtout. His figure said "stays" as plainly as figure could speak; he wore an eyeglass screwed into the brim of his very glossy hat; his eyes were half closed; his moustache was waxed and curled up at the ends like old-fashioned skates; and his carefully-trained whiskers lightly brushed their tips against his shoulders. And to set off such arrangements to the greatest advantage, he displayed a great deal of white wristband and shirt-front; his collar came down into the sharpest of peaks; and he rode in lemon-kid gloves and patent-leather boots.

"Hallo, Max!" exclaimed Charley, looking like some Colossus as he reined in by the side of the dandy, who was going in the same direction along a shady lane. "How are you? When did you come down?"

"So, so—so, so, mai dear fellow! Came down la-a-ast night. But pray hold in that confounded great beast of yours: she's making the very deuce of a dust! I shall be covered!"

Charley patted and soothed his fiery curveting steed into a walk, which was quite sufficient to keep it abreast of Maximilian Bray's ambling jennet, which kept up a dancing, circus-horse motion, one evidently approved by its owner for its aid in displaying his graceful horsemanship.

"Nice day," said Charley, scanning with a side glance his companion's "get-up," and evidently with a laughing contempt.

"Ya-a-s, nice day," drawled Bray, "but confoundedly dusty!"

"Rain soon," said Charley maliciously. "Lay it well."

"Bai Jove, no—surely not!" exclaimed the other, displaying a great deal of trepidation. "You don't think so, do you?"

"Black cloud coming up behind," said Charley coolly.

"Bai Jove, mai dear fellow, let's push on and get home! You'll come and lunch, won't you?"

"No, not to-day," said Charley. "But I'm going into the town to see the saddler. I'll ride with you."

"Tha-a-anks!" drawled Bray, with a grin of misery. "But, mai dear fellow, hadn't you better go on the grass? You're covering me with dust!"

"Confounded puppy! Nice brother-in-law! Wring his neck!" muttered Charley, as he turned his mare on to the grass which skirted the side of the road, as did Bray on the other, when, the horses' paces being muffled by the soft turf, conversation was renewed.

"Bai Jove, Vining, you'll come over to the flower-show to-morrow, won't you? There'll be some splendid girls there! Good show too, for the country. You send a lot of things, don't you?—Covent-garden stuff and cabbages, eh?"

"Humph!" growled Charley. "The governor's going to have some sent, I s'pose; our gardener's fond of that sort of thing. Think perhaps I shall go."

"Ya-a-s, I should go if I were you. It does you country fellows a deal of good, I always think, to get into society."

"Does it?" said Charley, raising his eyebrows a little.

"Bai Jove, ya-a-s! You'd better go. Laura's going, and the Lingon's girls are coming to lunch. You'd better come over to lunch and go with us," drawled the exquisite.

"Well, I don't know," said Charley, hesitating; for he was thinking whether it would not be better than going quite alone—"I don't know what to say."

"Sa-a-ay? Sa-a-ay ya-a-s," drawled Bray. "Come in good time and have a weed first in my room; and then we'll taste some sherry the governor has got da-awn. He always leaves it till I come da-awn from ta awn. Orders execrable stuff himself, as I often tell him. Wouldn't have a drop fit to drink if it weren't for me. You'd better come."

"Well, really," said Charley again, half mockingly, "I don't know what to say."

"Why, sa-a-ay ya-a-as, and come."

"Well, then, 'ya-a-as'!" drawled Charley, in imitation of the other's tone.

But Maximilian Bray's skin was too thick for the little barb to penetrate; and he rode gingerly on, petting his whiskers, and altering the sit of his hat; when, being thoroughly occupied with his costume, horse and man nearly came headlong to the ground, in consequence of the mare stumbling over a small heap of road-scrapings. But the little animal saved herself, though only by a violent effort, which completely unseated Maximilian Bray, who was thrown forward upon her neck, his hat being dislodged and falling with a sharp bang into the dusty road.

"All right! No bones broken! You've better luck than I have!" laughed Charley, as he fished up the fallen hat with his hunting-whip. "Nip her well with your knees, man, and then you won't be unseated again in that fashion. Here, take your hat."

"Bai Jove!" ejaculated the breathless dandy, "it's too bad! That fellow who left the sweepings by the roadside ought to be shot! Mai dear fellow, your governor, as a magistrate, ought to see to it! Tha-a-anks!"

He took his hat, and began ruefully to wipe off the dust with a scented handkerchief before again covering his head; but though he endeavoured to preserve an outward appearance of calm, there was wrath in his breast as he gazed down at one lemon-coloured tight glove split to ribbons, and a button burst away from his surtout coat. He could feel too that his moustache was coming out of curl, and it only wanted the sharp shower which now came pattering down to destroy the last remains of his equanimity.

"Bai Jove, how beastly unfortunate!" he exclaimed, urging his steed into a smart canter.

"Well, I don't know," said Charley coolly, in his rough tweed suit that no amount of rain would have injured. "Better to-day than to-morrow. Do no end of good, and bring on the hay."

"Ya-a-as, I suppose so," drawled Bray; "but do a confounded deal of harm!" and he gazed at the sleeves of his glossy Saville-row surtout.

"O, never mind your coat, man!" laughed Charley. "See how it lays the dust!"

"Ya-a-as, just so," drawled Bray. "I shall take this short cut and get home. Only a shower! Bye-bye! See you to-morrow! Come to lunch."

The ragged lemon glove was waved to Charley as its owner turned down a side lane; and now that his costume was completely disordered and wet, he made no scruple about digging his spurs into his mare's flanks, and galloping homewards; while, heedless of the sharply-falling rain, Charley gently cantered on towards the town.

"Damsels in distress!" exclaimed the young man suddenly. "'Bai Jove!' as Long-ears says. Taken refuge from the rain beneath a tree! Leaves, young and weak, completely saturated—impromptu shower—bath! What shall I do? Lend them my horse? No good. They would not ride double, like Knight Templars. Ride off, then, for umbrellas, I suppose. Why didn't that donkey stop a little longer? and then he could have done it."

So mused Charley Vining as he cantered up to where, beneath a spreading elm by the roadside, two ladies were waiting the cessation of the rain—faring, though, very little better than if they had stood in the open. One was a fashionably-dressed, tall, dark, bold beauty, black of eye and tress, and evidently in anything but the best of tempers with the weather; the other a fair pale girl, in half-mourning, whose yellow hair was plainly braided across her white forehead, but only to be knotted together at the back in a massive cluster of plaits, which told of what a glorious golden mantle it could have shed over its owner, rippling down far below the waist, and ready, it seemed, to burst from prisoning comb and pin. There was something ineffably sweet in her countenance, albeit there was a subdued, even sorrowful look as her shapely little head was bent towards her companion, and she was evidently speaking as Charley cantered up.

"Sorry to see you out in this, Miss Bray," he cried, raising his low-crowned hat. "What can I do?—Fetch umbrellas and shawls? Speak the word."

"O, how kind of you, Mr Vining!" exclaimed the dark maiden, with brightening eyes and flushing cheeks. "But really I should not like to trouble you."

"Trouble? Nonsense!" cried Charley. "Only speak before you get wet through."

"Well, if you really—really, you know—would not mind," hesitated Laura Bray, who, in spite of the rain, was in no hurry to bring the interview to a close.

"Wouldn't mind? Of course not!" echoed Charley, whose bold eyes were fixed upon Laura Bray's companion, who timidly returned his salute, and then shrank back, as he again raised his little deer-stalker hat from its curly throne. "Now, then," he exclaimed, "what's it to be?—shawls and Sairey Gamps of gingham and tape?"

"No, no, Mr Vining! How droll you are!" laughed the beauty. "But if you really wouldn't mind—really, you know—"

"I tell, you, Miss, Bray, that, I, shall, only, be, too, happy," said Charley, in measured tones.

"Then, if you wouldn't mind riding to the Elms, and asking them to send the brougham, I should be so much obliged!"

"All right!" cried Charley, turning his mare. "Max has only just left me."

"But it seems such a shame to send you away through all this rain!" said Laura loudly.

"Fudge!" laughed Charley, as, putting his mare at the hedge in front, she skimmed over it like a bird, and her owner galloped across country, to the great disadvantage of several crops of clover.

"What a pity!" sighed Laura to herself, as she watched the retreating form. "And the rain will be over directly. I wonder whether he'll come back!"

"Do you think we need wait?" said her companion gently. "The rain has ceased now, and the sun is breaking; through the clouds."

"O, of course, Miss Bedford!" said Laura pettishly. "It would be so absurd if the carriage came and found us gone;" when, seeing that the dark beauty evidently wished to be alone with her thoughts, the other remained silent.

"Who in the world can that be with her?" mused Charley, as he rode along. "Might have had the decency to introduce me, anyhow. Don't know when I've seen a softer or more gentle face. Splendid hair too! No sham there: no fear of her moulting a curl here and a tress there, if her back hair came undone. No, she don't seem as if there were any sham about her— quiet, ladylike, and nice. 'Pon my word, I believe Laura Bray would make a better man than Max. Seem to like those silver-grey dresses with a black-velvet jacket, they look so—There, what a muff I am, going right out of the way, while that little darling is getting wet as a sponge! Easy, lass! Now, then—over!" he cried to his mare, as she skimmed another hedge. "Wonder what her name is! Some visitor come to the flower-show, I suppose— *fiancée* of Long-ears probably. Steady, then, Beauty!" he cried again to the mare, who, warming to her work, was beginning to tear furiously over the ground; for, preoccupied by thought, Charley had inadvertently been using his spurs pretty freely.

But he soon reduced his steed to a state of obedience, and rode on, musing upon his late encounter.

"Can't be!" he thought. "A girl with a head like that would never take up with such a donkey! Ah, there he goes, drenched like a rat! Ha, ha, ha! How miserably disgusted the puppy did look! Patronising me, too—a gnat! Advising me to go into society, etcetera! Well, I can't help it: I do think him a conceited ass! But perhaps, after all, he thinks the same of me; and I deserve it.

"Dear old dad," he mused again after awhile. "Like to see me married and settled, would he? What should I be married for?—a regular woman-hater! Why, in the name of all that's civil, didn't Laura introduce me to that little blonde? Like to know who she is—not that it matters to me! Over again, my lass!" he cried, patting the mare as she once more bounded over a hedge, this time to drop into a lane straight as a line, and a quarter of a mile down which Maximilian Bray could be seen hurrying along—Charley's short cut across the fields having enabled him to gain upon the fleeing dandy.

"May as well catch up to him, and tell him what I've seen," said Charley, urging on his mare. "No, I won't," he said, checking. "Better too, perhaps. No, I won't. Why should I send the donkey back to them? Not much fear, though: he'll be too busy for a couple of hours restoring his damaged plumes—a conceited popinjay!"

He cantered gently on now, seeming to take the shower with him, for he could see, on turning, that it was getting fine and bright. But the rain had quite ceased as he rode up to the door of the Brays' seat—a fine old red-brick mansion known as the Elms—just as a groom was leading the ambling palfrey to its stable at the King's Arms—there not being accommodation in the paternal stables—a steed not much more than half the size of the great rawboned hunter favoured by Max's masculine sister.

"Why, here's Mr Charley Vining!" cried a shrill loud voice, from an open window. "How de do, Mr Vining—how de do? Come to lunch, haven't you? So glad! And so sorry Laura isn't at home! Caught in the shower, I'm afraid."

The owner of the voice appeared at the window, in the shape of a very big bony lady in black satin—bony not so much in figure as in face, which seemed fitted with too much skull, displaying a great deal of cheek prominence, and a macaw-beaked nose, with the skin stretched over it very tightly, forming on the whole an organ of a most resonant character—one that it was necessary to hear before it could be thoroughly believed in. In fact, with all due reverence to a lady's nose, it must be stated that the one in question acted as a sort of war-trump, which Mrs Bray blew with masculine force when about to engage in battle with husband or servant for some case of disputed supremacy.

"Ring the bell, girls," shrieked the lady; "and let some one take Mr Vining's horse. Do come in, Mr Vining!"

"How do, Vining—how do?" cried a little pudgy man, appearing at the window, but hardly visible beside his lady—Mrs Bray in more ways than one eclipsing her lord. "How do? How's Sir Philip?"

"Quite well, thanks; but not coming in," cried Charley, from his horse's back. "Miss Bray and some lady caught in the rain—under tree—bad shelter—want the brougham."

"Dear me, how tiresome!" screamed Mrs Bray. "But must we send it, Ness?"

Mr Bray, named at his baptism Onesimus, replied by stroking his cheek and looking thoughtfully at his lady.

"The rain's about over now, and they might surely walk," shrieked Mrs Bray. "Dudgeon grumbles so, too, when he has to go out like this, and he was ordered for two o'clock."

"Better send, my dear," whispered Mr Bray, with a meaning look. "Vining won't like it if you don't."

Mrs Bray evidently approved of her husband's counsel; for orders were given that the brougham should be in immediate readiness.

"They won't be long," she now screamed, all smiles once more. "But do come in and have some lunch, Mr Vining: don't sit there in your wet clothes."

"No—no. I'm all right," cried Charley. "I'm off again directly."

But for all that, he lingered.

"You'll be at the flower-show to-morrow, won't you?" said Mrs Bray.

"Well, yes, I think I shall go," said Charley. "I suppose everybody will be there."

"O, of course; Laura's going. I suppose you send some things from the Court?"

"Yes," said Charley; but he added, laughing, "What will be the use, when you are going to send such a prize blossom?"

"For shame, you naughty man!" said Mrs Bray. "I shall certainly tell Laura you've turned flatterer."

"I say, Charley Vining," squeaked a loud voice from the next window, "we're going to beat you Court folks."

"We are, are we?" laughed Charley, turning in the direction of the voice, which proceeded from a very tall angular young lady of sixteen—a tender young plant, nearly all stem, and displaying very little blossom or leaf. She was supported on either side by two other tender plants, of fourteen and twelve respectively, forming a trio known at the Elms as "the children." "I'm very glad to hear it, Miss Nell; but suppose we wait till after the judge's decision. But there goes the carriage. Good-bye, all!"

And turning his horse's head, he soon overtook the brougham, when, after soothing Mr Dudgeon, the driver, with a shilling, the progress was pretty swift until they reached the tree, where, now finding shelter from the sun instead of the rain, yet stood Laura Bray and her companion.

"O, how good of you, Mr Vining! and to come back, too!" gushed Laura, with sparkling eyes. "I shall never be out of debt, I'm sure. I don't know what I should have done if it had not been for you!"

"Walked home, and a blessed good job, too!" muttered Mr John Dudgeon.

"Don't name it!" said Charley. "Almost a pity it's left off raining."

"For shame—no! How can you talk so!" exclaimed Laura, shaking her sunshade at the speaker. "But I really am so much obliged—I am indeed!"

Charley dismounted and opened the carriage-door, handing in first Miss Bray, who stepped forward, leaned heavily upon his arm, and then took her place, arranging her skirts so as to fill the back seat, talking gushingly the while as she made play at Charley with her great dark eyes.

But the glances were thrown away, Charley's attention being turned to her companion, who bent slightly, just touched the proffered hand, and stepped into the brougham, taking her seat with her back to the horse.

"So much obliged—so grateful!" cried Laura, as Charley closed the door. "I shall never be able to repay you, I'm sure. Thanks! So much! Good-bye! See you at the flower-show to-morrow, of course? Good-bye!—*good-bye!*"

"She's getting a precious deal too affectionate! Talk about wanting me to marry *her*, why she'll run away with *me* directly!" grumbled Charley, as Mr Dudgeon impatiently drove off, leaving the young man with the impression of a swiftly passing vision of Laura Bray showing her white teeth in a great smile as she waved her hand, and of a fair gentle face bent slightly down, so that he could see once more the rich massive braids resting upon a shapely, creamy neck. "Have they been saying anything to her?" said Charley, as the brougham disappeared. "She's getting quite unpleasant. Grows just like the old woman: regularly parrot-beaked. Why didn't she introduce me? Took the best seat, too! Looks strange! I say, though, 'bai Jove'—as that sweet brother says—this sort of thing won't do! I should like to please the dad; but I don't think I could manage to do it 'that how,' as they say about here. She quite frightens me! Heigho! what a bother life is when you can't spend it just as you like! Wish I was out in Australia or Africa, or somewhere to be free and easy—to hunt and shoot and ride as one liked. Let's see: I shall not go over to the town now—it's nearly lunch-time, and I'm wet."

He had mounted his horse, and was about to turn homeward, when something shining in the grass caught his eye, and leaping down, he snatched up from among the glistening strands, heavy with raindrops, a little golden cross—one that had evidently slipped from velvet or ribbon as the ladies stood beneath that tree.

"That's not Miss Laura's—can't be!" muttered Charley, as he gazed intently at the little ornament. "Not half fine enough for her."

Then turning it over, he found engraved upon the reverse:

"E.B. From her Mother, 1860."

"E.B.—E.B.—E.B.! And pray who is E.B.?" muttered Charley, as, once more mounting, he turned his horse's head homeward. "Eleanor B. or Eliza—no, that's a housemaid's name—Ernestine, Eva. Who can she be? Not introduced—given the back seat—hardly spoken to, and yet so ladylike, and—There, get on, Beauty! What am I thinking about? We sha'n't be back to lunch."

He cantered on for a mile: and then as they entered a sunny lane—a very arcade of gem-besprinkled verdure—he drew rein, and taking the little cross from his pocket, once more read the inscription.

"'E.B. From her mother, 1860.' And pray who is her mother? and who is E.B.? Nobody from about here, I'll be bound. But what a contrast to that great, tall, dark woman! And they call her beautiful! Not half so beautiful as you, my lass!" he cried, rousing himself, and patting his mare's arched neck. "You are my beauty, eh, lass? Get on, then!"

But as Charley Vining rode on he grew thoughtful, and more than once he absently muttered:

"Yes; I think I'll go to the flower-show to-morrow!"

Chapter Six
A Second Meeting

Maximilian Bray, Esq., clerk in her Majesty's Treasury, Whitehall, sat in his dressing-room soured and angry. He had been hard at work trying to restore the mischief done by the rain; but in spite of "Bandoline" and "Brilliantine," he could not get hair, moustache, or whiskers to take their customary curl: they would look limp and dejected. Then that superfine coat was completely saturated with water, as was also his hat, neither of which would, he knew, ever again display the pristine gloss. And, besides, he had been unseated before "that coarse boor, Charley Vining," and the fellow had had the impertinence to grin. But, there, what could you expect from such a country clown? Altogether, Maximilian Bray, Esq., was cross—not to say savage—and more than once he had caught himself biting his nails—another cause for annoyance, since he was very careful with those almond-shaped nails, and had to pare, file, and burnish them afterwards to remove the inequality.

The above causes for a disordered temper have been recorded; but they were far from all. It is said that it never rains but it pours, and as that was the case out of doors, so it was in. But it would be wearisome to record the breaking of boot-loops, the tearing out of shirt-buttons, and the crowning horror of a spot of iron-mould right in the front of the principal plait. Suffice it that Maximilian Bray felt as if he could have quarrelled with the whole world; and as he sat chilled with his wetting, he had hard work to keep from gnawing his finger-nails again and again.

He might have gone down into the drawing-room, warm with the sun, while his northern-aspected window lent no genial softness; but no: there was something on his mind; and though he was dressed, he lingered still.

He knew that the luncheon bell would ring directly; in fact, he had referred several times to his watch. But still he hung back, as if shrinking from some unpleasant task, till, nerving himself, he rose and went to the looking-glass, examining himself from top to toe, grinning to see if his teeth were perfectly white, dipping a corner of the towel in water to remove the faintest suspicion of a little cherry tooth-paste from the corner of his mouth, biting his lips to make them red, trying once more to give his lank moustache the customary curl, but trying in vain—in short, going through the varied acts of a man who gives the whole of his mind to his dress; and then, evidently thoroughly dissatisfied, he strode across the room, flung open the door, and began to descend the stairs.

The builder of the Elms, not being confined for space, had made on the first floor a long passage, upon which several of the bedrooms opened; and this passage, being made the receptacle for the cheap pictures purchased at sales by Mr Onesimus Bray, was known in the house as the "long gallery."

Descending a short flight of stairs, Maximilian Bray was traversing this gallery, when the encounter which in his heart of hearts he had been dreading ever since he came down the night before was forced upon him; for, turning into the passage from the other end, the companion of Laura Bray's morning walk came hurriedly along, slackening her pace, though, as she perceived that there was a stranger in advance; but as their eyes met, a sudden start of surprise robbed the poor girl for a few moments of her self-control; the blood flushed to her temples, and for an instant she stopped short.

But Maximilian Bray was equal to the occasion. He had fought off the encounter as long as he could; but now that the time had come, he had determined upon brazening it out.

"Ha ha!" he laughed playfully. "Know me again, then? Quite frightened you, didn't I? Shouldn't have been so cross last time, when I only wanted to see you safe on your journey. Didn't know who I was, eh? But, bai Jove! glad to see you again—am indeed!"

There was no reply for an instant to these greetings. But as the flush faded, to leave the lace of her to whom they were addressed pale and stern, Maximilian Bray's smile grew more and more forced. The words were too shallow of meaning not to be rightly interpreted; and overcoming the surprise that had for a few moments fettered her, the fair girl turned upon Bray a keen piercing look, as moving forward she slightly bent, and said coldly in her old words:

"I think, sir, you have made some mistake."

"Mistake? No! Stop a minute. No mistake, bai Jove—no! You remember me, of course, when I startled you at the station. Only my fun, you know, only that young donkey must interfere. Glad to see you again—am, indeed, bai Jove! We shall be capital friends, I know."

As he spoke, he stepped before his companion, arresting her progress, and holding out his hand.

Driven thus to bay, the young girl once more turned and faced her pursuer with a look so firm and piercing, that he grew discomposed, and the words he uttered were unconnected and stammering.

"Sorry, you know, bai Jove! Mistook my meaning. Glad to see you again—am, bai Jove! Eh? What say?"

"I was not aware that Mr Maximilian Bray and the gentleman"—she laid a hardly perceptible emphasis on the word "gentleman"—"whom I encountered at that country station were the same. Allow me to remind you, sir, that you made a mistake then in addressing a stranger. You make another error in addressing me again; for bear in mind we are strangers yet. Excuse me for saying so, but I think it would be better to forget the past."

"Ya-as, just so—bai Jove! yes. It was nothing, you know, only—"

Maximilian Bray stopped short, for the simple reason that he was alone; for, turning hastily, his companion had retraced her steps, leaving the exquisite son of the house—the pride of his mother, the confidant of his sister, and the pest of the servants—looking quite "like a fool, you know, bai Jove!"

They were his own words, though meant for no other ears but his own, being a little too truthful. Then he stood thinking and gnawing one nail for a few moments before continuing his way down to the dining-room.

"So we are to be as if we met for the first time, are we?" he muttered; and then his countenance lighted up into an inane smile as he thought to himself, "Well, I've got it over. And, after all, it's something like being taken into her confidence, for haven't we between us what looks uncommonly like a secret?"

Chapter Seven
A Dawning Sense

They were rather famous for their flower-shows at Lexville, not merely for the capital displays of Nature's choicest beauties, educated by cunning floriculturists to the nearest point to perfection, but also for their wet days. When the exhibition was first instituted, people said that the marquee was soaked and the ladies' dresses spoiled, simply because the show was held upon a Friday. "Just," they said, "as if anybody but a committee would have chosen a Friday for an outdoor fête!"

But, if anything, the day was a little worse upon the next occasion, when Thursday had been selected, the same fate attending the luckless managers upon a Monday, a Tuesday, and a Wednesday. But now at last it seemed as if the fair goddess Flora herself had enlisted the sympathies of that individual known to mortals as "the clerk of the weather," and, in consequence, the day was all that could be desired. In fact, the weather was so fine, that the bandsmen of the Grenadier Guards, instead of coming down in their old and tarnished uniforms—declared, as a rule, to be good enough for Lexville—mustered in full force, gorgeous in their brightest scarlet and gold. The committee-men had shaken hands in the secretary's tent a dozen times over as many glasses of sherry, and forgotten to eat their biscuits in their hurry to order the cords of Edgington's great tent to be tightened, so potent were the rays of the sun; while within the canvas palace, in a golden hazy shade, the floral beauties from many a hot house and conservatory were receiving the last touches by way of arrangement.

Lexville was in a profound state of excitement that day, and Miss l'Aiguille, the dressmaker, declared that she had been nearly torn to pieces by her customers.

"As for Miss Bray," she said, "not another dress would she make for her—no, not if she became bankrupt to-morrow—that she wouldn't! Six tryings-on, indeed, and then not satisfied!"

However, Miss l'Aiguille's troubles were so far over that, like the rest of Lexville, she had partaken of an early dinner, or lunch, and prepared herself to visit the great fête.

Lexville flower-show was always held in the grounds of one of the county magistrates, the Rev. Henry Lingon, concerning whose kindness the reporter for the little newspaper generally went into raptures in print, and received orders for half-a-dozen extra copies the next bench-day. And now fast and furiously the carriages began to set down—the wealth and fashion of the neighbourhood making a point of being the earlier arrivals, so as to miss the crowd of commoner beings who would afterwards flock together.

"Ah, Vining! You're here, then, mai dear fellow! Why didn't you come to lunch?" exclaimed Maximilian Bray, sauntering up to the young man, who, rather flushed and energetic, was talking to a knot of flower-button-holed committee-men.

"How do, Max?" exclaimed Charley, hastily taking the extended hand, and giving it a good shake. Then, turning to the committee-men: "Much rather not—would, really, you know—don't feel myself adapted. Well, there," he exclaimed at last, in answer to several eager protestations, "I'll do it, if you can get no one else!—Want me to give away the prizes," he said, turning to Max Bray, who was gazing ruefully at his right glove, in whose back a slight crack was visible, caused, no doubt, by the hearty but rough grasp it had just received.

"To be sure—of course!" drawled Bray. "You're the very man, bai Jove! But won't you come towards the gate? I expect our people here directly."

Nothing loth, Vining strolled with his companion down one of the pleasant floral avenues, but seeing no flowers, hearing no band; for his gaze, he hardly knew why, was directed towards the approach; and though Maximilian Bray kept up a drawling series of remarks, they fell upon inattentive ears.

"Do you expect them soon?" said Charley at last, somewhat impatiently, for he was growing tired of his companion's chatter.

"Ya-as, directly," said Bray, smiling. "But, mai dear fellow, why didn't you come over and then escort them?"

Charley did not answer; for just then he caught sight of Laura, radiant of lace and dress, sweeping along beside Mrs Bray, who seemed to cut a way through the crowd at the farther part of the great marquee.

"Here they are," said Bray, drawing Charley along; "so now you can be out of your misery."

"What do you mean?" said Charley sharply.

"Bai Jove! how you take a fellow up! Nothing at all—nothing at all!"

Charley frowned slightly, and then suffered himself to be led up to the Elms party, Mrs Bray smiling upon him sweetly, and Laura favouring him with a look that was meant to bring him to her side.

But Laura's look had not the desired effect; for Charley stayed talking to Mrs Bray, after just passing the customary compliments to the younger lady.

A frown—no slight one—appeared on Laura's brow; but in a few seconds it was gone, and, walking back a few paces, she stayed by her younger sisters, with whom Charley could see the young lady of the previous day's encounter.

And now he would have followed Laura in the hope of obtaining an introduction, but he was arrested by a stout committee-man.

"Would he kindly step that way for a moment?"

With an exclamation of impatience, the young man followed, to find that his opinion was wanted as to the suitability of the site chosen for the distribution of the prizes.

"But surely you can obtain some one else?" exclaimed Charley.

"Impossible, my dear sir," was the reply.

So, after two or three unavailing attempts to obtain a substitute, Charley gave in; for the owner of the grounds, upon being asked, declared that a better choice could not have been made; the principal doctor shook his head; while Mr Onesimus Bray literally turned and fled upon hearing Charley's request. So, with a feeling of something like despair, the elected prize-giver began to cudgel his brains for the verbiage of a speech, telling himself that he should certainly break down and expose himself to the laughter of the assemblage; for the grandees from miles round had made their way to Lexville to patronise the flower-show; and at last, quite in despair, Charley walked hurriedly down one of the alleys of the garden, passing closely by the Bray party, and making Laura colour with annoyance at what she called his neglect.

But Charley Vining's perturbed spirit was not soothed by the anticipated solitude of the shady alley; for, before he had gone twenty yards, he saw Max Bray side by side with the lady who had occupied a goodly share of his thoughts since the encounter of the previous day.

Their backs were towards him, but it was quite evident that Mr Maximilian Bray was exerting himself to be as agreeable as possible to his companion, though with what success it was impossible to say. At all events, Charley Vining turned sharply round upon his heel, with a strange feeling of annoyance entirely new pervading his spirit.

"How absurd!" he muttered to himself. "What an ass I was to come to a set-out of this kind! No fellow could be more out of place!"

Turning out of the alley, he made his way, with rapid, business-like steps, on to the lawn, where the rapidly-increasing company were now gathering in knots, and listening to one of Godfrey's finest selections. To an unbiased observer, the thought might have suggested itself that there was as bright a flower-show, and as beautiful a mingling of hues, out there upon the closely-shaven turf, as within the tent; but Charley Vining was just then no impartial spectator; and, though more than one pair of eyes grew brighter as he approached, he saw nothing but two figures slowly issuing from the other end of the alley, where the guelder roses were showering down their vernal snows.

"I should uncommonly like to wing that Max Bray's neck!" said Charley to himself, as he threw his stalwart form into a wicker garden-chair, which creaked and expostulated dismally beneath the weight it was called upon to bear; and then, indulging in rather a favourite habit, he lolled there, muttering and talking to himself—cross-examining and answering questions respecting his uneasiness.

But the more he thought, the more uneasy he grew, and twice over he shifted his seat to avoid an attack from some conversational friend whom he saw approaching.

"There, this sort of thing won't do!" he exclaimed at last. "I'm afraid I'm going on the pointed-out road rather too fast. Suppose I take a dose of the Bray family by way of antidote."

So, leaving his seat, he strode towards where he could see Laura's white parasol; but his intent was baffled by a couple of committee-men, who literally took him into custody—their purpose being to give him divers and sundry explanations respecting the distribution of the prizes.

Chapter Eight
Shooting an Arrow

To have seen the company assembled in the Reverend Henry Lingon's grounds upon that bright afternoon, it might have been imagined that for the time being no marring shadow could possibly cross any breast; for, gaze where you would, the eye rested upon bright pleased faces wreathed in smiles, groups, whose aspect was of the happiest, setting off everywhere the Watteau-like landscape. But for all that, there were faces there wearing but a mask, and to more than one present that fête was fraught with *ennui* and disappointment. Toilettes arranged with the greatest care had, in other than the instance hinted at, been without effect; while again, where, in all simplicity, effect had not been sought, attentions had been paid distasteful even to annoyance. The Lexville flower-show had assembled together enough to form a little world of hopes and fears; and, fête-day though it had been, there were aching hearts that night, and tearful eyes moistening more than one pillow—the pillows of those who were young and hopeful still, in spite of their pain, though they were beginning to learn how much bitterness there is amidst the dregs of every cup—dregs to be drained by all in turn, earlier or later, in their little span.

But now the band was silenced for a while, and the company began to cluster around a temporary platform erected for the occasion, where the hero of the day was to distribute to the expectant gardeners the rewards of their care and patience.

Not that there is much to be called heroic in giving a few premiums for the best roses, or pansies, or stove-plants; but if the distributor be young, handsome, disengaged, heir to a baronetcy, and rich, in many eyes he becomes a hero indeed—a hero of romance; and bitter as were the feelings of Charley Vining, who declared to himself that his speech was blundering, that he had looked *gauche* and red-faced, and that any schoolboy could have done better, there were plenty of hearty plaudits for him, and more than one bright young face became suffused with the rapid beating of its owner's heart, as for a moment she thought that a glance was directed expressly at her.

Poor deluded little thing, though! It was all a mistake; for Charley Vining went through his business like an automaton, seeing nothing but a simple, half-mourning muslin dress, and a pale, sweet face in a lavender bonnet, which had appeared to him to have been haunted the whole day long by what he had once indignantly called "a tailor's dummy"—to wit, the exquisite and elaborately-attired form of Maximilian Bray.

But at length the distribution was at an end, and gardener, amateur, and cottager had been dismissed. Hot, weary, and glad to get away, Charley had hurried from the group of friends and acquaintances by whom he had been surrounded, when at a short distance off he espied Laura Bray, and his heart smote him for his neglect of the daughter of a family with whom he had always been very intimate.

"Too bad, 'pon my word!" said Charley hypocritically, for at the same moment other thoughts had flashed across his mind. However, he drew down that mental blind which people find so convenient wherewith to shadow the window of their hearts, and strode across the lawn towards Laura, who was apparently listening to the conversation of a gentleman of a more fleshy texture than is general with young men of three- or four-and-twenty.

"At last!" muttered Laura Bray, as Charley came smiling up to where she stood; and now beneath that smile the feeling of anger and annoyance at what she had looked upon as his neglect melted away. True, he owed her no allegiance; but she had set herself upon receiving his incense, and the afternoon having passed with hardly a word, a feeling of disappointment of the most bitter nature had troubled her: the music had seemed dirge-like, the brilliant flowers as if strewn with ashes. At times she was for leaving; but no, she could not do that. She had darted angry and reproachful glances at him again and again, but without effect, and then looked at him with eyes subdued and tearful, still in vain: he had seemed almost to avoid her, and such pains too as she had taken to make herself worthy of his regard! How she had bitten her lips till the blood had nearly started from beneath the bruised skin! Rage and disappointment had between them shared her breast. Then in a fit of anger she had commenced quite a flirtation with Hugh Lingon, the son of the owner of the grounds, a fat young gentleman from Cambridge, an ardent croquetist, but rather famed in his set for the number of times he had been "ploughed for smalls." Hugh Lingon had been delighted, smiling so much that the great creases in his fat face almost closed his eyes. He even went so far as to squeeze Laura's hand, and to tell her that the cup ought to have been presented to her as the fairest flower there; but Charley Vining had not seemed to mind the attentions in the least—he had not even appeared troubled; and at last poor Hugh Lingon was snubbed while uttering some platitude, and sent about his business by the imperious beauty, to make room for Charley Vining, whose pleasant smile chased away all Laura's care.

Of course she must make allowances for him. He had been busy and bothered about the prize-giving, so how could he attend to her? He was different from other men: so frank and straightforward and bold. She had always felt that he must love her; and after what Sir Philip Vining had hinted to papa, and papa had told mamma, and mamma had pinched her arm and told her in a whisper, what was there to prevent her being Lady Vining and the mistress of Blandfield Court?

"At last!" said Laura, and this time quite aloud, as Charley came up; when, taking his arm, she bestowed upon him a most reproachful glance. "I declare I thought your friends were to be quite neglected!"

"Neglected? O, I don't know," said Charley; and then there was a pause.

"Why, you grow quite *distrait*," said Laura pettishly. "Why, what can you see to take your attention there?"

She followed his gaze, which was directed towards a seat across the lawn, whereon were her companion of the day before, one of the "children," and Max Bray leaning in an attitude over the back.

"Shall we be moving?" said Charley abstractedly.

"O yes, please do!" said Laura. "I'm dying for want of an ice, or a cup of tea. I've been pestered for the last half-hour by that horrible fat boy!"

"Fat boy!" said Charley wonderingly.

"Yes; you know whom I mean—Hugh Lingon. So glad to have you come and set me free!"

Charley Vining did not say anything; but he led his companion towards the refreshment-tent, carefully avoiding the open lawn, and taking her, nowise unwilling, round by the shady walks where there were but few people, her steps growing slower, and her hand more heavy in its pressure. And still Charley Vining was quiet and thoughtful; but he led his companion to the refreshment-tent, handed the demanded ice, and then sauntered with her towards the lawn, still gay with fashionably-dressed groups.

"Had we not better get in the shade?" said Laura languidly. "The afternoon sun is quite oppressive."

"Let's cross over to Max," said Charley. "That seems a pleasant shady seat."

Laura did not speak, but she looked sidewise in his preoccupied countenance, and, evidently piqued at what she considered his indifference, allowed herself to be led across the lawn.

"By the way, Miss Bray," said Charley suddenly, "you never introduced me to your lady friend."

"Lady friend!" said Laura, as if surprised.

"Yes, the fair girl that friend Max there seems so taken with. Is it his *fiancée*?" Laura Bray's eyes glittered as she bent forward and looked intently in her companion's face; then a tightness seemed to come over the muscles of her countenance, giving her a hard bitter look, as a flash of suspicion crossed her mind. The next moment she smiled; but it was not a pleasant smile, though it displayed two rows of the most brilliantly-white teeth. But, apparently determined upon her course, she increased the pace at which they were walking till they stood in front of the seat where, with a troubled look in her eyes, sat, listening perforce to the doubtless agreeable conversation of Mr Maximilian Bray, the lady of the railway station, and the companion of Laura in the brougham.

It was with a look almost of malice that, stopping short, Laura fixed her eyes upon Charley Vining, to catch the play of his countenance as, without altering the direction of her glance, she said aloud:

"Miss Bedford, this gentleman has requested to be introduced to you—Mr Charles Vining." Then, with mock courtesy, and still devouring each twitch and movement, she continued: "Mr Charles Vining—Miss Bedford, *our new governess!*"

Chapter Nine
An Unexpected Protector

Mr Onesimus Bray led rather an uncomfortable life at home, and more than once he had confided his troubles to the sympathising ear of Sir Philip Vining. Laura was given to snubbing him; Max made no scruple about displaying the contempt in which he held his parent; while as to Mrs Bray, the wife of his bosom, the principal cause of his suffering from her was the way in which she sat upon him.

Now it must not be supposed that Mrs Bray literally and forcibly did perform any such act of cruelty; for this was only Mr Bray's metaphorical way of speaking in alluding to the way in which he was kept down and debarred from having a voice in his own establishment, the consequence being that he sought for solace and recreation elsewhere.

Mr Onesimus Bray was far from being a poor man; so that if he felt inclined to indulge in any particular hobby, his banker never said him "Nay," while if Mrs Bray's somewhat penurious alarms could be laid by the promise of profit, she would raise not the slightest opposition to her husband's projects. At the present time, Mr Bray's especial hobby was a model farm, in which no small sum of money had been sunk—of course, with a view to profit; but so far the returns had been *nil*. The old farmers of the neighbourhood used to wink and nod their heads together, and cackle like so many of their own geese at what they called Mr Bray's "fads"— namely, at his light agricultural carts and wagons; despising, too, his cows and short-legged pigs; but, all the same, losing no chance of obtaining a portion of his stock when occasion served.

Moved by a strong desire to possess the finest Southdown sheep in the county, Mr Bray had purchased a score of the best to be had for money, among which was a snowy-wooled patriarchal ram, as noble-looking a specimen of its kind as ever graced a Roman triumphal procession ere bedewing with its heart's blood the sacrificial altar. Gentle, quiet, and inoffensive, the animal might have been played with by a child before it arrived at Mr Bray's model farmstead; but having been there confined for a few days in a brick-walled pig-sty, the unfortunate quadruped attracted the notice of the young gentleman whose duty it was to clean knives, boots, and shoes at the Elms, and wait table at dinner, clothed in a jacket glorious with an abundant crop of buttons gracefully arranged in the outline of a balloon over his padded chest. It occurred to this young gentleman one afternoon when alone, that a little playful teasing of the ram might afford him some safe sport; so fetching a large new thrum mop from the kitchen, he held it over the side of the pig-sty, shaking it fiercely and threateningly at the ram, till the poor beast answered the challenge of the—to him—strange enemy by backing as far as possible, and then running with all his might at the suddenly-withdrawn mop, when his head would come with stunning violence against the bricks, making the wall quiver again.

The pleasant pastime used to be carried on very frequently, till most probably, not from soreness—rams' heads being slightly thick, and able to suffer even brick walls—but from disappointment at not being able to smite its adversary, the ram became changed into a decidedly vicious beast, and, as such, he was turned out into one of Mr Bray's pleasant meadows.

Now, as it fell upon a day, perfectly innocent of there being any vicious animal in the neighbourhood, Ella Bedford had passed through this very meadow during a walk with her three pupils. The morning was bright and sunshiny, and the sight of a fine snowy-wooled sheep cropping the bright green herbage was not one likely to create alarm. Had it been a cow, or even a calf, it might have been different, and the stiles and footpaths avoided for some other route; for the female eye is a strong magnifier of the bovine race, and we have known ladies refuse to pass through a field containing half-a-dozen calves, which had been magnified, one and all, into bulls of the largest and fiercest character.

There was something delightful to Ella in the sweet repose of the country around. The grass was just springing into its brightest green, gilded here and there with the burnished buttercups, while in every hedge-side "oxlips and the nodding violet" were blooming; the oaks, too, were beginning to wear their livery of green and gold. The birds sang sweetly as they jerked themselves from spray to spray, while that Sims Reeves of the feathered race—the lark—balanced himself far up in the blue ether, and poured out strain after strain of liquid melody. There was that wondrous elasticity in the air, that power which sets the heart throbbing, and the mind dreaming of something bright, ethereal, ungrasped, but now nearer than ever to the one who drinks in the sweet intoxicating breath of spring.

There was a brightness in Ella's eye, and a slight flush in her cheek, as she walked on with her pupils, smiling at each merry conceit, and feeling young herself, in spite of the age of sorrow that had been hers. For a while she forgot the strange home and the cool treatment she was receiving; the unpleasant attentions, too, of the hopeful son of the house; the meeting in the gallery. The wearisome compliments at the flower-show were set aside; for—perhaps influenced by the bright morning—Ella's cheek grew still more flushed, and in spite of herself she dwelt upon the scene where she pictured two beings addressed by a frank bold horseman; and as his earnest gaze seemed directed once more at her, Ella's heart increased its pulsations, but only to be succeeded by a dull sense of aching misery, as another picture floated before her vision, to the exclusion of the sunny landscape and the glorious spring verdure. The sweet liquid trill of the birds, too, grew dull on her ear; for she seemed once more to see the same earnest gaze fixed upon her face, and then to watch the start of surprise—was it disappointment?—as again Laura Bray's words rang on her ears:

"Miss Bedford, our new governess!"

It was time to cease dreaming, she thought.

Walks must come to an end sooner or later; and a reference to her watch showing Ella Bedford that they would only reach the Elms in time for lunch, they began to retrace their steps, when, to the young girl's horror, she saw that they had been followed by no less a personage than Mr Maximilian Bray, whose first act upon reaching them was to take his place by Ella's side, and send his sisters on in advance.

But that was not achieved without difficulty, Miss Nelly turning round sharply and declining to go.

"I shan't go, Max! You only want to talk sugar to Miss Bedford; and ma says you're ever so much too attentive—so there now!"

Ella's face became like scarlet, and she increased her pace; but a whisper from Max sent Nelly scampering off after her two sisters—now some distance in advance—when he turned to the governess.

"Glad I caught up to you, Miss Bedford—I am, bai Jove! You see, I wanted to have a few words with you."

"Mr Maximilian Bray will, perhaps, excuse my hurrying on," said Ella coldly. "It is nearly lunch-time, and I am obliged to teach punctuality to my pupils."

"Bai Jove! ya-as, of course!" said Max. "But I never get a word with you at home, and I wanted to set myself right with you about that station matter."

"If Mr Bray would be kind enough to forget it, I should be glad," said Ella quickly.

By Birth a Lady | 55

"Bai Jove! ya-as; but, you see, I can't. You see, it was all a joke so as to introduce myself like, being much struck, you know. Bai Jove, Miss Bedford! I can't tell you how much struck I was with your personal appearance— can't indeed!"

Ella's lip curled with scorn as she slightly bent her head and hurried on.

"Don't walk quite so fast, my dear—Miss Bedford," he added after a pause, as he saw the start she gave. "We shall be time enough for lunch, I daresay. Pleasant day, ain't it?"

Ella bent her head again in answer, but still kept on forcing the pace; for the children were two fields ahead, and racing on as quickly as possible.

"Odd, wasn't it, Miss Bedford, that we should have met as we did, and both coming to the same place? Why don't you take my arm? There's nobody looking—this time," he added.

The hot blood again flushed up in Ella's cheek as she darted an indignant glance at her persecutor; but there was something in Max Bray's composition which must have prevented him from reading aright the signs and tokens of annoyance in others; and, besides, he was so lost in admiration of his own graces and position, that when, as he termed it, he *stooped* to pay attentions to an inferior, every change of countenance was taken to mean modest confusion or delight.

"There, don't hurry so!" he exclaimed, laughing. "Bai Jove, what a fierce little thing you are! Now, look here: we're quite alone, and I want to talk to you. There, you needn't look round: the children are half-way home, and we shall be quite unobserved. Bai Jove! why, what a prudish little creature you are!"

Ella gave a quick glance round, but only to find that it was just as Max had said. There was a sheep feeding in the field, whose hedges were of the highest; and for aught she could see to the contrary, there was no assistance within a mile, while Max Bray had caught her hand in his, and was barring the route.

Regularly driven to bay, Ella turned upon him with flaming face, trying at the same moment to snatch away her hand, which, however, he held the tighter, crushing her fingers painfully, though she never winced.

"Mr Bray," she exclaimed, "do you wish me to appeal to your father for protection?"

"Of course not!" he drawled. "But there now—bai Jove! what is the use of your putting on all those fine airs and coy ways? Do you think I'm blind, or don't understand what they mean? Come now, just listen to what I say."

Before Ella could avoid his grasp, he had thrown one arm round her waist, when he started back as if stung, for a loud mocking laugh came from the stile.

"Ha, ha, ha! I thought so! I knew you wanted to talk sugar to Miss Bedford."

At the same moment Max and Ella had seen the merry delighted countenance of Nelly, who had crept silently back, but now darted away like a deer.

A cold chill shot through Ella Bedford's breast, and it was with the greatest difficulty that she could force back the angry tears as she saw that her future was completely marred at the Elms—how that she was, as it were, at the mercy of the young girl placed in her charge, unless she forestalled any tattling by complaining herself of the treatment to which she had been subjected.

"There, you needn't mind her!" exclaimed Max, who partly read her thoughts. "I can keep her saucy little tongue quiet. You need not be afraid."

"Afraid!" exclaimed Ella indignantly, as she turned upon the speaker with flashing eyes, and vainly endeavoured to free the hand Max had again secured.

"Handsomer every moment, bai Jove!" exclaimed Max. "You've no idea how a little colour becomes you! Now, I just want to say a few—"

"Are you aware, sir, that this is a cruel outrage?—one of which no gentleman would be guilty."

"Outrage? Nonsense! What stuff you do talk, my dear! I should have thought that, after what I said to you at the flower-show, you would have been a little more gentle, and not gone flaming out at a poor fellow like this. You see, I love you to distraction, Miss Bedford—I do indeed. Bai Jove, I couldn't have thought that it was possible for any one to have made such an impression upon me. Case of love at first sight—bai Jove, it was! And here you are so cruel—so hard—so—'Pon my soul I hardly know what to call it—I don't, bai Jove!"

"Mr Bray," said Ella passionately, "every word that you address to me in this way is an insult. As the instructor of your sisters, your duty should be to protect, not outrage my feelings at every encounter."

She struggled to release her hand, but vainly. Each moment his grasp grew firmer, and, like some dove in the claws of a hawk, she panted to escape. She felt that it would be cowardly to call for help; besides, it would be only making a scene in the event of assistance being near enough to respond to her appeal; and she had no wish to figure as an injured heroine or damsel in distress. Her breast heaved, and an angry flush suffused her cheeks, while, in spite of every effort, the great hot tears of annoyance and misery would force themselves to her eyes. She knew it not—though she saw the exquisite's gaze fixed more and more intently upon her—she knew not how excitement was heightening the soft beauty of her face, brightening her eyes, suffusing her countenance with a warm glow, and lending animation where sorrow had left all tinged with a sad air of gloom—an aspect that had settled down again after the brightness given by the early part of her walk.

"There now, don't be foolish, and hurt the poor little white hand! You can't get away, my little birdie; for I've caught you fast. And don't get making those bright eyes all dull and red with tears. I don't like crying—I don't indeed, bai Jove! Now let's walk gently along together. There—that's the way. And now we can talk, and you can listen to what I have to say."

In spite of her resistance, he drew the young girl's hand through his arm, and held it thus firmly. But to walk on, Ella absolutely refused; and stopping short, she tried to appeal to his feelings.

"Mr Bray," she said, "as a gentleman, I ask you to consider my position. You have already done me irreparable injury in the eyes of your sister; and now by this persecution you would force me to leave my situation, perhaps with ignominy. I appeal to your feelings—to your honour—to cease this unmanly pursuit."

"Ah, that's better!" he said mockingly. "But I'm afraid, my dear, you have a strong tinge of the romantic in your ideas. I see, you read too many novels; but you'll come round in time to my way of thinking, only don't try on so much of this silly prudishness, my dear. It don't do, you know, because I can see through it. There, now, don't struggle; only I'm not going to let you go without something to remember this meeting by. Now don't be silly! It's no robbery—only an exchange. I want that little ring to hang at my watch-chain, and you can wear this one for my sake. There!" he exclaimed triumphantly, as he succeeded in drawing a single gem pearl ring from her finger and placing one he drew from his pocket in its place, Ella the while alternately pale and red with suppressed anger, for she had vainly looked around for help; and now forcing back her tears, and scorning to display any farther weakness, she took off the ring and dashed it upon the path.

"What a silly little thing it is!" laughed Bray, who considered that he was honouring her with his attentions, however rough they might be. "But it's of no use: you don't go till that ring is on your darling little finger—you don't, bai Jove!"

Was there to be no help? A minute before, she would have refused assistance; for she did not believe that any one professing to be a gentleman would so utterly have turned a deaf ear to her protestations and appeals. From some low drink-maddened ruffian she might have fled in horror, shrieking, perhaps, for help; but here, with the son of her employers, Ella had believed that her indignant rejection of the insulting addresses would have been sufficient to set her at liberty. She was, then, half stunned as to her mental faculties on finding that her words were mocked at, her appeals disregarded, and even her indignant looks treated as feints and coyness. But then, poor girl, she did not know Maximilian Bray, and that his gross nature was not one that could grasp the character of a good and pure-hearted woman. It was something he could not understand. He measured other natures by his own, and acted accordingly. Once only the thoughts of Ella Bedford flew towards Charles Vining, as if, in spite of herself, they sought in him her natural protector, but only for an instant; and now, seriously alarmed, she gazed earnestly round for aid. She would have even gladly welcomed the mocking face of Nelly, and have called her to her side. But no, Nelly had hurried away, content and laughing at what she had seen: and now from the indignant flush, Ella's face began to pale into a look of genuine alarm. But help was at hand.

Still holding tightly by her hand, Max Bray stooped to recover the ring, when, suddenly as a flash of light, a white rushing form seemed to dart through the air, catching Max Bray, as he bent down, right upon the crown of his hat, crushing it over his eyes, and tumbling him over and over, as a fierce "Ba-a-a-a!" rung upon his astonished ears.

Set free by this unexpected preserver, Ella, panting and alarmed, fled for the stile and climbed it, when, looking back, she saw that she was safe, while Max Bray rose, struggling to free himself from his crushed-down hat; but only for his father's prize Southdown to dart at and roll him over again: when, once more rising to his feet, he ran, frightened and blindfold, as hard as he could across the field in the opposite direction.

Ella saw no more. It did not fall to her lot to see Max Bray make a blind bound—a leap in the dark—from his unseen pursuer, and land in the midst of a dense blackthorn hedge, out of which he struggled, torn of flesh and coat, to free himself from the extinguishing hat, and gaze through the hedge-gap at his assailant, who stood upon the other side shaking his head, and bucking and running forward "ba-a-a-ing" furiously.

For a few moments Max Bray was speechless with rage and astonishment. To think that he, Maximilian Bray, should have been bowled over, battered, and made to flee ignominiously by a sheep! It was positively awful.

"You—you—you beast! you—you woolly brute!" he stuttered at last. "I'll—I'll—bai Jove, I'll shoot you as sure as you're there!—I will, bai Jove!"

But now the worst of the affair flashed upon him, making torn clothes, thorns in the flesh, and battered hat seem as nothing, though these were in his estimation no trifles; but this was the second time within the past few days that he had been wounded in his self-esteem.

"And now there's that confounded coy jade run home laughing at me— I'm sure she has!" he muttered. "Not that there was anything to laugh at; but never mind: 'Every dog—' My turn will come! But to be upset like this! And—what? you won't let me come through!"

There was no doubt about it. The Southdown was keeping guard at the stile, and Max Bray, after trying to repair damages, was glad to make his way back to the Elms by a circuitous route, and then to creep in by the side-door unseen, vowing vengeance the while against those who had brought him to that pass.

"But I'll make an end of the sheep!" he exclaimed—"I will, bai Jove!"

Chapter Ten
Ella's Comforter

Most persons possessed of feeling will readily agree that scarcely anything could be more unpleasant than for a gentleman, bent upon making himself attractive to a lady, to meet with such a misfortune as to be taken, while in a stooping position, for a defiant beast, and to have to encounter the full force of a woolly avalanche, or so much live mutton discharged, as from a catapult, right upon the crown of his head. Max Bray was extremely sore afterwards—sore in person and temper: but the most extraordinary part of the affair is, that his head never ached from the fierce blow. It would perhaps be invidious to offer remarks about thickness, or to make comparisons; but certainly for two or three days after, when he encountered Ella Bedford, Max Bray did wear, in spite of his effrontery, a decidedly sheepish air. But not for a longer period. At the end of that time a great deal of the soreness had worn off, and he was nearly himself again.

But with Ella Bedford the case was different. She was hourly awakening to the fact that hers was to be no pleasant sojourn at the Elms; and with tearful eyes she thought of the happy old days at home before sickness fell upon the little country vicarage, and then death removed the simple, good-hearted village clergyman from his flock, to be followed all too soon by his mourning wife.

"I have nothing to leave you, my child—nothing!" were almost the father's last words. "Always poor and in delicate health, I could only keep out of debt. But your mother, help her—be kind to her," he whispered.

Ella Bedford's help and kindness were only called for during a few months; and then it fell to her lot to seek for some situation where the accomplishments, for the most part taught by her father, might be the means of providing her with a home and some small pittance.

By means of advertising, she had succeeded in obtaining the post of governess at the Elms, and it was while on her way to fill that post that she had encountered the hopeful scion of the house of Bray. It was, then, with a feeling almost of horror that she met him again at the Elms, and her first thought was that she must flee directly—leave the house at once; her next that she ought to relate her adventure to some one. But who would sympathise with her, and rightly view it all? She shrank from harsh loud-voiced Mrs Bray; and, almost from the first meeting, Laura had seemed to take a dislike to her—one which she made no scruple of displaying—while, as a rule, she tried all she could to how the immeasurable distance she considered that there existed between her and the dependent.

On the day of the sheep encounter, agitated, wounded, and with great difficulty keeping back her tears, Ella hurried on; and had Max Bray's position been one of danger, it is very doubtful whether any assistance would have been rendered him through Ella, so thoroughly was she taken up with her own position. She felt that she must be questioned respecting her charges reaching home alone; they would certainly talk about her staying behind with their brother, and the culminating point would be reached when Miss Nelly declared what she had seen.

Well might the poor girl's heart beat as she hastened on; for it seemed as if, through the persecution of a fop, her prospects in life were to be blighted at the outset. But there's a silver lining to every cloud, it is said; and before Ella had gone half a mile, to her great joy she saw Nelly seated with her sisters by a bank, gathering wild flowers, and then tossing them away.

Fortune favoured her too when they reached the Elms: luncheon—the children's dinner—had been put back for half an hour because Mr Maximilian had not returned.

"Mr Maximilian" did not show himself at all at table that day, and, glad of the respite, Ella sought her bedroom directly after, to think over the past, and try and decide what ought to be her course under the circumstances. What would she not have given for the loving counsel of some gentle, true-hearted woman! But she felt that she was quite alone—alone in the vast weary world; and as such thoughts sprang up came the recollection of the happy bygone, sweeping all before it; and at last, unable to bear up any longer, she sank upon her knees by the bedside, weeping and sobbing as if her poor torn heart would break.

She struggled hard to keep the tears back, but in vain now—they would come, and with them fierce hysterical sobs, such as had never burst before from her breast. Then would come a cessation, as she asked herself whether she ought not to acquaint Mrs Bray with her son's behaviour?—or would it be making too much of the affair? Then she reviewed her own conduct, and tried to find in it some flaw—some want of reserve which had brought upon her the insults to which she had been subjected. But, as might be expected, the search was vain, and once more she bowed down her head and sobbed bitterly for the happy past, the painful present, and the dreary future.

It was in the midst of her passionate outbursts that she suddenly felt some one kneel beside her, and through her tears she saw, with wonder, the friendly and weeping face of Nelly, who had crept unperceived into the room.

"O, Miss Bedford! Dear, dear Miss Bedford, please don't—don't!" sobbed the girl, as, throwing her long thin arms round Ella, she drew her face to her own hard bony breast, soothing, kissing, and fondling her tenderly, as might a mother. "Please—please don't cry so, or you'll break my heart; for, though you don't think it, I do love you so—so much! You're so gentle, and kind, and wise, and beautiful, that—that—that—O, and you're crying more than ever!"

Poor Nelly burst out almost into a howl of grief as she spoke; but, like her words, it was genuine, and as she pressed her rough sympathies upon her weeping governess, Ella's sobs grew less laboured, and she clung convulsively to the slight form at her side.

"There—there—there!" half sobbed Nelly. "Try not to cry, dear; do please try, dear Miss Bedford; for indeed, indeed it does hurt me so! You made me to love you, and I can't bear to see you like this!"

So energetic, indeed, was Nelly's grief, that, as she spoke, she kicked out behind, overturning a bedroom chair; but it passed unnoticed.

"They say I'm a child; but I'm not, you know!" she said half passionately. "I'm sixteen nearly, and I can see as well as other people. Yes, and feel too! I'm not a child; and if Laury raps my knuckles again, I'll bite her, see if I don't! But I know what you're crying about, Miss Bedford, and I saw you wanted to cry all dinner-time, only you couldn't; it's about Max; and you thought I should tell that he put his arm round your waist. But I shan't—no, not never to a single soul, if they put me in the rack! He's a donkey, Max is, and a disagreeable, stupid, cox-comby, stubborn, bubble-headed donkey, that he is! I saw him kiss Miss Twentyman, who used to be our governess, and she slapped his face—and serve him right too, a donkey, to want to kiss anybody—such stupid silly nonsense! It's quite right enough for girls and women to kiss; but for a man—pah! I don't believe Max was ever meant to be anything but a girl, though; and I told him so once, and he boxed my ears, and I threw the butter-plate at him, and the butter stuck in his whiskers, and it was such fun I forgot to cry, though he did hurt me ever so. But I'm not a child, Miss Bedford, and I do love you ever so much, and I'll never say a single word about you and Max; and if he ever bothers you again, you say to him, 'How's Miss Brown?' and he'll colour up, and be as cross as can be. I often say it to make him cross. He used to go to see her, and she wouldn't have him because she said he was such a muff, and she married Major Tompkins instead. But it does make him cross—and serve him right too, a nasty donkey! Why, if he'd held my hand like he did yours to-day, I'd have pinched him, and nipped him, and bitten him, that I would! He sha'n't never send me away any more, though; I shall always stop with you, and take care of you, if you'll love me very much; and I will work so hard—so jolly hard—with my studies, Miss Bedford, I will indeed; for I'm so behindhand, and it was all through Miss Twentyman being such a cross old frump! But you needn't be afraid of me, dear; for I'm not a child, am I?"

As Nelly Bray had talked on, fondling her to whom she clung the while, Ella's sobs had grown less frequent, and at last, as she listened to the gaunt overgrown girl's well-meaning, half-childish, half-womanly words, she smiled upon her through her tears; for her heart felt lighter, and there was relief, too, in the knowledge that Nelly was indeed enough of a true-hearted woman to read Max Bray's conduct in the right light, and to act accordingly.

"You darling dear sweet love of a governess!" cried Nelly rapturously, as she saw the smile; and clinging to her neck, she showered down more kisses than were, perhaps, quite pleasant to the recipient. "You will trust me, won't you?"

"I will indeed, dear," said Ella softly.

"And you won't fidget?"

"No," said Ella.

"And now—that's right; wipe your eyes and sit down—and now you must talk to me, and take care of me. But you are not cross because I came up without leave?"

"Indeed, no," said Ella sadly. "I thought I was without a friend, and you came just at that time."

"No, no, you mustn't say that," said Nelly, "because I am not old and sensible enough to be your friend. But it hurt me to see you in such trouble, and I was obliged to come; and now you won't be miserable any more; and you mustn't take any notice if Laury is disagreeable—a nasty thing! flirting all day long with my—with Mr Hugh Lingon," she said, colouring. "But there, I'm not ashamed: Hugh Lingon is my lover, and has been ever since he was fourteen and I was six—when he used to give me sweets, and I loved him, and used to say he was so nice and fat to pinch! And Laury was flirting with him all that afternoon at the show, when Max would hang about—a great stupid!—when I wanted to explain things; for you know she was flirting with Hugh because that dear old Charley Vining wouldn't take any notice of her. He is such a dear nice fellow! But I do not love *him*, you know, only like him; and he likes me ever so much. He told me so one day, and gave me half-a-crown to spend in sweets—wasn't it kind of him? He'll often carry a basket of strawberries or grapes over for me and the girls, or fill his pockets with apples and pears for us; when, as for old Max, he'd faint at the very sight of a basket, let alone carry it! You will like Charley. He *is* nice! Laury loves him awful—talks about him in her sleep! But I do not think he cares for her,—and no wonder! But I say, Miss Bedford, how nice and soft your hand is! and, I say, what a little one! Why, mine's twice as big!"

Ella smiled, and went on smoothing the girl's rough hair, but hardly heeding what she said—only catching a word here and there.

"I shouldn't never love Charley Vining," said Nelly, whose grammar was exceedingly loose, "but I should always like him; and if I don't marry Hugh Lingon, I mean to be an old maid, and wear stiff caps and pinners, and then—You're beginning to cry again, and it's too bad, after all this comforting up!"

"No, indeed, my child," said Ella, rousing herself. "I was only thinking that when things are at the blackest some little ray of hope will peep out to light our paths."

"I say," said Nelly, "is that poetry?"

"No," said Ella, smiling sadly.

"Ah, I thought it was," said Nelly. "But then I'm so ignorant and stupid! Mamma says I'm fit for nothing, and I suppose she's right! But there, I'm making you tired with my talking, and I won't say another word; only don't you fidget about Max—only snub him well; and I wouldn't tell pa or ma, because it might make mischief."

Hanging as it were in the balance, Ella allowed the advice of the child-woman at her side to have effect, and determined to say nothing—to make no complaints, trusting to her own firmness to keep her persecutor in his place until his visit was at an end. It was, perhaps, a weak resolve; but who is there that always takes the better of two roads? It was, however, her decision—her choice of way—one which led through a cloud of sorrow, misery, and despair so dense, that in after time poor Ella often asked herself was there to be no turning, no byway that should lend once again, if but for a few hours, into the joyous sunshine of life?

Chapter Eleven
Croquet and Roquet

"Bai Jove, seems a strange thing!" said Max Bray at breakfast-time, about a week after the events recorded in the last chapter—"seems a strange thing you women can't settle anything without showing your teeth!"

"You women, indeed! Max, how can you talk so vulgarly!" exclaimed Laura.

And then there was silence, for Ella Bedford entered the breakfast-room with her charges.

Strange or not, there had been something more than a few words that morning in the breakfast-room between Mrs Bray and her daughter, concerning a croquet-party to come off that afternoon upon the Elms lawn. As for Mr Bray, he had taken no part in the discussion, "shutting-up"—to use his son's words—"like an old gingham umbrella, bai Jove!"

However, hostilities ceased upon the appearance of Ella with the children; and Mrs Bray, after shrieking for the tea-caddy, sat down to the urn, and the morning meal commenced.

"Of course, mamma," said Laura suddenly, "you won't think of having the children on the lawn?"

"O, I daresay, miss!" cried Nelly, firing up. "Just as if we're to be set aside when there's anything going on! Charley Vining says I play croquet just twice as well as you can; and I know he's coming to-day on purpose to see me!" she added maliciously.

Mr Bray shook his head at her, and Ella slightly raised one finger; but as she made a rule of never correcting her charges when father or mother was present, she did not speak.

"Hold your tongue, you pert child!" exclaimed Laura, with a toss of the head. "You'll let Miss Bedford keep them in the schoolroom, of course, mamma?"

"Indeed, I don't see why they should not have a game as well as their sister!" shrieked Mrs Bray, from behind the urn; for after the hostilities of that morning mamma would not budge an inch.

The breakfast ended, Nelly ran round to give Mrs Bray a sounding kiss, and then danced after her sisters and their governess into the schoolroom.

"There, hooray! Beaten her!" shouted Nelly, clapping her hands. "I knew what she meant, Miss Bedford. She didn't want you to be on the lawn and come and play; and now she's beaten, and serve her right too! She's afraid Charley Vining will take more notice of you than he does of her, and I shall tell him."

"My dear Nelly!" exclaimed Ella, with a look of pain on her countenance; when her wild young charge dropped demurely into a seat, and began to devour French irregular verbs at a tremendous rate, working at them thoroughly hard, and, having a very retentive memory, making some progress.

These were Ella's happiest moments; for, in spite of their roughness, the three girls in her charge, one and all, evinced a liking for her; and save at times, when she broke out into a thorough childish fit, Nelly grew hourly more and more womanly under her care. But Ella was somewhat troubled respecting the afternoon's meeting, and would gladly have spent the time in solitude, for it was plain enough that she was to be present solely out of opposition to Laura; and in spite of all her efforts, it seemed that she was to grow daily more distasteful to the dark beauty, who openly showed her dislike before Ella had been in the house a week.

However, the schoolroom studies made very little progress that morning; for before long Mrs Bray entered to give orders respecting dress, sending Nelly into ecstasies as she cast her book aside; and at three o'clock that afternoon, as Laura swept across the lawn to meet some of the coming guests, there was a look of annoyance upon her countenance that was ill-concealed by the smile she wore.

"So absurd!" she had just found time to say to Mrs Bray, "bringing those children and their governess out upon the croquet-ground as if on purpose to annoy people, who are made to give way to humour their schoolroom whims!"

Mrs Bray's reply was a toss of the head, as she turned off to meet her hopeful son Max, who, after pains that deserved a better recompense, now made his appearance dressed for the occasion.

"Just in time, bai Jove!" he drawled; and then he started slightly, for, making a survey of the lawn, he suddenly became aware that Ella Bedford was seated within a few yards with her pupils. "O, here's Miss Bedford!" he exclaimed; "and, let's see, there's Laura; and who are those with her? O, the Ellis people. They don't play. I want to make up a set at once—want another gentleman. Why, there's Charley Vining just coming out of the stable-yard; rode over, I suppose. Perhaps he'll play."

Ella shrank back, and sent an appealing look towards Mrs Bray; but as Max had said Miss Bedford was to play, there was no appeal.

"Perhaps Miss Nelly here would like to take my place?" said Ella.

"O, dear me, no, Miss Bedford! Mr Maximilian selected you as one of the set, and I should not like him to be disappointed," said Mamma Bray.

"You'll play, Vining?" drawled Max.

"Well, no; I don't care about it," said Charley good-humouredly. "I'll make room for some one else."

"Ya-a-as, but we haven't enough without you," said Max. "You might take a mallet, you know, till some one else comes."

"O, very good," said Charley, who had just caught sight of Ella with a mallet in her hand. "I'm ready."

"Then we'll have a game at once before any one else comes. Now then, Laura, here's Charley Vining breaking his heart because you don't come and play on his side. I daresay, though, Miss Bedford and I can get the better of you."

But Max Bray's arrangement for a snug *parti* of four was upset by fresh arrivals—Hugh Lingon, looking very stout, pink, and warm, with a couple of sisters, both stouter, pinker, and warmer, and a very slim young curate from a neighbouring village, arriving just at the same time.

Then followed a little manoeuvring and arranging; but in spite of brother and sister playing into each other's hands, the game commenced with Max Bray upon the same side as Laura, one of the stout Miss Lingons, and the slim curate; while Charley Vining had Ella under his wing.

Croquet is a very nice amusement: not that there is much in the game itself, which is, if anything, rather tame; but it serves as a means for bringing people together—as a vehicle for chatting, flirting, and above all, carrying off the *ennui* so fond of making its way into social fashionable life. You can help the trusting friend so nicely through hoop after hoop, receiving all the while such prettily-spoken thanks and such sweet smiles; there is such a fine opportunity too, whilst assuming the leadership and directing, for enabling the young lady to properly hold her mallet for the next blow—arranging the little fingers, and pressing them inadvertently more tightly to the stick; and we have known very enthusiastic amateurs go so far as to kneel down before a lady, and raise one delicate *bottine*, placing it on the player's ball, and holding it firmly while the enemy is croque'd. *Apropos* of enemies, too, how they can be punished! How a rival can be ignominiously driven here and there, and into all sorts of uncomfortable places—under bushes and behind trees, wired and pegged, and treated in the most cruel manner!

And so it was at the Elms croquet-party. Looking black almost as night, Laura struck at the balls viciously—a prime new set of Jaques's best—chipping the edge of her mallet, bruising the balls, and driving Ella Bedford's "Number 1, blue," at times right off the croquet-ground. Not that it mattered in the least; for in spite of his self-depreciation, Charley Vining was an admirable player, making long shots, and fetching up Ella's unfortunate ball, taking it with him through hoop after hoop, till Laura's eyes flashed, and Max declared, "bai Jove!" he never saw anything like it; when Charley would catch a glimpse of Ella's troubled look, recollect himself, and perform the same acts of kindness for the plump Miss Lingon, to receive in return numberless "O, thank you's!" and "O, how clever's!" and "So much obliged, Mr Vining!" while "that governess," as Laura called her, never once uttered a word of thanks. As for Hugh Lingon, he was always nowhere; and as he missed his aim again and again, he grew more and more divided in his opinions.

First he declared that the ground was not level; but seeing the good strokes made by others, he retracted that observation, and waited awhile.

"I don't think my ball is quite round, Vining," he exclaimed, after another bad stroke.

"Pooh! nonsense!" laughed Charley. "You didn't try; it was because you didn't want to hit Miss Bray."

"No—no! 'Pon my word, no—'pon my word!" exclaimed Hugh, protesting as he grew more and more pink.

"Did his best, I'd swear—bai Jove, he did!" drawled Max, playing, and sending poor Lingon off the ground.

Then, after a time, Lingon had his turn once more.

"It's not the ball, it's this mallet—it is indeed!" he exclaimed, after an atrocious blow. "Just you look here, Vining: the handle's all on one side."

"Never mind! Try again, my boy," laughed Charley; and soon after he had to bring both his lady partners up again to their hoop, sending Laura's ball away to make room for them, and on the whole treating it rather harshly, Laura's eyes flashing the while with vexation.

"I like croquet for some things," said Laura's partner, the thin curate, after vainly trying to render her a service; "I but it's a very unchristian-like sort of game—one seems to give all one's love to one's friends, and to keep none for one's enemies."

"O, come, I say," laughed Charley, who seemed to be in high spirits. "Here's Mr Louther talking about love to Miss Bray!"

"Indeed, I assure you—" exclaimed the curate.

"But I distinctly heard the word," laughed Charley.

"Was that meant for a witticism?" sneered Laura.

"Wit? no!" said Charley good-humouredly. "I never go in for that sort of thing."

"Bai Jove, Vining! why don't you attend to the ga-a-a-me?" drawled Max, who was suffering from too much of the second Miss Lingon—a young lady who looked upon him as an Adonis.

"Not my turn," said Charley.

"Yes, yes!" said Hugh Lingon innocently. "Miss Bedford wants you to help her along!"

"Of course," sneered Laura. "Such impudence!"

But Charley did not hear her words; for he was already half-way towards poor Ella, who seemed to shrink from him as he approached, and watched with a troubled breast the efforts he made upon her behalf.

"Now it's my turn again," said Hugh. "Now just give me your advice here, Vining. What ought I to do?"

Charley interrupted a remark he was making to Ella Bedford, and pointed out the most advantageous play, when Hugh Lingon raised his mallet, the blow fell, and—he missed.

"Now, did you ever see anything like that?" he exclaimed, appealing to the company.

"Yes, often!" laughed Charley.

"But what can be the reason?" exclaimed Lingon.

"Why, bai Jove! it's because you're such a muff, Lingon, bai Jove!" exclaimed Max.

"I am—I know I am!" said Lingon good-humouredly. "But, you know, I can't help it—can't indeed!"

The game went on with varying interest, Charley in the intervals trying to engage Ella in conversation; but only to find her retiring, almost distant, as from time to time she caught sight of a pair of fierce eyes bent upon her from beneath Laura's frowning brows. But there was a sweetness of disposition beaming from Ella's troubled countenance, and the tokens of a rare intellect in her few words—spoken to endeavour to direct him to seek for others with more conversational power, but with precisely the contrary effect—that seemed to rouse in Sir Philip Vining's son feelings altogether new. He found himself dwelling upon every word, every sweet and musical tone, drinking in each troubled, trembling look, and listening with ill-concealed eagerness even for the words spoken to others.

"Bai Jove!" exclaimed Max at length, angrily to his sister, "what's the matter with that Charley Vining?"

"Don't ask me!" cried Laura pettishly, as she turned from him to listen to and then to snub the slim curate, who, after ten minutes' consideration, had worked up and delivered a compliment.

Once only did Ella trust herself to look at Charley, taking in, though, with that glance the open-countenanced, happy English face of the young man, but shrinking within herself the next instant as she seemed to feel the bold, open, but still respectfully-admiring glance directed at her.

Two other croquet sets had been made upon the great lawn; and, taking the first opportunity, Ella had given up her mallet into other hands—an act, to Laura's great disgust, imitated by Charley Vining, who, however, found no opportunity for again approaching Ella Bedford until the hour of dinner was announced, when, the major portion of the croquet-players having departed, the remainder—the invited few—met in the drawing-room.

Chapter Twelve
Cross Upon Cross

"Will you take down Miss Bedford, Max?" said Mrs Bray, according to instructions from her son, who, however, was not present, his toilet having detained him; and, therefore, trembling Ella fell to the lot of Charley Vining, whom, she knew not why, she seemed to fear now as much as she did Max Bray.

And yet she could not but own that he was only frank, cordial, and gentlemanly. Only! Was that all? She dared not answer that question. Neither could he answer sundry questions put by his own conscience, as from time to time he encountered angry, reproachful glances from the woman who sat opposite, but to whom, whatever might have been assumed, he had never uttered a word that could be construed into one of love.

Somehow or another, during that dinner, Sir Philip's words would keep repeating themselves to Charley, and at last he found himself muttering: "Shut myself out from an Eden—from an Eden!" while, when the ladies rose, and the door had closed upon the last rustling silk, a cloud appeared to have come over the scene, and he sat listening impatiently to the drawl of Max, and the agricultural converse of Mr Bray.

It was with alacrity, then, that Charley left the table, when, upon reaching the drawing-room, he found Laura hovering in a paradise of musical R's, as she sat at the piano, rolling them out in an Italian bravura song, whose pages, for fear that he should be forestalled by Charley Vining, Hugh Lingon rushed to turn over.

"Now Miss Bedford will sing us something," shrieked Mrs Bray; and not daring to decline, Ella rose and walked to the piano, taking up a song from the canterbury. But her hands trembled as a shadow seemed to be cast upon her; and without daring to look, she knew that Charley Vining was at her side, ready to turn over the leaves.

"If he would only go!" she thought; and then she commenced with tremulous voice a sweet and plaintive ballad, breathing of home and the past, when, living as it were in the sweet strain, her voice increased in volume and pathos, the almost wild expression thrilling through her hearers, till towards the end of the last verse, when forgetting even Vining's presence in the recollections evoked, Ella was brought back to the present with a start, as one single hot tear-drop fell upon her outstretched hand.

How she finished that song she never knew, nor yet how she concealed her painful agitation; but her next recollection was of being in the conservatory with Charley Vining, alone, and with his deep-toned voice seeming to breathe only for her ear.

"You must think it weak and childish," he said softly; "but I could not help it," he added simply. "Perhaps I am, after all, only an overgrown boy; but that was my dear mother's favourite song—one which I have often listened to; and as you sung to-night, the old past seemed to come back almost painfully. But I need not fear that you will ridicule me."

"Indeed, no!" said Ella softly. "I can only regret that I gave you pain."

"Pain! No, it was not pain," said Charley musingly. "I cannot explain the feeling. I am a great believer in the power of music; and had we been alone, I might have asked you to repeat the strain. I am only too glad, though, that my poor father was not here."

There was a pause for quite a minute—one which, finding how her companion had been moved, Ella almost feared to break; when seeing him start back, as it were, into the present and its duties, she made a movement as if to return.

"But one minute, Miss Bedford," said Charley. "You admire flowers, I see. Look at the metallic, silvery appearance of these leaves."

"Pray excuse me, Mr Vining," said Ella quietly, "but I wish to return to the drawing-room."

"Yes—yes—certainly!" exclaimed Charley. "But one moment: I have something to say to you."

"Mr Vining is mistaken," said Ella coldly; "he forgets that I am not a visitor or friend of the family. Pray allow me to return!"

"Of course—yes!" said Charley. "But indeed I have something to say, Miss Bedford. Look here!"

He drew the little gold cross from his pocket, and held it up in the soft twilight shed by the coloured lamps, when his companion uttered a cry of joy.

"I have grieved so for its loss!" she exclaimed. "You found it?"

"Yes; beneath that tree where you were taking refuge from the rain. I know it was my duty to have returned it sooner; but I wished to place it in your hands myself."

"O, thank you—I am so grateful!" exclaimed Ella, hardly noticing the *empressement* with which he spoke.

"I wished, too," said Charley, speaking softly and deeply, "for some reward for what I have done."

"Reward?" ejaculated Ella.

"Surely, yes," said Charley, laying his hand upon the tiny glove resting upon his arm. "You would accord that to the poorest lout who had been the lucky finder."

"Reward, Mr Vining?" stammered Ella.

"Yes!" exclaimed Charley, his rich deep voice growing softer as he spoke. "And but for those words upon the reverse side, I would have kept the cross as an emblem of my hope. I, too, had a mother who is but a memory now. But you will grant me what I ask?"

"Mr Vining," said Ella gravely, but unable to conceal her agitation, "will you kindly lead me back to the drawing-room?"

"I thank you for restoring me the cross, which I had never hoped to see again."

She held out her hand, and the little ornament was immediately placed within her palm.

"You see," said Charley, "I trust to your honour. I am defenceless now, but you will give me my guerdon?"

"Reward?" said Ella again.

"Yes," said Charley eagerly; "I do not ask much. That rose that you have worn the evening through: give me that—I ask no more."

"Mr Vining," said the agitated girl, "I am poor and friendless, and here as a dependent. I say thus much, since I believe you to be a gentleman. You would not wilfully injure me, I am sure; but this prolonged absence may give umbrage to my employers. Once more, pray lead me back!"

Charley was moved by the appeal, and he turned on the instant.

"But you will give me that simple flower?" he said.

"Mr Vining," said Ella with dignity, "would you have me lose my self-respect? I thank you for the service—indeed I am most grateful—but I cannot accede to your request."

"I had hoped that I might be looked on as a friend," said Charley gloomily, as he once more arrested his companion's steps; "but there, I suppose if it had been—Pish! forgive me, pray!" he exclaimed. "How weak and contemptible I am! Miss Bedford, I am quite ashamed to have spoken so. But tell me that you forgive me, and—"

"Is Miss Bedford so mortally offended?" said a voice close at their side. "I have no doubt we can manage to obtain her forgiveness for you, Mr Vining. But not to-night, as there will not be time.—Nelly wants you in the schoolroom, Miss Bedford, and then, as it is late, perhaps you had better not return to the drawing-room this evening."

Ella Bedford started, as, with flashing, angry eyes, Laura Bray stepped forward from behind the thick foliage of an orange-tree, and then, without a word—for she could not have spoken, so bitter, so cruel were the tones, and so deep the sting—Ella glided from the conservatory, leaving Laura face to face with Charley.

"I am sorry to have interrupted so pleasant a tête-à-tête!" exclaimed Laura tauntingly.

There was no answer. Charley merely leaned against the open window, and gazed out upon the starry night; for he could not trust himself to speak, since every humiliating word addressed to his late companion had seemed to cut into his own heart; and had he spoken, it would have been with some hot angry words, of which he would afterwards have repented.

"Had I known that Mr Charles Vining was so pleasantly engaged, I would not have come," said Laura again bitterly, and with reproach in every tone of her voice.

Again angry words were on Charley's lips; but for the sake of her who had left him he crushed them down, as he stood listening to the impatient foot of the angry girl beating the tiled floor, and seemed to feel her eyes burning him as they literally flashed with suppressed rage.

"Perhaps now that Mr Vining is disengaged he will lead me back to the drawing-room, as it might be painful to his feelings for people afterwards to make remarks upon our absence."

Charley started at this, and made a movement as if to offer his arm; but the remembrance of the cruel insult to the dependent yet rankled in his breast, and he seemed to shrink from the angry woman as from something that he loathed.

Laura saw it, and a sob of rage, disappointment, and passion combined burst from her breast. But even then, if he had made but one sign, she would have softened and thrown herself weeping upon his breast, reproaching, upbraiding, but loving still, and ready to forgive and forget all the past. But Charles Vining was touched to the quick, and, in spite of his calm unmoved aspect, he was hot with passion, wishing in his heart that Max had been the offender, that he might have quenched his rage by shaking him till those white teeth of his chattered again. Then came, though, the thought of Ella Bedford and her position. If he was cold and distant to Laura, would she not visit it upon that defenceless girl? Then he told himself she could behave with no greater cruelty, humiliate her no more, and he felt that he could not play the hypocrite. His growing dislike for Laura Bray was fast becoming a feeling of hatred, and facing her for a moment, he was about to leave the conservatory alone; but no, the gentlemanly courtesy came back—he could not be guilty of rudeness even to the woman he despised; and without a word, he offered his arm, and prepared to lead her back to the drawing-room.

For a moment Laura made as if to take the proffered arm; but at that moment she caught sight of Charley's frowning, angry face, when, with a cry of passionate grief, she darted past him, and the next instant he saw her cross the hall and hurry upstairs.

"Hyar—hyar, Vining, mai dear fellow, where are you?" cried a drawling voice from the other end of the conservatory.

"Confound it all!" ejaculated Charley, waking as it were into action at the tones of that voice, when with a bound he leaped from the window out on to the lawn, thrust out his Gibus hat, crushed it down again upon his head, and set off with long strides in the direction of the Court.

Chapter Thirteen
The Clearing of a Doubt

"My dear boy, yes—of course I will; and we'll have a nice affair of it! Edgington's people shall fit up a tent and a kiosk, and we'll try and do the thing nicely. You're giving me great pleasure in this, Charley—you are indeed!"

"Am I, father?" said Charley, whose heart smote him as he spoke, telling himself the while that he was deceiving the generous old man, with whom he had hitherto been open as the day.

"Yes, my dear boy—yes, of course you are! It's just what I wanted, Charley, to see you a little more inclined for society. You'll have quite a large party, of course?"

"Well, no, father," said Charley; "I think not. Your large affairs are never so successful as the small ones."

"Just so, my dear boy; I think you are right. Well, have it as you please, precisely, only give your orders. Slave of the lamp, you know, Charley—slave of the lamp: what shall I do first?"

"Well, dad," said Charley, flushing slightly, "I thought, perhaps, you wouldn't mind doing a little of the inviting for me."

"Of course not, my dear boy. Whom shall I ask first?"

"Well, suppose you see the Brays," said Charley, whose face certainly wore a deeper hue than usual.

"To be sure, Charley!" said the old gentleman, smiling.

"They've been very kind, and asked me there several times, so you'll ask them all?"

"Decidedly!" said the old gentleman.

"We must have Max," said Charley; "for he keeps hanging about here still."

"O, of course!" said Sir Philip.

"And Laura, I suppose," said Charley, feeling more and more conscience-stricken.

"By all means, my dear boy!" laughed the father.

"And then there are the three girls, *and the governess,*" said Charley.

"Should you ask them?" said Sir Philip.

"O yes, decidedly!" said Charley. "I'm very fond of that second girl, Nelly; she's only a child, but there's something nice and frank and open about her. She will be sure to make up for the unpleasantry of having Max."

"Very good, Charley—very good!" said Sir Philip.

"I wouldn't be put off with any of them," said Charley, in a curious hesitating way. "Perhaps they'll say that they had better not all come; but they can't refuse you anything, so insist upon them bringing the children and Miss Bedford."

"Miss who?" said Sir Philip.

"Miss Bedford—the governess," said Charley, who coughed as if something had made him husky. "I particularly wish for them all to come."

"It shall be just as you like, my dear boy," said Sir Philip gaily; "only let's do the thing well, and not let them go away and find fault afterwards."

Charley Vining left his father ill at ease and dissatisfied, for he felt that he was deceiving the old man; but, like many more, he crushed down the obtrusive thoughts, and, going round to the stable, he mounted his mare as soon as it could be got ready, and rode slowly and thoughtfully away.

"What's come to the young governor?" said one of the stablemen.

"O, the old game!" said another. "He's been betting heavy on the Derby, and lost, and the old gentleman won't pay his debts. I shouldn't be at all surprised if as soon as he comes in for the place, he'll make the money fly."

"Don't think it's that," said the other. "But he never takes a bit of notice of his 'orses now; if they look well, they do, and if they don't look well, they don't; but he's never got a word to say about them. There's something wrong, safe."

There was a good deal of truth in the remarks of the servants; for the Charley Vining of the present was certainly not the Charley Vining of a month before. Since the night of the croquet-party he had several times met Laura Bray, who, like himself, had endeavoured to ignore entirely their encounter in the conservatory, speaking in the most friendly manner, and endeavouring to the best of her ability to bring Charley more to her side. In fact, so completely was the past evaded, that Charley called several times, meeting a warmer welcome at every visit; but not once did he encounter Ella. He was very little more fortunate during his rides: once he pressed forward his horse upon seeing her at some distance down a lane with the "children;" but suddenly Max Bray made his appearance, as if by magic, and fixing upon him, kept by his side for quite an hour; another time Max was walking with his sisters and their governess; while upon a third occasion Max was coming in the other direction, as if purposely to meet them, and as Charley rode away his brow grew dark, and he asked himself what it meant.

In fact, watch as carefully as he would for a meeting, his efforts seemed in vain; while the more he was disappointed, the more eager he became.

It was upon one of these occasions that he had drawn up his horse by a hedge-side, gazing angrily after the distant party, consisting of Ella, two of the children, and Max, when, angry and disappointed, he was considering whether he should canter up after them or turn back.

"Why should I bother myself?" he muttered. "If she likes that donkey dangling after her, I'm quite convinced that she would not approve of rough unpolished me. I'll give up. Max shall have the field to himself, and I'll go back and ask the governor to let me live in peace. I've only been making a mistake, and neglecting everything for the sake of a pleasant-looking face. Hallo!"

"Ha, ha, ha!" rang out a merry laugh.

"Look at Sir Dismal, pausing thoughtfully beneath the trees."

Charley looked up, to see peering down upon him, from between the bushes on the high bank, the bright merry face of Nelly, with her hair tangled, her straw hat bent of brim, and a general aspect about her hot face and tumbled clothes of having been tearing through a wood.

"What, my little dryad!" laughed out Charley, brightening in an instant. "How is the little wood-nymph?"

"O, so jolly hot and tired, Charley! I've cut away from them, run up the bank, and scampered through Bosky Dell, and tore my dress ever so many times. But I wasn't going to stay; at least, I ought to have stayed," she added thoughtfully, "but I felt as if I couldn't, for old Max would have made me ill—he would, bai Jove!" she laughed, mocking her brother's drawl with all accuracy which delighted Charley.

"Been having a walk?" he said.

"Walk, yes," exclaimed Nelly; "and one can't stir without stupid old Max coming boring after us, bothering Miss Bedford to death with his drawling nonsense. She hates him, and he will follow us about, because he has grown so fond of his little sisters. But, I say, Charley Vining, do give me—no, not give, lend me sixpence to buy some sweets. We spent every halfpenny, and it isn't pocket-money till to-morrow night."

"I never give money to beggars at the roadside," laughed Charley, who seemed somehow to be brightening up under his young friend's revelations.

"Now don't be a nuisance," laughed Nelly, "or I'll tease you. I know why you were looking down the lane so miserably; it was because Max was along with—"

"Hold your tongue, do, you saucy puss!" roared Charley, with flaming face. "How dare you!"

"There! I knew I was right," laughed the girl. "I'm not a bit afraid of you, Charley Vining. But, I say, such a game: there, hold your arms, and I could jump down from here right on to the dear old mare just before you, and you could hold me tight, and we'd play at you being young Lochinvar, and gallop off with me. Wouldn't it be fun?"

"But there's no bridegroom to dandle his bonnet and plume," laughed Charley.

"There's an ungallant cavalier!" said Nelly, with her wicked eyes dancing with glee. "Now, if it had been Miss Bed—ha, ha, ha!" she shrieked, as Charley made a dash at her by forcing his mare half-way up the bank. "Don't you do that, Charley, or you'll go down again, and have to be carried on a gate—and I don't want you to be hurt any more," she said seriously. "But there, I must go back and save my poor dear darling Miss Bedford from being bored to death by old stupid. I'm glad I've seen you, though; it's done me ever so much good. I say, Charley Vining, isn't Miss Bedford nice?"

"I daresay she is; but I know very little of her," said Charley coolly.

"O, there's a story!" exclaimed downright Nelly. "I know you think ever so much of her, or else you would not stop looking miserable after her. There, I've done, and I won't tease you any more; but I do want to borrow sixpence. Old Max wouldn't lend me one if I was starving. Thank you! O, a shilling!" exclaimed Nelly, actively catching the coin he threw. "Now I'm going; but, I say, do come and see us. You would like my Miss Bedford so!"

Before Charley Vining could answer, Nelly had dashed off, taking a short cut, and he saw her no more; but from that day Charley's spirits rose; and when once or twice more he encountered the walking party, he did not feel so troubled of heart, but rode gaily up, saluting all, taking the first opportunity of frowning and shaking his head at merry laughing Nelly.

Chapter Fourteen
A Family Party

"Surely, Miss Bedford, you never think of going to Sir Philip Vining's party such a figure as that!"

It was the day of the Blandfield Court invitation, and the ladies were assembling in the drawing-room. For, some days before, in accordance with his promise, Sir Philip had been over to the Elms, taking Laura quite by surprise when he supplemented his invitation by a request that Miss Bedford might also be of the party.

"Miss Bedford—our governess!" stammered Laura, completely taken aback.

But she was herself again the next instant, as she saw through the arrangement.

"Sir Philip has been deceived," she thought; "but I am not so easily put off, nor yet cast off," she muttered.

What should she do? Display open anger, or temporise until Ella Bedford could be dismissed—ignominiously dismissed—from her situation?

Laura Bray was angry, and therefore she talked to herself in strong language, and called things by unpleasant names. But she must act in some way, she thought; it would never do for her to give up all for which her ambitious nature thirsted. She had set herself upon being Lady Vining, and after a fashion she loved Charley, who, from being free and friendly, and on happy laughing terms with her, seemed daily to be growing more and more distant; for she was not deceived by his assumed sociability. She herself had acted so as to try and efface the past; but there was still the recollection of the conservatory scene, and though she tried to set it down as merely a bit of flirtation—one that she ought to pass over without notice—her heart would not accept of the flattering unction; for she knew Charley Vining to be too sterling, too generous a man to trifle with the feelings of any woman.

Then why was he trifling with her? she exclaimed vehemently. Had she no claims to his consideration? There was a dull heavy feeling came over her, as she thought of how he had never been more than friend to her, and that the warmth had been entirely on one side.

But she felt that it would not do to show her anger—kindness would perhaps work a change; and until her rival—no, she would not dignify her with that title—till this governess had gone, she would assume an appearance of sorrow, trying the while to win Charley back from his passing fancy. She could have bitten her tongue for the ill-judged hasty words she had spoken; but O, if she could but detect this Miss Bedford in some light coquettish act, some behaviour too frivolous for her position, it should go hard with her!—for at the present—probably on account of the dislike openly shown—Mrs Bray and her hopeful son seemed disposed to treat their dependent with more consideration, which was really the case on the part of the former, whose mental constitution was such that she could not conceive the possibility of any one holding a paid position to perform certain duties possessing the sensitiveness and thoughts of a lady.

Laura had determined to temporise, and also to counterplot. It struck her that Sir Philip had been deceived, and hurriedly rising, she left the room.

It was evident to her sharpened perceptibilities that it was Charley's doing that Miss Bedford was invited; and she determined Sir Philip Vining should see who was the lady his son wished to be of the party.

Laura's heart beat quickly, as, with assumed kindness and gentleness of mien, she returned from the schoolroom with Ella, and introduced her to Sir Philip.

"I thought that Miss Bedford would like to thank you herself, Sir Philip, for your kind invitation," she said, by way of explanation of her sudden act; and then she watched attentively the effect produced.

She was right. Sir Philip was startled, and as he rose to cordially greet and repeat his invitation, he gazed almost wonderingly at the sweet mien and gentle face before him, raising Ella's hand, and with all the grace of an old courtier, kissing it respectfully, moved by the true homage he felt for so much youth and beauty. But as he released her hand, there was a troubled puzzled look in the old gentleman's face—a look that was still there when at last he took his leave to go thoughtfully homeward; for now it again struck him that Charley's impressive demand that the governess should be asked was a little strange, though here was the key.

Sir Philip dismissed the thought that oppressed him, though. Charley was too noble to be moved by any disloyal acts; and as to stooping—pooh! it was absurd! He was growing an old woman, full of nervous fears and fancies; and casting his "whimsies," as he called them, away, he entered with all his heart into the preparations for the little fête.

And now the day had arrived, and the ladies were assembling in the drawing-room, where Mr Bray and "Mr Maximilian" were already waiting. Mrs Bray had sailed and rustled into the room in a tremendously stiff green brocade dress, to be complimented by her lord as resembling a laurel hedge, and by her son for her May-day aspect and Jack-in-the-green look. But Mrs Bray was satisfied, and that was everything. Her satisfaction was evident by the way in which she swept round the room, making a vortex that caught up the light chairs and loose articles that came within its reach.

"Bai Jove, there, why don't you mind!" exclaimed Max, as the glossy hat left upon the couch was sent spinning across the room. "Why don't you sit down?"

Mrs Bray did not reply, but she would not have sat down in that dress, save in the carriage, upon any consideration—at all events, not until after it had been seen at Blandfield.

Max's hat was made smooth sooner than his temper, and he was still muttering and grumbling when Nelly and her sisters came bounding in, like three tall, thin, peripatetic tulips, followed closely by Laura, glorious with black hair, flashing eyes, amber moiré, and black lace.

Mr Onesimus Bray placed his hands in his pockets and walked smilingly round his daughter, in whom he took immense pride; but the attempt that he made to kiss her was received with a shriek of horror, his daughter darting back beyond his reach, and at the same time bringing forth an oath from her brother's lips, as she swept the glossy, newly-brushed hat from the marqueterie table whereon it had been placed for safety.

"For shame, Max!" exclaimed his mother.

"Bai Jove, then, it's enough to make an angel swear! How would you like a fellow to tread on your bonnets?"

The ladies shuddered.

"Never mind, then—a poor old Max!" exclaimed mischievous Nelly, who had but a few minutes before been snubbed by her brother; and, stooping down, she picked up the unfortunate hat, and, before she could be arrested, carefully brushed all the nap up the wrong way, Max sitting completely astounded the while at the outrage put upon him.

What he would have said remains to this day unknown. His mouth had gasped open after the fashion of an expiring aquarium pet, and he was about to ejaculate, when he stopped short; for Ella Bedford came quietly into the room, the centre, as it were, of a soft cloud of grey barège, which gave to her pale gentle features almost an ethereal expression, but which called forth from the gorgeous amber queen the remark standing at the head of this chapter:

"Surely, Miss Bedford, you never think of going to Sir Philip Vining's party such a figure as that!"

Ella coloured up, and then said gently: "Shall I change the dress for a plain muslin, Miss Bray?"

"O, I'm sure I don't know!" exclaimed Laura, with a toss. "I think—"

"I think the dress looks uncommonly nice, Miss Bedford—I do, bai Jove!" drawled Max, fixing his glass in his eye, and staring furiously.

It was the first act of kindness Max Bray had done for many a long day; but it caused a shrinking sensation in her for whom it was intended, while Laura darted at her a fierce look of hatred, and then an angry glance at her brother.

Ella looked inquiringly at Mrs Bray, as if for instructions; but that lady always sided with son Max, as did Mr Bray, as far as he dared, with his daughter.

"I almost think—" he ventured to observe.

"Don't talk stuff, Ness!" shrieked his lady. "What do you know about a lady's dress? If it was a fleece or a pig—There, I think Miss Bedford's things will do very nicely indeed; and if some people would only dress as neatly, it wouldn't half ruin their parents in dressmakers' bills."

Laura did not condescend to answer, but throwing herself into a chair, she took up a book, pretending to read, but holding it upside down, till Nelly laughingly called attention to the fact.

"Pert child!" exclaimed Laura fiercely.

"Don't care!" laughed Nelly. "So the book *was* upside down; and I'd rather be a pert child than a disagreeable, sour old maid!"

"You'd better send that rude tom-boy to bed—you had, bai Jove!" drawled Max.

"Ah!—and I'd rather be a rude tom-boy than a great girl, bai Jove, Mr Max!" cried Nelly; whereupon Mr Bray laughed, Mrs Bray scolded, and Nelly pretended to cry, directing a comical look the while at her father, who, whatever his weakness, was passionately fond of his girls.

The crunching of the gravel by the wheels of the wagonette put a stop to the rather unpleasant scene, when, to Laura's surprise, Max jumped up and handed Ella down to the carriage, returning afterwards for his sister, who favoured him with a peculiarly meaning look; one which he replied to in as supercilious a manner as he could assume.

"What does it mean, Max?" she whispered, as they descended the stairs. "More affection for your little sisters?"

"My dear Laura," drawled Max, "will you take my advice and adopt a motto?"

"Motto?" said Laura inquiringly.

"Ya-as, bai Jove! the very one for you—just suited to the occasion: *Laissez-aller*. Do you understand?"

Laura looked at him meaningly, but made no reply, for they had reached the carriage.

Chapter Fifteen
Charley's Fête

In spite of her annoyance, Laura's eyes sparkled when they reached the Court; for Sir Philip hurried to the carriage, welcoming the party most warmly, and, handing her out, he led her himself to the beautiful little kiosk, and then took her from place to place, according to her attentions that made more than one match-making mamma with marriageable daughters look meaningly at the same daughters, and then think of Charley Vining with a sigh.

But if Laura was in high glee, so was not Max, who had to stand by while Charley carried off Ella Bedford, Nelly laughingly fastening upon his other arm.

"A rude coarse beast, bai Jove!" muttered Max elegantly, as he tried vainly to get the little button of his glove secured. "Let him have a fall again, and see if I'll go to his help!"

"I shall come with you if I may," said Nelly demurely.

"To be sure!" laughed Charley, whose heart throbbed with pleasure as he felt—nay, hardly felt—the light pressure of the grey glove upon his arm. "Miss Bedford won't mind, I hope. Do you know, Miss Bedford, I'm rather glad you are with us? I'm almost afraid Nelly means some inroad upon my purse."

"No, I don't," said Nelly, "so don't be afraid;" and then she walked very demurely by their side, Charley encouraging her to stay upon observing Ella's constraint and troubled looks.

"She'd be off like a frightened pigeon—dove, I mean!" muttered Charley, as he looked down at the almost painful face beside him. But a little quiet conversation upon current topics seemed to set her more at ease, and, after a while, Hugh Lingon approaching, Charley Vining whispered, loudly enough, though, for Nelly to hear:

"Now I'm going, Miss Bedford, for here comes Nelly's intended. I hope you will play the *chaperone* most stringently."

Nelly rewarded him with a sharp pinch as he left them, Hugh Lingon taking his place; and Ella, whose heart beat almost painfully, asking herself the reason why.

But Charley Vining had laid his plans that day, and he felt he must proceed with caution. So hurrying himself, he acted the part of host with admirable tact, picking out the ladies who seemed neglected, forming sets for croquet, handing refreshments, or escorting little parties to the lake-like river for boating; distributing himself, as it were, throughout the grounds, and at last interrupting a tête-à-tête between Laura and Hugh Lingon, who had soon forsaken the ladies left in his charge.

Laura commenced a little *minauderie*, professing to be unable to leave Mr Lingon; but she gave up directly she saw Charley's laugh, for she knew that it would be—nay, was—seen through. She knew Charley Vining to be different from most men of her acquaintance; and accepting his offer, she gladly took his arm, making the match-making mammas to whisper, as the handsome couple passed through the grounds, "There, didn't I tell you so?" and then to gossip about how they had had their suspicions concerning the purpose of the fête.

But Laura's pleasure was but short-lived; for though Charley was pleasant, gay, and chatty, he was nothing more, and though he carefully avoided referring to the croquet-party, she felt that he was not as she could wish.

"He'll go back to her as soon as, with any decency, he can," she thought; and her teeth were set, and her fingers clenched, pressing the nails almost through her gloves, as she forced back a sigh.

But she soon cheered up, for she told herself it was not for long, and determined to try if gentleness would gain the day; she listened to all her companion said, striving the while, without being obtrusive, to obliterate her past words of anger.

Laura was wrong; for it was not for a considerable time, and until he had played cavalier to many a lady—winning the thanks and smiles of Sir Philip, who was delighted at his son's efforts—that he sought once more Ella Bedford, followed by Sir Philip's eyes; the old gentleman gazing uneasily after him as he went up and offered his arm, which was reluctantly taken.

"I'm going now," said Nelly, who had kept with her guard the whole time; "I want something to eat. I declare, Charley Vining, I've only had one thin slice of butter spread with bread-crumbs, and a cup of tea;" and before a word could be said, she had darted off.

Sir Philip's were not the only eyes that followed Charley Vining to where sat Ella Bedford; for as Max Bray followed him at a distance, as if by accident Laura did the same, and brother and sister gave genuine starts as they encountered at the union of two alleys.

"Grows quite romantic, bai Jove!" sneered Max; but he relapsed into an uncomfortable look on seeing the penetrating gaze directed at him by his sister.

"Let me take your arm," she said coldly; and then, as the shades of evening were fast falling, they walked slowly on together, towards a part of the grounds now apparently deserted.

Meanwhile Charley Vining had led Ella across the lawn, pressing her to partake of some refreshment, but in vain; and at last, in spite of herself, she found that she was alone with him, in a secluded part of the grounds.

"There is a seat here," said Charley. "Shall we rest for a few minutes?"

"It would hardly be advisable," was the quiet reply; "the evening is damp." And then for a few moments there was a pause, as they still walked slowly on, Charley with his heart beating heavily, and Ella eager to return to the throng upon the lawn—a throng that the afternoon through she had avoided—and hardly liking to speak, lest she might betray her agitation, and that she looked upon this otherwise than as an ordinary attention of host to one of his guests.

For Ella was not blind: her woman's instinct had whispered to her respecting the many attentions pressed upon her, and she trembled as she recalled the night when the cross was returned; for her heart told her that such things must not be—that she must be cold and cautious, guarding and steeling herself against tender emotions, for she was but the poor paid governess, and this man, whose arm she lightly touched, was almost engaged to Laura Bray.

But the silence was broken at length by Charley, who spoke deeply, as he stopped short by a standard covered with pale white roses, whose perfume seemed shed around upon the soft night air.

"Miss Bedford," he said, "I have been in pain, almost in agony, for many days past; and till I found that I had been wronging you, it seemed to me that life was going to be unbearable."

"Pain!—wronging me!" exclaimed Ella.

"Yes," he said; "but hear me out. I am no polished speaker, Miss Bedford—only a simple, blunt, and I hope honest and truthful man. A week or two since I believed that you favoured the suit of Max Bray: to-night I will not insult you with questions, but tell you honestly I do not believe that to be the case; and when the conviction flashed upon me that I was wrong, I tell you frankly my heart leaped with joy. You may ask why: I will tell you."

"Mr Vining," exclaimed Ella, "this must not be; you forget yourself, your position—you forget me when you talk so. Pray lead me back."

"You speak as if my words pained you, Miss Bedford," said Charley huskily. "Pray forgive me if they do. Nay, but a few minutes longer."

He caught one hand in his, and as she glanced for an instant in his direction, the rising moon gleaming through the trees lit up his handsome earnest face, photographing it, as it were, upon her brain; for to her dying day she never forgot that look—that countenance so imploringly turned upon her.

"Miss Bedford—Ella," he whispered, "I love you tenderly and devotedly! This is no light declaration: till I saw you, woman never occupied my thoughts. You see by my brusque ways, my bluntness, that I have been no dallier in drawing-rooms, no holder of lady's silk. Till now, my loves have been in the stables, kennels, fields. Blunt language this—uncomplimentary perhaps; but I am no courtier. I speak as I feel, and I tell you that to win your love in return would be to make me a happy man."

"Mr Vining," exclaimed Ella, vainly trying to release her hand, "lead me back, pray!"

"Nay," said Charley, with sadness in his tones, "I will not force you to listen to me;" and he released her hand. "I was hopeful that you would have listened to my suit."

"Indeed—indeed," said Ella, "I cannot, Mr Vining: it can never be. You forget—position—me!"

She could say no more—her words seemed to stifle her; and had she continued speaking, she felt that she would have burst into tears.

"I forget nothing," said Charley, almost sternly. "How can I forget? How can I ever forget? But surely," he said, once more catching her hand in his—"surely you cannot with that sweet gentle face be cruel, and love to torture one who has spoken simply the truth—laid bare to you his feelings! You believe what I say?"

"Yes, yes!" almost sobbed Ella. "But indeed—indeed it can never be. Do not think me either harsh or cruel, for I mean it not."

"What am I to think then?" said Charley bitterly. "Is it that you reject me utterly, or am I so poor a wooer that you would have me on my knees, protesting, swearing? No; I wrong you again: it is not that," he exclaimed passionately. "Look here, Ella"—he plucked one of the white roses, tearing his hand as he did so, the blood appearing in a long mark across the back—"emblematic," he said, smiling sadly, "of my love. You see it has its smarts and pains. You refused me so slight a gift once, but take this; and though I am a man I can freely say that my love for you is as pure and spotless as that simple flower. You will not refuse that?"

He could see the tears in her eyes, and that her face was drawn as if with pain; but one trembling hand was extended to take the flower; then, before he could recover from his surprise, she had turned from him and fled; when, with almost a groan, he threw himself upon the garden-seat, remaining motionless for a few moments, and then rising to hurry back to the marquee.

Chapter Sixteen
The Echoes of Charley's Declaration

Two minutes had scarcely elapsed before there was the faint rustling of a lady's dress and the creaking of a boot, and then two pale faces—those of brother and sister—appeared from a neighbouring clump of evergreens, gazed cautiously about for a few moments, and then moved away in another direction; the moon just beginning to cast their shadows upon the dewy lawn upon whose turf they walked, perhaps because it hushed their footsteps.

They had hardly disappeared before there was another faint rustling, and, eagerly peering about, Nelly Bray appeared, her girlish face looking half merry, half anxious, in the moonlit glade.

"A nasty, disagreeable, foxy pair of old sneaks!" she exclaimed—"to go peeping and watching about like that, and all because they were as jealous as—as jealous as—well, there, I don't know what. I know I was watching too, but I wouldn't have done so for a moment, if it hadn't been to see what they were going to do. I wouldn't have been so mean and contemptible—that I wouldn't! But O, wasn't it grand!" she exclaimed, clasping her hands. "Ah, don't I wish I was like Miss Bedford, to have such a nice boy as Charley Vining to fall in love with me and tell me of it, and then for me to reject him like that! I don't believe she meant it, though, that I don't. She couldn't! Nobody could resist Charley Vining: he's ever so much nicer than Hugh Lingon, and I'd run away with him to-morrow, if he asked me—see if I wouldn't! But there ain't no fear of that. I knew he was in love with her—I was sure of it. And didn't he speak nicely! Just as if he felt every word he said, and meant it all—and he does, too, I know; for he's a regular trump, Charley is, and I shall say so again, as there's no one to hear me—he's a regular trump, that he is; and I don't care what any one says. Wouldn't it be nice to be Miss Bedford's bridesmaid! I should wear—Here's somebody coming!"

Nelly darted off, reaching the door just as leave-takings were in vogue; Sir Philip and Charley handing the Bray family to the waiting carriages; but in spite of then efforts, there was an appearance of constraint visible.

"Why, here's the little rover!" exclaimed Charley, as Nelly appeared. "Where have you been?"

"Looking after and helping my friends, as a rover should, Mr Croquet-player!" exclaimed Nelly pertly, as she looked Charley full in the face; while, as he was helping her on with a shawl, she found means to make him start by saying:

"Look out! Max and Laura were listening!"

The next moment the carriage had driven off, leaving Charley standing motionless, and thinking of the pale-faced girl who had leaned so lightly upon his arm as he handed her to the carriage, and wondering what would follow.

"Charley, my dear boy, the Miss Lingons!"

So spoke Sir Philip, rousing the young man from his abstraction, when he hastened to make up for his want of courtesy as guest after guest departed, till the last carriage had ground the gravel of the drive, for the fête was at an end. But as Sir Philip sat alone in his library, thoughtful and fatigued, it seemed to him that the affair had not been so successful as he could have wished; and that night—ay, and for many nights to come—he was haunted by a vision of a fair-haired girl, with soft grey eyes which seemed to ask the protection of all on whom they rested; and somehow Sir Philip Vining sighed, for he felt troubled, and that matters were not going as he had intended.

Meanwhile the Brays' wagonette rolled on till it reached the Elms. Hardly a word had been spoken on the return journey; for Mr Bray was hungry, Mrs Bray cross, and Max and his sister thoughtful, as was Ella Bedford. Nelly had spoken twice, but only to be snubbed into silence; and it was with a feeling of relief shared by all, that they descended and entered the house.

Mrs Bray and her lord directly took chamber candlesticks, Mr Bray whispering something to the butler respecting a tray and dressing-room. Ella hurried away with her charges, while Max opened the drawing-room door and motioned to his sister to enter; but she took no heed of his sign, as, with angry glances, she followed Ella till she had disappeared.

"Come here," said Max. "I want you."

"I'm tired," said Laura. "You must keep it till the morning."

"I tell you I want you now!" he exclaimed almost savagely, the man's real nature flashing out as he cast the thin veil of society habit aside, and spoke eagerly.

"Then I shall not come," said Laura, turning away.

"If you dare to say a word about all this, I'll never forgive you!" he whispered.

"I can live without Mr Max Bray's forgiveness," said Laura tauntingly.

"Confound you, come down!" he exclaimed, as Laura ascended the stairs. "I will not have her spoken to about it unless I speak."

"Good-night, Max," was the cool reply; and he saw her pass through the swing door at the end of Mr Bray's picture-gallery; while foaming and apparently enraged, he made a bound up a few stairs, but only to descend again, enter the drawing-room, and close the door.

The door had hardly closed before Laura appeared again, without a chamber candlestick, to lean over the balustrade eager and listening as she peered down into the hall. But there was not a sound to be heard; and hurrying back along the gallery, she stopped at Ella's door, and then, without knocking, turned the handle and entered.

Chapter Seventeen
A Vial of Wrath

"And, pray, what are you doing here?" exclaimed Laura Bray, as she saw the tall slim form of her sister Nelly standing between her and the object of her dislike.

"Talking to Miss Bedford, if you must know, my dear sister," said Nelly pertly; but the next moment she encountered a glance from Ella, in obedience to which she was instantly silent; and, crossing over, she kissed the pale girl lovingly, and said, "Good-night."

But all this was not lost upon Laura, who bit her lips till Nelly had half hesitatingly quitted the room.

"What sweet obedience!" she then said sarcastically. "Really, Miss Bedford, you must give me some lessons in the art of winning people's affections. I have no doubt that papa will satisfy you if there is any extra charge."

Ella did not speak; but her gentle look might have disarmed animosity, as she turned her soft eyes almost appealingly towards her irate visitor. She was in some degree, though, prepared for what was coming, for Nelly had lingered behind to place her on her guard; and as she stood facing Laura she did not shrink, neither did she make answer to the taunts conveyed in those bitter words.

"I trust that you have enjoyed a pleasant evening, Miss Bedford," continued Laura, who seemed to be working herself up, and gathering together the battalions of her wrath, ready for the storm she meant to thunder upon the defenceless head before her. But still there was no reply in words—nothing but the calm pleading gaze from the soft grey eyes.

"Can we make arrangements for you to be introduced to some other family, where you can carry on your intrigues?"

Still no answer—only a pitiful, almost imploring look that ought to have disarmed the most wrathful. But at this moment Ella involuntarily raised a white rose, which till then had remained concealed, as her hand hung down amidst the soft folds of her dress; and no sooner did Laura catch sight of the blossom than, interpreting the act to be one of insolent triumph, she threw herself upon the shrinking girl, tore the flower from her hand, and flung it upon the floor, where she crushed it beneath her foot as she stamped upon it furiously.

"How dare you!" she almost shrieked, in tones that bade fair some day to rival those of Mamma Bray. "Such cowardly—such insolent acts! To dare to insult me after practising your low cunning to-day, laying your snares for my poor unworldly brother, and then setting other traps—to—to—inveigle—to entrap—There, don't look at me with that triumphant leer! You shall be turned out of this house, into which you have gained entrance by false pretences, so as to act the part of a scheming adventuress!"

For a few moments Laura seemed as if she would strike the object of her resentment, so fierce was the burst of passion that came pouring forth—the unlucky act having roused every bitter and angry feeling in her breast: disappointed love, ambition, hatred—all were mingled into a poison that was like venom to her barbed and stinging words, as she stooped even to abusing the innocent cause of her dislike.

At length Ella raised her hands, and spoke deprecatingly; but each appeal only seemed to rouse Laura to fresh outbursts of violence, so that at last the bitter taunts and revilings were suffered in silence, the angry woman's voice rising louder with her victim's patience, till, alarmed by her daughter's angry, hysterical cries, Mrs Bray hurried into the room.

"What is the meaning of all this?" she shrieked. "Laura!—Miss Bedford! Are you both mad?"

Ella was about to speak, but Laura fiercely interrupted her.

"Speak a word if you dare!" she said. "I will not have anything said! Such insolence is insupportable."

"But what has Miss Bedford been doing?" shrieked Mrs Bray. "You are alarming the whole house. What does it mean?"

"Nothing. Let it rest," cried Laura, cooling down rapidly, but with face a-flame; for she could not bear her mother to be a witness to her humiliation, there being, based on Laura's slight exaggerations of one or two attentions, a full belief in the Bray family that even if the question had not been put by Charley Vining, matters had so far progressed that he was sure to be her husband: hence her objection to a word being uttered; and, shrinking back, Ella stood with bended head, while a passage of arms took place between mother and daughter, Mrs Bray's curiosity increasing with Laura's reticence.

Finding though, at last, that nothing was to be gained, Mrs Bray followed Laura from the room; and Ella, trembling with excitement and the agitation of many painful hours, was about to welcome the solitude hers at last, when once more the door opened, and, pale and wild-looking, so that she felt to pity her, Laura again appeared, closing the door carefully behind her, and then standing to gaze thoughtfully in Ella's face.

She had come to threaten—to try and enforce silence; but her voice was husky; the fierce passion which had before sustained her had now passed away, and the weak woman, cut to the heart by disappointment, was once more asserting herself.

For quite five minutes she stood with heaving breast, trying to speak, but the words would not come; and at last, dreading to let the woman she hated and despised, one whom she looked upon as full of deceit and guile, gaze upon and triumph in her tears, Laura turned and fled from the room; and once more Ella was alone.

Chapter Eighteen
Analysis of the Heart

Alone—alone once more in her bedroom, the scene of so many bitter tears, Ella stood with flushed cheeks, and eyes that seemed to burn, thinking of the words that had been uttered to her that day. She held the crushed rose in her hand—the flower Laura had with cruel hand snatched away and cast down, and upon which she had trampled with as little remorse as upon her feelings. But the agitated girl had once more secured the torn blossom, to stand gazing down upon its bruised petals.

What did he say? That he loved her—her whom he had seen so few times! He loved her: he, the heir to a baronetcy, loved her—a poor governess, the persecuted, despised dependent of this family—that his love for her was as pure as that white blossom! It could not be. And yet he had spoken so earnestly; his voice trembled, and those low soft utterances so tenderly, so feelingly whispered, so full of appeal and reverence, were evidently genuine. They were not the words of the thoughtless, the lovers of conquest, the distributors of vain compliments, empty nothings, to every woman who was the toy of the hour. And he was no weak boy, ready to be led away by a fresh face—no empty-headed coxcomb, but a man of sterling worth.

There was a plain, straightforward, manly simplicity in what he had said that went home to her heart; there was a nobility in his disappointment and anger which made her thrill with the awakening of new thoughts, new senses, that had before lain dormant in her breast; there was the sterling ring of the true gentleman in his every act and look and word, and—Ah, but—no—no—no! She was mad to harbour such thoughts, even for an instant; it was folly—all folly. How could she accept him, even if her heart leaned that way? It would be doing him a grievous wrong, blighting his prospects, tying him down to one unworthy of his regard. She could not—she did not love him. Love! What was it to love? She had loved those who were no more; but love him, a stranger! What was it to love?

Beat, beat!—beat, beat!—beat, beat! Heavy throbbings of her poor wounded heart answering the question she had asked, plainly, and in a way that would not be ignored, even though she pressed that flower-burdened hand tightly over the place, and laid the other upon her hot and tingling cheeks. But even if she knew it, could she own to it? No! impossible; not even to herself. That was a secret she could not ponder on, even for an instant.

And yet he had said that he loved her! What were his words? She must recall them once more: that his love for her was as truthful and as pure as that flower—that poor crushed rose.

As she thought on, flushed and trembling, she raised the flower nearer and nearer to her face, gazing at the bruised petals, crushed, torn, and disfigured. It was to her as the reading of a prophecy—that his pure love for her was to become torn and sullied, and that, for her sake, he was to suffer bitter anguish, till, like that flower, his love should wither away. But there would still be the recollection of the sweet words, even as there stayed in the crushed blossom its own sweet perfume, the incense-breathing fragrance, as she raised it more and more till the hot tears began to fell.

No, she did not love him—she could not love him: it was folly—all a dream from which she was awaking; for she knew the end—she knew her days at the Elms must be but few—that, like a discarded servant, she must go: whither she knew not, only that it must be far away—somewhere to dream no more, neither to be persecuted for what she could not help.

No; she did not love him, and he would soon forget her. It could be but a passing fancy. But she esteemed him—she must own to a deep feeling of esteem for one of so noble, frank, and generous a nature. Had he not always been kind and gentle and sympathising—displaying his liking for her with a gentlemanly respect that had won upon her more and more? Yes, she esteemed him too well, she was too grateful, to injure him ever so slightly; and her greatest act of kindness would be to hurry away.

The fragrance from the poor crushed flower still rose, breathing, as it were, such love and sweetness; recalling, too, the words with which it was given so vividly, that, betrayed beyond her strength to control the act, for one brief instant Ella's lips were pressed softly, lovingly, upon the flower—petals kissing petals—the bright bee-stung and ruddy touching the pale and crushed; and then, firmly and slowly, though each act seemed to send a pang through her throbbing heart, Ella plucked the rose in pieces, telling herself that she was tearing forth the mad passion as she went on showering down the creamy leaflets, raining upon them her tears the while, till the bare stalk alone remained in her hands—her cruel hands; for had she not been tearing and rending her own poor breast as every petal was plucked from its hold? For what availed the deceit? The time had been short—they had met but seldom: but what of that? The secret would burst forth, would assert itself; and she knew that she loved him dearly—loved him so that she would give her life for his sake; and that to have been his slave—to have been but near him—to listen to his voice—to see his broad white forehead, his sun-tinged cheeks, and clustering brown hair; not to be called his, but only to be near him—would be life to her; while to go far—far—far away, where she might never see him more, would be, as it were, tottering even into her grave.

No; there was no one looking: it was close upon midnight, but she glanced guiltily round, as with burning cheeks she sank upon her knees, whispering to that wild beating heart that it could not be wrong. And then she began to slowly gather those petals, taking them up softly one by one, to treasure somewhere—to gaze upon, perhaps, sometimes in secret; for was it not his gift that she had cast down as if it had been naught? She might surely treasure them up to keep in remembrance of what might have been, had hers been a happier lot.

Then came once more the thoughts of the past evening, and more than ever she felt that she must go. She would see him no more, and he would soon forget it all. But would she forget? A sob was the answer—a wild hysterical sob—as she felt that she could not.

One by one, one by one, she gathered those leaflets up to kiss them once again; and that night, flush-cheeked and fevered, she slept with the fragments of the blossom pressed tightly to her aching breast, till calm came with the earliest dawn, and with the lightening sky dreams of hope and love and happiness to come, with brighter days and loving friends, and all joyous and blissful. She was walking where white rose petals showered down to carpet the earth; the air was sweet with their fragrance, and she was leaning upon his stout arm as he whispered to her of a love truthful and pure as the flowers around; and then she awoke to the bare chill of her own stiffly-papered, poorly-furnished room, as seen in the grey dawn of a pouring wet morning, with the wind howling dismally in the great old-fashioned chimney, the rain pattering loudly against the window-panes, and hanging in great trembling beads from the sash. It was a fit morning, on the whole, to raise the spirits of one who was dejected, spiritless, almost heart-broken; find it was no wonder that Ella Bedford's head sank once more upon the pillow, which soon became wet with her bitter tears.

For how could she meet the different members of that family? She felt as if she was guilty; and yet what had she done? It was not of her seeking. She could have wept again and again in the despair and bitterness of her heart;

but her eyes were dried now, and she began to ponder over the scenes of the past night.

She rose at last to go down to the schoolroom, for it was fast approaching eight, and as she descended, her mind was made up as to her future proceedings. She would go carefully on with her duties; but in the course of the morning, if not sent for sooner, she would herself seek Mrs Bray, and ask to be set at liberty, so that she might elsewhere seek a home—one that should afford her rest and peace.

Chapter Nineteen
The Making of a Compact

Breakfast over at the Elms, and no improvement in the weather. Maximilian Bray said that it was impossible to go out, "bai Jove!" so he was seated in a low *bergère* chair in the drawing-room. He had taken a book from a side table as if with the intention of reading; but it had fallen upon the floor, Max Bray not being at the best of times a reading man; and now he was busy at work plotting and planning with a devotion worthy of a better cause. His head was imparting some of its ambrosia to the light chintz chair-cover, for he had impatiently thrown the antimacassar under the table. Then he fidgeted about a little, altered the sit of his collar and wristbands, and at last, as if not satisfied with his position, he removed his chair farther into the bay, so that the light drapery of the flowing curtains concealed his noble form from the view of any one entering the room, when, apparently satisfied, he gazed thoughtfully through the panes at the soaked landscape.

Max Bray had not been long settled to his satisfaction when Laura entered, shutting the door with a force that whispered—nay, shouted—of a temper soured by some recent disappointment. She gave a sharp glance round the room, and then, seeing no one, threw herself into a chair, a sob at the same moment bursting from her breast.

"She shall go—that she shall!" exclaimed Laura suddenly, as she gave utterance to her thoughts. "Such deceit!—such quiet carneying ways! But there shall be no more of it: she shall go!"

Laura Bray ceased speaking; and, starting up, she began to pace the room, but only to stop short on seeing her brother gazing at her with a half-mocking, half-amused expression of countenance from behind the curtain.

"You here, Max!" she exclaimed, colouring hotly.

"Bai Jove, ya-a-as!" he drawled. "But, I say, isn't it a bad plan to go about the house shouting so that every one can hear your bewailings, because a horsey cad of a fellow gives roses to one lady and thorns to another?"

"What *do* you mean, Max?" said Laura.

"What do I mean! Well, that's cool, bai Jove! O, of course nothing about meetings by moonlight alone, and roses and vows, and that sort of spooneyism! But didn't you come tearing and raving in here, saying that she should go, and that you wouldn't stand it, and swore—"

"O, Max?" cried Laura passionately.

"Bai Jove! why don't you let a fellow finish?" drawled Max. "Swore, I said—swore like a cat just going to scratch; and I suppose that you would like to scratch, eh?"

"But, Max, did you really hear what I said?" cried Laura.

"Hear? Bai Jove! of course I did—every word. Couldn't help it. Good job it was only me."

"How could you be so unmanly as to listen!" cried Laura.

"Listen? Bai Jove, how you do talk! I didn't listen; you came and raved it all at me. And so she shall go, shall she?"

"Yes!" exclaimed Laura, firing up, and speaking viciously, "that she shall—a deceitful creature! I see through all her plots and plans, and I'll—"

"Tear her eyes out, won't you, my dear, eh? Now just look here, Laury: you think me slow, and all that sort of fun, and that I don't see things; but I'm not blind. So the big boy has kicked off his allegiance, has he? and run mad after the little governess, has he? and the big sister is very angry and jealous!"

"Jealous, indeed!" cried Laura—"and of a creature like that!"

"All right; only don't interrupt," said Max mockingly. "Jealous, I said, and won't put up with it, and quite right too! But, all the same, I'm not going to have her sent away."

"And why not, pray?" cried Laura with flashing eyes.

"Because I don't choose that she shall go," said Max coolly.

Laura started, and then in silence brother and sister sat for a few moments gazing in each other's eyes, a flood of thought sweeping the while across the brain of the latter as she recalled a score of little things till then unnoticed, or merely attributed to a natural desire to flirt; but, with the key supplied by Max Bray's last words, Laura felt that she could read him with ease, and her brow contracted as she tried to make him shrink; but that did not lie in her power.

"Max!" she exclaimed at last, "I'm ashamed of you! It's mean, and contemptible, and base, and grovelling! I'm disgusted! Why, you'll be turning your eyes next to the servants' hall!"

"Thank you, my dear!" drawled Max. "Very high-flown and grand! But I shall be content at present with the schoolroom. And now suppose I say I'm ashamed of you; and, bai Jove, I am! A girl of your style and pretensions, instead of winking at what you've seen, or coming to your brother for counsel, to go howling about the house—"

"Max!" half shrieked Laura. "I don't care—bai Jove, I don't!" he exclaimed. "So you do go howling about the house like a forlorn shepherdess, bai Jove, so that every one can see what a fool you are making of yourself!"

"And pray what would my noble brother's advice be?" cried Laura sarcastically.

Max Bray was another man for an instant, as, starting up in his chair, he caught his sister by the arm, drawing her towards him until she sank down in a sitting position upon the ottoman at his feet, when, with the drawling manner and affectation gone, he leaned over her, talking in a low earnest voice, and so impressively, that Laura's mocking smile gave place to a look of intense interest. She drew nearer to him at length, as he still talked on eagerly; then she clasped her hands together, and rested them upon his knees.

"But no!" she exclaimed, suddenly starting as it were from something which seemed to enthral her, "I will not be a party to it, Max!"

"Very good, my dear," he said cavalierly; "then you shall have the pleasure of watching progress, and seeing yourself thrust out, if you please. Bai Jove, though, Laury, I did think you were a girl of more spirit! Seems really, though, a good deal smitten, does Charley."

Laura's countenance changed, and her teeth were set together.

"I shall let him go on, then, for my part, if you choose it to be so."

"I choose!" cried Laura, with the tears in her eyes. "O, Max, why do you torture me?"

"Then look here!" said Max.

And once more he leaned over towards her, assuming a quiet ease, but at the same time it was plain to see that he was greatly excited. He talked on and on impressively, with the effect of making Laura's lips part and her eyes to glisten with a strange light. Then a pallor overspread her countenance, but only to be swept away by a look of exultation as Max still talked on.

"But it is impossible, Max!" cried Laura, at length.

"Perhaps you'll leave me to judge about that, and think only of your own part!" he said coolly. "Is my advice—are my offers—worth accepting?"

"O yes, Max, yes!" cried Laura excitedly; "I'd do anything!"

"I don't want you to do anything," said Max, smiling with triumph; "only what I advise. Help me, and I will help you with all my heart. But I always knew that you would. You say that you don't like my choice. Well and good; I might say that I don't like yours. Perhaps my affair will come to nothing; but, anyhow, you are the gainer. I won't say anything about hating, but let you have your selection. Now let me have mine. But if you have anything better to propose, I am ready to listen."

"But I have no plans, Max. I only thought of her being sent away; I'm half broken-hearted and worn-out with disappointment!"

"Yes, just so. I expected as much, and I was waiting here to see you," said Max. "I'm not blind, Laury, nor deaf either. I heard you two shouting across the hall. So you've been telling the old lady that some one shall go, have you?"

"Yes, I have!" exclaimed Laura, ignoring the past conversation; "and she shall go too! Mamma did promise me."

"Ya-a-as, I know," said Max, relapsing into his drawl; "but that was before she promised me. The second will counts before the first made. But, as I said before, and we understand now, she's not going—so there's an end of it."

"O, of course!" cried Laura passionately. "Everything must be as mamma's dear boy wishes! He shall have everything he likes, and do as he likes, and say what he likes, and every one else is to give way to him!"

"Bai Jove, now, don't be an idiot!" exclaimed Max. "What's the good— now that I'm working on your side, and we have got to understand one another—of running back like this? I'm obliged to speak plain, and to tell you that you are only a stupid child, Laury, and that you've taken a liking for another stupid child—and there's a pair of you; but all the same, if you do as I tell you, all will come right!"

Laura tossed her head, and seemed somewhat mollified, perhaps from being reminded of her folly.

"There," said Max, "that will do for this morning; so now do just as I tell you, and leave all the rest to me. But is it a bargain?"

Laura Bray was thoughtful for a few minutes. She was placed in a position which required consideration: the languid brother, whom she had hitherto almost despised, was asking her to forego one purpose for the sake of an equivalent; but it was the fact of his asking her to trust herself entirely to his guidance that troubled her; and for a while she shrank from yielding.

"Well," he said again, "is it a bargain?"

Still Laura did not answer, but remained gazing fixedly at the speaker, who watched her as attentively, his flushed cheek and eager eyes displaying the interest he took in the affair. At last, though, she leaned forward, and taking one of his arms between her hands,

"I never trusted you yet, Max," she said.

"Sisterly, very—but perfectly true," he exclaimed, laughing.

"But I will, Max, this time. But if you play me false—"

"Hush!" ejaculated Max, throwing himself back in his chair, and forcing his glass beneath his brow to stare at the new-comer; for at that moment the drawing-room door opened, and Ella Bedford stood upon the threshold.

Chapter Twenty
Ella's Resolve

"I beg pardon," said Ella, upon seeing who occupied the room. "I thought that Mrs Bray would be here."

"No, not here now, Miss Bedford," said Max, in his best style. "But take a chair; she won't be long first. Don't run away, Laury."

"I must; I have a letter or two to write," said Laura, trying hard to appear calm, and play into her brother's hand. But so far the efforts of brother and sister were without effect; for, with a few words of thanks, Ella withdrew; and a minute after the tones of Mrs Bray's voice were heard in loud expostulation, and coming nearer and nearer, till the door was flung open, and she entered, literally driving Ella before her.

"There, only think, Maximilian dear," shrieked Mrs Bray; "here's Miss Bedford been to say she must go!"

"Quite out of the question," said Max. "Bai Jove, what can you be thinking of, Miss Bedford? Why, poor Nelly would break her heart."

Ella started slightly, for Max Bray had touched a tender chord, and she remained silent, with the tears standing in her eyes, as the form of Nelly forced itself upon her imagination.

"It would be so inconvenient," shrieked Mrs Bray; "and you suit us so very well. I was only yesterday saying to your master—I mean, to Mr Bray—that the way in which those children have improved is perfectly wonderful."

"Perhaps Miss Bedford will reconsider her sudden determination," said Laura, in a voice which trembled with the struggle she had with self to obey the intelligent look darted at her by her brother.

"I have quietly thought it over," said Ella, looking with wondering eyes at the last speaker, as she felt unable to comprehend this sudden change, "and it is really absolutely necessary that I should leave."

"I'm sure you never will with my consent," shrieked Mrs Bray. "I think you a very nice young person indeed, Miss Bedford; and even Mr Maximilian made the remark this very morning, how pleased he was with the way in which you manage the children. And really, Miss Bedford, if it is a matter of two pounds more in your wages, I'm sure Mr Bray won't object to raising you. It's so troublesome to have to change, you see. But now that you are aware how much we are disposed to keep you, I think you will alter your mind."

"Indeed, madam—" cried Ella.

"There, there, there—pray don't be hasty!" shrieked Mrs Bray. "That's what I always say to the servants: 'Don't do anything without plenty of consideration.' You are young yet, Miss Bedford, and have not yet learned how much easier it is to lose than to gain a situation. Now take my advice, and go and think it over. No, I won't hear another word now; only remember this: I wish you to stay, and so does Mr Maximilian, who takes great interest in the studies of his sisters, as well as in their welfare, as you must have found out before now."

"Bai Jove, yes!" murmured Max, unabashed by the sharp glance sent flashing at him by his sister.

"I'm afraid," said Laura with an effort, "that it is all due to my hasty words, spoken in anger last night. I'm sure I beg your pardon, Miss Bedford: I'm afraid I was in error—labouring under a mistake—been deceived—" She hesitated here as for an instant she encountered Ella's candid, wondering look; but feeling reassured by the thought that Ella did not know how she had played the spy, Laura plucked up courage, and joined with Mrs Bray in requesting that Ella would quietly reconsider the matter, playing the hypocrite admirably, and little thinking how those soft eyes read the deceit.

"I quite agree with mamma, that you had better calmly think the matter over," said Laura after a pause.

"Bai Jove, yes!" said Max, rising and going to the door. "There, I'll leave you all to talk it over." And, with a parting glance at Ella, he left the room; but no sooner was the door closed than Ella started again, for Max was heard loudly calling, "Nelly! Nelly!" Then there was the noise of a scuffle, a smart slap, and two or three "I won't's!" and "I sha'n't's!" in the midst of which Max returned, dragging in Nelly, very hot and wild-looking; for her conscience told her that she was to be taken to task for listening amongst the shrubs the night before.

"There!" said Max, "I've got another voter, bai Jove, Miss Bedford! Here, Nelly, Miss Bedford says she wants to go away from the Elms; it won't do—"

"What!" cried Nelly, her eyes flashing as she darted to Ella's side.

"You should say, 'I beg your pardon,' or 'I did not catch your words,' my dear," shrieked Mrs Bray—"not 'what!'"

"Miss Bedford wants to go!" cried Nelly, not heeding Mamma Bray's words. "Then you and Laury have done it between you, and it is cruel and wicked, and—and—shameful, and—and beastly—that it is!" cried Nelly, bursting out into a passion of weeping. "But if she is sent away, I'll run away too, and never come back any more."

"But, bai Jove! we want her to stop," cried Max, "don't you see?"

"Then she will stop," cried Nelly; "won't you, Miss Bedford?"

"There, I'm off; I see you womenkind will settle it amongst you," said Max; and, satisfied that what had threatened to be a check to his plans had been most likely averted, he left the room and sought the solace of a cigar.

VOLUME TWO

Chapter One
Clouds at the Court

"Well, Charley my boy," said Sir Philip Vining, a few mornings after, "you must keep the ball rolling. You are going along swimmingly. But ladies like plenty of attentions. What are you going to do next? Can't you get up something fresh? Don't spare for money, my boy: I've—that is, we've plenty, you know; and I like to be lavish as far as the income allows. It's an old-fashioned idea of mine, Charley, that it is the duty of a landlord, deriving a handsome revenue from a neighbourhood, to spend that revenue liberally in his district. It's no waste, you know; it is all distributed amongst the people, and does some good. By the way, though, I think you might be a little more attentive to Laura. She's a fine girl, Charley: perhaps a little too masculine; but it's surprising how love and matrimony soften down that class of women. I saw you with her yesterday along with that Miss Bedford or Rutland—which was her name?"

"Bedford," said Charley quietly.

"To be sure—Bedford," said the old gentleman; "and the children. Seems a very ladylike young person. I was rather taken with her nice, sad, gentle face. One can almost read trouble in it. Pity a girl like her should have to lead such a life as that of a governess!"

Charley was silent; and Sir Philip, seeing him thoughtful, took up the paper.

And indeed Charley Vining was thoughtful and troubled in mind. He had encountered Ella twice since the day of the fête, to find her cold and distant. But then she had been in the company of Laura. All the same, though, it struck him as strange that the haughty beauty should have taken it into her head to accompany her in her walks: it looked like supervising her actions; and again and again Charley reverted to Nelly's warning, and longed for a few words with her; but so far it was in vain. He had called twice, to meet Laura and Mrs Bray, Max having returned to town. His reception had been most flattering, and there was a gentle, retiring way with Laura that troubled him; for he felt that he must be giving her pain, and his was too generous a disposition to suffer in peace the knowledge that he was causing others trouble or care. But call or walk, save in the society of Laura, neither Nelly nor Ella could be seen; and leaving Sir Philip immersed in the day's news, Charley left the room, went round to the stables, and had his mare saddled.

Still no luck. He did not even see them that day; and time slipped by without fortune smiling upon him. He called again and again at the Elms; but Nelly and her governess were always invisible, while Laura was still more gentle and retiring. Once he asked to see Nelly, and she was fetched down, evidently longing to take him into her confidence; but opportunity was not afforded; and at last one morning, with the feeling strong upon him that Laura was playing a part, and that he was being debarred from seeing Ella alone, Charley sat listening to the pleasant banter of Sir Philip over the breakfast-table, till, seeing his son's moody looks, the old gentleman became serious; for his conversation had all turned upon Charley's visits to the Elms, and his great love for woodland and meadow rambles.

"Why, my dear boy," Sir Philip had said, "I'd no idea that I was going to make such a solemn fellow of you. Certainly matrimony should be taken *au sérieux*; but I'm afraid the lady is hard to win."

A few minutes after Sir Philip rose; for Charley had turned uneasily in his chair, so that his face was averted.

"My dear Charley," said the old gentleman, going round the table, and making the young man start as he felt that loving hand laid upon his shoulder,—"my dear Charley, I have hurt your feelings in some way. Pray forgive me."

Charley groaned.

"My dear boy," said Sir Philip, "what does this mean? Surely my old-womanish babbling has not upset you like this! It was only lightly meant. Or is there something wrong?"

Charley turned his face to his father's for an instant, but only to avert it again.

"Is it anything to do with money, Charley?" said the old gentleman. "But pooh—nonsense! It isn't that, I know. Your personal expenses are ridiculously small. Why, I expected that by this time you would have half ruined yourself in jewellery presents. What is it, Charley? Can you not confide in me?"

"No, father," cried Charley, starting angrily to his feet, and overturning his chair; "I have been showing you for the past month that I cannot. But I can stand this no longer," he cried, striding up and down the room; "for it is not in my nature to play the hypocrite!"

"Hypocrite, Charley! My dear boy, what is it?"

"What is it!" exclaimed Charley fiercely. "You think that I am going day after day to some assignation with that—that—that—with Laura Bray!"

"Good heavens, Charley! what does this mean?"

"Mean, father! Why, that I am a hypocrite, and deceiving one who has always been generous and kind. It means, too, that my life has been turned to gall and bitterness; for I am going about like some puling boy, seeking in vain for a kind word from the woman who has robbed me of all that seems bright in life."

"But, Charley, what does this mean? I thought—I felt sure—"

"Yes," cried Charley bitterly; "and I was so mean, so base and contemptible, as to let you believe that I loved Laura Bray, and ask her here, as if—Heaven forgive me!—I blushed for my love for a woman who—There, I can't talk of it—I can't enter into it. Father, why did you stop the even tenor of my life? But no!" he cried, as he recalled his first meeting, "it was not your doing. I am half mad with disappointment, and know not what I say. A few weeks ago, and I could mock at the word Love, while now it is as though something was robbing me of sleep by night, rest by day, and my old zest for life. Father, I tell you I love—and love almost madly—a woman who rejects my suit, who turns from me, while every effort to see her now seems to be frustrated."

"But, Charley," cried the old man, his hands trembling with agitation, as, following his son about the room, he sought to drive away the suspicion that was beginning to enlighten him, "who is this lady? You are too timid— too diffident. Surely no one we know would refuse *you*. Pooh! my dear boy, you have taken the distemper almost too strongly," he continued, with a forced laugh. "But who is it?—one of the Miss Lingons?"

Charley turned angrily upon him, as if suspecting him of banter, but only to see truth and earnestness in the old man's troubled countenance.

"Father," he said calmly, "I love Ella Bedford."

"Who? Miss Bedford?" cried the old man excitedly. "You are joking with me, my boy," he said huskily; "and it is ungenerous, Charley. You know how I have set my mind on this—on your marriage—our pedigree, my son, our ancient lineage. Think, Charley, of your position."

"I do, father," said Charley sternly.

"But, my boy," exclaimed Sir Philip angrily, "it is madness! You, soon to be a baronet, with one of the finest rent-rolls in the county, and to stoop to a governess!"

"To a lady, father!" cried Charley fiercely now, as he stood facing Sir Philip. "You told me you wished me to marry. Can I govern my own heart? I told you once that I did not believe so good and pure a woman as my dear mother lived on this earth. I retract it now, and own, father, that it was said in the blind ignorance of my foolish conceit; for I know now that there are women walking this lower earth of ours whom I cruelly calumniated, for they might be taken as the types of the angels above. Father, I love one of these women with a strong man's first fierce love—with the passion long chained, now almost at your bidding let loose, and before heaven I swear that—"

"For heaven's sake be silent, Charley, my dear child!" cried Sir Philip almost frantically, as he laid his hand on his son's lips.

Then with a groan he shrank away, staggered to his chair, and buried his face in his hands, while with face working, brow flushed, and the veins standing out in his forehead, Charley stood struggling between the two loves, when he turned; for the door opened, and the servant handed to him a letter that made his face flush a deeper hue.

Chapter Two
Nelly a Correspondent

Charley Vining took the letter with trembling hand from the silver salver upon which it lay, glancing the while at the superscription, written in an awkward scrawly character, as if the sender had been possessed of a wild unbroken colt of a pen, which would shy and buck and dart about as it should not; but as well as if some one had been present to whisper to him that that letter contained trouble, its recipient knew it, and hesitated to tear open the envelope. He gazed at the address once more, then at the bent figure of his father, and took a step forward to speak—but no, he could not. He felt half unmanned, and that his words would be choked in their utterance; and turning hastily round, he hurried from the room, his last glance showing him Sir Philip with his face still covered by his hands; and Charley's heart smote him as he thought of the pain he had inflicted upon that noble heart.

Unintentionally, upon hurrying out of the house, Charley made his way to the part of the grounds where stood the rose-tree from which he had plucked that blossom—the spot where he had told his love, believing that it fell only upon the ears he wished, but all the same in the presence of three witnesses—the false and the true. But the roses were gone—only a few brown withered petals yet clung to the branches; and recalling how Ella had fled from him, he once more threw himself into the garden seat, and with an effort tore open the letter.

And then he could not read it; for the characters swam before his eyes, till savagely calling himself "girl!"

"Idiot!" and setting his teeth firmly upon his nether lip, he read as follows:

"My Own Dearest Charley Vining,—This is not a love letter, though I do indede love you very much indede (and those are both spelt wrong; only if I smudge them over and alter them, they will be so hard to read). I do love you very much indede, though not in that way, you know, but as I should love brother Max if he wasn't such a donkey. I've been wanting to speek to you so *verry, verry, verry* bad, but Laury has watched me and Miss Bedford just like two mice (I mean like a cat, only my eyes are so swelled up with crying that I don't hardly know what I'm saying or doing), and I have such a lot to tell you, enough to brake your hart, and I'm speling this worse and wors, though Dear Miss Bedford took such pains with me, and it's all about her I want to talk to you, only I won't say what, in case you don't see this yourself. So you must please come and meet me to-night in Gorse Wood, and it won't be rong, for I'm only a girl and a child; yet sometimes though I can't help feeling womanish, and feeling half and half too. But you always did play with and pet me, Charley, and i know you love somebody else verry much, and so do I, so that it won't be wrong, only candlestine. Mind and come at 7, whilst they're at dinner, and I shall tell Milly and Do that I'm going to get some pairs. So plees to fill both of your pockets verry full of those early ones, same as you gave me last year. And plees excuse all mistakes, for i write in a great hurry, and don't forget to come, for I've got to tell you all about some one you gave the rose to when you thought No one was looking.

"Mamma and Papa desire their best compliments, and with best love, i am, deer Charley Vining,

"Youre afectionate friend,

"Nelly Sophia Bray.

"P.S. That's all nonsense about Ma and Pa sending their complements, only it sliped in, and if I smudge it out, the letter looks so bad; and it don't mater, does it? for I haven't got time to write another letter, only don't forget to come."

Charley Vining was too troubled at heart to smile at poor Nelly's letter, as, doubling it back into its former folds, he sat wondering what news the girl could have for him. He did not like the idea of obeying her wishes, but he felt that he must go: the hints the letter contained were too strong to be resisted. If they were seen, what would it matter after all? for Nelly was but a child, he told himself—the great tomboy whom he had romped and played with again and again. There was something about it, though, that he did not like, but a re-perusal of the letter decided him; and more for a means of passing the time than for any other purpose he went round to the stables, and mounting his favourite, rode slowly away, heedless that, looking ten years older, Sir Philip Vining was watching him from the study window.

Chapter Three
Reversed Proceedings

Some people might have called Charley Vining a spoiled child, who had had everything he wished for from his earliest days, and now, at the first disappointment in life, was turning pettish and angry. True enough so far, his every whim had been gratified, and perhaps this made him feel the more bitterly that this newly-awakened desire should be thwarted on every side.

Try what he would, all seemed against him—father, friends, even the object of his choice herself; and he needed no one to tell him that the greatest care was taken to prevent all interviews. That Laura had a great deal to do with it he was sure, with out Nelly's confirmatory words. Max too might have some influence; but it was in vain that he thought—matters would only look more and more rugged on ahead; and at length, longing, in spite of his dislike to the meeting, for the evening to come, he cantered away.

"I only wish I were clever," he muttered. "Some men would scheme a score of plans; but as for me, I understand horses and dogs, and that is about—"

Charley's thoughts were directed the next moment into another channel; for turning a corner sharply, he came upon a family party from the Elms, consisting of Laura Bray and her two youngest sisters, with Max angrily stamping, clenched of fist and with his face distorted with rage.

"It's all a confounded plot of yours, Laury—it is, bai Jove!" he screamed in an excited voice, the very counterpart of his mother's.

"Indeed, indeed, Max, you wrong me," she cried. "It was not—Hush! here's Charley Vining."

"How do, Miss Bray?" he said, reining in, and trying to be cordial.— "Ah, Max, I thought you were in town.—Well, little ones, how are you off for fruit?"

"Nelly's going to have lots to-night," said Do, the youngest "child;" and the blood flushed up in Charley's face as he thought of the note he had received,—for he was as transparent as a girl.

"Bai Jove! ya-a-s," said Max. "Been in town, but thought I'd run down again for a bit."

"What for?" said Charley Vining's jealous heart, as he recalled the excited way in which Max had been gesticulating before his sister.

Max looked half disposed to be sulky; but he caught a meaning glance from Laura, when, feeling that he could not afford to fall off from his part of the compact he had made with her, he commenced talking to his youngest sister, just as Charley's eyes flashed, his nostrils distended, and, evidently moved by some strong emotion, he leaped from his horse, gazing eagerly the while at Max's watch-chain, and then at Max himself, with a fierce questioning look; which the exquisite responded to with a quiet self-satisfied smirk, ran his fingers along the chain, played with the locket and other ornaments to it attached, and then, with a side glance of insolent triumph, he thrust the little finger of his kid glove into a ring which hung there, turned it about a few times, and then walked on with the girls.

Charley Vining's heart felt as if something were making it contract, as if he were seized by some fearful spasm; for that ring—he would swear it—that ring had once encircled Ella Bedford's finger, and had lain in his palm. He had noticed it particularly, as he had longed to press his lips to the hand it graced—no, that graced the little bauble. What did it mean, then?—what was Nelly's news that she had to communicate? He could have groaned aloud as his heart whispered that he was—not supplanted—but that that empty-headed conceited dandy had been able to carry off the prize he had so earnestly sought—that heartless boasting fop, who esteemed a woman's purest best feelings as deeply as he did the quality of his last box of cigars. It was plain enough the ring was a gift, and had been replaced by another.

"I *am* a fool—a romantic boy!" thought Charley to himself; "and there is no such thing as genuine passion and feeling in this world; at least, I am not discriminating enough to know it. Here have I been grasping at the shadow when I could have possessed the substance. But, O!" he mentally groaned, "how sweet was that shadow, and how bitter is the substance!"

"Have I offended you, Charley?" said a deep soft voice at his ear—a voice trembling with emotion; and starting back to the present, the muser saw that Max had walked on some yards in advance with the girls, and that, with his horse's bridle over his arm, he was standing by Laura, whose hand was half raised, as if ready to be laid upon his arm, while her great dark eyes, swimming with tenderness, were gazing appealingly in his.

There was something new in Laura's manner, something he had not seen before. She was quiet, subdued, and timid; there was a tremulousness in her voice; and with the feelings that agitated him then swaying him from side to side, it was with a strange sense of trouble that he turned to her, half flinching as he did so.

"Have I hurt your feelings in some way?" she said, for he did not reply, and her voice was lower and deeper. "You seem so changed, so different, and it grieves me more than you can think."

It was very dangerous. There had been a sudden discovery coming directly upon Nelly's announcement that she had something grievous to impart. He had evidently been looked upon as a rude uncultivated boor, and this London exquisite had been preferred before him. In his poor country ignorance, he had been looking upon Ella Bedford's words as the utterances of a saint, gazing at her every act through a *couleur de rose* medium, till now, when he was rudely awakened from his simple love-dream; while, as if offering balm for the wound, here was a passionate loving woman talking, nay, breathing to him in whispers her tender reproaches for what she evidently looked upon as his neglect.

What could he do? He felt that his faith to one he loved would be firm as a rock; but he owed no allegiance—he had been played with—and this woman to whom he had breathed his love had preferred gloss and polish to his simple homely ways.

It was thus that Charley Vining reasoned with himself, as slightly raising his arm he, as it were, made the first step towards a future of trouble; for the next instant Laura's hand was laid gently upon that arm, and they were sauntering slowly along. She, trembling and excited; he, swayed by varied emotions—disappointment, rage, bitterness, and added to all, the knowledge that he had left that gentle loving old man heart-broken at his persistence in what he now owned to himself had been a wild insane passion.

"You do not speak you say nothing to me," said Laura softly, as she turned slightly, so as to look in his face. "I must in some way have unwittingly caused you annoyance. But there, Charley, I will not dissemble; I know why you are angry, and I must speak. You will think lightly of me—you will even sneer," she said, and he could see that the tears were running down her cheeks, and that her breast heaved painfully; "but I cannot help it; I must speak now that for once there is an opportunity. You are vexed with me because I was so madly angry with you for flirting. But you would not be, Charley, if you knew all. I don't think you would willingly hurt any one; but thoughtless acts sometimes give great pain."

Charley did not reply, but his arm trembled as they walked on, Laura's passionate words being very truthful, as by a bold stroke she tried to recover the ground she told herself that she had lost.

"See how humble I am. I never, that I can remember, asked pardon before of any one, but I do of you; and I feel humbled and abased as I think, for I know it is enough to make you mock at me. But though you refuse to know my heart, I know yours well, and that it is too much that of a gentleman for you ever to make me repent of what I say."

Still Charley was silent, though Laura paused to hear him speak. This interview had been unexpected, and had come upon her by surprise; but, led away by her feelings, words in torrents were pressing upon one another ready to pour forth, and she had to struggle hard to keep those words within due bounds, lest in her agitation she should make a broader avowal than that already uttered, and cause him to turn from her in disgust.

"Have I so deeply offended you? Can you not pardon me? Is mine such a sin against you, Charley, that I am always to suffer—suffer more deeply than you can believe?"

"I am not offended," he said gently. "Indeed, you mistake me."

"Charley!" she exclaimed in a burst of passionate emotion; for the soft, gently-spoken words seemed to sweep away the barrier that she should have more sternly supported—"I cannot help it; I am half heart-broken. You have been cruel to me; you have maddened me into saying things, and treating you in my rage in a way that has torn my own breast. But you will forgive me—you will be to me as you were a few months back—and, above all, promise me this, that you will not think lightly of me for this. Indeed, indeed, I cannot, cannot help it; I—I—"

Laura's voice was choked by her passionate sobs; and trembling himself with emotion, mingled of sorrow, pity, and an undefined sense of tenderness evoked by what he had heard, Charley Vining was moved to say a few words perhaps more warmly than under other circumstances he might have done. He did not love Laura Bray—he almost disliked her; but if there was any vanity in his composition, it was sure to be stirred now, when a young and ardent woman was, in the most unmistakable terms, telling him of her love, and imploring his forgiveness for her past resentment.

Charley Vining was but human. His heart had been deeply torn; and in spite of himself his voice softened, and he was about to say words that might have been too sympathising in their nature, when Laura's eyes flashed with bitterness and mortification. Had she possessed the power, she would have turned her to stone where she stood; for, with a laugh half merry, half sad, Nelly came running up, and pressing herself between him and the horse, she caught hold of Charley's other arm.

Charley gave a sigh of relief, as rousing himself, he exclaimed, "ah, Nelly!"

"I didn't mean to go for a walk," said Nelly; "but thought I'd come and meet them; and I can't walk with Milly and Do, because of old Max; so I've come here."

They say that two are company, three none: and if ever those words were true, they were so here. But, in spite of her mortification, and the agitation brought on by her imprudent avowal, Laura's heart bounded; for she read, or thought she read, on parting, what she called her pardon in Charley Vining's eyes.

Chapter Four
The "Candlestine" Interview

Sir Philip Vining ate his dinner alone that day, for his son was an absentee. In fact, a good half-hour before the appointed time Charley Vining was in Gorse Wood walking up and down, crushing the thin grass and trampling through the undergrowth, as he vainly sought to control the impatience of his spirit.

But he was in no controllable humour, and the more he tried to beat down the feelings that troubled him, the more fretful his spirit grew. It had been a day of misery and disappointment, such as he had never thought to see, and he was bitterly mortified with his own conduct. He told himself that it was his duty to have sternly answered Laura Bray, whereas he had allowed her to go on till, as they parted, her look of intelligence seemed to intimate that she was happy and satisfied, and that he had been making love to her, when—

When? Why should he trouble himself about a light frivolous girl, who gave love tokens to a tailor's dummy—a contemptible jackanapes? But all the same, there was no reason why he should marry Laura Bray, and give up his happy independent life.

"A fig for all womankind!" said Charley at last, out loud; "but then the poor old gentleman!"

Charley's face darkened as he thought of his father and his wishes. What should he do? Let matters run their course?

He asked himself that last question rather grimly, as he thought of how easily he could be in accord with all Sir Philip wished. A few quiet tender words to Laura Bray, and all would go on satisfactorily. And why should he not utter them? She would be well content, and he need trouble himself no farther, but seek in his old amusements *délassement* and balm for the disappointment he had met with.

How plain it all was! Max had come down again on Ella's account. Why, he had not spent so much time down at Lexville since he was a boy!

Of course, the Brays would not sanction it; but, anyhow, it was another of Mr Maximilian Bray's conquests.

"Ah, well," said Charley, as he stood leaning against an oak, "it's the old story: one's boy love never does come to anything!—What, my little wood-nymph!"

"O, Charley, Charley, Charley!" cried Nelly, running up to him panting, "what shall I do? I am *so, so* miserable; and they think I'm in the schoolroom now; and I can't bear it, and I hate it; and I've run out through the side gate and over the elm meadow like a mad girl, for they all watch me; and I stay in my bedroom most of the time; for since Miss Bedford's gone—"

"What?" roared Charley, seizing Nelly's arm.

"Don't frighten me, Charley, and please don't pinch so! That's what I wanted to tell you. That Laura led her such a cruel life with her temper, and Max was such a horrible donkey, that she told ma she would rather not stay, and—O, O, O!" sobbed Nelly, crying out aloud, "she's gone away, and I didn't say good-bye; for she went early in the morning, and came and kissed me when I was asleep; and me such a thickheaded, stupid old dormouse that I never knew—knew it—or—or I'd have put my arms so tightly round her neck that I'd never have left go."

"But where has she gone?" cried Charley fiercely.

"I don't know," sobbed Nelly—"nobody knows. She would not say a word even to mamma; and mamma said it was very obstinate, and that she was obstinate altogether."

"Do you think—" said Charley huskily, and then he stopped as if he could not utter the words—"do you think she told Max?"

"Told Max!" said Nelly, almost laughingly; "no, she wouldn't tell him. She hated him too much, for he was always worrying her, when all the time she was ever so fond of you, Charley. I knew it, though she never said so. Pah, she would never tell such a donkey as that, when she would not tell me! They think I'm very stupid; but I know well enough why she wouldn't stay, nor yet say where she was going: it was all because of Max, so that he should not bother her any more."

"Go on, pray!" exclaimed Charley.

"I have not got anything more to tell you," said Nelly pitifully, "only that there was such a scene over and over again; for at the last Laury and Max both wanted her to stay, and Laury asked her over and over again; but I could see through that: it was because Max made her, for some reason of his own."

Here was a new light altogether: Laura and Max both asking her to stay, and the poor girl led such a life that she was compelled to leave. Why had she not confided in him, then, when he had implored her to listen to him? But that ring?

Troubled in spirit, Charley began to stride up and down the wood, but only to stop once more in front of Nelly.

"When did she go?" he asked.

"Yesterday morning," said Nelly; "but I couldn't send you word till to-day. And now I want to ask you something, Charley."

"Quick, then!" he said hoarsely, as he turned to go.

"Will you try and find out where Miss Bedford is gone, and then tell me when you know?"

"Yes, yes!" cried Charley, rushing off.

"Yes, yes, indeed!" cried Nelly; "that's a pretty way to leave a lady who has given him a mysterious assignation in a wood; and—There, now—what shall I do? If I haven't forgotten all about the pears!"

Chapter Five
Mr Maximilian Beginneth to Show his hand

Gone without leaving a trace behind! Would she take another engagement, and write to Mrs Bray for a recommendation? She might, or she might not. She had taken the train at Lexville station after Dudgeon had, by Mrs Bray's gracious permission, driven the light cart in with "the governess's boxes;" but upon Mr Dudgeon being favoured with five shillings by Charley Vining, he shook his head.

"Sutternly, sir, I did see her boxes in the station, but I didn't read the directions."

Foiled there, Charley inquired of the booking-clerk.

"O yes, sir; remember it perfectly well. Mr Max Bray asked the very same question only this morning. She took a ticket for London, sir."

"Max Bray asking," mused Charley. "Then he did not know where she was, and there could be no undercurrent at work there. Max wanted to know her address, confound him! He had better mind how he stood in his way."

But, save when his thoughts turned in the direction of Laura Bray, which complication in his affairs troubled him, Charley Vining felt lighter of heart; for though Max held that ring, and so ostentatiously displayed it, there was no reason why he might not have obtained it by some hazard, as he himself had once gained possession of a plain golden cross. Matters were not so desperate after all, and he need not give up hope. And yet what misery for her to leave Lexville like that, without one word of farewell—flying, as it were, from his persecution, as well as from that of Max Bray!

Thinking over the words, too, of Nelly, how he could imagine the wretched life the poor girl must have led! and then, with brightened eye, he determined to find out where she had taken refuge. But London—the place of all others where a quest seemed vain.

Charley's musings were interrupted by one of the servants handing him a letter.

"John Dudgeon, Mr Bray's man, sir, gave it to our Thomas this morning."

Charley hastily tore open the thimble-sealed epistle, to find it written on a very dirty sheet of paper, and in a character that was almost undecipherable; but fortunately the note was not long, and he read as follows:

> "Hon'd Sur, — This comes hoppin to fine you verry wel, as it leves me at presen. Mr Maxy Million comes a hordrin an a swerin at a pore suvvant lik ennythink, an thare aint know pleesing im. An that ante the wa 2 get ennythink out of him as nose. E say wairs Mis Bedfors bocksis drecty 2, an off korse I wasn goin 2 tel he; but mi gal jain, she se an rede em bofe, an I lik doin gents a good turn as has sivil tungs for a por suwant, and shes gon to missus Brandins Kops all laintun; an if Mr Macks Million wan 2 no, dont let im kum to ure umbel suwant to kommarn,
>
> "Jhon Dugegin.
>
> "P.S. Wich you wone sa i tole u, ples, or yung marsta wil get me the sak."

Mrs Brandon's, Copse Hall, Laneton! Why, across country that was, not above a dozen miles off, on a branch of the South Midland Railway. Nothing could have happened more fortunately. He would have the dogcart and drive over at once—no, not at once: he would go the next day; and, come what might, he would see her again. Surely she would not be so hard, so cruel, with him—

His musings were brought to an end by the entrance of Sir Philip with a note in his hand.

The old gentleman looked pale and troubled, but his words were gentle, as he said: "A note from Mr Bray, Charley: he asks us to dinner there to-morrow. Shall I say that we will go?"

"To the Elms?—to-morrow?" said Charley. "No, I cannot; I have an engagement."

"An engagement!—to-morrow, Charley!" said Sir Philip sadly.

"Yes, I am going out—I cannot go," said Charley hastily.

Sir Philip said no more, but he sighed deeply as he turned and left the room to decline the invitation, thinking bitterly the while of her who had robbed him of his son's confidence and affection; for hitherto father and son had lived almost for one another, and now there was coldness and estrangement.

Laura Bray's eyes sparkled as she saw the servant returning on horseback with the reply from Blandfield Court, for there was a strange excitement now pervading her. In obedience to her brother's wish she had consented to try and prevail upon Ella Bedford to stay; but it was a source of infinite pleasure to her when she had written to tell Max, in London, that, in spite of all persuasion, Miss Bedford had insisted upon leaving, and had gone—bearing his reproaches and anger with the greatest of patience, when he came down by the fast train, and abused her, and charged her with counterplotting, in the midst of which scene he was interrupted, as we know, by the coming of Charley Vining. As for the events of the next quarter of an hour, they were burned in Laura's memory; and, her rival gone, her heart was light, and she had sat longing for the time when she should next see him who so engrossed her thoughts.

It was at her instigation that a dinner-party had been arranged at the shortest of short notices, ostensibly so that Maximilian Bray might have Charley Vining to see him—a pleasant fiction, which formed the text for much good-humoured banter at the Bray table, while Laura blushed and looked conscious.

The man was a terrible while before he took in that letter, and Laura's colour came and went a score of times. Then it seemed as if the footman would never bring the letter up. But at last it was handed to Mr Bray, who was so long getting out his glasses, that Laura, unable to contain herself, exclaimed:

"Let me look for you, papa."

Seizing the letter, she tore it open, read a few lines, and then dropped it with a look of the utmost disappointment. Then she walked to the window; but only to hurry the next moment from the room, so as to conceal her tears.

Max joined her, though, ten minutes after. "I thought you two had made it up?" he said inquiringly.

"Yes—no—I don't know," she answered passionately.

"He's going out to-morrow, is he?" continued Max musingly. "What's he going to do?—where's he going?"

"Have you found out what you want?" said Laura, to turn the current of the conversation.

"Not yet," he said. "You ought never to have given me the trouble. But I am at work, and so is he."

"What!" cried Laura eagerly, as she caught her brother's hand.

"He's at work too," said Max. "Bai Jove! he thinks himself very cunning, but he won't get over me."

"But you do not mean to say that he is trying to get that creature's address?" cried Laura pitifully.

"Raving mad after it, bai Jove!" said Max. "You see you want me, Laury. I must take her out of your way altogether, or it's no good. He won't throw her up till he hears something."

"Hears something?" said Laura slowly.

"Yes," said Max in a whisper; "hears something. I had nearly ripened my plans, only this evasion of hers disturbs them, and now I have to begin all over again."

"But are you sure he has been trying to find out where she is gone?"

"Certain of it; yes, bai Jove, I am!"

"How cruel!—how treacherous!" muttered Laura.

"There, don't go into the high flights, and spoon!" said Max roughly. "Set your wits to work. And look here, Laury, take my advice. Now, then, are you listening?"

"Yes—yes!" cried Laura, for she had been pressing her hands abstractedly together.

"Then look here. Don't show that you either hear or see anything. I have him on the hip in a way he little thinks for. What you have to do is to meet him always with the same gentle unvarying kindness. Wink at everything you hear about him; and even if he comes to you straight from her, you must receive him with open arms. Do you hear me?"

"Yes," said Laura bitterly; "I hear."

"For, bai Jove! he's not the man to be played with! Any show of jealousy, or whim, or snubbing, or any of that confounded tabby-foolery you women are so well up in, will drive him away."

Laura sighed.

"There, don't be a fool, Laury! Bai Jove, I'm ashamed of you! I thought you were a woman of more spirit. But look here: I was put out—I was, bai Jove!—when I came down and found the little dove had spread her soft little wings and flown away, for it put me to a great deal of trouble and inconvenience and expense; but you trust to me, and you shall be Lady Vining—of course, I mean when the old gentleman drops off. But Charley will come back to you like a great sheep as he is."

"How dare you, Max!" cried Laura, firing up.

"O, there, I don't want to upset the fair sister's sweet prejudices," said Max, with a sneer. "There, we'll call him the noble baronet-apparent. He'll come back to you by and by to soothe the pains in his great soft heart, and you shall heal them for him."

Laura bit her pocket—handkerchief fiercely, and kept tearing it again from between her teeth.

"I have him, I tell you; and, bai Jove! the day shall come when he shall frown at the very mention of the little soft dove's name!"

"But when—when?" cried Laura.

"When!" said Max coolly; "bai Jove! how can I tell? I shall work hard as soon as I have found out the address, and when the proper time comes, my charming sister, I shall want your help in a scene I have *in petto*. It may be a month, or it may be two, or perhaps three; but," he said excitedly, as he again threw off the drawl, and effeminate way, to let flash out the evil passions of his heart, "I am in earnest, Laury, and I'll have that address before many days are gone by."

"But how—how will you get it?" cried Laura.

"Well," said Max, sinking back into his old way, "I've got a plan for that too—one that will give but little trouble, and so I don't mind telling you."

"Well—quick, tell me!" cried Laura.

"Bai Jove! how excited you are!" said Max, laughing insolently, and taking evident delight in probing his sister's wounds. "Charley is hard at work trying to find out her address."

"Yes, yes!" cried Laura, pressing her hand to her side.

"And he'll be sure to find it sooner or later."

"Yes, yes!" cried Laura pitifully, her eyes flashing with jealous hate the while she stood before her brother, the style of woman who, had she lived at an earlier period, would have gladly taken a leaf from the book of Lucrezia Borgia, and ridded herself of her rival.

"Well," said Max coolly, "I said he'd be sure to find it out, didn't I?"

"Max—Max! why do you torture me?" cried Laura. "Tell me how you will manage, when you say that you will leave him to find out what should be yours to do, if there is to be any faith in your promise!"

"Faith!—yes, bai Jove, you may have faith in me! And there, I won't hurt your feelings any more. Charley will find out the address, and so shall I."

"But how?" cried Laura passionately, stamping her foot.

"How? Why, bai Jove, *I shall watch him!*"

Chapter Six
The New Home

John Dudgeon was right. Ella Bedford's luggage was directed to Mrs Brandon's, Copse Hall, Laneton, to reach which, unless a fly had been engaged to convey her across country, Ella had to go up to town by one line, and then take her ticket by another. This she did, and reached Copse Hall, a gloomy-looking dwelling, late one evening, her heart sinking as the station fly conveyed her down a muddy lane, on the Croppley Magna road. The hedges were heavy, and the trees seemed all weeping—drip, drip, drip—while an occasional gust of wind drove the rain against the fly window.

Cold, sombre-looking, and bare was the house; and feeling that the refuge she had sought by means of advertising would be to her as a prison, Ella descended from the fly. A tall hard-looking footman opened the door, and kept her standing on the mat of a great bare hall, whose floor was polished oak, and whose ornaments were a set of harsh stiff-backed chairs, that looked as if they had been made out of old coffin boards, while the cold wind rushed through and shut a door somewhere in the back regions with an echoing bang.

"There'll be a row about that," said the hard-faced footman, as he set down the second trunk and closed the door, and the flyman drove off. "Missus hates the doors to bang, and they will do it when the wind's in the south. You're to come in here, please, Miss—Dedford, isn't it?"

Trembling, in spite of her efforts to be calm, Ella responded to his query, and then followed the footman to a great gaunt-looking door. He opened it, and announced, "Miss Bedford." She advanced a few steps, seeing nothing for the blinding tears that would stand in her eyes—tears that she had much difficulty to keep from falling. Then the door was closed behind her, and she felt two warm soft hands take hers, and that she was drawn towards a great glowing fire.

"Why, my dear child!" said a pleasant voice, "you are chilled through. Come this way."

Then, as in a dream, she felt herself placed in a soft yielding easy-chair, her bonnet and mantle removed, the same soft hands smoothing back her hair, and then, as a pair of warm lips were pressed to hers, the same voice said gently:

"Welcome to Copse Hall, my love! I hope it will prove to you a happy home."

Ella started to her feet as those words thrilled through her; words so new, so tender, so motherly, that she could no longer restrain her feelings, but threw herself, sobbing violently, upon the gentle breast that seemed to welcome her; for two arms pressed her tightly there for a few moments. Then there were soothing whispers, soft hands caressing her; and at last Ella was seated calm and tranquil at Mrs Brandon's feet, feeling that, after the storms of the past, a haven of safety had been reached; and long was the converse which followed, as ingenuously Ella told all to her new friend, whose hand still rested on, or played with, the soft glossy bands of hair.

"We will not make a host of promises," said Mrs Brandon cheerfully; "but see how we get on. You were quite right to leave there: and I had such a kind letter from the Reverend Henry Morton, that I was glad to secure your aid for my children's education."

"Mr Morton was very, very kind," said Ella, "and offered me a home when poor mamma died; but I thought that I ought to be up and doing, though I did not expect so much trouble at the outset."

"Trouble, my child," said Mrs Brandon softly, — "the world is full of it;" and Ella, looking up, glanced at the widow's weeds. "Yes, seven years ago now," she continued, interpreting Ella's glance. "But the troubles here could be lessened, if we studied others more and self less. But there, bless me, you haven't seen the children!" and jumping up, she rang, and the hard-faced footman appeared.

"Tell Jane to bring in the young ladies, Edward," said Mrs Brandon; and, five minutes after, two bright happy-looking girls of eight and ten came running in. "There, my dears, that is Miss Bedford — your new governess."

The two girls went smiling up to offer their hands and kiss her, the younger clinging to her, and reading her face with a curious childish gaze.

"They are both totally spoiled, Miss Bedford," said Mrs Brandon, gazing fondly at her children; "and they're behindhand and tomboyish, and will give you no end of trouble. But you must rule them very strictly; and as they've not been quite so bad to-day, they may have tea with us this evening."

The girls clapped their hands, and over that pleasant meal it seemed to Ella that she must have been there for months; while, when Mrs Brandon accompanied her to her bedroom that night—a snug pleasant chamber, with a fire, books, and a general aspect of comfort—and left her alone with the sense of the warm kiss on her lips—a friendly pressure on her hand, Ella sank upon her knees, and the tears would for a while flow—tears this time, though, of thankfulness for the refuge she had found.

Two days of happiness had passed like a dream, in spite of sad thoughts and an undefined dread that all was too bright to last, when, seated in the drawing-room with Mrs Brandon, Ella's heart leaped, and then the blood seemed to rush to her heart, for the clangour of the hall bell proclaimed a visitor. The next minute the hard footman entered with a card upon a salver.

"Gentleman wishes to see Miss Bedford," he said; and Ella with trembling hand took the card, to read thereon:

"Mr Charles Vining, Blandfield Court."

Chapter Seven
Mrs Brandon's Receptions

Mrs Brandon made no movement as the card was handed to Ella; but a look of firmness seemed imperceptibly to sweep across her pleasant matronly face, and one skilled in physiognomy would have said that she was waiting anxiously to see how the young girl would act, under what threatened to be very trying circumstances. Then, glancing at Ella, she saw her standing, pale as ashes, with the card in her hand.

"Where have you shown the gentleman, Edward?" said Mrs Brandon.

"Breakfast-room, ma'am," said the hard footman.

"Very good; you need not wait," said Mrs Brandon; and the next moment they were alone, when, with pleading eyes, Ella held out the card.

"Indeed, indeed, ma'am, I could not help this," she whispered. "I hoped that my retreat would not have been known."

"My dear child," said Mrs Brandon kindly, "I do not blame you;" and she also rose and passed her arm round Ella's waist. "But you would like to see him?"

"No, no, *no!*" cried Ella hastily. "I must not—I would rather not—it cannot be! I hoped to have been left here in peace, and free from persecution. I cannot see him; I must never see him again."

"You wish, then, that Mr Charles Vining should be told that you decline to see him, and you beg he will not call again?" said Mrs Brandon softly, as she drew the fair girl nearer to her.

"I would not willingly hurt him," said Ella hoarsely; "but I have told you all, and what else can I do? It can never be!"

"My child," said Mrs Brandon tenderly, "I don't know how it is, but you seem to have even in this short time made yourself occupy the place of a daughter. You are quite right, and this gay gallant must be checked and kept in his place. We cannot have hawks here to flutter our dovecot. I will go and see him—that is, if it is indeed your honest wish and desire that he should see you no more."

"Yes, yes, it is indeed!" said Ella, with a sob that tore its way from her breast. "I can never see him more."

Mrs Brandon made a movement to leave the room, but Ella clung to her.

"Do you repent of what you have said?" Mrs Brandon quietly asked.

"No, no!" said Ella half hysterically: "but—it is very kind of you to see him—but—but you will speak gently to him—you will not be harsh or cruel; for he is good and noble, and true-hearted and manly, and I believe he feels all this deeply."

Mrs Brandon smiled incredulously, but there was pity in her words as she bent over Ella, and tried to calm her.

"Is it really then like that, my poor, weak, gentle little dove?" she whispered. "Has he then made so firm a footing in this poor soft yielding heart? But you are quite right; you must not see him, and the soreness will soon wear off. You do not know the ways of the world, and of these gay, insidious, smooth-tongued gallants, born with the idea that every pretty face beneath them in station, forsooth, is to minister to their pleasure. I see—I see; and I don't blame you for believing all he said."

"But I think you mistake his character," said Ella pleadingly.

"Perhaps so," said Mrs Brandon, smiling; "but will you leave your welfare in my hands, Ella?"

It was the first time Mrs Brandon had called her by her Christian name, and the young girl looked up with, a sad sweet smile.

"I am very young, very helpless, and quite alone in the world," she said softly; "and I have met here with kindness such as I have not before known since *they* died. I was so happy, so hopeful, so trustful that happier days were coming; and, indeed. I wish to be grateful."

Mrs Brandon kissed her again, and made a movement once more to leave; but Ella made a clutch at her hand.

"Shall I stay?" said Mrs Brandon softly. "Will you see him yourself?"

Ella was silent for a moment, for there was a great, a wild struggle in her breast; but she conquered, and drawing herself up, she stood, pale and cast-down of eye, with one hand resting on a chair-back.

"Do I understand you, Miss Bedford?" said Mrs Brandon.

"Yes, yes," said Ella, in a calm sad voice. "I must never see him again."

Mrs Brandon moved towards the door, and laid her hand upon the lock, making it rattle loudly as she turned to gaze at Ella; but the latter never moved; and as the door closed, Mrs Brandon's last glance showed her Ella pale and motionless as a statue.

"Now for this lordly gallant!" muttered Mrs Brandon, as she stood for a moment in the gaunt hall; "now for this sportive disturber of young hearts! If I had my will," she exclaimed, her handsome matronly features flushing up, "I'd have them all banished—I would!"

Then, with a firm step, and her head drawn back, she crossed the hall, threw open the door, and entered the room where Charley Vining was impatiently walking up and down.

Chapter Eight
Mrs Brandon's Receptions: First Visitor

Charley Vining started as, instead of Ella Bedford, he was confronted by a tall, handsome, middle-aged lady, who bowed stiffly, and motioned him to a seat, taking one herself at the same time.

"I have the pleasure of addressing—?" said Charley inquiringly.

"Mrs Brandon," was the reply.

"And Miss Bedford is not ill, I trust?" said Charley anxiously.

"Miss Bedford has requested me, as her particular friend, to meet you, and answer any questions upon her behalf."

"But she will see me, will she not?" said Charley earnestly. "Her leaving us was so sudden—I was taken so by surprise. You say, madam, that you are her friend?"

Mrs Brandon bowed, and Charley wiped the dew from his forehead.

"May I then plead for one interview, however short?"

Mrs Brandon frowned, and then rising, she stood with one hand resting upon the table.

"Young man," she said firmly—and Charley started as she looked down almost fiercely upon him, "you are the son of Sir Philip Vining, I believe?"

"I am," said Charley, slightly surprised.

"A worthy old country squire, whose name is known for miles round in connection with kindly deeds."

"My father," said Charley proudly, "is, in every sense of the word, a gentleman."

"Then why is not his son?" said Mrs Brandon fiercely.

"Me? Why am not I?" said Charley, in a puzzled voice.

"Yes, sir, you!" exclaimed Mrs Brandon angrily. "Why should not the only son be as the father?"

"Because," said Charley proudly, once more, "it does not befall that there should be two such men for many generations."

"It seems so," said Mrs Brandon bitterly; "but the son might learn something from the father's acts."

"Good heavens, madam! what does this mean? What have I done that you should speak to me thus?" cried Charley earnestly.

"What have you done!" exclaimed Mrs Brandon, standing before him with flashing eyes. "You pitiful coward! you base scoundrel! how dare you come before me with your insidious, plausible, professing ways—before me, a mother—the wife of an English gentleman, who would have had you turned out of the house! Silence, sir!" she exclaimed, as Charley rose, now pale, now flashed, and looked her in the face. "You shall hear me out before you quit this room. I say, how dare you come before me here, and parade your interest, and the trouble you are in because *she* has left the Elms? Do you think I do not know the ways of the world—of the modern English gentleman? You pitiful libertine! If I were a man, my indignation is so hot against you, that I should even so far forget myself as to strike you. Could you find no pleasanter pastime than to insinuate your bold handsome face into the thoughts of that sweet simple-minded country girl—a poor clergyman's daughter—a pure-hearted lady—to be to her as a blight—to be her curse—to win a heart of so faithful and true a nature, that once it has beaten to the command of love, it would never beat for another? I can find no words for the scorn, the utter contempt, with which you inspire me. But there, I will say no more, lest I forget myself in my hot passion; but I tell you this, she has been here but a few hours, and yet, few as they are, they have been long enough to show me that she is a pearl beyond price—a gem that your libertine fingers would sully. She has won from me a mother's love, I may say; and wisely trusting to me, she bids me tell you that she will see you no more!"

"She bade you tell me this?" said Charley hoarsely; "and have you poisoned her ears against me thus?"

"Poisoned her ears!" exclaimed Mrs Brandon, forgetting her *rôle* in her excitement, "poor, innocent, weak child! She believes you to be perfection, and but a few minutes since was imploring me to be gentle with the gay Lothario who has so basely deluded her, though she had the good sense and wisdom to seek another home. What—what!" cried Mrs Brandon, "are you so hardened that you dare smile to my face with your nefarious triumph?"

"Smile!" said Charley slowly, and in a strange dreamy way; "it must be then the reflection of the heart that laughs within me for joy at those last words of yours. Mrs Brandon," he exclaimed, firing up, "but for the proud knowledge that your accusations are all false, the bitter lashing you have given me would have been maddening. But you wrong me cruelly; I deserve nothing of what you say, unless," he said proudly, "it is wrong to purely love with my whole heart that sweet gentle girl. Mrs Brandon, you are a woman—you must once have loved," he cried almost imploringly. "What have I done that I should be treated so? Why should she meet me always with this plea of difference of worldly position? You see I am not angry—you have made my heart warm towards you for the interest you take in her. It may be strange for me to speak thus to you, a stranger, but you broke down the barrier, and even if it be simple, I tell you that I am proud to say that I love her dearly—that I can know no rest till she is mine. Indeed, you wrong me!" he cried, catching her hand in his. "Intercede for me. This indignation is uncalled for. Yes; look at me—I do not flinch. Indeed my words are honest!"

Mrs Brandon gazed at him searchingly, but he did not shrink.

"I am no judge of human hearts," said Charley earnestly, as he continued pleading; "but my own tells me that one so easily moved to indignation in a righteous cause must be gentle and generous. You have shown me how you love her, and that, in spite of your cruel words, draws me to you. Think of my pain—think of what I suffer; for indeed," he said simply, "I do suffer cruelly! But you will let me see her—you will let me plead my own cause once more, as I try to remove the impression she has that a union would blight my prospects. It is madness! But you will let me see her?"

For the last five minutes Mrs Brandon had been utterly taken aback. Prejudging Charley from her own experience, she had emptied upon his defenceless head the vials of her wrath, while ever since the first burst of indignation had been expended, the thought had been forcing itself upon her that she had judged rashly—that she was mistaken. No frivolous pleasure-seeking villain could have spoken in that way—none but the most consummate hypocrite could have uttered those simple sentiments in so masterly a fashion. And surely, her heart said, this could be no hypocrite— no deceiver! If he were, she was one of the deceived; for his upright manly bearing, his gentle appealing way, the true honest look in his eyes, could only have been emanations from a pure heart; and at last, overcome by her emotion, Mrs Brandon sank back in her seat, as, still grasping her hand tightly, Charley stood over her.

"Have I, then, wronged you?" she faltered.

"As heaven is my judge, you have!" cried Charley earnestly. "I never loved but one woman before."

"And who was that?" said Mrs Brandon anxiously.

"My dead mother; and her I love still!" said Charley earnestly.

"Mr Vining," said Mrs Brandon, "I beg your pardon!"

"What for?" cried Charley; "for showing me that Miss Bedford has found a true friend? Heaven bless you!" he said; and he raised her hand to his lips before turning away and walking to the window.

At the end of a minute he was back at her side.

"Mrs Brandon," he said, "will you also be my friend? Will you act as counsel and judge for us both? I will leave my fate in your hands. Think quietly over it all, talk to Ella, and see what is right. You will not judge me wrongly again," he said, smiling.

"I cannot think calmly now," she said; "I am agitated and taken aback. I thought to castigate a libertine, and I have been, I fear, lacerating the heart of a true gentleman! Go now, I beg of you!"

"But you will let me see her once—but for a minute?" pleaded Charley.

"No!" said Mrs Brandon firmly. "It is her wish, *and mine*, that you should not see her now."

"Now!" said Charley, catching at the word. "Then I may call again—to-morrow—the next day?"

"No!" said Mrs Brandon thoughtfully; "no! be content. I am but a weak woman, and I have shown myself to be no judge of human character. I must have proof and the words of others; when, if you come scatheless from the ordeal, I will be your friend."

"You will!" cried Charley joyfully, as he caught her hands in his; and then what more he would have said was choked by his emotion. "When may I come again?" he said at last.

"To see *me*?" queried Mrs Brandon smilingly.

"Yes," replied Charley, with a sigh.

"This day week," said Mrs Brandon. And five minutes after Charley's mare was galloping at such a rate that her rider did not see the grinning face of Max Bray peering at him from over a hedge. In fact, Charley saw nothing but his own thoughts till he reached the Court, where he encountered his father on the steps.

"Where have you been?" said the old gentleman sternly, but with a shade of sadness in his voice.

"To Copse Hall, Laneton," replied Charley boldly.

"Is that where Miss Bedford now resides?" said the old gentleman, watching the play of his son's features.

"Father," said Charley, "I never deceived you yet."

"No, Charley," said Sir Philip with trembling voice. "Is it there?"

"Yes!" replied the young man; and he turned away.

Chapter Nine
Mrs Brandon's Receptions: Second Visitor

Mrs Brandon returned to the drawing-room after Charley Vining's departure, to find Ella as she had left her, standing cold and motionless, supporting herself by one hand upon the chair-back, but ready to confront Mrs Brandon as she entered the room.

"Has he gone?" whispered Ella, with a strange catching of the breath.

"Yes," said Mrs Brandon, who watched her keenly; and then, as a half-suppressed sob forced itself from the wounded breast, Ella turned and began to walk slowly from the room.

"My child!" whispered Mrs Brandon, hurrying to her side, and once more passing a protecting arm around her.

Ella turned her sad gentle face towards Mrs Brandon with a smile.

"Let me go to my own room now," she said. "You are very good. I am very sorry; but I could not help all this."

Mrs Brandon kissed her tenderly, and watched her as she passed through the door, returning herself to sit thoughtfully gazing at the floor, till, taking pen, ink, and paper, she wrote three hurried notes, and addressed them to various friends residing in the neighbourhood of Blandfield Court. One will serve as an example of the character of the others. It was addressed to an old intimate and schoolfellow—Mrs Lingon; and ran as follows:

"My dear Mrs Lingon,—Will you kindly, and in strict confidence, give me *your* opinion respecting the character and pursuits of a neighbour—Mr Charles Vining. I have a particular reason for wishing to know. With kind love, I am yours sincerely, Emily Brandon."

The answers came by the mid-day post on the second afternoon, when, Ella being pale and unwell, one of the upper servants had been sent with the children for their afternoon walk.

Mrs Brandon was evidently expecting news; for, after sitting talking to Ella in a quiet affectionate way for some time, she rang the bell, and the hard footman appeared.

"Has not Thomas returned from Laneton with the letter-bag?"

"Just coming up the lane as you rang, ma'am," said the man, who then hurried out, to return with several letters, three of which Mrs Brandon read with the greatest interest and a slight flush of colour in her cheeks, when, with a gratified sigh, she placed them in a desk, and closing her eyes, leaned back quiet and thoughtful, till her musing was interrupted by the reappearance of the footman, with salver and card.

"Gentleman wishes to see Miss Bedford," said the man, handing the card.

"Not the same gentleman?" exclaimed Mrs Brandon excitedly, and as if annoyed at what she looked upon as a breach of faith.

"No, 'm; 'nother gentleman—a little one," said the hard footman.

"That will do," said Mrs Brandon quietly; and the man left the room, as, with the colour mounting to her cheeks, Ella handed the card just taken.

"Mr Maximilian Bray," said Mrs Brandon, glancing at the delicate slip of pasteboard, enamelled and scented. "That is *the* Mr Bray you named?"

Ella bowed her head, and then, as if transformed into another, she said hastily,

"Mrs Brandon, I think you give me credit for trying to avoid this unpleasantly; you know I cannot help these calls. It will be better," she said huskily, "that I leave here, and at once."

"Give you credit? Of course, child!" said Mrs Brandon quietly. "Sit down, you foolish girl. So, this is the dandy—the exquisite! I think we can arrange for his visiting here no more. That is," she said playfully, "unless *you* wish to see him."

Ella's eyes quite flashed and her nostrils dilated as she recalled past insults; all of which was duly marked by Mrs Brandon, who smiled once more as she rose to leave the room.

"I need not spare his feelings, I presume?" she said.

"What excuses can I offer you?—what thanks can I give you?" cried Ella earnestly.

"Just as many as I ask you for," said Mrs Brandon, smiling, and then kissing her affectionately. "I believe you are a little witch, my child, and that you are charming all our hearts away. Why, the cook has been civil ever since you have been here; and Mary the housemaid has not said a word about giving warning; and as for Edward, he has not let the great passage-door slam once. But, bless me, child!" she said merrily, as she glanced at the mirror in front, "am I in fit trim to present myself before the great Mr Maximilian Bray?"

But Ella could not smile: her heart beat fast, and she was troubled; and, in spite of Mrs Brandon's affectionate behaviour, she feared that this persecution might tend to shorten her stay at Copse Hall. A sense of keen sorrow pervaded her at such a prospect—at a time too when it seemed that she had found a haven of peace, where she might bear the sorrows of the past; and as Mrs Brandon left the room, she sank down in her chair, and covered her face with her hands.

There was a smile upon Mrs Brandon's countenance as she entered the breakfast-room, to find Max busy before a glass, battling with a recalcitrant stud.

Most men would have been slightly confused on being found in such a position; but not so Max. He turned round slowly, displaying the manifold perfections of his exquisite toilet, smiled, showed his fine white teeth and pearl-grey gloves, and then advanced and placed a chair for Mrs Brandon, taking the one to which he was waved by the lady of the house, who was still smiling.

"Charming weather, is it not?" said Max in his most fascinating tones, as he caressed one whisker, and placed boot number one a little farther out in front, so that the fit might be observed. "Pleasure of addressing Mrs Brandon, I presume?"

Mrs Brandon bowed.

"Ah! ya-as, bai Jove! mutual acquaintance, and all that. Heard the Lingons speak of you, and being riding this wa-a-ay, took the liberty—"

"Yes!" said Mrs Brandon rather sharply.

"Ya-as, just so, bai Jove!" said Max obtusely. "Took the liberty of giving you a call. Country's ra-ather dull just now: don't you find it so?"

"Not at all," said Mrs Brandon, who was evidently highly amused.

"Just so! ya-as, bai Jove!—of course!" said Max. "Miss Bedford be down soon, I suppose? Hope you like her—most amiable girl."

"I quite agree with you," said Mrs Brandon.

"Ya-as, just so—of course!" drawled Max, who either could not or would not see the half-amused, half-contemptuous way in which his remarks were received. "Thought I'd call and see her," he continued. "We all thought a deal of her; but she would go."

"Indeed!" said Mrs Brandon.

"Ya-as," drawled Max. "Fancy it was some annoyance she met with from young Vining: not that I wish to say anything—bai Jove, no!"

"I'm sure Miss Bedford will be delighted to hear of the kind interest you take in her," said Mrs Brandon.

"O, I don't know so much about that!" said Max; "but we were always very good friends."

"You puppy!" muttered Mrs Brandon.

"Always liked her because of the interest she took in a sister of mine. Down soon, I suppose?"

"Who—Miss Bedford?" said Mrs Brandon.

"Ya-as," drawled Max; "should like to have a quiet chat with her;" and he directed one of his most taking glances at the lady, who, all smiles and good-humour, had been studying his manners and dress in a way that Max set down for admiration, and presuming thereon, he grew every moment more confidential. "You see, when she was at home, Mrs Brandon, I felt a natural diffidence."

"I beg your pardon," said Mrs Brandon.

"Natural diffidence—kind of drawing back, you know," explained Max. "Didn't seem the sort of thing, you see, to be too attentive to the governess; but—er—er—must own to a sort of weakness in that direction. Nature, you see—bai Jove!—and that sort of thing, for she is a dooced attractive girl."

"Very," said Mrs Brandon; and Max went on, for he was in his blind-rut mood—a rut in which he could run on for hours without ever seeing that he was being laughed at.

"Glad you think so—I am, bai Jove! Very kind of you too, to be so cordial and—"

"Pray do not imagine—" began Mrs Brandon.

"No, no. Don't make any excuses, pray," said Max, interrupting her. "You see, I've been candid, and I've no doubt that you'll give me your permission to call frequently.—But is Miss Bedford coming down?"

Mrs Brandon did not reply; but still smiling pleasantly, she rose, rang the bell, and then resumed her seat.

"Bai Jove! don't trouble yourself—I can wait," said Max. "Ladies' toilets do take a long while sometimes."

Mrs Brandon smiled, and then rose again, as the hard-faced footman opened the door.

"Edward," she said in the coolest and most cutting manner, "do you see this gentleman?"

"Yes, ma'am, I see him," said the astonished servant.

"He has made a mistake in coming here."

"Yes, ma'am," said the footman.

"Show him to the door; and if ever he has the impertinence to call here again, either to ask for Miss Bedford or me, order him off the premises; and if he does not immediately go, send for the policeman."

"Bai Jove!" drawled the astonished Max, "what does this mean?"

"You will show him out directly," said Mrs Brandon, who would not turn her face in his direction, but continued to address the man; "and give him fully to understand what will be his fate if he should have the insolence to call any more."

"Yes, ma'am," said Edward, trying to keep back a grin.

"Bai Jove, she's mad!" ejaculated Max.

"Now then, sir; this way, please," said the hard-faced footman, whose countenance, if stony before, was now adamantine.

"Hyar, I say, you—Mrs Brandon!" ejaculated Max, "what does this mean?"

"Air you coming, sir, or airn't you?" said the footman angrily. Then, opening the door to its widest extent, he placed a chair against it, and advanced so fiercely towards the unwelcome visitor, that, to give him his due, more from dread of a disarrangement of his attire than fear of the man, he retreated round the table, stumbling once over a chair as he did so, and then in his confusion halting in the doorway. The next moment he was hurried into the great hall, and backed out by Edward, who, enjoying his task, proved himself to be the most uncompromising of footmen, and slightly exceeded his duty by slamming the hall-door after his discomfited guest with all his might, just as his mistress crossed and entered the drawing-room, where, pale and excited, Ella sat awaiting her.

"There, my child, that's over!" exclaimed Mrs Brandon; and then, in spite of Ella's troubled face, she leaned back in her chair, and burst into an uncontrolled fit of laughter, till, seeing how disturbed her companion looked, she sat up once more.

"I meant to have been angry, and given him a tremendous snubbing," she said; "but, as he says, 'bai Jove!' it was impossible. Of all the consummate puppies I ever beheld, I think he is the quintessence. And he is so dense too, he seems to have not the slightest idea when you are laughing at him. There, my dear Ella, never wear that troubled face about the donkey. He is not worthy of a moment's thought; and besides, he will never show his face here again."

"I cannot help feeling troubled about him," said Ella slowly, and as if she were telling her thoughts. "I fear him; and, dear Mrs Brandon, you do not know his character. It seems to me that that artificial glaze covers much that is gross, and unprincipled, and relentless. It has been my misfortune to have attracted his notice, and I never think of him without a shiver of dread. He seems to have cast a shadow across my path; and a dread of coming evil in some way connected with him—a strange undefined sense of peril— haunts me again and again."

"There, there; what nonsense!" laughed Mrs Brandon merrily. "We'll watch over you like dragons, and no one shall molest you; or, if it should come to the worst, we will set one chivalrous knight against the other—in plain English, Mr Charles Vining shall trounce, or call out and shoot, or do something to Mr Maximilian, the scented. Bah! he is in my nostrils now! But who is to be the next? Really, I am hard set to keep my little acquisition. How many more visitors of the masculine gender will there be, Miss Bedford?"

Ella looked at her so pitifully, that she directly ceased her light bantering tone, and changed the subject; while, perfectly astounded at the unexpected termination of his reception, Max Bray rode slowly home.

Chapter Ten
Mrs Brandon's Receptions: Third Visitor

Mrs Brandon's was a genuine feeling of affection for the gentle motherless girl who strove so hard and not unsuccessfully to gain the love of her pupils. She had called herself a poor judge of human nature, and had doubtless erred with regard to Charley Vining; but her estimation of Ella Bedford's worth, quickly as it was arrived at, was correct; and many an hour were her thoughts devoted to the best means of serving her protégée.

It need hardly be stated that Charley Vining too occupied no slight share of her thoughts—thoughts that now inclined in one, now in the other direction. They loved; that was evident. Both were young, true-hearted, handsome. They would make an admirable couple. Why should there not be an engagement? Then the balance was on the other side—of difference of position, the slighting treatment that might be met with from wealthy relations; and all at last ended with a sigh, as she told herself that the only way in which she could act was to be a watchful friend to her protégée, and to let matters shape themselves as they would, hoping always that the course they would take would be the best.

Meanwhile, during one of her walks with the children, Ella had a narrow escape from an encounter with Max Bray; and after staying within doors for a couple of days, she again had to hurry back; but this time not without his company for a part of the distance—a fact which Ella was not slow in announcing to her protectress, who bit her lip with annoyance, and tried to form some plan for putting a stop to these importunities; but, strangely enough, all Mrs Brandon's plans ended with thoughts of Charley Vining—when she gave up.

The day at last came when, in accordance with the given consent, Charley was to call; and Mrs Brandon sat turning matters over in her mind as to what she should do—what plan she should adopt. The week had slipped away, and, in spite of her cogitation, she was still undecided. "What should she do?" she asked herself for the hundredth time. She had not even acquainted Ella with the fact that he was coming again; and in a few hours he would certainly be there, beseeching her to stand his friend.

"What should she do?" she asked herself again; and she was just about to send to request Ella to come to the drawing-room when a carriage drove up to the door, there was a peal at the bell, and directly after Mrs Brandon felt that matters had indeed now come to a crisis; for the footman came in and announced Sir Philip Vining.

"To see Miss Bedford, Edward?" she asked eagerly.

"No, ma'am; to see you."

And this time, with no slight feeling of trepidation, Mrs Brandon requested that the visitor might be shown in there, and prepared herself for what she conceived would be an anxious scene.

The old baronet bowed with all a courtier's grace, and then, taking the indicated seat, immediately opened the business upon which he had come.

"You are doubtless surprised at this call, Mrs Brandon," he said, "for we are not acquaintances, and our homes are far removed; but I will be frank with you. You have a young lady here as governess—a Miss Bedford?"

"Yes," said Mrs Brandon quietly, as she waited to see what course she ought to pursue.

"I come to ask your permission for an interview with that young lady," said Sir Philip.

"It was unnecessary, Sir Philip Vining," said Mrs Brandon, rising. "I will at once send Miss Bedford to you."

"Stay, stay a little, I beg of you," said Sir Philip; and Mrs Brandon resumed her seat. "I must tell you, in the first place, that my son—my only son—has formed a most unfortunate attachment in that quarter—an attachment which it seems to me will blight his prospects in life. Mind, madam," he added hastily, "I make no attack upon the lady, who may be one of the most estimable of women; but it would grieve me sorely if such an alliance were to be formed. It may seem to be weak, but I have a certain pride in our old pedigree, and it is the earnest wish of my heart that my son should marry well."

He paused for a moment.

"I was aware of this," said Mrs Brandon quietly.

"Indeed!" said Sir Philip. "But I need not be surprised: Miss Bedford has, perhaps, confided to you my son's offer."

"Yes," said Mrs Brandon, "and so did your son."

"He was here a week ago," said Sir Philip. "Has he been since?"

"I expect him this afternoon to ask my cooperation; and I confess I am much troubled thereby."

"Your cooperation," said Sir Philip; "but I see, the lady is perhaps coy. Mrs Brandon, I must ask your aid on my side. This marriage is impossible—it would be an insane act, and can never take place. Will you ask that Miss Bedford may be sent here?"

"Will you see her alone?"

"No, no! I would rather you were present, Mrs Brandon. You know all; and perhaps, as a mother, you may be able to sympathise with another parent."

"Sir Philip Vining, you are placing me in a most difficult position. How am I to divide sympathies that are with all of you? But I will ring. Let us have Ella here; and I tell you candidly that I am glad to be free from a responsibility that threatened to fix itself upon my shoulders."

"Ask Miss Bedford to step this way," said Mrs Brandon as the man appeared.

And five minutes after, very pale, but quite collected, Ella was ushered into the room.

Mrs Brandon advanced to meet her, and led her to Sir Philip, who saluted her gravely, and then placed for her a chair.

Then for a few minutes there was an embarrassed silence, broken at last by Sir Philip Vining.

"Miss Bedford," he said, "I am an old and prejudiced man; proud of my wealth, proud of my estate, proud of my position in the county. I have, too, an only son, whose life and future are dearer to me than my own. For many years past my sole hope has been that he would form some attachment to a lady of his own rank in society; one who should be to him a loving wife—to me a daughter in whom I could feel pride."

"Hear me out," he continued, rising and standing before Ella, in almost a piteous and pleading attitude, while Mrs Brandon sank upon her knees by the fair girl's side, and placing one hand around her, took Ella's with the other.

"Hear me out," said Sir Philip; "and forgive me if my words sound harsh and cruel. On an unfortunate day he beheld you—fair, beautiful, as was his sainted mother—a woman to be seen but to be loved; and though I came here hot and angered against you, I tell you frankly that I am weak and disarmed. Had it been some proud scheming woman, I could have acted; but I find you sweet, gentle, pure-hearted, and one who gains the good word and love of all with whom you come in contact. He tells me boldly that he loves you. I do not ask you if you love him. No one could know his frank honest heart without giving him their love. But I ask you, hoping that any affection you may bear him may be slight, to make some sacrifice for his sake—for my sake—the sake of an old man who will give you his blessing. You must esteem him, even if you do not love. Think, then, of his prospects—think of his position. You see I humble myself, for his sake, to plead to you—to implore that this may go no farther. I came as a last hope; for I find that he has sought you out—that he will be here again to-day."

"He here to-day!" exclaimed Ella, starting, her wounds reopened by the cruel ordeal she was called upon to suffer. Then calmly rising, she stood before the old man, looking down at his feet, as, clearly and distinctly, she said, "Sir Philip Vining—his father!—I love him too well—with too pure a love—a love that I dare here avow to you—to wrong him either in thought or deed! I have told him it is impossible; I have avoided—I have fled from him. I have done all that woman can do to prove to him that we are separated by a gulf that cannot be crossed. I came here seeking rest and peace; but it was not to be: and in a few days I will go—go somewhere where he shall see me no more! You need not fear for me. I would not listen to him—I will not listen to him; and I thought that all that was at an end. It is nothing!" she said with a gasp, turning with a smile to Mrs Brandon. "I think I am weak. I wish to be alone. Sir Philip Vining will excuse me perhaps; but I have had much trouble lately. Thanks; I am better now!"

She tried to withdraw her hand; but Sir Philip took it, and raised it to his lips.

"Heaven bless you, my child!" he said, his voice trembling as he spoke. "I have wronged you bitterly in thought; but you must pardon me. I came, thinking to meet an ambitious aspiring woman; but I find an angel. Would to heaven that it could have been otherwise—or," he muttered, "that this pride was humbled! I feel," he continued aloud, "that I am playing a hard part; but you will forgive me."

Ella turned her face towards him with a sad and weary smile, and then one arm was thrown over Mrs Brandon's shoulder, the little head drooped down as droops some storm-beaten flower, and, as it touched Mrs Brandon's breast, there was a faint gasping sigh, and Sir Philip started forward.

"You had better leave us, Sir Philip Vining," said Mrs Brandon gravely; "the poor child has fainted."

And pale, trembling, and looking years older, Sir Philip walked with tottering steps to the door, paused, looked round, came back, and then kneeling, pressed his lips twice upon Ella's glossy hair, before, with a sigh, he tore himself away, and was rapidly driven off.

At that self-same hour, light-hearted and hopeful, Charley Vining mounted his favourite mare to ride over to Laneton.

Chapter Eleven
Kitchen Canvassing

"Now do tell us, there's a dear man," said cook, alias Sarah Stock, to Edward, the hard-faced footman, as he sat in front of the kitchen fire at Copse Hall, gently rubbing his shins and ruminating; while the housemaid, with her workbox on the table, was pretending to be busy over some piece of useful needlework, though she was watching Edward the hard-faced with all her might.

For it was that cosy half-hour after supper when all was at peace in the mansion; when the late dinner things had all been washed up, the kitchen tidied, and cook had performed the operation which she called setting herself straight—a manifest impossibility, for she was a circular woman of at least sixteen stone weight. All the same, though, she had changed her dress, polished her face till it shone, and then crowned herself with a gorgeous corona of lace and bright-hued ribbons and net-work, an edifice which she called her cap. The cat sat and purred upon the round smooth centre of the bright steel fender, winked at the fire, twitched its ears, and purred and ruminated at intervals; for it was fast nearing the hour when it would be shown the door for the night; so that it was getting itself thoroughly warmed through. The firelight danced in the bright tin dish-covers hung upon the wall, and then gleamed off, and dodged about from bright stewpan to brass candlestick, and back again to the clean crockery and the dresser; the old Dutch clock swung its pendulum busily to and fro, as if labouring under the mistake that it had nearly done work for the day; and altogether the place looked bright and snug, and spoke of the approaching hour of rest, when cook, having tapped the fire playfully here and there, to the destruction of several golden caverns in the centre, and taking up an apparently interrupted conversation, said, as above:

"Now, do tell us, there's a dear man;" when the housemaid gave her head a toss, as much as to say, "What indelicacy!—don't think I endorse that expression!"

Then she smiled with a kind of pitying contempt, for, according to her notions, cook and Edward were courting; and of course, if he chose to prefer a great fat coarse woman like that, he had a right to. An the slim maiden of thirty-eight bridled and looked almost as hard-faced as Edward himself. For though cook called him a dear man, it almost seemed at first as if she were bantering him, till it was taken into consideration that every eye forms its own beauty. In fact, just then Edward looked more hard-faced and grim than ever.

"You will tell us all about it, now won't you?" said cook, for Edward remained silent.

"'Tain't likely," said Edward at last.

"Why not?" said cook.

"There was two buttons off my shirt in the very worst places on Sunday morning."

"I *am* sorry!" exclaimed cook.

"Don't believe it!" said Edward; "and it's mean and unfair. Didn't you say, if I'd always get your coals in, you'd always see to my buttons and darn my stockings? And at this present moment there's a hole as big as a shilling in them as I've got on."

"But it shan't never occur again, Eddard, if you'll only tell us; for Mary and me is as interested as can be."

"O, I don't care about knowing, if Mr Edward don't choose to tell," said the housemaid, with a toss of her head.

"Who's trying to pick a quarrel now?" retorted Edward; "when missus said we was always to be peaceful and orderly in the kitchen."

"Not me, I'm sure," said the housemaid. "I wouldn't bemean myself to quarrel."

"Now don't, dear," said cook; "Mr Eddard's agoin' to tell us all about it, and really, you know, if it ain't for all the world like chapters out o' that book as missus had from Mugie's libery—the one you brought up out of the drawin'-room, and read of a night when we was in bed."

"Stuff!" said the housemaid tartly.

"Now, don't say so, dear," said the cook, who was particularly suave for once in her life. "There she is, just like a herrowine, and a nice-looking one too."

"Get out! call her good-looking?" said the housemaid.

"Well, 'taint to be denied as she has what some folks would call good looks. Then you see she's pussycuted by one lover, and another loves her to distraction, and his father won't hear of it; and first one comes and then another, and then the father, and frightens the poor dear into fits, and goes away fainting—no, I mean goes away leaving her fainting away, and wanting salts and burnt feathers, and all sorts. Why, it's for all the world like a real story in a book, that it is; and I declare the way Mr Eddard has told us all about it has been beautiful."

"There's soft soap," growled the hard-faced footman, smiling grimly.

"That it ain't now, I'm sure," said cook. "It really was beautiful, and almost as good as seeing or reading it all. I'm sure I never lived in a house before where there was such goings on. I declare that bit where you told us about how you took the dandy by the scruff of his neck, and says to him, 'Now, out you go, or I'll stuff you up the chimney!' was as exciting as could be. And so it was where you dragged him across the hall, and pitched him neck and crop down the front steps. I could a'most see it; and we both of us did hear the door slam."

"Mr Eddard," who had been slightly adding to the history of Ella's visitors, smiled a little here, and his face relaxed somewhat from its stern expression.

"Lor', what a nice clear fire!" said cook, who had detected the melting sign. "Let me hot you a sup of beer in a little stoopan, with a bit of nuckmeg and ginger, and a spoonful of sugar. Don't say no, Eddard."

"Yes, I shall," said Edward, who was tightening up again. "I sha'n't have none unless you two join with me."

"Well, if it comes to that," said cook, "sooner than you should go without, I'll have the least taste in the world."

The housemaid shook her head as if despising such excuses; but ten minutes after, when a mug of the hot sweet-scented compound was placed before her by cook, who winked at Edward as she did so, the lady of the dustpan and brush condescended to simper, and say, "O, the very idee!" Then she smiled, and at the end of another ten minutes the trio were all smiling as they sat with their feet on the fender, Edward regaling himself and his fellow-servants with an account of what had taken place during the afternoon.

"I should say it was as near as could be three o'clock," said Edward punctiliously; "it might have been a little after, though I hadn't heard it strike, or it might have been a little before: I ain't certain. Anyhow, it was as near as could be to three o'clock when the front-door bell rings.

"'Visitor for Miss Bedford,' I says to myself, laughing like, and meaning it as a joke; for as we'd had one that day, I didn't of course expect no more."

"What time was it as Sir Philip Vining went away?" said cook, who was deeply interested.

"O, that was before lunch," said Edward.

"To be sure, so it was," said the housemaid.

"Well, I slips on my coat—for I was dusting the glasses over before going to lay the dinner-cloth—and up I goes."

"And up you goes," said cook; for Edward had paused to soften his hard face with a little more of the stewpan decoction.

"Yes, up I goes, to find it was Mr Charles Vining, looking as bright and happy as could be—quite another man to what he was when he come last week.

"'Ah,' I says to myself, 'you don't know about your governor being here afore lunch, young man, or you'd be laughing the other side of your mouth.' But I says aloud:

"'To see Miss Bedford, sir?'

"'No, my man,' he says; and he looked at me very curious and hesitating, as if he'd like to have said 'yes.'

"'Show me in to your mistress,' he says."

"Now it's a-coming!" said cook, rocking herself to and fro with excitement, and rubbing her hands softly together.

"Now what's a-coming, stoopid?" said Edward gruffly. "What d'ye mean?"

"I—I only meant that the interesting bit was now coming—the denowment, you know," said cook humbly, and seeking to mollify the insulted narrator by emptying the little stewpan, cloves, bits of ginger, and all into his mug.

"If you're so precious clever, you'd better tell it yourself," growled Edward fiercely, "instead of keeping on interrupting like that. Who's to go on, I should like to know?"

"O, I'm sure cook didn't mean nothing, Mr Eddard," said the interested housemaid. "Do go on!"

"What's she want to say anything for, if she don't mean anything then, eh?" grumbled Edward. "I hate such ways."

Cook looked at housemaid, and slightly raised her hands, while the offended dignitary sipped and muttered, and muttered and sipped, and his audience waited, not daring to speak, lest they should miss the rest of the expected treat.

"I wouldn't say another word if I hadn't begun, that I wouldn't!" growled the hard-faced one. "Now, then, where'd I got to?"

"'Show me in to your mistress,'" exclaimed cook; when "Mr Eddard," turning round upon her very sharply, she shrunk as it were into her shell, and nipped together her lips.

"I tell you what it is," said Edward viciously; "if I'm to tell this here, I tells it, but I ain't going to be driven wild with vexatious interruptions. Do you both want to know it, or don't you?"

"O yes, please, Mr Eddard, we do indeed," exclaimed the two domestics; "so please go on!"

Thus adjured, and apparently mollified by the respect paid to him, as much as by the stewpan essence, "Mr Eddard" continued: "Well, I shows him into the breakfast-room, and then goes in to missus, who had just come down from Miss Bedford's room; and looking all white and troubled, she goes across the hall, and I opens the door for her, and up comes my gentleman with a rush, catches her hand in his, and kisses it.

"'That's making yourself at home anyhow, young man,' I says to myself, backing-out of the room; and I can't say how it happened, but the corner of the carpet got rucked up, so that I was ever so long before I could get the door shut, and they would keep talking, so that I couldn't help hearing what they said."

"And what did they say?" said cook.

"Ain't I a-coming to it as fast as I can?" said Edward angrily. "What an outrageous hurry you always are in with everything, except getting the dinner ready in time!"

"Now don't be cruel, Mr Eddard," said the housemaid, tittering, when "Mr Eddard" himself condescended to laugh at what our Scotch brethren would call his own "wut," to the great discomfiture of cook, who wanted to fire-up and give them a bit of her mind, but did not dare, for fear of losing the end of the coveted history. The consequence of her reticence, though, was that "Mr Eddard" grew exceedingly amiable, and went on with his account.

"That door being shut," he said, with a grim smile, which was meant to be pleasant, but was the very reverse, "I didn't want to go; for I put it to you now, under the circumstances, was it likely as he'd stay long?"

"Of course not!" said cook.

"Not likely!" said the housemaid.

"Well, then," continued Edward, "where was the use of me going back to my pantry only to be called directly? So I took his hat and brushed it, and when I'd brushed it and set it down, I set to and brushed it again, and so on half a dozen times, while—it was very foolish of them if they didn't want other people to hear—they kept on talking louder and louder.

"'Mr Vining,' says missus, 'I must ask you as a gentleman to come no more.'

"'But, in 'evin's name,' he says, 'what have I done that you should turn upon me like this?'

"'Nothing,' says missus; 'nothing at all. I pity you from the bottom of my heart, as much as I pity that sweet girl; but it cannot be. You must come here no more.'

"'Are you a woman?' he says. 'Have you feeling? Can you form any idea of the pain your words are giving me?'

"'Yes, yes, yes,' says missus. 'Mr Vining, why do you force me to speak? I do not wish to cause trouble, but you drive me to do so.'

"'Speak, then,' he says, quite in another voice, 'unless you wish to drive me mad, or to something worse—' There, I'm blessed," continued Edward, breaking short off in his narrative, and pointing to the cook, "did you ever see such a woman? Why, what are you snivelling about?"

"I—I—I c-c-c-can't help it, Eddard, when I think of what those poor things must be suffering," sobbed cook, with a liberal application of her apron to her eyes.

"Suffer, indeed—such stuff!" said Edward.

"Ah, Eddard," said cook, turning upon him a languishing look, "if I have saved up forty-seven pound ten in the savings bank, I've a heart still, and know what it is for it to bleed when some one says a hard word to me."

The housemaid sniffed.

"I'm a going on," said Edward, who was evidently moved by the culinary lady's remarks.

"'Drive you,' says Mr Vining, 'to speak! Why, stay!' he says excitedly, as if a thought had struck him. 'Why, yes; I'm sure of it. My father has been here to-day.'

"'He has,' says missus solemnly.

"'It was cowardly and cruel!' cries Mr Vining, quite shouting now, for his monkey was evidently up. 'And pray, madam, what is the result of his visit? There, I can answer it myself: Miss Bedford refuses to see me; you decline to receive me into your house.'

"'Mr Vining,' says missus softly, and I could fancy that she took his hand, 'I grieve for you, as I do for that suffering girl.'

"'What!' cries Mr Vining, 'is she ill? Let me—let me see her—only once—for a minute, dear Mrs Brandon! Pray—on my knees I beg it of you! You cannot be so cruel, so hardhearted, as to refuse!' And then I heard a loud sobbing wail as of a woman crying, and—There, I'm blest if I go on, if you will keep on snivelling. Why, blame the women, you're both on you at it!"

"We—we—we—we—we're—only a-blowin' our noses," sobbed the housemaid.

"Never see such noses!" growled Edward, who then continued:

"Well, directly after, as if in a passion, Mr Vining says:

"'Mrs Brandon, this is cruel and harsh. I left you last week with my hopes raised; to-day you dash them to the ground.'

"'Mr Vining—Mr Vining!' she says softly.

"'I tell you this,' he says, shouting again; and hearing his words, you could almost see him stamping up and down the breakfast-room—'I tell you this, Mrs Brandon: the ties of duty are strong, but the ties formed by the heart of a man newly-awakened to love are stronger. To win Ella Bedford, my own love, I will give all—time, hope, everything; I will leave no stone unturned—I will stop at nothing! I see that she has been coerced—that she has been, as it were, cruelly stolen from me by external pressure; and it shall be my task to win her back. I had hoped to have had you on my side; as it is, I must begin my battle by myself. I thank you for your patient hearing of my words; but before I go I tell you this—that *till I learn that, by her own act, she gives herself to another*, I will never cease from my pursuit.'

"The next minute he was in the hall, and I handed him his hat, brushed as he never had it brushed before; when, even then, upset as he was, he puts his hand in his pocket, and pushed something into my fist.

"'Sixpence,' I says to myself, as I shut the door after him, and him a-walking away like mad."

"Sixpence!" echoed the cook.

"Sixpence!" squeaked the housemaid.

"Well, it did feel like it, sutternly," said Edward; "but it was arf a suffrin'."

"But what did he mean by never ceasing from the pursuit till she gave herself to another? Would she give herself to another?" said cook, who was very moist of eye.

"No, I should say not—never!" said the housemaid.

And so said, mentally, Charley Vining as, disappointed and half maddened, he galloped homeward that afternoon; but the day came when, bitterly laughing to himself, he said otherwise, and hummed with aching heart the words of the old song:

> "Shall I, wasting in despair,
> Die because a woman's fair?"

And then he turned over and over in his hand—what?

A wedding-ring!

Chapter Twelve
More Passion and Little Progress

"Bai Jove! she's about the most skittish little filly I ever met with in the whole course of my experience," muttered Max Bray; and then he went over mentally the many rebuffs he had encountered. Forbidden Mrs Brandon's house, he had all the same gone over day after day to Laneton, for the purpose of impressing Ella with a sense of the value of his attentions; but still, though he displayed as much effrontery as a London rough, all went against him, and he found that, so far from meeting with a kindly greeting, his appearance was ever the signal for an immediate retreat.

"But you won't tire me—bai Jove, you won't!" said Max. "I've set my mind, and it will keep set."

And still day after day he rode over to Laneton, till not a walk could Ella take without catching sight of his mincing step and gracefully-attired figure; while, in spite of every effort, there were times when she could not avoid his addresses, as he stubbornly persisted in walking by her side.

"Bai Jove! it's of no use for you to harry and worry me," drawled Max to Laura. "I'm getting on as fast as I can."

"But are your visits having any effect?" said Laura eagerly.

"Well, I'll be candid with you," said Max. "Not so much as I could wish in one quarter; but, bai Jove! I'm doing you a good turn in the other direction. He's as jealous as Othello—he is, bai Jove! He meets me now with a scowl like a stage villain, confound him! But he gets on no better there than I do."

Max Bray was very decided in what he said; but though debarred from visiting, like himself, at Copse Hall, Charley Vining was under the impression that he did get on much better than friend Max. The very sight of Ella, even at a distance, was to him a pleasure; and in spite of many disappointments, he was never weary of his twenty-four-mile ride, counting himself a happier man when, by a lucky chance, he was able to catch a glimpse of Ella, if but for a minute. While upon the day when Max made the above remarks, Charley Vining had not only seen, but spoken to Ella—not only spoken to, but won from her—But stay—we are premature.

Weeks had passed since, exactly as had been described by Edward the hard-faced footman, Charley Vining had had an interview with Mrs Brandon, to learn that in future he must never call there, nor expect the slightest aid to be given to him, or even to have his suit countenanced; and then it was that, angry and determined, the young man had left, the house with the intention of leaving no stone unturned to win an answer to his love.

To this end, day after day he would watch the house, thinking nothing of the weary waiting hours, though it seemed that as little heed was paid to the distance by Max Bray, who now made no secret of his pursuit, carrying it on in open defiance of his rival—the two meeting constantly, but never speaking. In fact, Charley was rather glad of this; for after the last interview with Laura, it had seemed to him that he must be for the future upon unfriendly terms with the Bray family, though Laura, whenever they met, was more gentle and pleading than ever, although she must have seen that Charley shrank from her.

"*Nil desperandum*" seemed to be the motto adopted by all; and at length came the day when Charley's heart leaped, for he told himself that his perseverance was to have its reward.

He had ridden over as was his custom, put up his horse at Laneton, and was then listlessly strolling towards Copse Hall, in the hope that he might be favoured by, at all events, a glimpse of Ella, when he turned from the road, leaped a stile, and took a path which led through the copse from which the Hall was named.

There was no especial reason for going that way, only that he was as likely to encounter Ella walking—which was not often—in one direction as another; so he made up his mind to go through the copse by the broad winding path which led round the back of the Hall, then to make his way into the lane by Croppley Magna, walk on and see the old lady who had received him into her house when he had his bad hunting fall, and then return to where his horse awaited him.

He had entered the copse, walking very slowly, and thinking deeply of the unsatisfactory state of affairs, when suddenly he was awakened from his musing by the sound of merry childlike laughter. A little girl dashed round a bend of the walk, closely followed by another, and then, passing him quickly, they were out of sight in an instant, just as, dreamy and thoughtful, Ella, with her head bent down, came round the bend of the path—came slowly on, nearer and nearer to where Charley stood, with palpitating heart;

and the next moment, as she started from her reverie, it was with Charley holding her hand tightly in his.

"Ella!" he said, the word being as it were forced from his panting breast.

"Mr Vining!" she exclaimed softly, as for a moment she met his gaze, starting not from him, neither struggling to release her hands, but looking up at him with a soft pleading look, that seemed to say, "You know all that I have promised. Why do you persecute me?"

"Ella," he said again, "at last!"

"Mr Vining," she said wearily, "please loose my hands and let me return. This is folly; it is unjust to me and to Sir Philip Vining. You know what I have promised to him."

"I know what was cruelly wrung from you," he said bitterly; "but I cannot think that you will adhere to it. Ella, dearest Ella, do you doubt my love?"

She turned her eyes sadly to his for a moment, as he still held her a prisoner.

"You believe me, then! You know how earnest I am!" cried Charley.

"Yes—yes!" she answered, her face bearing still the same sad weary expression.

"Listen to me, then," continued Charley, his words sounding deep and husky. "If we were what you would call equals in station—an utterly false position—if I were some poor penniless tutor or curate telling you of my love, pleading to you earnestly, showing you in every way how dear you were to me, would you then—could you then—return that love?"

There was a silence for a few moments, and then, in a weak unguarded moment, Ella raised her eyes once more to his, to gaze, in spite of herself, fondly and earnestly, as she faintly breathed the one word "Yes."

The next moment she had repented; for he had clasped her in his arms, to kiss her fondly again and again, as frightened and struggling she strove to escape.

"Pray—pray, Mr Vining," she sobbed; "this is cruel—it is unfair to me;" and then she upbraided herself for her weakness.

But the next moment he was walking by her side, holding one hand still captive, as he urged and pleaded with a love-awakened earnestness, while Ella thought of all she had promised to Sir Philip Vining, and upbraided herself bitterly for not leaving Copse Hall, though the blame, if any, was not hers, since Mrs Brandon had again and again refused to hear of her departure. At last she roused herself, and for the next five minutes it was another spirit that contended with that of Charles Vining.

"Mr Vining," she said, as quietly but firmly she withdrew her hand; and he saw that, though deeply moved, there was a quiet determined will in existence—"Mr Vining, you tell me that you love me."

"And you believe me," cried Charley hastily.

"And I believe you," said Ella steadily and hurriedly. "For the sake, then, of that love—for my sake and my future welfare in this world, leave me—try to see me no more—strive to forget all the past, and let these words of yours be to you as some sad dream."

"If I forget all this—"

"Hush!" she exclaimed firmly; "and remember my prayer to you. I ask you to do all this for my sake—for the sake of the love you bear me. I have promised that I would meet you no more, and that promise I must keep."

"Stop!" cried Charley angrily, for she had turned to go. "I love you well, as you know—too well to accede to what you ask—and I tell you now, as I have told those who have importuned me so to do, that I will never, so long as I can see the faintest spark of affection for me, give you up. I go now, Ella, to wait—to wait patiently, even if it be for years. If rumours, set afloat by interested people, meet your ears, credit nothing that tells of want of faith on my part to you. I will be patient, and wait till you are less cruel—till you relent towards me: for now you are to me, I may say, harsh. But recollect this: by your treatment you condemn me to a life of misery and wretchedness, for I can never again know peace. You wish me to leave you?"

"Yes," said Ella hoarsely; and without another word, he turned and strode away, his brow knit, and the veins swollen and knotted; but had he turned then, in the midst of his hot anger and disappointment at what he called her cold heartless cruelty, he would have seen so pitiful, so longing a look in Ella's eyes, that he would the next moment have been asking pardon at her feet.

But he did not turn; and the next moment the bend in the pathway hid him from her sight, as with a sigh that seemed to cut its way from her heart, she, too, slowly turned, pressed her hands together, and walked sadly back to Mrs Brandon's, closely followed by her charge.

Chapter Thirteen
For Another Campaign

Three months had glided away with, at the end of that time, matters still in the same unsatisfactory state. There had been no open collision between Max Bray and his sturdy rival; but Laura had long since learned that, while Max persisted in his present course, there was no prospect for her to be even on friendly terms with Charley Vining. She had told her brother this; but he had angrily bade her be silent and wait, when all would be right in the end.

So Laura waited, to find that Charley now totally ignored her existence, spending his time either in sitting moodily in his own room, or else in riding over to Laneton.

But Max Bray was not idle: he literally haunted Laneton; so that at last Ella was quite confined to the house, and Mrs Brandon had looked grave.

Then came a visit from Sir Philip Vining, who again saw Ella, to part from her with a kind, gentle, fatherly farewell; and this was the result:

There were tears flowing fast at Copse Hall; for her few months' stay at Mrs Brandon's had been sufficient to endear Ella to all there.

Edward, the hard-faced, had confided to cook that he didn't know how things would go now; while upon cook weeping, and drying her eyes with her apron, he told her that her conduct was "childish, and wus."

The housemaid looked as if she had a violent cold in her head; while the children sobbed aloud; for the day had arrived when Ella Bedford was to leave Copse Hall; Mrs Brandon, though knowing well enough for some time past that such a course would be the better, yet only now having given her consent, and that too most unwillingly.

Ella Bedford was to leave Copse Hall, but only for a year. Mrs Brandon declared a twelvemonth would no doubt serve to alter the state of affairs, and then she could return.

"For I shall never be happy till I get you back again, child!" Mrs Brandon exclaimed. "And mind this, my love: I hope that you will be happy with Mrs Marter, who is a distant relative of my late husband; but, come what may in the future, there is always a home for you here. Write and say you are coming, or come without writing, and you shall always find a warm welcome. These are no unmeaning words, child, but the utterances of one whom you have made to feel sincerely attached to you."

"I know that," said Ella softly, as she clung to the motherly arm at her side.

"I would never have consented to your going, only I cannot help thinking that it may be for the best in the end; though really, now it has come to the point, I don't know what I can have been thinking about, not to decide and leave here myself for a few months. But you promise me faithfully that you will write often, and that at any time, if there is any unpleasantry, you will acquaint me?"

"Yes," said Ella, smiling sadly, "I promise."

"I think you will find Mrs Marter kind to you; and I have said everything that I could."

There was an affectionate leave-taking; and then, once more, Ella awoke to the fact that she was driven from the home where she had hoped to be at rest. But this time she bore up bravely, in the hope that the end of a year would again find her an occupant of Mrs Brandon's pleasant home, where unvarying kindness and consideration had been her portion from the day when, low-spirited and desponding, she had first entered what seemed to be the gloomy portals of a prison.

She told herself that, with the battle of life to fight, she must not give way to despondency; and nerving herself for all that she might have to encounter, she sat back in the fly, glancing anxiously from side to side, to see if she were observed, and in spite of her efforts trembling excessively, lest at any moment a turn of the road should reveal the figure of Max Bray or Charley Vining. It did not matter which should appear, she felt equal dread of the encounter; but upon that occasion she was not called upon to summon up her often-tested resolution.

The station was reached in safety, her modest luggage labelled for London; and this time she had taken the precaution of having no farther address, to act as a clue for those who sought her.

The train sped on, and in due course, and without farther adventure, she reached the terminus, engaged a cab, when, breathing freely, under the impression that she had thoroughly escaped pursuit, she was soon being rattled over the stones of the great metropolis.

Chapter Fourteen
A New Home

Poor Ella! in her happy innocence she did not know that she was as surely leaving a trail by which she could be tracked, as did the child in the story, who sprinkled a few ashes behind her from time to time as she went through the wood. Poor girl! she did not even notice the railway company's official, book in hand, taking the number of each cab, and asking the drivers where they were to set down.

No, she was free this time; but she said those words with a strange feeling of sadness as she leaned back. But the next minute she summoned resolution to her aid, and sat gazing from the window at the hurry and bustle around.

Crescent Villas, Regents-park, the residence of Mrs Saint Clair Marter, was Ella's destination. By rights it was Mr Saint Clair Marter's house, but his lady always spoke of it as her place; and as he dared not contradict her, so the matter rested.

Ella entered a pleasantly-furnished hall neatly floorclothed, and with groups of flowers and statuary, all in excellent taste. There was an air of luxury and refinement in the place, which was, however, totally spoiled by the tawdry livery of the footman, who muttered and grumbled a good deal about having to lift in the boxes, to the great amusement of cabby, who kindly advised him not to over-exert himself, for the reason that good people were very scarce.

But the door was closed at last, and the footman departed to announce the new-comer.

"Let her wait a bit!" said a sharp voice, as the door was held open; and the "bit" the young traveller had to wait was about three-quarters of an hour, for no earthly reason save that Mrs Saint Clair Marter wished, as she said, "to teach her her place."

But at last there was the tinkling of a bell somewhere in the lower regions; the footman ascended, entered what Ella supposed to be the drawing-room, and then returned to say gruffly, "Now, miss, this way, please!"

And Ella was shown into the presence of her new mistress.

As a rule, no doubt, a young lady engaged to act as governess in a family would speak of the feminine head of that family as her employer, or the lady whose daughter she instructed. She might easily find some other term that would avoid that word which expresses the relation between hirer and servant; but Mrs Saint Clair Marter always spoke of herself as the mistress of the ladies she engaged to act as governess to her children, and therefore we say that Ella was shown into the presence of her new mistress.

Mrs Saint Clair Marter was a very diminutive lady, with a flat, countenance, and very frizzly fair hair. She gave a visitor the idea of having been a small negress carefully bleached or made "beautiful for ever;" while the first glance told that, had she really been a sufferer from the slave-trade, whatever others may have valued and sold her at, her purchase at her own valuation would have been a ruinous speculation. She was dressed in the height of ultra-fashion, and reclined upon a couch perfectly motionless, evidently for fear of making creases; for her dress was carefully spread out over the back and foot, with every fold and plait arranged as may be seen any day behind plate glass at the establishments of Messrs Grant and Gask, Marshall and Snellgrove, or Peter Robinson; and upon Ella's entrance, Mrs Marter inspected her for full a minute through a large gold-rimmed eyeglass.

"Ah!" she said at last, with an expiration of the breath, and a look as if she had just made a discovery, "you are the young person recommended to me by Mrs Brandon?"

Ella bowed.

"Exactly. I have a good deal to say to you about the young ladies, but I'm afraid my memory will not allow me to recall it at present. I daresay, though, that I shall recollect a little from time to time."

Ella remained standing; for Mrs Marter, doubtless from having to recall so much, entirely forgot to invite her dependent to a seat.

"I am very particular about my governesses, Miss Bedford," said the lady; "and mind, I don't at all approve of their making friends of, or associating with, the other servants. I expect, too, that the young person I have in the house to superintend my children's education will rise early. The young ladies' linen, of course, you will keep in order, and assist the nurse in dressing them of a morning. Let me see, I think Mrs Brandon said you understood German?"

"Yes," said Ella quietly.

"And Italian?"

"Yes," was the reply.

"French, and music, and singing, of course you know; but really I must make a point of examining you in these subjects, for the trouble one has with governesses is something terrible. They all profess to know so much, and all the while they know next to nothing. Where were you educated?"

"Principally at home," said Ella patiently.

"At home!" exclaimed Mrs Marter. "Dear me; I'm sorry to hear that. I don't think much of home education. I ought to have seen you and talked matters over; but I trusted entirely to Mrs Brandon, as you were so far off. However, I suppose we must see how you get on."

"I will do my best to give you satisfaction," said Ella meekly, though her heart sank the while she spoke.

"Yes, that's what Miss Tuggly said; and before she had been here a week, she actually contradicted me to my face—before the young ladies, too. Ah! there's another thing, too, I may as well say: Mr Marter likes to be read to of an evening, and you will have to do that, for my lungs are in such a state, that I cannot read half a page without a fit of coughing. And of course you will have to come into the drawing-room tidy; but mind, I don't approve of dress, and governesses imitating their employers. I think it better to say these few words, so that there may be no unpleasantness after."

Ella bowed again, and sought in her inward spirit for firmness to bear all that might fall to her lot during the next twelve months.

"You may go now, Miss Bedford," said Mrs Marter, letting fall her great eyeglass with a loud rattling of gold chain; and Ella turned to leave.

The next instant she was summoned back.

"O! really, Miss Bedford," exclaimed the lady, "that will never do! Just what I feared when you told me of your home education. Not the slightest deportment! Pray, how can you ever expect to teach young ladies, when you do not know how to leave a room decently yourself? Pray be careful for the future, whatever you do! A ladylike bearing is so essential, as you must be aware! There, you may go now. Thomas will show you to the schoolroom, and you may ask the upper housemaid to take you to your bedroom, which, by the way, I visit myself once a week. I say that as a hint respecting the way in which I expect it to be kept. That will do, Miss Bedford."

Ella again turned to leave, but only to be staved once more.

"O, by the way, Miss Bedford, I have a great objection to my servants—I mean, to those in my employ—having followers; I mean visitors. Of course, upon some particular occasion, if I were asked, I should not say no to your mother and father visiting you; but what I mean, Miss Bedford, is that I do not allow young men followers."

Ella's face was now aflame, partly at the coarseness of the words, partly at the remembrance of the way in which she had been visited while at Mrs Brandon's; and she trembled as she thought of the consequences of her retreat being discovered.

"I think that is all I have to say now," said Mrs Marter. "But stay: the young ladies may as well be summoned before you go away. Have the goodness to ring that bell."

Ella obeyed, and the result was the coming of the footman in drab and scarlet, with dirty stockings, and an imperfectly-powdered head—that is to say, it was snowy in front, and greasy and black in the rear.

"Let the young ladies know that I wish to see them directly, Thomas," said the lady.

"Yes, mum," said Thomas, who, on turning, winked at Ella, not from impertinence, but from an ignorant desire to be upon friendly terms.

Five minutes of utter silence now ensued, when there was a distant squeal, a rush of feet, then a noise as of some one falling downstairs, followed by a loud howl.

"Bless me—those children!" said Mrs Marter faintly; and directly after the young ladies came tumbling into the room.

Chapter Fifteen
The Young Ladies

Ella Bedford might well be excused for looking with astonished eyes at the three juveniles to whom she was expected to teach deportment in connection with music and language—British and foreign; for the first that presented herself was a square-shaped child of about six, very red-eyed and smudgy from the application of a pair of grubby fists to remove the tears not yet dry, evidently on account of the absence of a pocket-handkerchief, which absence was also plainly otherwise manifested.

Number two, about a year and a half older, was a young lady gifted with a perpetual sniff, in which she indulged as she stood and stared at the new governess, an operation she was abetted in by number three, a young lady of ten, with tousley hair, and an inclination to rub one ear with a bony bare shoulder, which was continually hitching itself out of the loose shoulder-straps, and rising up as its owner gave herself a writhe, and then lolled against the drawing-room table, which creaked audibly at the infliction.

"This, my dears," said Mrs Marter, pointing at Ella with her gold eyeglass, and speaking in an imposing showman-like voice, as if she was exhibiting some new curiosity—"this, my dears, is Miss Bedford, your new governess. Eleonora, you may shake hands with her."

Thus adjured, Eleonora, the eldest and tousley of head, gave her shoulder a hitch out of the straps, and sulkily held out a hand elegantly veined and marbled from the want of saponaceous applications.

"Alicia, you may shake hands with your new governess," said Mrs Marter again, evidently addressing the second daughter, who did not move. "Alicia, did you hear me? Go and shake hands with your new instructress."

"Sha'n't?" said Alicia, twisting her feet about so as to loosen a shoe, and sniffing directly afterwards in a defiant manner.

"What do I hear?" exclaimed Mrs Marter. "Go correctly, and shake hands with Miss Bedford!"

"Shan't!" said Alicia, tucking her hands behind her, and sniffing again abundantly, as she, to show her dislike to governesses in general, made what is termed "a face" at the new-comer—that is to say, she contracted the skin of her little snub nose, half-closed her eyes, and lolled out her tongue in a most prepossessing manner; though Ella, not being of the medical profession, could very well have dispensed with the last attention.

"Alicia, I've told you before that that is very coarse and vulgar," said Mrs Marter mildly, for the young lady's back being turned, she did not see the physiognomical contortions. "You must not say 'sha'n't!' but, if you do not wish to shake hands with Miss Bedford: 'I would rather not,' or, 'I do not wish to do so.'—Selina, my darling, you will do as mamma tells you—won't you? Now, my love, you go and shake hands with your new governess."

Ella took a step forward, and held out her hand, when mamma's darling's face contracted, and directly after she spat fiercely at the new-comer, and then ran howling behind the sofa.

"Naughty Seliny—naughty Seliny!" said Mrs Marter. "You see, Miss Bedford, you are strange to them yet. They will know you better soon."

"I sha'n't do no lessons," said Alicia defiantly; "and I've burnt my book."

"Fie, fie!" said Mrs Marter sweetly.

"Licy pushed me downstairs, mar," said the darling behind the sofa.

"No, I didn't," shouted Alicia; "she tumbled."

"There's a big story!" cried Eleonora. "She put her hands on her back, mar, and pushed her as hard as she could—"

Smack!

"Boo—boo—bo—oh!"

Before Miss Eleonora had finished her sentence, her sweet sister had smitten her upon the mouth so sharply, that her lip bled, and she burst forth into a loud howl.

"There, my dears, I cannot have this to-day.—Miss Bedford, be kind enough to see them into the schoolroom.—There, it's of no use, Selina; if you will not go, you must be carried.—There, for goodness' sake, Miss Bedford, what are you thinking about? Take her up in your arms and carry her."

Ella obeyed; for Miss Selina had refused to leave the room, clinging tightly to mamma's skirts till she was carried off, fighting furiously, and slapping and scratching at her bearer's face in such a way that, could Charley Vining have been a spectator, he would have been frantic.

"Never mind her scratching," said the eldest girl; "she always does like that. This way."

And in a few moments more Ella was able to deposit her precious charge in the schoolroom, where, set free, the sweet innocent revenged herself again by spitting, till the upper housemaid was summoned, and led Ella to her own room.

"I pity you, miss, I do," said the woman kindly. "You're no more fit to manage them young rips than nothing. They're spoilt in the drawing-room, and encouraged in everything."

"Thank you," said Ella gently; "you mean kindly, I am sure; but pray say no more. Let me find it out by degrees."

"Well, that's best, certainly, miss," said the woman, who eagerly assisted her to take off her things, and then hurried down to help get up the luggage; while Ella—did she break down and burst into weak tears?

No; smiling sadly, she determined to bear the burden that was to be hers, and nerved herself for the coming battle; so that when the housemaid returned and helped uncord the luggage, she was rewarded with a sweet and cheerful smile, which was repeated when she said she would go down and make Miss Bedford a cup of tea.

Ten minutes later, when, after coaxing the kettle to boil with a few pieces of bundle London fire-wood, she was making that infusion that is considered by the fair sex to be a balm and refreshment for every pain and fatigue, she expressed herself loudly to her fellow-servants, to the effect that "that was quite an angel they had got upstairs. But it's my belief," she added, "that the poor thing don't know what she's got to put up with."

Chapter Sixteen
Change of Scene

It was not until Ella had been gone a fortnight that Charley Vining learned the news of her departure; as it happened, upon the same day that it was brought home to Max Bray that his visits to Laneton were of no effect.

But he was shrewd, was Max Bray; and encountering Charley directly after, and reading his disappointment in his face, he assumed an air of perfect contentment himself, played with the ring upon his watch-chain, and passed his rival with a mocking smile.

Five minutes after, Charley was at Copse Hall face to face with Edward the hard, who encountered him with a shake of the head.

"Show me in to your mistress," said Charley hoarsely; and it was done.

Mrs Brandon was seated working, but she rose, evidently much agitated, as her visitor entered to catch her hands in his, and look imploringly in her face.

"I have only just learned the news," he said. "Dear Mrs Brandon, you know why I have come! Be pitiful! See how I suffer! Tell me where she is gone!"

"I cannot," was the gentle reply, as, with a mother's tenderness, Mrs Brandon pressed him back into a seat. "You forget that I have given my word to Sir Philip."

Charley groaned bitterly.

"You are all against me!" he cried reproachfully. "You measure me by others. You do not know the depth of my feelings towards her. You all think that in a few days—a month—a year—all will be forgotten; but, Mrs Brandon, it grows upon me with the obstacles I encounter. But you will at least tell me to what part of England she has gone?"

Mrs Brandon shook her head.

"It was her wish—her express wish—that her retreat should not be known, Mr Vining; and, in addition to what I promised to your father, I must respect that wish."

Charley looked sternly at her for a moment, and then rose, and without a word left the room; Mrs Brandon following him with a sympathising look, till the door closed upon him.

"I must be a boy—a simple boy!" muttered Charley fiercely; "for they treat me as such. My father, this Mrs Brandon, and even Max Bray laugh at me! But," he muttered fiercely, "I may be a boy; but these bitternesses will soon make me a man—such a man as they do not dream of! Give her up? Yes, when I see her in Max Bray's arms—not before!"

Then he laughed, almost lightly, at the utter impossibility of such a termination, and returned to Blandfield after vainly trying to obtain information at the Laneton station of Ella's whereabouts. He could find that a young lady answering his description had taken a ticket for London; that was all; and in spite of his laugh of assurance, that was all the information that had so far been obtained by Max Bray.

But there are ways and means of finding all who play at hide and seek; England, as a rule, proving to be too small a place to conceal those who are diligently sought.

Max Bray knew that well enough; and returning to town, he sat tapping his white teeth as he made his plans; on the whole feeling very well satisfied at the change in the base of operations, since, in spite of his hippopotamus hide, he was beginning to be a little annoyed at the notice taken of his visits to Laneton. Old women were in the habit of thrusting their heads out of their cottage doors to watch him; servant-girls would titter; and on more than one countenance of the male sex there would often be a stolid grin.

It was satisfactory, then, on the whole, for London presented many advantages to a scheming mind; but the first thing to be found out was whether Ella were in London.

Max was seated in one of the windows of his club, as he ran over his arrangements; then rising, he ordered a cab, and drove away, ignorant of the fact that the hall boy was imitating his gestures for the benefit of the porter, who was convulsed with laughter.

That same day, without a word to Sir Philip, Charley started for town.

A week later, and, to his surprise, Charley Vining, who was staying at Long's, involuntarily raised his hat as the Brays' carriage passed him, with Mrs Bray and Laura on the back seat, Nelly and a stranger on the front. So introspective was Charley as he stood upon the hotel steps, that the carriage would have passed him unnoticed if a loud shrill voice had not shouted his name, when, starting and looking up, he saw Nelly, flushed and excited, leaning over the side of the barouche, as if ready to jump into his arms. But the carriage passed on; and though by a little exertion he might easily have overtaken it in the crowded street, beyond raising his hat, Charley made no movement.

Ten minutes after, an empty hansom passing, Charley hailed it, gave his orders, and was soon being spun along through the streets, thinking over the encounter he had just had, and wondering whether Sir Philip Vining would be the next to make his appearance.

"To see what I am doing!" said Charley bitterly. And then his thoughts reverted to the past, and he came to the conclusion that it does not fall to the lot of any of us to pass a life of uninterrupted happiness, such as his had been until he first set eyes upon Ella.

"Branksome-street, sir?" cried the driver through his little trap-door. "Number nineteen, sir?"

"How did you know that I wanted number nineteen?" said Charley pettishly; "I did not name a number."

"Lor' bless you, sir, this makes, I should think, a score of times I've been here in the course of a couple of years' hansom-driving. I never come wunst when it was a growler I druv. You want number nineteen, sir—private-inkviry orfice—that's what you want."

"And how did you know that?" said Charley, who could not help feeling amused.

"How did I know that, sir?" grinned the man. "It's a sort of instinkt, sir, as is only possessed by drivers of kebs. Here you are, sir—number nineteen. Up on the first floor for Mr Whittrick."

Charley leaped out, ran up the stairs indicated; and directly after he was in the office of Mr Whittrick, of private-inquiry celebrity.

Chapter Seventeen
Private-Inquiry

Waiting your turn in a dull cheerless room along with half a dozen more people who always seem oil to your water or *vice versa*, so as to insure non-mixing, is about one of the most unpleasant things in life. It is bad enough at the doctor's, where you sit and wonder what is the matter with your neighbours right or left, and whether their complaints are infectious; but at a private-inquiry office at a busy time it is ten times worse. There is such a general disposition evinced by everybody to turn his back on everybody else; an act which the actor soon finds out to be an utter impossibility; for though he gets on very well with respect to two or three, he soon finds that, however clever a mathematician he may be, he cannot place himself in the required position; and, as a matter of course, he turns rusty, and resents the presence of the other waiters—waiters, of course not in the hotel and coffee-room sense of the term.

To do Charley Vining justice, he was as ill-tempered as any one present; but he refrained from showing it, and tried to tranquillise his mind into a state of wonderment as to the business of others present. Was there any one seeking the address of some daughter or sister very dear?—was any one moved by the tender passion? It did not seem like it, judging from the countenances around.

One lady of vinegary aspect was evidently in search of a husband who had vanished; while on the other side was a little squeezy mild man, who might have come on a similar errand respecting a wife. The gentleman in speckless black, with papers in his hand tied with red tape, looked legal, and took snuff or pounce frequently from a small box, which he tapped with considerable grace, so as to bring the dust from the corner into a heap in the centre. His mission was evidently respecting a legatee, heir-at-law, administrator, executor, or assign, whose presence was necessary for the completion of some deed, document, or preamble as aforesaid.

What a wheezy stout man wanted was doubtful; but it was evident that the quiet-looking unassuming man who came out softly from the inner sanctum, and in one glance took down and mentally recorded all who were present, had something to do with order as well as law.

And it was so, in fact; for the quiet unassuming man was Mr Orger, of the detective department of Great Scotland-yard, who, after a fortnight of unavailing search for some gentleman who was wanted, did not think it derogatory to his dignity to seek counsel—on the principle of two heads being better than one—from his old friend and fellow-inspector Mr Whittrick, of the detective force formerly, but now professionally engaged upon his own account.

Charley's turn at last, just as he had come to the conclusion that he would wait no longer, but call another day, when there were not so many private inquirers.

Obeying a signal, he was shown into a well-furnished room with a couple of tables, at one of which, whose top was covered with papers, sat a very ordinary-looking man, in a black-velvet cap; at the other, which bore a telegraphic dial, were a couple of clerks busily writing.

"Perhaps you will step this way," said the man of the black-velvet cap, mentally photographing his visitor the while; and Charley followed him to an inner room, where, taking the seat offered, he paid certain fees and stated his case.

"Young lady—deep mourning—fair—grey eyes—luxuriant hair," muttered the private-inquiry high-priest, as he took notes during Charley's explanations, trying hard to suppress a smile as he saw his client's earnestness. "Came up from Laneton on the 9th, to the South Midland Terminus," he continued.

"Well, Mr Vining?"

"Well," said Charley, "I must have her address found!"

"The information you give is very meagre, sir," said Mr Whittrick quietly.

"It is, I know," said Charley impetuously: "but I must have that address.

"Here," he exclaimed, drawing out his porte-monnaie and placing a couple of crisp new ten-pound notes upon the table, "do not stand for expense. That is all I have with me; but tell me what you require, and you shall have it."

"Thanks, sir," said Mr Whittrick quietly, as he transferred the notes to his pocket-book, after entering the transaction and the numbers in a book. "But you give us the credit of great powers, sir."

"Well," said Charley, "you have great powers: telegraphy and a cordon of spies, I have no doubt. All you require is something to set the mechanism at work, and I tell you frankly I am ready to supply that something liberally."

"You would not consider those two notes ill spent for a little certain information, I suppose, sir?"

"No, nor double!" said Charley hastily.

"Good," said Mr Whittrick; and rising, he took a whistle from the mouth of a speaking-tube in the wall, whispered a few words, and then applied his ear.

The answer came in half a minute; and then he gave some other order, replugged the tube, and sitting down, made some remark touching the present ministry.

"But I am keeping you," said Charley, who took the remark as an intimation that he might go. "Tell me when I may come again?" he said, rising.

"Stop a bit—stop a bit, Mr Vining: I never like doing things in a hurry. Let's economise time; and we can now you are here," said Mr Whittrick. "It may save my sending to Long's Hotel, and wasting time, and men, and cab-hire, and perhaps not then to find you. I shall have a reply directly to a question I have asked. And, besides, you have entirely omitted to give me the young lady's age and name.—Ah, Smith, that will do," he said, as a clerk entered the room with a sheet of paper.

The clerk left the room; and then, after running through the manuscript note, Mr Whittrick took out a double eyeglass, rubbed it leisurely, and then fixed it by its spring upon the bridge of his nose.

"You'd be surprised, Mr Vining," he said, "what a deal of difficulty I have to get clerks who write a plain legible hand. I'm a terrible scrawler myoelf; but then my writing has to keep up with my thoughts, and has to struggle hard, with the certainty of failure always before it. But my clerks are well paid to do nothing else but copy; and really at times, either from hurry or carelessness, their stuff is almost undecipherable. But let me see; I think I have managed this, though."

"Is that anything relating to my search?" said Charley excitedly.

"Stop a minute, my dear sir, and we'll see," said Mr Whittrick; and then he held the slip of paper in his hand as if about to read aloud.

Chapter Eighteen
Second-Hand

At the last words uttered by Mr Whittrick, Charley Vining started forward, and gazed at the speaker as if he would have devoured the ordinary-looking slip of paper rustling before him. It was with the greatest difficulty that he refrained from snatching the memorandum from its holder; for in every respect save one, Mr Whittrick, of the black-velvet cap, was outwardly an excessively slow man. He had crawled to the speaking-tube and crawled back, and when he took the slip of paper from the clerk, it was as if the effort was too much for him—so much, in fact, that he had hard work to wipe his double eyeglasses.

But we said that there was an exception, and this lay in Mr Whittrick's eyes, which gave a sharpness to his whole appearance, as they twinkled and darted and played as it were, while they displayed the activity of their owner's brains.

But, apparently satisfied that if he kept him waiting half an hour longer, Charley Vining would not say anything that would be of service for information of any kind, Mr Whittrick commenced reading:

"9th instant. Miss Ella Bedford, age about twenty; fair; grey eyes; thick braided hair—*not false*; height about five feet two; dressed in deep mourning; arrived by forty-five, a.m., train from Laneton. Robert Wilks, porter, Number 93, called four-wheeled cab, V.R. 09876, John Round driver. Luggage: canvas-covered box, black enamelled bag, and leather wallet, *not addressed*. Set down at 19 Crescent Villas, Regent's-park—Mr Saint Clair Marter's. Cab man paid. No farther communication; but footman averse to taking in luggage, whether from idleness or particular reasons not known; shall know shortly, if necessary. Cab returned to terminus."

"Let me see," continued Mr Whittrick, turning the paper on the other side. "No, that is all we know at present;" and he looked at Charley, who, mute with astonishment, was staring hard at him.

"Why, good heavens! how did you know that?" he cried. "That is all I wanted to know."

"At present—at present!" said Mr Whittrick, with a smile.

"But I expected days of waiting and anxiety," cried Charley, eagerly seizing the paper.

"Possibly," said Mr Whittrick; "but there are times, you see, when we are speedy in our movements."

"But I am astounded!" cried Charley. "You make me almost to believe in magicians."

Mr Whittrick smiled deprecatingly and shrugged his shoulders.

"How did you obtain the information?" cried Charley.

"My dear sir," said Mr Whittrick, "that is my profession. If you go to a doctor and he gives you a prescription which cures you, do you ask him how he discovered his drugs? Of course not. You came to me for assistance, and showed me that you were ready to pay liberally for that assistance, and, of course, I set to work instanter."

"But is that—are you sure—that Miss—that the young lady is there?"

"Certainly not," said Mr Whittrick; "some time has passed since then. But I am ready to make affidavit that she was there. Now then, sir, what can I do for you next?"

"Nothing more," said Charley; "I am quite satisfied."

"Do I understand you to say you consider my efforts sufficient?"

"Quite," said Charley.

"Very good, my dear sir," said Mr Whittrick; "then all I can say is, that it has been a most satisfactory interview for both parties; only recollect that you may want me again, and that you have paid me so liberally, that there is a large balance in your favour, which I am ready to devote to you at a moment's notice."

"You would rather not inform me how you obtained that information, I presume?" said Charley, turning on the threshold, to display to the high-priest of private-inquiry a thoroughly mystified countenance.

"Quite out of the question," said Mr Whittrick, smiling; and the next minute Charley was bowed out, to descend the stairs, taking no heed of the scowls of those who had been kept waiting during the long interview.

"Where to next, sir?" said a voice; and Charley started to find that the cabman, who had not been paid, was naturally enough waiting the return of his fare.

"19 Crescent Villas, Regents-park," said Charley abstractedly; but the next moment he had altered his mind, and changed his order for Long's Hotel, where he arrived elate, but confused, so utterly incomprehensible seemed the power of the private inquirer.

Light came through at last, and seemed to cut through his brain with a sharp pang. It was all plain enough now: another had been seeking information, even as he had sought it, and the news he had obtained was only second-hand. But who had been beforehand with him, while he had been wasting time with his own ineffectual unassisted efforts?

There was no need for much consideration. The reply to his question was quick enough in arriving, burdened too with bitterness: and the answer was—

"Max Bray!"

Chapter Nineteen
At Crescent Villas

Keeping to her determination, Ella wrote cheerfully to Mrs Brandon, making the best of everything, and then devoted herself energetically to the task of trying to shape the rugged children in her charge. The days glided by, and ever striving to be hopeful she toiled on, driving away all thoughts of the past, and rejoicing in her freedom from persecution.

But her rejoicings were but short-lived; for one day, upon returning from a walk, there, once more, was Max Bray to meet her, and salute her with all the familiarity of an old acquaintance, just in front of the windows of Mrs Saint Clair Marter's house, and at a time, too, when that lady herself was gazing from a window.

Ella crimsoned with vexation, and escaping as quickly as possible, she entered the house, to learn from Thomas that there had been "a gent to see her; but as she was out, missus had seen him instead."

How was it all to end? she asked herself, as, angry now, she hurried to her room, expecting momentarily a summons to the presence of Mrs Marter.

But it did not come; and it was with beating heart that she descended to the drawing-room in the evening. Had there come a message soon after she returned, it would have been when, driven as it were to bay, she would have had spirit to defend herself; but now she was tremulous and weak, and as she took her place and began to read, her voice shook so that she was afraid it would attract attention.

"By the way, Miss Bedford—" said Mrs Marter suddenly.

It was coming, then, at last, and in an instant Ella saw herself once more driven to seek a home—saw herself harried and persecuted at situation after situation; and it was with a faint giddy sensation, making everything look confused and indistinct, that she listened to Mrs Marter's words, and tried to find words to reply.

"By the way, Miss Bedford, as you are aware, a gentleman called this afternoon while you were absent with the young ladies. I have always said that I would never encourage anything of the kind; but when a gentleman of good family comes to me, and in a proper way, I must say that I feel disposed to be lenient. I must say, though, that I consider you a very fortunate girl; and though this has come upon me very suddenly, yet I shall not be harsh; and if your conduct continues satisfactory, I shall give you every encouragement."

Ella was astounded: the words were so thoroughly opposed to those she had expected, that for a few moments she could not speak, and her silence was immediately interpreted to mean modest confusion.

"I did know some branches of the Bray family at one time," continued Mrs Marter, "and Mr Maximilian puts me very much in mind of them. I must say that I very greatly approve of your choice, for he is a most gentlemanly man: there is so much the tone of one accustomed to good society. Really I cannot help congratulating you."

"Indeed, indeed, madam—" exclaimed Ella earnestly.

"Hush, child, hush. I will not hear a word. I have said all that need be said upon the subject, except that I have given Mr Maximilian Bray my full consent to his calling here as frequently as he likes."

Again Ella essayed to speak, but only to be checked, and almost ordered to go on with her reading, which was kept up for two hours, till Mrs Marter and her lord were both comfortably asleep, when the reader was left alone with her thoughts.

Two days passed, and then she was summoned to the drawing-room to meet Mr Maximilian Bray. In the interim she had twice approached the subject—the first time to be checked good-humouredly, the second time to be told that her conduct was bold and forward, words which effectually sealed her lips for the future; while it was with a feeling of hot indignation that she descended to the drawing-room, to find Mrs Marter laughing at some remark just made by the exquisite, who rose on Ella's entrance to salute her in a quiet, respectful, friendly way, that she told herself it would be folly to resent. Then, chattering quietly, more to Mrs Marter than herself, his behaviour was sufficient to make Mrs Marter at his departure praise him earnestly, but at the same time refuse to hear a word in return.

What did it mean? Was Mrs Marter siding with him? What, then, should she do? It seemed nothing so long as such visits as those were paid.

From twice in a week Max's visits grew to three, and soon to one a day; but always towards her there was a quiet gentlemanly reserve, and once, and once only, when they were left alone for a minute, did Max say words that gave her cause for thought.

"Nice woman, Mrs Marter," said Max quietly, "only she keeps twitting me with my frequent visits. She will have they are for an end, while really, Miss Bedford, my sole end now is a little friendly feeling. O, here she comes back. Can't you give us a little music? I do find it so dull here in town!—Just asking Miss Bedford to give us a little music, Mrs Marter," said Max, raising his voice as that lady re-entered the room.

"O, yes, of course," said Mrs Marter; and Ella was obliged to go to the piano.

She could not help wondering at times whether Charley Vining had ever tried to find out her address, a strange thrill passing through her frame at the thought; but the next moment she had crushed that thought out, and was sternly occupied over some task in connection with her duties.

At one time she thought of telling Mrs Brandon of Max's visits, but as they seemed to grow daily more and more addressed to the lady of the house, there seemed to be no necessity; for there were days when hardly half-a-dozen words passed between her and Max during a visit, and she had not worldly wisdom enough to see that Max Bray was awaiting the time when it would suit him best to make his spring.

Chapter Twenty
A Rival Encounter

The day following his visit to Branksome-street, Charley made his way to Crescent Villas, and sent up his card to Mrs Marter.

The footman returned at the end of a few minutes to say that Mrs Marter was not at home.

Was Miss Bedford at home?

Thomas did not know, but he would go and see; which he did, to return shaking his head.

Charley said he would call again, which he did, with precisely the same result.

Nothing daunted, he repeated his calls, till it was perfectly evident that neither Mrs Marter nor Ella would see him; and he was coming away knit of brow one day, when he started with anger on seeing a cab trundle by with Max Bray as its occupant.

It was most repugnant to his feelings to play the spy; but in despite of himself he followed the cab till he saw it stop at Crescent Villas, and Max spring out, run up the steps and ring, to be the next minute admitted, the cab being driven off.

One hour, two hours, three hours, did Charley Vining wait, when, it being evident that Max was dining there, he returned to his hotel; and then, in a state of mental anguish that he could not control, he wrote a long and earnest letter to Ella, imploring her to see him, telling of his sufferings, and of how he had been refused entrance again and again.

He waited three days and there was no response, when he wrote again—a bitter angry letter this time, to have it returned to him unopened by the next post, the direction, he felt sure, being in Max Bray's handwriting.

Maddened now by the jealous feelings that assailed him, he watched the house till he saw that Max Bray was a constant visitor. Then came a night when a brougham was at the door, and he saw Max hand down two ladies, one of whom was Ella. Then taking his place, the door of the brougham was closed, and it was driven off.

"Follow that fly," said Charley to a cabman; and the man drew up at last by the Piazza in the Haymarket, and Charley leaped out just in time to see Max disappearing in the stall-entrance of Her Majesty's Theatre, Mrs Marter upon one arm, Ella upon the other.

Dressed as he was, it was with some difficulty that Charley secured a place where he could, unobserved, watch the movements of the party. Max's quiet gentlemanly attentions were directed to both alike, the passing of the book of the words, the seeking places, and lastly the replacing of the opera-cloak upon Ella's gracefully rounded shoulders.

They passed close to him where he stood muffled up and with flashing eyes, Ella's cloak brushing his coat on the way to the brougham; and then they were driven off.

He wrote again after a sleepless night, telling of what he had seen, and imploring Ella to send him if but a line to assure him that his suspicions were false. "I have fought against them till it seems to me that it would require more than human strength," he said naïvely, "while now I feel almost driven to believe."

The same result: the letter returned unopened, and redirected in a hand that he was certain was Max Bray's.

Furious now with rage, he took a cab and drove to Max's lodgings in Bury-street, Saint James's, to arrive in time to see two ladies descend the steps—one of whom was Ella—Max handing them into a waiting brougham, and kissing his hand as they were driven off.

"Ah, Charley Vining, how do?" he exclaimed, smiling pleasantly as he encountered the fierce angry face at his side. "Bai Jove, what a stranger you are! Haven't set eyes on you for months."

"I want a few words with you, Max," said Charley harshly.

"Many as you like. Bai Jove, I don't care how much any one talks to me, so long as they don't want me to talk to them! Come upstairs."

Charley followed him into his sybaritish bachelor rooms, where Max threw himself on a couch.

"Cigar or pipe, Vining—which will you have? I've some capital Saint Julien, and a decent bottle or two of hock. Which shall it be? Bai Jove, man, what's the matter? Anything upset you?"

"Max Bray," said Charley, striding up to the sofa and towering over its occupant, "I want to know who those ladies were that you handed into that brougham."

"Bai Jove, mai dear fellow, what an uncouth kind of catechism! And suppose I don't choose to tell you?"

"Curse you! I'll wring it out of you!" cried Charley fiercely.

"No, bai Jove, you won't do anything of the kind," said Max coolly. "Gentlemen don't act like confounded cads. Why, man alive, I did not say I would not tell you. I'm open as the day. Do you want to know?"

Charley made an impatient gesture.

"Well, bai Jove, if you must know, one is a friend of mine, Mrs Marter, of Regent's-park."

"And the other?" said Charley hoarsely.

"The other," said Max, quietly lighting a cigar, "is another lady friend of mine—one Miss Bedford."

Max must have seen those clutching fingers that moved as if about to seize him by the throat; but he did not shrink, he did not waver for an instant, but lit his cigar unmoved, and then sank luxuriously back upon the couch to smoke and stare nonchalantly in his visitor's face.

That cool matter-of-fact way staggered and disarmed Charley. Had he seen the slightest sign of cowardice, he would have seized Max, and shaken him savagely; but that cool insolence seemed to the stricken man to tell of success and safety of position—the sense of being able to deal pityingly with an unfortunate rival; and it was in altered tones that Charley tore a letter from his breast, and threw it upon the table.

"Who redirected that letter?" he exclaimed.

Max smoked for a few moments in thoughtful silence, then, casting off all affectation, he said quietly:

"Would it not be better to change the subject, Vining? It is not every horse that wins. The favourite is a dangerous nag to place your money on, as you must know. We are old friends, Vining, and I am sorry to run counter to you. Say what you will, I shall not quarrel."

"Who redirected that letter?" repeated Charley, again more fiercely.

"Bai Jove, Vining, this is going too far!" said Max in injured tones. "You have no right to come to a gentleman and ask him such questions."

"Who redirected that letter?" Charley cried for the third time.

"Well there, then, if you will have it—I did," said Max quietly.

"And any others?"

"Yes, all of them."

"And by whose authority?"

"Bai Jove, it's too bad!" exclaimed Max—"I will not say another word. I will not be cross-examined like this. You've made misery enough, Vining, bai Jove, you have! You throw over poor Laura in the most heartless way; you come between me and some one; and now, when matters are once more running smoothly, you come here more like a mad bull than anything. I don't care; it's the truth, and you can't deny it!"

The moment was critical again; for blind with rage, Charley Vining seized Max by the throat, and placed his knee upon his chest as he lay back on the couch; but again the latter was equal to the position, and he did not attempt to free himself.

"Don't be a brute, Vining!" he said quietly. "I'm not afraid of you; but you have double my strength."

Charley started back as he was met by those cool collected words, and catching up his letter, he tore from the place, leaving Max with a quiet contented smile upon his face, smoking till he had finished his cigar, when he threw away the end, rose, rearranged his slightly disordered shirt-front, and rang for a cab, being driven to Austin's Ticket-Office, where he secured seats for a concert to be held that night at Saint James's Hall; returned, made a most elaborate toilet, and then, not knowing, but careless, whether or not he was watched, he made his way to Crescent Villas, dined there, and that same evening Charley Vining saw him seated beside Ella Bedford in the reserved scats at the great hall, while, pale and careworn in the balcony, the young man again and again saw Ella smile at something her companion uttered.

"I'll not give up yet," said Charley hoarsely. "I made a vow, and I'll keep to it!"

Chapter Twenty One
(-?-)

"La Donna e Mobile," hummed Charley again and again, as he sat in the smoking-room of his hotel. He had paid no heed to the concert, his eyes being fixed all the while upon Max and his two companions; but that air had been sung by one of the great artistes, and words and music had forced themselves upon him so that they seemed for hours after to be ringing in his ears.

"La Donna e Mobile." Yes, it was all plain enough, and it was nothing new. He had made an impression at first, and she had seemed to love him—perhaps, after her fashion, had loved him—but woman's love, he said, required feeding. The fuel absent, the flame must become extinct.

He laughed bitterly, and a waiter came up.

"Did you ask for something, sir?"

"No!" roared Charley savagely; and the man shrunk away.

"I'll pester her no more," he said; "let things take their course. I'll go down home and see the poor old gentleman to-morrow. I may just as well, as hang about here torturing myself over a slow fire. I wonder how the mare looks. A good run or two would do me no end of good. I'll pack up and run down to-morrow."

Then he laughed bitterly, for he knew that he was playing at self-deceit; he felt that he could not stir from London—that he was, as it were, fixed, and without a desire to leave the spot where he could feel that she was near.

"No," he said, after a while; "I'll not give up yet. I made a vow, and I'll keep it. She is not his yet. She may have been—she must have been—deceived. I have been condemned. No; she would not listen. I don't know—there, I think I'm half mad!"

Just then his hand came in contact with a couple of letters which had been awaiting him on his return, and which one of the waiters had handed to him, to be thrust unnoticed into his pocket.

"Bills," said the waiter, to one of his fellows. "How nice to be tradesman to those young swells! I s'pose some of them must pay, some time or other, or else people couldn't live."

"O yes," said the other; "some of them pay, and those who will pay, have to pay for those who won't."

"Through the nose," said number one with a wink.

"To be sure," said his confrère; and then they laughed at one another, and winked again.

But the waiter was wrong: those were not bills; one being a long and affectionate letter from Sir Philip Vining, telling Charley that he would be in town the next day, and asking if it would be convenient for his son to meet him at the station. The other was from Laura Bray, saying that they had heard from Sir Philip that he would be in town the next day, and asking that he and Charley would dine in Harley-street, where was the Brays' town house, on the next day but one.

The above was all formal, and written at mamma's command, but Laura had added a postscript, asking that Charley would come for the sake of the old times when they were friends. Max would be away, and the party very small.

Then came a quiet reminder of the encounter, and a word to say that the writer had looked out day by day, in the expectation of receiving a call, while poor Nelly was *au désespoir*.

Charley smiled grimly as he read the letter over, and then carelessly thrust it back into the envelope with the bold address which waiter number one had kindly taken for a tradesman's hand.

"Take the good the gods provide one," said Charley with a bitter laugh, as he smoked furiously, and tossed down glass after glass of claret to allay the fevered rush of thought through his brain.

"I'll go," he said at last, "and see little Nell. Poor little wiry weedy Nell!—what a genuine, free-hearted, jolly little lass it is! But there, if I do, shell only make some reference to the past."

Charley Vining's thoughts came so fast that night, that they jostled and stumbled over one another in the most confused way imaginable, till once more, shining out like a star amidst the surrounding darkness, the light of Ella's face seemed to slowly rise, and he sat there thinking of her till the waiters yawned with misery because he did not retire.

But he went at last; and Ella's name was on his lips as he fell off into a heavy weary sleep, as it was the first word he uttered when waking.

The next day Sir Philip was in town, surprised and shocked to see the alteration in his son's face; for Charley looked haggard and worn, and as if he had been engaged in a long career of dissipation. He laughed, though, when Sir Philip reverted to it, and seemed most assiduous in his endeavours to promote the old man's comfort.

"About this dinner at the Brays', Charley: I should like to go," Sir Philip said—"that is, if you will go with me."

"Do you particularly wish it, sir?" said Charley.

"It would give me much pleasure, if you have no other engagement."

"Engagement!" said Charley, with a bitter laugh that shocked Sir Philip. "No, father, I have no engagements. I'll go."

"But, my dear boy, what have you been doing with yourself?—how do you pass your time?"

"Preparing myself for a private lunatic asylum, father," said Charley, with a cynical laugh; and the old man felt a swelling in his throat as he thought of the alteration that had taken place since the morning of the memorable conversation in the library.

There was a something in Charley's looks that troubled Sir Philip more than he cared to intimate: had the young man sternly refused to visit the Brays, or to accede to his wishes in any way, he would not have been surprised; but his strange looks, his bitter words, and ready acquiescence alarmed Sir Philip; and when, an hour after, Charley left the room, the old gentleman looked anxiously for his return, till, unable to bear the suspense any longer, he rang and summoned a waiter.

"Has my son gone out?" he asked.

"Think not, Sir Philip. I'll make inquiry."

Five anxious minutes passed, and then the man returned.

"No, Sir Philip, he went up to his bedroom."

Pale and trembling, Sir Philip rose and hurried upstairs. He knew that Charley had had some more than usually bitter reverse, and a horrible dread had invaded the troubled father's breast, so that when he reached his son's room door, he feared to summon him; but at last he knocked, and waited for a few moments before he struck again upon the panels, this time more forcibly.

There was no reply.

Chapter Twenty Two
Accident or Design?

Sir Philip Vining tried the door again and again, shaking it loudly, and repeating his son's name; but there was no reply.

What should he do—summon assistance and have the room broken open? He dreaded calling for aid, to bring up the curious to gaze upon his anguish, and perhaps upon—

He seemed to check his thoughts there by a tremendous effort, and turning round, he gazed in both directions along the well-lit thickly-carpeted corridor.

There was no one in sight, neither could he hear a sound.

Then he tried to look through the keyhole of the door, but something arrested his vision. He knocked and called again and again, but there was not even the sound of breathing to be detected on the other side; and at last, roused to frenzy. Sir Philip turned the handle, and then dashed his shoulder with all his might against the panelling.

He was not strong, but the sudden sharp shock made the little bolt by which the door was secured give way, when, rushing in, Sir Philip hastily closed the door behind him, anxious even now to hide from the public eye any blur that might have fallen upon the Vinings' name.

There was a small globe lamp burning upon the table, but the room seemed empty, and the bed was impressed; but on hurrying round to the foot, there on a couch lay Charley, his coat and vest thrown off, his collar and neckband unfastened, and his pale handsome face turned towards the light. His lips were just parted, and his leaden-hued eyelids barely closed; but upon Sir Philip throwing himself on his knees by the figure of his son, he could just detect a faint breathing, and upon hastily drawing his watch and holding it near his lips, the bright gold back was slightly dimmed.

"O, that it should have come to this!" groaned Sir Philip; and raising his clenched hand, for a moment it was as though he were about to call down Heaven's bitterest curse upon the head of the gentle girl to whom he attributed all this pain and suffering. But as he did so, his hand fell again to his side, and the recollection of the fair, soft, pleading face he had last looked upon, with its gentle eyes and pale cheeks, and then the scene of her fainting when he tottered back to kiss her glossy hair—all came back most vividly, and he groaned aloud.

And then he seemed to awaken to the necessity for instant action, and running to the bell, he tore at it furiously.

But there was pride still busy in the old man's brain, in spite of the shock: the world must not know what was wrong; and hastily looking round, he saw upon the dressing-table, lying in company with the young man's watch, with the thick gold chain carelessly thrown around it, a small graduated bottle—Time and Eternity, so it seemed, side by side.

Sir Philip was not surprised. He seemed to know intuitively what was coming. He had suspected it when downstairs, but in a more horrible manner; and as soon as he had thrust the bottle into his pocket, he shudderingly closed and locked the dressing-case upon the table, where, glittering and bright, lay amongst velvet several unused keen-bladed means of avoiding the pains and suffering of this world.

The next minute there was a knock at the bedroom-door, and the chamber-maid appeared.

"Quick!" exclaimed Sir Philip—"the nearest doctor directly. My son is dangerously ill!"

The woman hurried out, but returned directly.

"I have sent, sir. But can I do anything? Has he taken too much?"

"Too much! Too much what?" cried Sir Philip angrily, resenting the remark. "What do you mean, woman?"

"He has been taking it now for above a fortnight, sir," said the maid. "Poor gentleman! he's in trouble, I think, and takes it to quiet himself."

"What?" cried Sir Philip, but this time with less anger in his tones.

"Morphy, I think it's called, sir—a sort of spirits of laudanum; and I suppose it's awful strong. Surely, poor gentleman, he ain't over-done it!"

"Are you sure that he has been in the habit of taking it?" said Sir Philip.

"O, yes, sir. I've often seen the bottle on the dressing-table. 'Morphy: to be used with great care,' it said on the label. I don't fancy he's so bad as you think, sir."

Sir Philip, still trembling with anxiety, knelt by his son's couch, to be somewhat reassured by a deep sigh which the young man now drew; and five minutes after, the doctor came in, black, smooth, and silent—a very owl amongst men—bowed to Sir Philip, and then looked at his patient.

"How long has he been like this?"

"I found him so a quarter—half an hour since," said Sir Philip. "He had left me an hour before that."

"Humph!" said the doctor. "Any reason for thinking he would commit suicide?"

"H'm—no!" said Sir Philip, hesitating; "but he has, I fear, been suffering a great deal of mental pain."

"Any bottle or packet about?" said the doctor—"bottle, I should say. No strong odour existent; but it seems like a narcotic poison at work."

"I found this," said Sir Philip, producing the little flask he had taken from the table.

"To be sure—exactly—graduated too! My dear sir, I don't think there is any cause for alarm. He has evidently taken a strong dose; but, you see, here are ample instructions, and the bottle is nearly empty."

"But he may have taken all that," said Sir Philip anxiously.

"My dear sir," said the doctor, "if he had taken one-eighth part, he would not be lying as you now see him. Depend upon it, that after a few hours he will wake calm and composed, when, if you are, as I suppose from the likeness,"—here the doctor bowed,—"his father, a little quiet advice would not be out of place. It is a bad sign for a fine young man like this to be resorting to such subtle agencies to procure rest. Depend upon it, his brain is in a sad state. I should advise change."

"But do you not think that you had better wait?" said Sir Philip anxiously.

"I would do so with pleasure," said the doctor; "but really, my dear sir, there is not the slightest necessity, and, besides, I am within easy call."

The doctor departed softly, as he had arrived; and taking his seat by the couch, Sir Philip watched hour after hour, forgetful of his own fatigue, till towards morning, when Charley turned, sighed deeply, and then sat up to gaze anxiously in his father's face.

"You here, dad?" he said lightly.

"My dear boy—at last!" cried Sir Philip. "You have alarmed me terribly! Why do you take that?" And he pointed to the bottle.

"To keep myself sane, father," said Charley sadly—"because I have lain here night after night waiting for the sleep that would not come. I've smoked; I've drunk heavily; I've walked and ridden till so tired I could hardly stand; and then I've lain here through the long dreary nights, till I felt that I should lose my head altogether."

The old gentleman rose and began to pace the room.

"But there," cried Charley cheerfully, "I've kept you up too. So now go to your room, and I'll turn over a new leaf, dad. Look here!"

As he spoke, he took up the little bottle from where it had been placed by the doctor, and threw it sharply into the grate, where it was smashed to atoms.

"There, I'll be a coward no longer, sir! I'm going to begin a clean page of the book to-morrow. No more blots and random writing, but all ruled fair and straight. There, good-night, or, rather, good-morning! Breakfast at ten, mind!"

Sir Philip left the room, and Charley plunged his face into a basin of cold water before sitting down quietly to think; and as he thought, he turned over and over again his intentions for the future.

It did seem now certain that Max Bray had supplanted him—there could be hardly a doubt of it, but still there was that shade; and till he was certain he would still hold to his faith. He told himself that he was wanting in no way, that he had done all that man could do; but still he must have the final certainty before he would hide for ever in his breast the sharply-cut wound, and trust to time to do something towards alleviating his suffering.

Then he thought of Max Bray, and his brow lowered as he recalled his words, till those floated before his mind respecting Laura, and his treatment of her.

It was absurd, certainly, but the whole family must have supposed that he had intended to ask her hand. But he had never said word of love to her. What, though, of the lady? There was no doubt that Laura did love him, poor girl! perhaps very earnestly; and if so, he was sorry for her; for it was not his wish to give her pain.

Then once more he thought of Ella. Would she have accepted him, he would have set the world at defiance; but no—under the guise of a modest retirement, she had rejected him to accept Max Bray.

But was it so? No, *no*, no! He would not believe it. He would hold to his faith in her till the last came, and then he knew that he should be a changed man.

Once more he asked himself whether he had done all that man could do; and his heart honestly replied that he had—everything.

"Then my policy now is, to wait and see," said Charley aloud, and with a bitterness in his tones that told how what he had seen rankled in his breast. Then, throwing himself on his bed, he said once more aloud, "It can't be long now before I have some proof, and after that—"

He did not finish his sentence—he could not; for "after that" seemed to him to be such a weary blank, that he almost wondered whether he would be able to live through it all. And there he lay, sleepless now, awaiting the convincing proof; a proof that was to come sooner even than he anticipated.

Chapter Twenty Three
Nelly's Confidence

The Brays' mansion in Harley-street, and as grand a dinner as had been in the long, gaunt, dreary place for months past. Sir Philip and Charley had called the morning before, and Nelly had planted herself by Charley's side, to keep there the whole time. Not that Laura seemed to mind; for she was gentle, slightly constrained, but there was a saddened suffering look in her countenance which lighted up whenever Charley said a few words.

For some reason she kept glancing at him with a troubled air—perhaps from some dread in connection with her plain avowals; but Charley was the quiet gentleman in every word and look; and before they left, all seemed to be quite at ease, so that the young man was almost angry with himself for feeling so quiet and happy during the half-hour or so the visit had lasted, besides which he had been merrily laughing two or three times with Nelly.

"Do, do, please!" Nelly had whispered; and those whispers had made Laura's breast heave as she interpreted them to relate to Ella Bedford, whose name, however, had not been mentioned.

"I daren't," said Charley laughingly, in answer to Nelly's appeal.

"O do—*do*—do!" whispered Nelly again. "You owe me ever so much for being your friend."

Charley's face darkened.

"Please I didn't mean to hurt you," said Nelly gently; "don't be angry with me," for she had seen the cloud cross his countenance.

"I'm not angry, my child," he said, smiling again.

"That's right!" whispered Nelly. "I do love to see you laugh; it makes you look so handsome. I say, Charley, I do wish you had been my brother! But now, I say, do declare you won't come unless they let me dine with you all. I am so sick of the schoolroom."

Poor Nelly! Inadvertently she kept touching chords that thrilled in Charley Vining's breast; but he beat back the feelings, and laughingly said aloud that he thought he should not be able to come.

"O, really," shrieked Mrs Bray, "I shall be so disappointed!"

Laura looked pained, but she did not direct her eyes Vining-ward.

"I find that a particular old friend of mine is not coming to dinner," said Charley, "and therefore I shall decline."

"O, really, my dear Vining," said Mr Bray, ceasing to warm the tails of his coat, "don't say so; give us his name, and we'll invite him at once."

"'Tain't a him at all," cried the ungrammatical one, jumping up, laughing, and clapping her hands; "it's a her, and it's me; so there now — you must have me to dinner, after all. And why not, I should like to know. I'm only an inch shorter than pa."

So Nelly dined with them that day, and Charley took her down, and sat between her and Laura, "behaving more jolly than ever he did before," so Nelly vowed; while Laura could not but own to the quiet, staid, gentlemanly tact with which he avoided all the past; and trembling and hopeful, she watched him unseen the whole evening.

He did not, neither did she, seek a *tête-à-tête*; but at the first opportunity Nelly dragged him aside in one of the drawing-rooms, under the pretence of showing him pictures; and though Laura saw all, she did not stir.

"That's pretty, ain't it?" said Nelly. "I sketched that." Then in a low voice, "You like me, Charley, don't you?"

"Yes, very much, my child," said Charley quietly. "Do you want me to do something for you?"

"No," said Nelly; "I only want to say something."

"Go on, then."

"You will not be cross?"

"No."

"Are you sure?"

"Yes, yes, my child," said Charley sadly.

"It's about that I wanted to talk to you," said Nelly. "I don't like seeing you so low and dumpy when you ought to be jolly and happy. You know you are miserable about some one that I got to love very — very much."

Charley was silent; but his breath came thick and fast.

"And do you know, I'm sure that, if she had been left alone she would have been all that's wise and good and dear? May I go on?"

"Yes," said Charley, with quite a hiss.

"I thought you would like me to say anything, when you wouldn't hear it from any one else. Do you know, Charley, you mustn't be miserable about Miss B — any more? and if I wasn't going to have Hugh Lingon when

I get big—I mean old enough—I should ask you to let me love you, and try and comfort you, and make you happy. I do love you very much now, you know, but I mean the other way."

She was silent for a few moments, while he went on turning over the pictures.

"Charley," she then said earnestly, "I don't think she has done right; but whether she's been persuaded, or somebody's told stories about you. Max goes to see her very often—nearly every day now—and she writes to him lots of letters. O Charley, dear Charley!" she half sobbed, "what have I done? Pray!—please don't look like that! I thought telling you would make you leave off looking miserable, and ready to be happy again when you knew you couldn't have her. But pray—pray don't look like that!"

For the young man's ghastly face had frightened her, as he stood gazing full in her eyes, crushing the while one of the drawings in his hand.

"How do you know that?" he whispered hoarsely.

"I heard Max tell Laury; and one day, when I went with her to his rooms, there was a whole heap of little narrow envelopes directed to him, and they were all in her handwriting. But please try and not fret, or I shall be so—so unhappy."

Charley drew a deep long breath, and for the space of a good minute he stood there supporting himself by, and gazing blankly down at, the table, for a sharp pang had shot through him, and he felt giddy; but the next minute it passed off, as he muttered to himself:

"Not yet, not yet. I must have farther proof!"

Then, by an effort, he recovered himself, and leading Nelly to the piano, he sat by her while she sang. A few minutes after, he was by Laura's side, talking to her quietly and gently, as he would have talked to any other lady.

And she knew the while what had passed in the farther drawing-room—knew as well as if she had listened; for she knew that Nelly had heard her brothers words, and, in spite of Nelly's quickness, Laura had seen her looking at the letters that were in Ella's handwriting.

Laura's breast heaved as Charley sat beside her, and again she trembled, and her heart smote her as she saw how deeply that wound had been cut. But though she pitied, she was hopeful; for she said to herself, "The day must come when Max's words will be true, and he will run to me for solace. The day must come! But when?"

Chapter Twenty Four
Mr Whittrick Again

During the rest of the evening at the Brays' party Charley was lively and chatty. By an effort he seemed to have cast aside the feelings that oppressed him; and as they went back to the Bond-street hotel, Sir Philip felt quite hopeful, as it seemed to him that his son was indeed going to turn over the fresh leaf.

The next day Charley was off betimes to Branksome-street, where he was fortunate in getting an immediate interview with the great Mr Whittrick.

"You received my letter, posted two days since?" asked Charley.

"Same evening, sir," said Mr Whittrick.

"You grant, I suppose, that it is as I said—Mr Maximilian Bray had been here before me?"

"My dear sir," said Mr Whittrick, with a smile, "when a gentleman pays me certain fees for certain services, he has bought those services—they are his private property, and I have done with them—that is all finished. Do you understand? This is a private-inquiry office, and every client's business is private. What I might divulge upon that pleasant old institution the rack, I can't say—that being enough to make any man speak; but I believe I should do as many another man did."

"What was that?" said Charley, smiling

"Tell any lie the inquisitors wished," said Mr Whittrick. "But as we have no rack nowadays, only moral thumbscrews, why, we are not forced to speak at all. No, sir; if there is such a person as Mr Maximilian Bray, or Cray, or Dray, or whatever his name is, and he came here on business, if we could, we did his business—we can't always, you know—and there was an end of it; but if you want me to private inquire him, I'll do it, just the same as if he came here and wanted me to private inquire you, I should do it—both together if it was necessary—though I don't think I should say anything about visits here," he said, with a slight twinkle of one of his dark eyes. "So now, my dear sir, what's it to be? Shall we report to you upon this gentleman's proceedings? Let me see," he said, referring to the letter, "Bury-street, Saint James's, isn't it? Yes, quite right. Well, sir?"

"Yes," said Charley; "and set about it at once."

"How often, and how much, would you like to know?"

"How often!" cried Charley fiercely. "Every day—every hour if it is necessary. Write, send, telegraph to me. I want to know his every act and deed, till I tell you to leave off, if you can do it."

"I think we can manage it, sir," said Mr Whittrick, with a quiet smile. "Not quite so quickly as we did the last, though."

"Then set about it at once," said Charley. "It will be rather expensive work, sir," said Mr Whittrick quietly.

Charley drew a blank cheque, signed by Sir Philip, from his pocket-book.

"What shall I fill this up for, Mr Whittrick?" said Charley.

"O, really, Mr Vining, I did not mean that," said Mr Whittrick. "With some clients, of course, we make sure of the money before acting; but I am in your debt still. What I meant was, are you disposed to go to the expense of men, day after day, the whole of their time on your business?"

"Yes, certainly," said Charley, taking pen and ink. "Shall I fill this up for a hundred pounds?"

"No," said Mr Whittrick quietly: "fifty will do for the present. But stay—let me see: make it to bearer, sir—Mr Smith or bearer; it might not be pleasant to Sir Philip Vining to have it known at his banker's that I am transacting family business. You see, sir, mine's a very well-known name, and one that has been blown upon a good deal, and some people are rather fastidious about it. And to tell the truth, sir, I really am agent sometimes in rather unpleasant matters. Thank you—that will do, sir. You shall have some information to-night, and of course, under these circumstances, a great deal may seem very trivial; but you must not mind that, for sometimes very trivial acts turn out to be the most important in the end, while again noisy matters turn out empty bangs. I think we understand one another so far; but would you like a few attentions to be paid to the lady?"

"What?" said Charley abruptly.

"Would you like one of my agents to give an eye to Number 19 Crescent Villas, Regents-park, Mr Vining?"

"No," said Charley sternly; "certainly not!"

"Very good, sir," said Mr Whittrick, in his quiet way. "Have you any farther commands?"

"No," said Charley, taking the hint, and rising; and the next minute he was face to face with Sir Philip Vining in the street.

For a few moments father and son stood quite taken aback at the suddenness of the encounter; but Charley was the first to recover from his surprise.

"There is only one house here, sir, that you would visit," he said quietly; "and there is no necessity. You were going to Whittrick's?"

Sir Philip bent his head.

"Let us go back to the hotel," said Charley; and without a word they entered the cab Sir Philip had in waiting, and were driven back to Bond-street.

Not a word was spoken during the backward journey; but as soon as they were alone in their private room, Charley placed a chair for his father, and then seated himself opposite to him.

"You were going to have me watched, father," he said calmly.

"My dear boy—my dear boy, it is for your own sake, and you drive me to it!" exclaimed Sir Philip.

"There is no need, father," said Charley. "We will have no more estrangement. You have wronged me cruelly to gratify your pride, but— There," he exclaimed hastily, "I said there was no need for my being watched. I will be open with you as the day: ask me anything you will, and I will answer you freely. To begin with: I have been there this morning for the purpose of having Max Bray watched: one proof—only one more proof, father—of what I am seeking for, and your wishes will be accomplished— there will be no fear of the Vinings' escutcheon being lowered. One thing more," he said hoarsely, and forcing his words from his lips, "and I have done; and we will return to Blandfield, where you shall help me to begin life again, father."

"My dear Charley," groaned the old man, "if I could but see you happy!"

The young man turned upon him a wistful mournful look before speaking.

"Let the past be now!" he said sternly. "It cannot be altered. Only leave me free for the present—don't hamper me in any way."

"But, Charley—"

The old gentleman whispered a few words in his son's ear.

"No," said Charley, shaking his head; "there will be none of that. If I were to knock Max Bray down," he said, with scornful contempt, "he would send for a policeman. My dear father, you are thinking of your own days: men do not fight duels now in England. Let us go out now—this place seems to stifle me. But don't be alarmed, sir; if I am beaten in the race, whether it be by fair running or a foul, I shall give up. I know that I have run the course in a manly straightforward manner, according to my own convictions, and as, father, I felt that I must. But the running is nearly over, sir, and I shall give you little more pain."

"Charley, my dear boy—" began Sir Philip.

"Hush, father!" said Charley, checking him. "The time has nearly come for burying the past. Let us hope that some day the grass may grow green and pleasant-looking over its grave. At present, I see nothing but a black yawning pit—one which I shrink from approaching."

Chapter Twenty Five
Coming Round

"From the Brays, Charley?" said Sir Philip, as they sat over their breakfast at Long's about a month after the meeting in Branksome-street.

"Yes," said Charley. "Mr Bray has taken a private box at Her Majesty's for to-night, and will we have an early dinner with them and go?"

"My dear boy, I trust you will accept the invitation."

"Do you wish me to, father?" said Charley.

"Yes, certainly," cried Sir Philip; "but not in that dreadfully resigned spirit."

"All right, sir!" said Charley, with a smile that he tried to make cheerful; and tossing the letter carelessly aside, he went on with his breakfast.

"You will write an answer, and send it by a commissionaire, of course?"

"No," said Charley. "I'll ride up there before lunch, and tell them. I want to see if my little maid Nelly has come back yet: she seems to make the Brays' place more bearable when one goes there."

Charley burst out laughing the next moment to see his father's serious face.

"Well, really, my dear father," he said, as he interpreted his look, "I how can you expect me to play the hypocrite?"

Sir Philip was troubled, but he said nothing; and soon after Charley retired to his own room, where, over a cigar, he sat turning about the various reports he had received from Branksome-street, wondering the while why none had come in the night before.

"Nothing of sufficient importance to send in, I suppose," he muttered; and then he sat musing and thoughtful, reading here that Mr Maximilian Bray went to his office, dined out at Crescent Villas, went to Saint James's Hall in the evening in company with Mrs M. and Miss B., returned to C.V., then back to lodgings; there, that Mrs M. and Miss B. called at Bury-street, and Mr Maximilian Bray accompanied them to the House of Commons.

Day after day the reports were of a similar nature, all tending to show that Max was a most constant visitor at Crescent Villas, but little more.

Charley sat so long that he had to give up his projected ride, and sent a messenger with a note to say that Sir Philip and he would dine with the Brays at six, and accompany them afterwards to the opera. They were punctual to their time; and Laura, handsomer than ever, and most tastefully dressed, greeted Charley shrinkingly, while, going up to Sir Philip, there was something very winning in the way in which she offered him her cheek, and the old gentleman saluted her.

"Nelly come back?" said Charley quietly, as he took Laura down to dinner.

"No," said Laura; and as she spoke, there was a tremor in her arm. "I am to meet her to-morrow at Paddington-station. I thought perhaps—"

"I would go with you," said Charley smilingly. "To be sure I will. What train?"

"Fifty-five minutes past four," said Laura huskily.

"I'll be with you," said Charley, "at, say, four or half-past three. I want to see her again."

Laura looked now pale, now flushed; and Sir Philip told her she had never appeared more handsome. Then, the dinner past, the carriage arrived, and they were driven to the Haymarket. Sir Philip had passed in with Mrs Bray, and Charley was handing out Laura, when he felt a slight touch on the arm, and a note was passed into his hand; but the bearer, unless it was the stolid policeman at his side, had disappeared.

In spite of himself, Charley uttered a faint ejaculation of surprise as he took the note, and then looked round for the giver; and this was not lost upon Laura, who directly became fearfully agitated, leaning heavily upon his arm, so that he was compelled to half carry her into the crush-room.

"It is nothing; I shall be better directly," she whispered. "A sudden spasm—faintness; but it is going off fast;" and all the while she gazed in her companion's face with a terrified aspect, as if trying to read therein something that was certainly not visible.

"Suppose I leave you five minutes with the attendant, and get you an ice or a cup of coffee?" said Charley.

"No, no!" exclaimed Laura; "do not go—"

But her words were too late: he had passed through the door, staying for a moment to read the note placed in his hands.

"Nothing last night. To-night Her Majesty's Theatre. Stalls, Numbers. 24, 5, and 6. Mr M.B. and the ladies. Tickets procured at Andrews's in Bond-street."

A complete work of supererogation; for the next moment a voice speaking loudly made Charley shrink back, and press his crush-hat down over his eyes.

"Bai Jove, no! Capital time, I'm sure," And the next moment Ella Bedford's white-muslin skirt had swept against Charley as he stood stern and motionless as a statue.

Quite five minutes had elapsed after Ella had disappeared before Charley moved. His teeth had been set, and a feeling of rage, bitterness, and hatred combined, had surged up in his breast. Had he liked, he could have stretched forth his hand and touched her; but he did not stir. But he was himself again as he felt a trembling hand laid upon his arm, and a voice that he hardly knew said softly: "Had you forgotten me?"

"No," said Charley earnestly, as, turning, he saw Laura at his elbow, very paler and with a strange shiver passing from time to time through her frame.

"Are you unwell?" he said kindly, as he drew her hand through his arm.

"No, no," she exclaimed, brightening in an instant, as she leaned heavily upon that arm, and gazed almost imploringly in his face, her great dark eyes wearing a fascinating aspect that he had never seen there before; and thinking that he read all they would say, he turned frigid in an instant, and led her to the corridor, whence they were soon ushered into the private box.

But Charley Vining had not read those beseeching eyes. The interpretation was not for him then, or, in his mad anger, woman though she was, he would have dashed her to the ground, and fled from her as from something too hideous to live upon this earth. He did not read them then, for the key was not his; but, satisfied in his own mind that she was agitated on his account, he was coldly polite all through the first act.

Chapter Twenty Six
Trembling

Disturbed as Laura evidently was by some powerful motive, it was not long before her eye rested upon the occupants of the stalls immediately below, but two or three tiers nearer the stage. It almost seemed as if, as they sat side by side, she and Charley had seen them at the same moment; for involuntarily they both leaned forward, but only to draw back the next instant for eye to meet eye.

Surely enough, there was Max Bray seated between Mrs Marter and Ella Bedford, who, with their backs to them, had not seen the occupants of the private box. As for Mrs Bray, she had preferred a back seat, in which she was followed by Sir Philip, who insisted upon Charley taking the front, he caring very little now for the opera; while Mrs Bray found much more gratification in the ladies' dresses than in what she called, in private, "a parcel of squalling," and employed her lorgnette accordingly.

Laura's next act was to glance round uneasily at Mamma Bray and Sir Philip; but there was nothing to fear there: their attention was taken up by the audience, and from their position it was impossible for them to see where Max and his companions were seated.

The next moment Laura's eyes were directed towards Charley, as he sat sternly, fiercely looking down again, and then, softly, tremulously, and as if even the delicately-gloved hand deprecated what it was about to attempt, she laid that hand upon his stalwart arm, and he turned once more, frowning heavily, to encounter those great eyes, pitiful, imploring, swimming in tenderness. It seemed to him that it was pity for him, sorrow for the pain he was suffering; and as the frown passed from his brow, he returned her gaze till her eyes sank shrinkingly before his, and the great long dark lashes fell to curtain them from his sight.

But her hand still rested upon his arm, pressing it more and more tightly; and again her eyes were raised to his for him to read in them once more the same expression.

Yes, it must be pity, sorrow for him; and he read them so, as, forgetful of all—opera, the hundreds around, even those in the box with them—Laura came nearer and nearer to him, till he felt her soft breath upon his cheek as she whispered:

"Charley, I can bear this no longer. Will you take me home?"

They rose together, and Laura whispered a few words to Mrs Bray; the next minute they were in the corridor, and then what followed seemed to Charley like a dream—the coldness of air as they passed through swing—doors, the fastening of cloak and adjustment of hood, the descent of stairs, and the rattling of wheels; and then, with the recollection of what he had last seen—Ella Bedford's face turned smilingly towards Max—Charley Vining was seated in a street cab, rattling over the stones, with Laura Bray still clinging to his arm, to utter his name once in a hoarse whisper, as, in spite of all he could do to prevent it, she flung herself on her knees in the rough straw, her rich evening dress forgotten, as she clung to his hand and pressed it to her burning forehead, kissed it, deluged it with her scalding tears, while, as he bent over her, he could feel that her sobs shook her frame as they burst from her labouring breast.

At length, partly by a few deeply-uttered words, partly by passing his arms round and lifting her, Charley Vining had the passionate girl at his side; but only for her to cling to him, sobbing fearfully, till they neared the house.

It was barely half-past nine, and as he handed her out, he would have parted from her; but she clung to his hand, and together they went up into the drawing-room, where, once more alone, Laura threw herself at his feet, clinging to him, sobbing hysterically, imploring him to forgive her, to be lenient to her; it was all for love of him—the love she had borne him so long without a tender word in return. She accused herself of want of womanly feeling, of baseness, of treachery, lashing herself with fierce words in her passion, till, moved by pity, maddened by despair and disappointment, Charley Vining began to feel that he was but weak—that he was but man, after all. The icy coldness gradually melted away, and he whispered first a few words, then one arm was passed round the kneeling form.

"Forgive me—forgive! It is all for the love of you!" sobbed Laura with a fierceness of emotion that startled him.

"Forgive you?" he said; "I have nothing to forgive."

And then Ella, the past, all was forgotten, as his other arm drew her nearer to him as she knelt, and the next moment, with a wild sigh, Laura's arms were tightly clasping his neck, and her face was buried in his breast. Then a click of the door-handle, a stream of light, and Laura was upon her feet, tall, proud, and defiant.

"Did you ring for candles, ma'am?" said the voice of the butler.

"Set them down," was the reply; and the man withdrew.

Charley had risen too, and was standing by her side.

"Go, now," she said, in a choking voice; "I can bear no more to-night. But tell me—O, tell me," she cried, throwing herself at his feet, and clasping his knees—"tell me that you forgive me!"

"Forgive you, my poor girl?" said Charley softly, as he bent down to her, once more to pass his arms round her lithe form, when, with a bound, she was again nestling in his breast, but with her face turned towards his, and for a moment their lips met.

The next, Laura had hurried from the room; while, with every pulse in his frame beating furiously, Charley walked down to the hall, accepted the footman's assistance with his coat, and then he made his way-out into the great deserted street, to walk staggering along like one who had drunk heavily of some potent liquor. But Charley Vining's was a maddening sense. What had he done? He had not waited for the proof. He had been weak and vile in his own sight; and as he staggered along, he anathematised himself again and again, and, as if appealing to some great power, he called upon Ella to save him from the degradation of his heart.

"False!—false!—false to her! A coward—a scoundrel—a villain! Why was I made with such a weak and empty heart?"

Then he walked on faster and faster for long enough, not heeding where he went, but muttering still:

"Fate, fate, fate! And I have done all that mail can do. I must submit, and I love her not. Do I not hate her—or has she conquered?"

"Hadn't you better take a cab, sir?" said a rough voice; and a policeman's hand was laid upon his arm. "It's too bad, r'aly, sir; but you gents will do it. Now, only think of coming into a place like this here, reg'lar lushy, and with diamond studs and gold watches and chains shining out in the light, and asking poor starving men to steal them!"

"I'm not drunk, my man," cried Charley, himself again in a moment. "Thank you; get me a cab. Not a savoury locality!" and he glanced round at the dark lane and the ill-looking figures about.

"This way, then, sir," said the man; and he led him into a wider thoroughfare, where, a cab being called, and the policeman substantially thanked, Charley Vining was driven to his hotel, his brain a very chaos of doubt, despondency, and rage at what he called his baseness and falseness to his vows.

VOLUME THREE

Chapter One
In the Balance

As if to show him how long he had been heedlessly wandering through the streets, Charley found Sir Philip quietly seated at the hotel on his return; and though his father carefully forbore to make any reference to the past, Charley fancied that he could detect a sense of elation on the old gentleman's part—one which seemed to anger him more as his heart kept reproaching him for the evening's lapse.

But Sir Philip made not the slightest reference to the events of the evening, not even remarking upon Laura's indisposition; but there was an impressive way with which Sir Philip parted from his son that night, that Charley interpreted to mean satisfaction, and he frowned heavily as he sought his own room.

In spite of his troubled mind, without recourse to narcotics, the young man slept soundly and long, waking, though, with a strange heavy sense of oppression troubling him, as the thoughts of the past night's events came upon him slowly one by one, till he was half maddened, hating himself for the part he had played, or, rather, for his weakness.

Then he recalled Ella's quiet peaceful face as he saw her turn round to Max; and he asked himself why he should consider himself as in any way bound to her who refused to hold him by any ties. Morally he knew that he was quite free, and that, bitterly as he regretted the last night's tête-à-tête with Laura Bray, he had shed sunshine upon her heart, and left her happy and exultant.

Then he remembered his promise to accompany her to the terminus at Paddington. He could not go—he would not go! But that was some hours distant yet, and for a while he felt that he need not trouble himself about it.

But what should he do? Write a long letter to Laura, telling her that she was to forgive his weakness of the past night, and bid her farewell for ever, while he made immediate arrangements for going abroad somewhere? Was it too late in life for him to get a commission? If he could, he would have to wait months perhaps, and he wanted to leave England at once. Africa seemed to present the field that would afford him the most variety and change. He would go there for a few years. He could soon make arrangements; and in the excitement of hunting, he would find the diversion he so much required.

But then about Laura? He recalled the scene at Lexville, where she had hung upon his arm and wept; and then the events of the past night flashed upon him, and he groaned as he told himself that he had been cowardly and weak—that as yet he had had no proof that Ella was lost to him for ever.

What was the last night's scene, then?

He stamped upon the floor with impotent rage, and determined at last to forswear all ties. He went out directly after lunch to make preliminary inquiries respecting the means for leaving England. Paddington, Laura, Max, Miss Bedford, were driven from his mind, and he hurried along, but only to hear his name uttered as he passed an open carriage; and starting and turning round, there was Laura, flushed and happy-looking, sitting with her hands outstretched to him.

He could not help himself, though he called himself weak and folly-stricken, as he took her hand in his, watching the bright flush give way to a deadly pallor.

"How she loves me!" thought Charley, as he leaned on the side of the barouche; and it was from no vanity or conceit; he was too true-hearted and genuine, too honest and simple-minded. "Why should I make her unhappy, perhaps for life, when, by a sacrifice, I can send joy into her heart—into the heart of that loving old man? What have I to care for, what to live for, that I should hesitate?"

"Ella!" his conscience whispered; but the whisper was very faint; it was hardly heard amidst the tumult of contending thoughts. The African scheme was forgotten, and Charley Vining was in the balance. One vigorous pressure on either scale would carry the beam down. How was it to be?

How was it to be? The indicator was pointing directly upwards, each scale poised and motionless. Coldness, distant behaviour, returned letters, an evidently favoured rival—a man almost beneath contempt—misery for those who loved him, and more bitterness: all these in one scale; and in the other—

A passionate determined love, strong as his own, a woman pleading to him for what he had so long refused, warmth, tenderness, no rivalry, gratification to Sir Philip, and, above all, the knowledge that on the past night he had allowed himself to be betrayed into a warmth for which he had been blaming himself as though he had committed a grievous sin.

Which was the scale to go down, when Laura was in trembling tones, and, in a retiring way, asking him to take the seat by her side, for the time would soon be at hand for the visit to Paddington?

Her voice trembled audibly as she spoke, but the latter scale did not go fiercely down: the indicator only moved slightly in Laura's favour, as, remembering his promise of the day before, Charley said he would go, and took his seat by her side. It was only a slight motion, and the faintest breath from Ella's lips would have sent that scale up—up—up rapidly, till it kicked the beam.

But there was no breath there, though Charley's heart still clung to Ella fondly. Laura's scale wanted a strong impulse in her favour, and as, half triumphant, half sad, she felt Charley Vining take his place by her side, she flushed, then paled, and again and again a strange shiver of dread passed through her frame. Once even her teeth chattered, as if some fearful illness was attacking her. But the disease was only mental, and, seeking Charley's hand, her own nestled in it—clung to it convulsively, as if she dreaded even now that she would lose him, when so very, very near the goal of her hopes, of her plotting and scheming; and yet she had not known of his anger against self, and the plans for going abroad; though had she known them, she could have trembled no more.

Laura's scale was growing heavier; for Charley did not withdraw his hand, but let hers rest therein. It only wanted one addition either way now, for the weighing was just at hand—the scales were no longer evenly poised. Which was to sink boldly? The striking of the clock at five would decide it, and it was now four.

Chapter Two
The Weighing

If any one will take the trouble to refer to *Bradshaw's Guide*—that fine piece of exercise for the brain—for the month in the year in which the events being recorded took place, he will find, in connection with the Great Western Railway service, that whereas the down express left Paddington at 4:50 p.m., there was an up train due at the platform at 4:55.

It was to meet this latter train that Mr Bray's barouche was being rattled over the newly macadamised roads, with Charley Vining and Laura therein.

No one could have sat by Laura's side for an instant without remarking her extreme agitation; and as Charley turned to gaze in her pleading face, he felt something like pity warming his breast towards her—her agitation was so genuine, and she had shown him the night before how earnest and passionate was her love.

Pity is said to be very nearly akin to love, and Charley's pity was growing stronger. Why should he not take the good the gods provided him? She asked no more. But no; there was that one great proof wanted; and his words were quite cold and commonplace as he said to her, "You seem unwell. Do you not think it would be better to return home? Why, this poor little hand is quite chilly, and you shiver. You must have taken cold last night."

"Cold? Last night? No, no," she said hoarsely; and he felt the pressure upon his hand tighten. "We must meet Nelly, and I am quite well, Charley. I never felt more happy."

He encountered her glance, but it awoke no response in his breast; and as he read her countenance, he saw there the tokens of a terrible agitation, and surely he may be excused for imagining himself the cause.

"At last!" said Charley impatiently, as he handed Laura out, trembling violently; but the next moment, though she was deathly pale, the agitation seemed to have passed away, and taking his arm, she held to it tightly.

"Ten minutes too soon," said Charley. "Shall we go round to the waiting-room?"

"Yes, please," cried Laura eagerly; and walking round, he stopped to read a waybill.

"Let me see," he said; "this train leaves first. Ours comes in five minutes after."

"Take me into the waiting-room," said Laura anxiously. "It is cold out here."

"I fear that you are going to be unwell," he said, attending to her request.

"No; indeed, indeed I am quite well, dearest Charley," she whispered, and an impatient frown crossed his brow; but he said no more, only half led, half followed her to a window looking out upon the platform, where there was the customary hurry previous to the departure of a train, when the first bell has rung. Porters running here and there with luggage, cool passengers, excited passengers, box- and wrapper-laden ladies'-maids seeking second-class carriages; footmen bearing fasces of umbrellas and walking-sticks; heavy swells seeking smoking-compartments; Smith's boys shouting the evening papers; and as they gazed through the great plate-glass window of the waiting-room, the hurry and bustle seemed to have an interest for Charley he had never known before.

"We shall be in plenty of time when this train has gone," said Laura; and she clung very tightly to his arm. "I long to see Nelly again. Don't you think she improves?"

"Very much. I quite love that child!" said Charley with some animation. "She is so piquante, and fresh, and genuine!"

A sort of gasping sigh escaped from Laura's breast, but he would not heed it.

And now the bustle was nearly over; the last bell had rung, the inspector had taken his last glance, the doors were banging, and the guard's whistle was at his lips, when the inspector held up his hand, as there came the pattering of hastening feet on the platform.

"Bai Jove, portare, make haste, or we shall miss it!" cried a familiar voice.

"This way, sir," was the reply; and an official trotted by with a black portmanteau on his shoulder and a bag in his hand; and Charley started as if he had received a fatal stab, for directly following, clinging to Max Bray's arm, shawled and muffled, and pale as ashes, Ella Bedford passed the window.

"Max!" exclaimed Laura excitedly, while, as Charley made a movement to reach the door, she clung to his arm. "Dearest Charley," she whispered in low impassioned tones, "my own love, my dear life, do not leave me! pray, pray do not leave! I love you dearly, more dearly than ever, and my heart bleeds for you—truly—faithfully!" She could say no more, for her emotion choked her utterance; but she clung to him wildly, as he stood, now pale and motionless as a statue, gazing through the window. And in those brief moments what had he seen?

Ella handed into a first-class compartment, Max following her, while her pale face was directly opposite to Charley, and only a couple of carriage-lengths distant. Then came the bang of the door, the piping whistle, the shriek of the engine, then the rapidly increasing panting snorts as of impatience to be off; the carriages glided by; and where Ella Bedford's face had been the moment before, was first one and then another, strangers all; then the guards own, then blankness—a blankness that seemed to have made its way to his soul, till looking down he became aware of the stony face gazing up into his, the wild eyes, the parted lips, and the arms clinging to him so tightly.

His face softened as he gazed down at her, and then a sigh tore its way from his breast; a sigh that seemed to bear with it the image of a pale sweet face; and from that moment it was to Charley Vining as if he had been transformed into another man.

"My poor girl!" he said softly, more than pityingly, as he drew her arm closer to his breast.

"Charley!" she sighed gently; but there were volumes in that one word; and had they been alone, she would have thrown herself upon his breast, where she felt now she might cling. Then her eyes closed, a faint hysterical sob passed her lips, and she smiled, as if from a sense of ineffable satisfaction, as she felt his strong arms supporting her—that he was bearing her towards the inner room; and then all was blank.

Ten minutes after, Laura unclosed her eyes, to find herself upon a couch, with Nelly and Charley at her side; and starting up, she rested upon one elbow. Then she fixed her eyes upon the latter, and caught at his hand.

"You will not leave me?" she gasped hoarsely.

"No!" he whispered almost tenderly. "I feared that you were unwell." And he passed his hand across her damp brow, smoothing back the raven hair; and Laura sank back, her eyes closed and a smile upon her lip, drawing with her his hand, which she held tightly in both hers; for, saving Nelly, they were now alone.

A quarter of an hour passed in silence, and then Charley Vining said gently:

"Do you think you can bear to be moved?"

"Yes," she said, rising eagerly and fixing her eyes upon his, "if you are with me. But," she said, leaning towards him and whispering, "do not be angry; only tell me, to set me at rest—tell me that you will not—Max—dear Charley, you know what I mean."

"Follow Max—your brother?" said Charley sternly; "no!"

The next minute Laura was leaning upon his arm, and they sought the carriage, Nelly taking Charley's other arm, and whispering to him as he turned towards her with a sad smile on his lip, "I'm so sorry, Charley, and yet so glad, and I don't know how I feel; but tell me, is it to be *brother* Charley?"

"Hush!" said the other sternly, as they reached the carriage.

Had he not been so preoccupied, Charley Vining would have seen that a strange man, rather shabbily-dressed, was close beside him, vainly attempting to gain his attention; for, after handing Laura and her sister into the barouche, he was about to leave them to return alone; but the imploring look of dread in Laura's eyes stayed him, and yielding to her outstretched hand, he leaped in and took his place opposite.

Upon reaching Harley-street the strange man seemed to be there before them, and Charley would again have left, but Laura begged him to go with her upstairs; and seeing how pale and disturbed she was, he accompanied her to the drawing-room.

"There!—need I tell you on my honour," he said, taking her hand gently, "you need be under no fear."

"And—and, Charley," she said appealingly, "you will not judge me harshly?"

"Judge you harshly?" he said; "no." And as she held out her hands to him, he took her gently to his breast and kissed her.

"Do you know how happy you have made me?" she whispered, clinging to him and gazing up in his pale honest face.

"No," he said in the same tone; "but I fear I have pained you sorely."

"Charley!"

"Laura!"

There was no other sound heard in that room but those softly uttered words; and when, a minute or two after, Mrs Bray quietly opened the door unobserved, she stepped back again on the points of her toes smiling with a satisfied air, and posted herself as a sentinel upon the stairs.

And all this while that strange man was impatiently watching the windows from the other side of the street.

"Couldn't get to see you before, sir," said a voice, as Charley Vining left Mr Bray's house in Harley-street. "Perhaps you'll run over that while I follow you and wait for farther orders."

Charley started, and looked up to see that a rather shabbily-dressed man was walking away from him, after placing a note in his hands.

"Mr M.B. went to Crescent Villas at nine this morning, stayed ten minutes, returned to Bury-street, left Bury-street at three in a cab with a black portmanteau, and was driven to the front of the Colosseum. Waited an hour, and was then joined by Miss E.B. carrying a small black bag—very pale, and evidently been crying. Mr M.B. said aloud, 'At last!' as he handed her into the cab. Driven rapidly to Paddington-station. Took first-class tickets to Penzance, and left by 4:50 express. Are we to follow?"

So read Charley Vining, the letters at times swimming before his eyes. He glanced round, and the bearer was a dozen yards in his rear. But he waved him back. A quarter of an hour ago, and he had told himself that he was free; but the suggestion at the end of the letter whispered him that some links of his old chains still clung around. But no; he would not have them followed. Why should he? What was it to him? But for his infatuation, he might have known to what all was tending. It was nothing to him now; but a sigh that was almost a sob escaped from his breast, as, once more turning, he waited till the man was alongside.

"Tell Mr Whittrick he need take no farther steps," said Charley in a voice that he hardly knew for his own; and touching his hat, without another word, the man glided off, disappearing round the corner of the next street so rapidly, that when, upon second thoughts, Charley would have set him another task, and hurried after him with that intention, he was out of sight.

Five minutes after, Charley was in a cab and on his way to Crescent Villas; where, after a little parley, he was now admitted to the presence of Mrs Marter, red-eyed, furious, and ready, apparently, to make an onslaught upon the first person who offended her.

Before he had been there long, the rapid flow of the angry woman's words told of how, by cunning, flattering, and attention, Max Bray had gained a footing in the house; the weak vain woman believing that his visits were all upon her account, and willingly accepting the presence of Ella as a blind. Her only sin was a love of flattery, attention, and Max Bray's escorts to the various places of amusement; but now the veil had dropped from her eyes, and she spoke.

"It has all been planned for long enough," she exclaimed passionately, "and they have gone off together." And then she burst forth into a furious tirade against deceit, forgetful entirely of how she was hoist with her own petard.

Charley could hear no more, but hurried away, confused, doubting, heart-sick. What faith could he place in any one again? He had gone to Crescent Villas in the hope that he was, after all, wrong; that there was some mistake which might be cleared up; and according to this woman the idol of his heart had been a monster of treachery and deceit.

He was ready to make any allowance for the mad passion of a woman who found that she had been made the tool of the designing; but, after all, what could he say to his wounded heart after the scenes he had witnessed? What right had he now to trouble himself, though—what was it to him? There was nothing to palliate what he had seen; and now he must begin life afresh. What he had to do was to draw a line across the mental diary of his life—a thick black mark between the present and the bygone—and at that line he told himself his thoughts must always stay; for upon that past he could not bear to dwell.

Forgive her? He had nothing to forgive. She had always told him, from the first, that it could not be; while he had blindly and impetuously rushed on to his heart's destruction.

Chapter Three
Beginning Again

And how about Laura? Well, she loved him, and it was his father's wish. He had committed himself to it now, too; and if he were to marry, why not her as well as any other woman?

So mused Charley Vining, weakly enough; but he is here held up as no model—simply as a weak erring man, whose passions had been deeply moved. He had been, as it were, in a fearful life-storm, to be left tossing, dismasted, and helpless, now that a calm had come. Here, too, was the friendly consort offering her aid to lead him into port—the port that he had hoped to enter gallantly, with ensign flowing. But now, as this was impossible, he would let matters take their course.

He met Sir Philip Vining at dinner; and though the old gentleman studiously avoided all allusion thereto, yet he marked the change in his son, and was inwardly delighted thereby.

"Father," said Charley, as they sat over their wine, "I'm about tired of town. When shall we go back home—home—home?" he said, repeating the word. "How pleasant that seems to sound!"

"My dear boy, when you like; to-morrow, Charley, if you wish." And the old gentleman spoke earnestly, for of late his heart had pricked him sorely; and had his son now brought Ella to his side and said, "Father, I shall never love another; this must be my wife," he would have struggled with himself, and then given up and blessed them. But now it seemed that there was a change; the attentions to Laura had been marked; and, hushing his conscience, the old man told himself that matters would soon come right after all, and he spoke cheerfully.

"Well, let's go back to-morrow, then," said Charley. "I want to see the old place again."

"You are not ill, Charley—you don't feel in need of advice?"

"Ill?" said Charley, "not at all! I want a change, and to see the old place."

"By the way, Charley, Bray called here to-day; he wanted me to dine there again, but I declined, as you said you would be back. I said, though, that I would go up in the evening. We are discussing the drainage question of Holt Moors. You will not mind my leaving you. I thought, too, that perhaps—"

"I would go too," said Charley smilingly. "Well, yes, I've no objection; little Nell is come back. Do you know, dad," he said cheerfully, "I should like to give that girl a nice little well-broken mare? She would ride splendidly. Couldn't we pick up something before we go down, and let it be for a surprise? A nice little thing that would hunt well, without pulling the child's arms off."

"My dear Charley, you give me great pleasure, you do indeed. We'll see about it first thing in the morning. My dear boy," exclaimed the old man, rising, and crossing to his son's chair to rest his hands upon his broad shoulder, "Heaven bless you, my dear boy! Are the old times coming back?"

"I hope so, father," said Charley, smiling; but there was something very sad in his tone.

"Not in that way, my dear boy," said the old man tenderly. "Indeed, indeed, Charley, my every act and desire has been for your good."

"Father," said Charley sternly, "do you see that?" And he made a mark on the white cloth.

"My dear boy, yes."

"That must divide the past from the present. All on that side is to be forgotten. Let it be as if dead. Now for the clean blank page of the future."

He held out his hand, which was eagerly taken by Sir Philip, and then they were silent for some time; when, in quite changed tones, Charley said, looking at his watch, "Eight o'clock, dad! Shall I ring for a cab?"

Sir Philip did not speak; he only bowed his head, and then wringing his son's hand, he left the room.

Chapter Four
Of What are Men's hearts Composed?

"Hooray, here's Charley Vining!" cried Nelly, as Sir Philip and his son entered the Brays' drawing-room; and bounding over the carpet, she ran up, and caught the latter by the hand; but as Charley shook both her thin hands warmly, he glanced across the room to where Laura was standing, flushed and happy.

"Are you better?" he said, as he crossed over.

"Better? yes," she said softly; "and so happy!"

There was such a look of intensified joy in Laura's face, that as he took his seat beside her, Charley Vining smiled pleasantly. He was accepting his fate.

And why not, he asked himself, when, with all their eccentricities, the family seemed ready to worship him? Sir Philip and Mr Bray had no sooner taken their places in a corner of the lesser drawing-room, and commenced their discussion upon the projected improvements, than Mrs Bray crossed over to where Charley was seated, and probably for the first time in her life forbore to shriek, and, leaning over him, actually whispered, as she stooped and kissed him on the forehead.

"Bless you, Vining! you have made us all so happy! But I have not said a word to him."

Charley felt disposed to frown; but there was a genuine mother's tear left upon his forehead, and he pressed Mrs Bray's hand as she left him, carrying off Nelly at the same time.

It was all settled, then; it was to be. And why not? Let it be so, then. Some people said there was no fate in these things; what, then, was this, if it were not fate?

But he accepted it all, asking himself the while, could the gentle tremulous woman at his side be the Laura of old? How she drank in his every glance, eagerly listening for each word! Could he, as he had said he would, thoroughly dismiss the past, life might, after all, be endurable.

So he reasoned, as the evening passed away.

They had had tea, and Nelly had been sent to the piano to play piece after piece, not one of which was listened to, for those present were intent upon their own affairs. Charley talked in a low voice to Laura, Mrs Bray dozed in an easy-chair, and Nelly kept to her music.

Meanwhile the question of draining Holt Moors had been discussed and rediscussed. Farming matters had been talked over, and the state of Blandfield Park; Mr Bray strongly advising a particular breed of sheep for keeping the grass short and lawnlike, giving his opinions freely, and at the same time listening with deference to those of his old friend.

At last, during a pause, Sir Philip caught Mr Bray's eye, and nodded towards the other room.

"That's a picture, Bray!" he said. "Ah," said Mr Bray, as he gazed for a few moments at where—a noble-looking couple—Charley and Laura sat together in the soft light shed by the lamps, "I wish, Vining, I had had such a son. It seems hard to speak against one's own flesh and blood, but my Max—"

He did not finish his sentence, but shrugged his shoulders, laughing pleasantly, as tall thin Nelly came and rested her weak loose body against his shoulder, before laying her cheek against his bald head, afterwards polishing the shiny white hemisphere with her little hand, rubbing it round and round, round and round; while, apparently approving thereof, Papa Bray drew his child upon his knee, and went on talking.

But suddenly he ceased; for, rising, and with her hand in his, and one arm round her waist, Charley Vining walked with Laura towards where the old men sat, and Nelly, with the tears in her eyes, glided away to the seat just vacated.

"Mr Bray—father," said Charley quietly, as he stopped in front of them, "Laura has promised to be my wife: have you any objection?"

The next moment Sir Philip Vining had folded Laura in his arms, kissing her lovingly, as Mr Bray caught Charley's hands in his, shaking them warmly.

"My dear boy," he exclaimed, "you make me very proud—happiest day of my life!"

"Charley, my son," said Sir Philip, stretching out one hand to take his son's, and speaking in a voice that showed how he was moved, "thank you, thank you; you have made me very happy."

Half an hour after, they were leave-taking; and as Charley kissed Nelly and bade her warmly "good-night," there was a tear left upon his lips.

"What, little one!" he said gaily, "in trouble? What is it? You don't think I've jilted you, do you?"

"Don't talk stuff, Charley!" she said gravely. "I'm very happy; but I feel like marble—just as if there were dark veins running all through me."

"Marble? veins?" said Charley in a puzzled tone.

"Yes; dark veins, like sorrowful thoughts; for though I'm very glad that you are going to be my own dear brother—and something like a brother too!—I can't help feeling sorry about my poor Miss Bedford."

Charley started from her as if he had been stung; but no one but Nelly noticed it. Five minutes after, Sir Philip and he were in the Brays' carriage, and on their way home, for Mr Bray had insisted upon their having it in place of a cab.

There was no farther talk of going back to Blandfield Court till the Brays left town next week, and to all intents and purposes the Vinings lived in Harley-street. But Charley found time for a visit to Mr Whittrick, to see if there was any payment due.

"Happy to attend upon you, if you require my services again, Mr Vining," he said, as he pocketed a cheque; and then he bowed his client out.

It was that same morning that, returning to lunch in Harley-street, Charley found Laura seated frowningly over a note, which she made as if to conceal upon his entrance; but directly after, as if blushing for her weakness, she stood up, holding the letter in her hand.

"Am I to be jealous?" he said laughingly, as he saluted her.

"I was afraid it might hurt your feelings, Charley," she said, as her arms were resting on his shoulder. "Can you bear to hear its contents? It is from Max."

"Yes," said Charley moodily, and with the veins in his forehead swelling.

"He asks me to try and mediate—to try and make you think less angrily of him."

"Where is he?" said Charley abruptly.

"I do not know," said Laura. "Somewhere in the west of England. The postmark is Plymouth."

"Laura," said Charley sternly, "I cannot forgive him. Max and I must never meet! Don't look so serious—I cannot help it. I am, I know, hard and unrelenting—But there, no tears! Why, you are trembling. I am not angry."

"No, no; I know you are not," she whispered, nestling closer to him. "You must not be. I shall be so glad to get down to the old place again."

"And I as well," said Charley.

And, probably in deference to their wishes, both families started on the following day for their country seats.

Chapter Five
Preparing the Rivets

"*Con*-gratulate you, my dear Vining! do, indeed," said Hugh Lingon, coming up to Charley in the hunting-field, when he had been home about a fortnight.

"What about?" said Charley, who had attended every meet, and tried his best to break his neck as he rode straight, taking everything that came in his way.

"What about?" said Lingon. "Why, about your coming marriage, to be sure. Haven't seen you before, or I should have given you a word or two. Rather too bad of Laura Bray, though."

"What was?" said Charley very impatiently.

"Why, making such a pair of tongs of me, with which to fish for her hot roast chestnut—meaning you, of course, Charley," said Lingon, with a laugh.

"Don't be a fool!" said Charley gruffly.

"Not if I can help it," said Lingon good-humouredly. "But you know how I was made a fool of, and then pitched over at any time, when your sultanship thought proper to be attentive."

"Long time finding a fox this morning," said Charley impatiently, as he turned his horse along by the side of a spinney. But Hugh Lingon was not to be shaken off, and trotting up to his side, fat and good-tempered, he talked on.

"I should have expected that you'd have given up all this sort of thing now, old fellow," said Lingon; "but I suppose you are having your run out before the knot is tied. I say, though, how well Laura looks!"

"Does she?" said Charley absently; and it was very evident from his quiet abstracted manner, that he was thinking upon other matters.

"Does she! Ah, I think so. But mind you, I've an idea that Nelly will grow into a handsomer woman altogether. I like Nelly," he added simply.

"So do I," said Charley, starting from his reverie. "She's a lovable girl."

"I say, young man," exclaimed Lingon, "that won't do; you can't have them both."

"Pish!" exclaimed Charley, putting the spurs to his mare. "There, I'm going on. Good-morning, Lingon."

"But I'm going your way, Charley," cried the other, spurring up alongside. "Don't be in such a hurry, man! It isn't often one sees you now. I want to know when it's to be. Our girls are sure to ask me, for they're all red-hot about it."

"When what's to be?" said Charley, with a wondering gaze.

"O, come, I say, now, that's a good un!" laughed Hugh Lingon, till his fat face was full of creases and rolls, some of which threatened to close his little twinkling eyes. "Going to be married, and got it all settled, and not know the day! Ha, ha, ha! Charley Vining, that is a good one! I do like that!" And he gave his friend a hearty slap on the back. "Come, I say, tell us, old fellow!"

"This day month, I believe—there!" said Charley viciously; and again he essayed to leave his friend behind.

"By the way, Charley," said Hugh, continuing alongside, "I want you to do me a favour."

He spoke so earnestly, that the other drew rein and turned to him.

"What is it?" he said.

"Well, I hardly like to ask you, but just now I'm in a fix."

"Well, but what is it? How do you mean?" said Charley.

"Well, you see, I'm short of money, and I'm a good deal bothered; for I'd promised to pay my tailor, and now I can't do it."

"How much do you want?" said Charley quietly. "I've none here; but I'll draw you a cheque when I get home."

"O! I'm much obliged—I *am*, 'pon my word!" said Lingon. "Don't I wish, though, that I could draw cheques, and come that sort of thing! I'm quite ashamed to ask you. But it isn't my fault; for you see I had the money, and was going to send it, when who should pop down but Max Bray, and ask me to lend it to him—five-and-twenty pounds, you know. He wanted fifty; but of course that was out of my reach altogether. I lent him all I had, though; for he said that he should only want it for two days, when he'd be sure and send it back. Nelly's brother, too, you see, so that I couldn't well refuse him."

Hugh Lingon did not see the black angry look upon Charley's face, and he went on.

"He went to the governor after he left me, and got fifty pounds out of him; so I found out this morning when I went into the study to see if I could raise the wind myself, for I had an awful dunning letter from my tailor for breakfast, and there was the governor in no end of a rage—put on that grand magisterial air of his, and begins to talk to me like he does to the clodhoppers who have been having a drunk and a fight. And, lo and behold, it comes out that Mr Max promised to send his back the next day without fail; and the governor swears he'll make old Bray pay up, if Max doesn't answer his last letter, for he has written three, and had no reply. The last one he read me the copy of—all about ungentlemanly dishonourable behaviour, and so on. I believe the old chap would like to commit him for obtaining money under false pretences. But, I say, don't run away, Charley. I may come and have the cheque, mayn't I? for it's of no use to try the governor again till Max Bray has paid up."

"Yes, yes; come when you like!" cried Charley, turning and breasting his mare at a high hedge on the left, which the gallant beast cleared, but with hardly an inch to spare; and then they went crashing through the copse, and were out of sight in a minute.

"Well, that's one way of giving a fellow the go-by!" muttered Hugh Lingon. "Why? I wouldn't try that leap for five hundred pounds! nor would any one else who had the least regard for his neck. What did he fire-up about as soon as I mentioned Max Bray's name? By Jove, though, as Max says, he don't seem highly delighted about his good fortune!"

Other people made the same remark about Charley Vining, and also noticed how hard he hunted, riding in the most reckless way imaginable, but always seeming to escape free of harm, when more cautious riders met with the customary croppers, bruises, contusions, and broken limbs.

Chapter Six
Had She Won?

It was one of the things generally known in the neighbourhood of Blandfield, that Sir Philip Vining gave up the Court to his son, who, in a very short time, was to confer upon it a new mistress in the shape of Laura Bray.

Every one said that it was an admirable match; and old ladies, who had set themselves up for prophets, laughed and nodded together, and reminded one another of how they had always said so. That croquet-party at the Court was not for nothing, they knew!

Then came a round of congratulatory calls, and a general disposition amongst the callers to declare that they had never heard of anything that had given them more pleasure.

"Really," they said, "it was exquisite, and just the thing that was wanted to make the Lexville circle complete. For, you see, Sir Philip was indeed most charming, but he gave so few dinner-parties!"

"But what Charles Vining could see in that great, tall, coarse woman, when there were my nice quiet gentle girls, I don't know. But there, every eye forms its own beauty!"

So said Mrs Lingon; and, in fact, allowing for a little variety, so said every mother of marriageable daughters; but all the same, at the end of a fortnight Laura Bray was to be Mrs Charles, and in future Lady Vining, always allowing, of course, that nothing occurred to put off the wedding, that every one declared to be, on the whole, rather hurried.

There was certainly, too, a little disappointment felt by some of the marriageable young ladies; but that was soon mastered: for there was to be the wedding, after all, if they were not to be the principals in the thrilling ceremony; and also, after all, there was not one of them who might not be asked to act as bridesmaid.

It was the theme of discussion throughout the district. Even gentlemen had their say, as they hoped that Vining wouldn't be so shabby as to cut off his subs. to the hounds, even if he had no more idea of hunting. While, as for the ladies, they knew to an inch how many yards of white gros-de-Naples there would be in Laura's wedding-dress; how many breadths there would be in the skirt; and that Miss Bray had decided not to have it gored.

"And quite right too," said some with a titter, "with such a figure as she has!"

"Don't you think Laura Bray looks quite yellow and thin?" said the elder Miss Lingon, who was certainly neither yellow nor thin, but very plump, fair, and dumplingy.

"O, decidedly!" said her sister. "She looks anxious and worried, too."

"Well, no wonder," said the elder Miss Lingon, with a sigh. "Any stupid would know that it is a most anxious and trying time for her. She is about to take a step which—"

"There's not much fear of your taking, Miss Fan," said her sister spitefully. "And how you should know anything about its being an anxious time, I'm sure I don't know, without you read it in a book."

The elder Miss Lingon tossed her head.

"But I know why she's anxious," said the second Miss Lingon. "Hugh told me. It's because he will hunt so recklessly now."

"I don't believe that's it. All gentlemen hunt," said the other.

"You can believe what you like," was the snappish answer. And there the matter dropped, as each lady waited anxiously for the request that should make her a bridesmaid.

But, all the same, Laura did look thin and anxious. Not that Charley Vining was wanting in attention, for he was constantly at the Elms; but there was a great dread always oppressing her, that the wedding would not take place. Each day that passed without adventure, she reckoned as so much gained; and though Miss l'Aiguille was engaged with her staff especially on Miss Bray's account, and dresses for bride and bridesmaids were in rapid progress, yet would Laura start at the slightest sound, and tremble as every letter came to the house.

She counted the days and the hours that must intervene, and mentally checked them off as they passed away. She clung nervously to Charley as he left her at night, and seemed loth to let him leave her, though he smiled at her anxiety and tried to seem happy, but all the while there was an aching void in his heart, as he told himself that he was about to be guilty of a wrongful act.

And still the time glided on. A few more days, and Laura told herself that she could be at rest.

"At rest?" She shivered as she repeated the words, and then tried to look pleased at the rich presents sent by Sir Philip Vining, or brought to her by Charley himself to swell the bridal trousseau.

But she could not conceal the agitation she felt; for ever, by night and day, thrown athwart the light of her understanding was the dark shadow of a peril to come—a peril coming as surely as day would succeed unto night.

Costly preparations at Blandfield Court; painters and decorators busy; fresh carpets here, and fresh carpets there; Laura fetched over by Sir Philip to give her opinion upon this, her consent to that, or to choose something else. The old gentleman seemed never happy save when he was superintending some fresh arrangement that should add to the pleasure and comfort of his fixture daughter-in-law. He was almost angry at times on seeing how little interest was taken in such matters by his son; but ever ready with an excuse, he set it down to Charley's renewed pleasure in the sports of the field.

Laura did not complain, although Nelly, but for her youth, might have been taken for the favoured one, since she was constantly Charley's companion, to the great astonishment of Hugh Lingon. For the little well-broken mare had been purchased, and had come down to Blandfield, where, one day when Nelly was over with her sister, Charley proposed a ride, the horses were brought round, and Nelly's rough black pony sent back, to her utter astonishment; while, when informed that the graceful little creature that stood arching its neck, and softly pawing at the gravel, was her own, Nelly's joy knew no bounds, as, in turns, she literally smothered Sir Philip and Charley with kisses.

It was not from mortification at being so unceremoniously left that Laura turned pale; but, in her nervous state, it seemed that the danger she apprehended—the peril that should stay the wedding—might come from any direction, and that a delay of a month, a fortnight, or even of a week, might be fatal to her prospects; for might not Charley alter his mind? or— no, there was no fear of that now. But might not this prove a danger that should delay that which she so ardently prayed for? Nelly might meet with an accident, and be brought back half-killed.

There was certainly some foundation for Laura's fears; for had Miss Nelly been left to herself, in her wild exhilaration she would most probably have come to grief; in fact she tried her best to get thrown; but there was ever a strong hand ready to be laid upon her rein, so that, in spite of Laura's forebodings, she was brought back in safety.

Laura counted: six days—five days—four days—three days before—two days before—one day before the wedding; and all this time Max Bray might have been forgotten, for his name was never once mentioned at the Elms. Hugh Lingon, though, on making an excuse for not having repaid Charley's loan, mentioned having felt sure that he had seen Max in London, but that he had been unable to overtake him before he disappeared, but that, after all, he was not sure.

That news slightly disturbed Charley, and he winced as he thought upon the probable future fate of Ella Bedford; his brow contracted too, as he seemed to see a pale face appealing to him for help, and he shuddered slightly as he drove away the thoughts.

He spent the evening with Sir Philip at the Elms, and all seemed to be working to the one end.

Nelly was in a tremendous state of excitement, and displayed it as she darted about with brightened eye and flushed cheek; but now that the time was so near, Laura had so nerved herself that she was calm and composed in appearance, though her heart was agitated by varied emotions.

But what cause could there be for fear? Had not the woman who had been her rival fled, in, apparently, a most discreditable manner, with her own brother? Was not Charles Vining, if not a warm and passionate, at all events a most respectable lover as to his attentions? Surely she could wish for nothing more, if the proverb be true, that the hottest love the soonest cools.

And, besides, how gleefully were all the preparations being made! Gunters were providing the breakfast, and even then the men were in the house. The wedding garments were waiting, and Miss l'Aiguille was coming herself in the morning to superintend the dressing, to the great disgust of Laura's maid. The wedding was expected to be one of the grandest that had been in the neighbourhood for some years; and the weather had been for many days past so settled and bright, that there was every prospect of the bride being bathed in the sunshine of good fortune.

"Good-night, for the last parting!" said Charley, as he held Laura in his arms, previous to taking his departure; and she clung to him, for he was more tender and gentle to her.

He must love her, she felt, or he could not have spoken as he had.

Only a few more hours, then, and the suspense would be at an end. The wedding-breakfast over, dresses changed, the carriage would be in waiting to convey them to the station. They were to pass the first night in London, and depart by tidal boat the next morning for Paris, Marseilles,

Hyères, Genoa, Rome—a month of pleasant touring in Southern Europe; and in that period old sorrows would be forgotten, and her husband's heart would have warmed to her.

But still Laura trembled, for she had been gambling for a great stake.

Had she won?

It seemed so; for once more he repeated those words, "Good-night, for the last parting!" as they stood in the hall.

"But you'll have to put up with me, my dear!" said Sir Philip, kissing Laura in his turn; "but I won't bother you—I won't interfere in any way—only let me have my study fire in the cold weather; and don't stop away from home too long. I say so now, because I shall have no chance to-morrow. There, good-bye!"

They were gone; and, proud and elate, Laura returned to the drawing-room. The victory was nearly won, and the happy congratulatory looks of friends and those who were to act as her bridesmaids seemed to be mirrored in her face, as they clustered laughingly round her—Mrs Bray forbearing to shriek, and little pudgy Mr Bray disregarding her evening dress as he caught her in his arms, to give her a sounding kiss on either cheek.

Meanwhile Sir Philip and Charley were returning in their carriage to Blandfield: the former light-hearted and chatty, the latter quiet, but apparently content. He had weighed all well, and pondered the matter again and again, and still his heart told him that it was his duty. The faint spark of his old passion, as he called it, that would still keep showing, in spite of his efforts to crush it out, he told himself would soon be extinct—hiding the fact that that spark was a consuming fire that was not even smouldering, but though concealed, eating its way fiercely to the light.

"Good-night; heaven bless you, my dear boy!" said Sir Philip, as he stood, candle in hand, in the hall. "It will be hard work sparing you, Charley, for I'm an old man now, and growing feeble, and in want of humouring. You may have your month, but don't exceed it."

Charley did not answer; but shook his father's hand warmly, and they parted.

Chapter Seven
On the Point

The wedding-morning, with all its flutter, flurry, and excitement! The bride pale, but collected; Nelly and her sister bridesmaids appealing vainly to one another for help; hair, that at any other time would fall into plait, or bandeau, or roll, with such ease, now obstinate and awkward, and requiring to be attended to again and again; hair-pins becoming scarce, and, where plentiful, given to bending; eyes with a disposition to look red; hands ditto—for it is winter; while, as if out of sheer spite, more than one nose follows suit, and is decidedly raw and chappy.

"O, do, do, do fetch a knife!" whimpered Nelly. "I shall never be dressed in time! I must have a knife to open these horrible old hooks, that have flattened down when 'Lisbeth ran an iron along the back plait. O, what shall I do? I shall never be ready! And the old chilblains have swelled up on my heels, and I can't get on those little satin boots; and I can't go in my others, because they haven't got high heels. I could sit down and have a good cry— that I could! Here, 'Lisbeth—'Lisbeth! why don't Miss l'Aiguille come and help some of us?"

"Lor, miss, how you do talk!" cried the excited 'Lisbeth. "And is that what you called me back for? Miss Luggle's a-doing of Miss Lorror, and couldn't leave her, was it ever so. There, don't stop me, miss; they're waiting for pins, and there'll be no end of a row if I don't go."

"But, please, come and do my back hair, 'Lisbeth," cried one of the bridesmaids—a cousin, who was staying in the house.

"Lor, miss, I can't. You must ask Miss Nelly!" cried 'Lisbeth, vainly struggling to get out, for Nelly was holding on with both hands to her dress, and dragging her back.

"There, do let go, Miss Nelly—pray! Here, miss, ask your cousin to leave go, and come and do it. She'll put it right—beautiful!"

"But she has done it twice," cried the other; "and see how it has come tumbling down again; it's worse now than if it hadn't been touched!"

"I don't care; I shan't try any more," whimpered Nelly. "I can't get dressed decent. But you'll all have to wait for me; for I'm sure Charley Vining won't go to be married if I ain't there."

"For goodness gracious' sake, now just look there, Miss Nelly, at what you've been and done! You've pulled all the gathers out of my frock!"

"Don't care!" said Nelly, throwing herself down, half-dressed, into a chair. "Fasten 'em up again: you've got lots of pins."

"'Lisbeth—'Lisbeth!" was shouted from the passage, and the girl disappeared.

We have nothing to do with the bride's mental sufferings at present, the remarks now made appertaining to dress alone; but she must have borne something at the hands of Miss l'aiguille and her staff of assistants, before, tall, dark, and handsome, she stood amidst a diaphanous cloud of drapery, which floated from and around her, descending, as it were, from the orange wreath twined amidst her magnificent raven ringlets.

Miss l'aiguille clasped her hands, and went down upon one knee in an ecstasy of admiration at the glorious being she had made, as a gentle chorus of "O!" and "O, miss!" was raised by her satellites; while, wonderful to relate, when she descended to the drawing-room, she was not the last, for two of the bridesmaids were not ready.

But Mrs Bray was there, gorgeous to behold, bearing upon her everything in the shape of costly dress that money would purchase. To describe her costume would be simply impossible, save to say that it was as solid-looking as her daughter's was light and airy—the plaits and folds of her silken robe literally creaked and crackled as she moved, which was all of a piece. Colour there was too; but what, it would be impossible to say, the prevailing hue being warm scarlet, which was shed upon Mr Bray, whose white vest was so stiff and grand, that nothing could have been whiter and stiffer and grander, unless it was the tremendous cravat that held his head as if he was being garotted—symptoms of strangulation being really visible in the prominence of his eyes. But then, as he said, in regard to his sufferings, he did not have a daughter married every day.

"I should have liked for Mr Maximilian to have been here," said Mrs Bray, as they were waiting for Nelly, who, now under the hands of Miss l'Aiguille, was being made up rapidly—her thin bony form growing quite graceful under the dressmakers fingers.

"Bless me, though, what is the matter?" cried Mrs Bray. "Laura my dear, pray don't faint in those things, whatever you do!"

"Hush!" cried Laura hoarsely, as, by a strong effort, she recovered herself. "Did you—did you say Max was here?"

"No—no! I said I wished he was here," said Mrs Bray pettishly. "I do not see what you have got to turn queer about in that. Your own brother too!"

Laura gave a sigh of relief and then closed her eyes for a few moments.

"Only a little while now," she thought.

The hour was very near, and surely nothing could stay the event.

Then, summoning her resolution she began to pace slowly up and down the room. No tremulous maiden now, but a firm determined woman, who told herself that she had persevered and won the lover—the husband soon.

"What are we waiting for?" said Mr Bray.

"Two bridesmaids," said Mrs Bray: "Nelly and Miss Barnett. But we have plenty of time; and the Miss Lingons are not here yet. O, here they are, though!"

The young ladies were set down at the door as she spoke; and soon the Bray drawing-room was well filled.

The horses were pawing up the gravel, to the disgust of the gardener, who thought of the rolling to be done; but went and drowned his sorrows in some of the beer on the way, with ample solids, in the Bray kitchen.

A bright brisk winterly day, with a wind that kissed each cheek as bride-elect and bridesmaids descended the steps, and entered the carriages drawn up in turn. Rattle, rattle, bang! went steps and doors; footmen were more upright than ever, and raised their chests into glorious hills, crowned with white satin-and-silver wedding-favours—Mrs Bray insisting upon their being mounted at once.

A grinding of the gravel, and first one and then another carriage departing, Laura, with Mr Bray, completing the cortege; Mrs Bray going before, after declaring that she ought to have stopped behind to superintend the wedding-breakfast arrangements.

And proud was Mr Bray of the stern handsome girl before him; for he had given up the whole of the back seat to his daughter—and her dress. The pallor and look of dread seemed now to have passed away, as if Laura, by her determination, had exorcised the phantom of coming ill; and well-merited were the remarks made, as a glance was obtained at the beauty "arrayed for the bridal."

People had plenty of ill-natured things to say when the wedding was first settled; but now all these remarks were forgotten; and again and again, as the Bray carriage rolled on towards the church, there was a cheer raised; while, on coming abreast of the Lexville Boys' School, there was a tremendous scattering volley of shouts, followed by a rush, for the boys were to have a holiday for the occasion; and away they went to the churchyard, to cluster thickly on walls, tombstones, and iron railings—wherever they could find a post of vantage.

Carpet rolled down to the church-gate, and the clerk in a state of fume and worry, that brought him, in spite of the wintry day, into a profuse perspiration, because, no matter how he "begged and prayed," people would walk over the carpet, and print upon it the mark of their dirty boots.

The church was filled in every part where a view of the communion-table could be obtained; and the pew-openers gave up at last in despair, for the people would stand on the cushions. The organist was ready with the "Wedding March"—Mendelssohn's, of course—and the ringers were already giving those thirsty lips of theirs a dry wipe, in anticipation of the beer to be on the way by and by, when they made the town echo with a peal of bob-majors and grandsire-caters. While last, but not least, and posted side by side with panting Miss l'Aiguille, who had run down, and was now promising him an account of each lady's dress, with the proper terms to be applied thereto—was the reporter of the local paper, busy at work with a spikey pencil.

He had already put down a list of the notabilities present—people whom "we observed"—and had added the name of the officiating clergyman, who was to be assisted by a couple more; the two being now engaged in robing in the vestry.

There was no mistake about its being a errand wedding; for the covers were off the communion hassocks—those worked by the Lexville ladies—and people were on the tiptoe of expectation, for the hour was at hand.

Wheels!

"Here they come: the bridegroom, of course!" "'Tain't. It's some ladies!" "'Tain't, I tell you; the bridegroom always comes first." "Sir Philip's chariot is to have four horses, and the first and second grooms are to ride post in blue and silver, and black-velvet caps." "There, I was right—they are ladies."

Such were a few of the buzzing remarks made as the leading carriage drew up to the gates, and the first batch of friends and bridesmaids descended, hurried up to the old church porch, shook out their plumage, and then swept gracefully up the nave, while remarks full of admiration were passed by those excited fair ones who would not miss a wedding on any consideration, and had duly posted in their mental ledgers the account of every affair that had taken place at Lexville church for the last twenty years; though, during all that long space of time, no one had ever asked them to take the little journey for the purpose of saying, "I will."

Wheels again, and another buzz of excited voices, for this time there is a volley of cheers faintly heard.

This is the bridegroom, then; and there is a perfect rustle amongst the ancient and modern doves of Lexville to catch a good glimpse of the stalwart handsome heir of Blandfield.

But the next minute the rustle subsides, for the carriage that stopped at the gate only brought friends and bridesmaids. And so did the next, and the next, till the chancel began to wear a goodly aspect, though every face was turned now towards the entrance, and all were upon the extreme point of the tiptoe of expectation.

"The bridegroom ought to be here now," said some one in the chancel.

"Isn't Charley Vining here, then?" whispered Nelly to her cousin.

But there was no answer.

Chapter Eight
Was it an Accident?

Wheels again, and louder cheers than ever; a rolling scattering volley from a hundred young throats.

"Here he is then, now," said some one. "The Vinings are so popular!"

More bustle, and pressing, and confusion; the steps round the font invaded, and two small boys mounted on the stove to get a good view, while no one interrupts them; the organ-gallery crammed as it never was on Sundays; and the organist hard put to it to keep people from invading his own little sanctum behind the red curtains, and treading upon the pedal keys.

The boy at the bellows has already pumped the wind-chest full, and there is a wheezing sound of escaping air. But the excitement down below is now at its height, and a murmur of admiration is heard as pudgy Mr Bray, hat in hand, leads in Laura—proud, sweeping, stately, and with her eyes cast down, but her head thrown back.

No modest retiring bride she, though the lids do droop and the long black fringes conceal the dark flashing eyes. For she has arrived at the moment of her triumph, and there is a curl to her upper lip as she leads, rather than is led, and passes between scores of the envious.

The chosen one of Charles Vining of Blandfield, the heir to the old baronetcy, Laura knows that there is many a one present who would give ten years of her life to exchange places—to become the future Lady Vining, the leader of the society of the district for miles round. How could she think of the past, when so bright a future was before her? How could she trouble now about forebodings and shadows of coming evil? All were forgotten as she swept down the long nave, each moment more queenly of aspect.

The chancel screen was passed, and the chancel entered—the chancel filled with friends, who smilingly part to allow her to pass to where the invited hedge-in the bridesmaids—a light and cloudy bevy of eight, all white and pale blue, and pale blue fading into white. Dainty forget-me-nots hidden here by lace, or peeping out there from amidst transparent tissue, while every cheek is tinged with the bright damask-rose hue of excitement. The flowers in the bouquets tell tales of the hands that hold, for they tremble and nod; and more than one of those white-gloved hands has drawn out the end of a delicately-scented and laced pocket-handkerchief, so as to have it ready for the tears that will be sure to flow anon; but for a moment the tears, are forgotten, as the bride appears.

"Are you ready?" whispers a voice; and the horribly incongruous-looking clerk comes bustling out of the vestry as the smiling pew-opener dabs the hassocks about, and then smoothes herself down and smirks at everybody, as she wonders how much the wedding will be worth to her.

"Shall I tell them to come?" says the clerk again, smiling so that you can see the two yellow teeth in his top jaw, and the one and a half below. "They're waiting to come and begin."

These remarks of course relate to the clergymen in the vestry, who are warming their boot-toes as they stand in front of the fire, like three shut out ghosts, and discuss the amount of the Vinings' fortune, and talk of Laura Bray's lucky hit. But as the questions are put in a general fashion by the clerk, no one conceives it to be his duty to answer, and consequently there is a dead silence; and now Laura feels, as it were, an icy hand slowly passing towards that heavily-throbbing heart of hers, nearer and nearer, as if about to clutch it, only holding off for a few moments to add to her torture in that dreadful pause, broken at length by an ominous whisper that runs through the length and breadth of the church:

"Where is the bridegroom?"

That pause must have lasted some thirty seconds; but to those in waiting it seemed an hour. Laura's eyes were not cast down, but flashing fiercely, and the hand at her heart—the icy cold hand—now moved as if to clutch it, when she drew a long sighing breath of relief; for though hurt at the apparent neglect, she was once more elate and proud; for a voice at the entry was heard to cry, "Here they come!" and overbearing the whispers of the expectant crowd could be heard the rapid beat of galloping horses and the whirl of wheels.

"They're a-coming down the road as hard as ever they can gallop," whispered a man at one of the windows which commanded the way to Blandfield.

"But is it them?" said another aloud.

"Them! Of course it is; chariot and four; blue and silver. And, my word, how they are going it!"

It was an insult, certainly, his not being there in time—a cruel insult to his bride-elect; but Laura would forgive anything, for he had much to forgive in her, she whispered to herself.

"It's all right," said Mr Bray, nervously looking at his watch. "Blandfield time is always correct; but this church-clock is a perfect disgrace, although we are so foolish as to set our watches by it. Here he is, though!"

Cheering from the boys; galloping horses; whirring wheels, and a rapid rattling rush; and a chariot and four had dashed past the church-gates, and away down the High-street of Lexville, as fast as four well-bred horses could tear.

Away it went, swaying from side to side on its springs, faster and faster as the horses warmed to their work; and those nearer to the door ran out into the churchyard.

"They've taken fright and run away!"

"The horses were too fresh; they've done no work lately."

"Why didn't they have post-horses from the Lion?"

"Sir Philip and Master Charles were both in it!"

"They weren't: there was only one."

"I tell you the chariot was empty."

"Them two grooms have been at the 'all ale, that's about it."

"The carriage must be smashed!"

Remarks in a perfect, or rather imperfect, chaos jumbled one another as opinions were passed. But at last the news was taken to where, with the icy hand now clutching her heart, stood Laura, not fainting, but stern, pale, and erect, that there was nothing to fear, the grooms had evidently been drinking, and the horses had taken fright, but that the chariot was empty.

"Yes, yes, it's all right. Here they come!" cried a voice at the door; and two bridesmaids about to faint, refrained—"here's the barouche, and one, two—yes, there's four inside."

And once more there was a buzz of expectation. Such an accident couldn't have been helped, of course; horses would be restive sometimes, but it *was* hard on the poor bride. But, all the same, those who took more interest in the smashing of a carriage than the linking together of hearts, set off at a brisk run down the High-street.

Chapter Nine
Resignation

There was a look of calm resignation on Charley Vining's face as he met his father at their early breakfast that morning, to which he had descended without a trace of excitement. He was certainly carefully dressed, his dark-blue morning coat and vest and grey trousers fitting his fine figure admirably, while the utter want of constraint displayed told of breeding as plainly as did his well-cut handsome features.

Well might Sir Philip gaze with pride in his son's face, lit up now by the pleasant smile of greeting; and even he, the smooth cleanly-shaven old courtier of a bygone school, owned to himself that it would be a sin and a shame to cut off even a hair of the crisp golden beard that swept down upon his son's breast.

Charley's face was paler now than when we first met him. The ruddy tan had disappeared, to leave his skin pure, fair, and soft as a woman's; but there was no show of effeminacy there. His firm look of determination swept that away, and he was, indeed, that morning a bridegroom of whom any woman might have been proud.

"A good half-hour yet," said Charley, referring to his watch. "I shall have a cigar in the shrubbery before we start, dad." And he nodded to his father and the friends who were to accompany them. "Shall you have both carriages?"

"Yes, my dear boy, yes!" exclaimed Sir Philip nervously, as his snuff-box came out as if by instinct. "But, Charley!" he said in a whisper, "you won't—I don't think I'd smoke this morning!"

"Not smoke, dad!" laughed Charley. "Why not? Perhaps as soon as the knot is tied, I may be forbidden."

"Stuff, my dear boy! But this morning, think of the odour; the ladies, Charley, the ladies!"

"My dear father," laughed the young man quite merrily, "surely you are not going to sprinkle that elaborate frill with snuff. Think, dad, the ladies, the ladies!"

"Go and have your havana," laughed Sir Philip. "I daresay the fresh air will take off the smell."

"You won't smoke, of course?" said Charley to his friends.

"O, no, not this morning, thank you," said one. "We'll pay attention to your boxes when we come back."

Charley nodded carelessly, strolled out in his wedding trim, stood upon the broad façade, and lit a cigar, and then walked slowly down towards the avenue.

"Mind, Charley, at half-past ten precisely. Don't forget the carriages!" cried Sir Philip, throwing up a window as his son passed.

"All right," said Charley quietly; and the next instant he had disappeared among the trees.

Chapter Ten
Not by Post

The sun shone brightly through the bare branches, and the soft blue vapour from Charley Vining's cigar floated upwards, but without poisoning the atmosphere, as red-hot opponents of tobacco—the disciples of the British Solomon, the counter-blaster—so strongly assert. In fact, Charley's pure havana was fragrant to inhale, and under its soft seductive influence the young man strolled on and on, forgetful of everything but the train of thought upon which his ideas were gliding back into the past.

For as he strolled onward, sending light cloud after light cloud to the skies, there came to him a sense of sadness that he could not control: Laura, the wedding, passed away as that fair reproachful face floated before him, the soft grey eyes fixed on his, and the white lips seeming to quiver and tremble. He tried angrily to crush it out from his mental sight; but its gentle appealing look disarmed his anger, and back came gently all that he had seen of her, all he had heard, all that she had said to him; and now, for the first time, he asked himself whether his eyes had not deceived him, whether it was possible that she, Ella, so pure, so holy, could have been the woman who hurried by, leaning upon Max Bray's arm.

Sorrow, sorrow, a strange feeling of regret, almost of repentance, seemed to come upon him, as for an instant he recalled the fact that this was his wedding-morn, that a great change was about to be made, and that henceforth even the right would not be his to dream upon the past. He felt then that he must dream upon it now by way of farewell; and again that soft, appealing, pleading face fleeted before him, so that a strange shiver, almost of fear, passed through his frame.

What did it mean? he asked himself. Was there such a thing among the hidden powers of nature as a means by which soul spake to soul, impressing it for good or bad, unless some more subtle power was brought to bear? If not, why did the past come before him as it did? for there again was that night when in the pleasant summer time he had told her of his love, and pressed upon her that rose.

Yes, but that was in the pleasant summer time, when there was a summer of hope and joy in his heart, when he believed that there was truth where he had found naught but falsity; while now it was winter, and all was cold and bleak and bare. He had been thoroughly awakened from his dream; but he would not blame her for what was but his own folly.

Heedless of wet grass and fallen leaves, he struck off now across the park, walking swiftly, as if seeking in exertion to tame the wild flow of his thoughts; and at last calm came once more, and after making a long circuit he entered the park avenue, intending to return to the house.

His cigar was extinct, and it was time now to return to life and action. He must dream no more.

Time? He drew out his watch, and a flush of shame and vexation crossed his countenance, as he saw that it was close upon the hour when he should be at the church.

"I must be mad!" he exclaimed; and then he started aside, as close behind came the sound of galloping hoofs from the direction of Lexville. "They are coming to seek the tardy bridegroom," he said with a little laugh; "but *she* will forgive me."

"Is this the way to the house—Mr Charles Vining's?" cried a voice roughly.

"Yes; what do you want?" said Charley. "I am Mr Vining."

"Letter, sir," said the man hastily. "I was to ride for life or death; and I was afraid I should be too late."

"Too late for what?" said Charley hastily.

"To catch you before you went to church, sir," said the man. "I heard as I came through that there was a wedding."

The next instant Charley had taken the letter, and was gazing at the direction; but he did not recognise the hand.

"Where do you come from?" he said. "Is it very important? I am engaged."

And then he stopped; for he hardly knew what he was saying, and he dreaded to open the letter.

"Better read and see, sir," said the man gruffly. "My horse is dead beat."

Rousing himself, he tore open the envelope, and read a few lines, reeled back on to the sward by the road, struggled to regain his firmness, and then, with a countenance white as ashes, he read to the end, when a groan tore its way from his breast.

That, then, was the meaning of the strange forebodings, of that soft pleading face; and now it was too late, too late!

"Curses, the bitterest that ever fell, be on them!" he muttered, grinding his teeth, and in his clenched fists that letter was crushed up to a mere wisp. "And now it is too late! No, not yet;" and to the surprise of the messenger he turned and dashed off furiously towards the house, where upon the broad entrance steps stood Sir Philip and the two friends anxiously awaiting him, the former watch in hand. The chariot with its four fine horses, and postillions in their gay new liveries of blue and silver, was at the door, and another open carriage behind; while a couple of servants were running at a distance in the park, evidently in search of him.

"My dear Charley, we shall be late," cried Sir Philip, as, wet and spattered with mud, his son dashed furiously up. "How you have excited yourself to get back! Pray make haste."

"Stand back!" cried Charley hoarsely, as, bounding up to the steps, he tore open the chariot-door and leaped in, dragging the door after him.

The next moment he had dashed down the front window, and shouted to the postillions to go on.

The men turned in their saddles, touched their caps, and before Sir Philip and his friends could recover from their surprise, the carriage was going down the avenue at a sharp trot.

"Poor boy, he was excited at being so late. Ah, to be sure, here's a messenger who has evidently come to seek him. It must be later than I thought, for our time must be slow. I must ride with you, gentlemen, instead of with him. Make haste, or we shall be too late."

In less than a minute the barouche was in motion, and as they passed the messenger, Sir Philip leaned over the carriage side, and shouted a question to the man:

"Did you bring a message for Mr Charles Vining?"

"Yes, sir," shouted the man in answer; and the next moment they were out of hearing.

"Good heavens, though," exclaimed Sir Philip anxiously, "look at him!" And at a turn of the road Charley could be seen in the distance leaning out of the carriage window, fiercely gesticulating to the postillions, who, apparently in obedience to his orders, had broken into a smart gallop, and the chariot was being borne through the lodge-gate at a rapid rate.

It was a two-mile ride to Lexville church, and as Sir Philip's carriage passed the lodge-gate in turn, he caught one more glimpse of the chariot ascending a hill in front, not at a moderate rate, but at a furious gallop, the vehicle swaying from side to side, till it crowned the hill and disappeared.

"I suppose it is excusable," said Sir Philip, turning pale with apprehension; "but what a pity that he should have gone out!"

Directly after, though, the old gentleman smilingly observed to his friends that they would only be in at the death; and then speaking to the coachman, that functionary applied his whip, and the horses went along at a brisk canter.

"More behind even than I thought for," said Sir Philip anxiously, as the carriage drew up to the churchyard gates, amidst a burst of cheering from the crowd, and then, smiling and raising his hat, Sir Philip walked up to the church, as there was a loud cry of "Here they are!" passed along the nave, entered the chancel, and taking Laura's hand in his, kissed it with a mingling of love and respect.

"But surely you have not got it over? Where is Charley?" exclaimed the old man.

It was Nelly who gave the sharp cry as he made the inquiry, while Laura stood the image of despair as a rumour ran through the church.

"Was he—was he in the chariot?" whispered Mr Bray, catching his old friend by the arm.

"Yes, yes; where is he," cried Sir Philip, trembling as he spoke.

"They say the horses must have taken fright and galloped away. The chariot dashed by here a few minutes ago; but they said it was empty."

"Mr Charles Vining in the carriage, and borne away at that mad rate!" was the whisper through the church, which soon did not contain a man who had not hurried down the road in the expectation of coming at every turn upon the wreck of Sir Philip Vining's chariot, with horses and men in a tangle of harness and destruction.

But before those on foot had gone far, they were passed by Sir Philip Vining and Mr Bray in the barouche; for they had hurried away from the scene in the church, where Laura was seated, pale, despairing and stony, Nelly sobbing violently, and a couple of bridesmaids had fainted.

"It all comes of having such horrible wild horses," said Mrs Lingon, whose conveyance was a basket carriage, drawn by a punchy cob, given to meditation and genuflections. "But there, I hope the poor young man isn't hurt; and on his wedding-morning, too!"

"Will you hold your tongue?" exclaimed Mrs Bray fiercely. "Do you think matters are not bad enough without prophesying ill? There, there, my darling, don't cry," she said softly the next moment to Nelly, who was sobbing convulsively, as she trembled for the fate of him whom she indeed loved as a dear brother. But at last the Reverend Mr Lingon and his aides appeared upon the scene, and pending the arrival of news, the wedding party were screened from curious eyes by the refuge offered to them in the vestry, till twelve o'clock striking, carriages were summoned, and, sad and disappointed, all returned to The Elms.

Chapter Eleven
In Chase

Those who ran off on foot, upon first seeing the carriage clash by, gave up after a two-mile race, and the most impetuous of them were standing at a corner when the barouche came in view.

"What is it? Have you seen them?" cried Sir Philip, who was standing up in front, and holding on by the driver's seat, directing him so that the horses were now arrested.

"No, Sir Philip," said one man, "they've gone right on ahead, but they were nearly over here." And he pointed to the wheel-marks, which, in the sudden curve, showed that the chariot must have torn round at a fearful rate; so swiftly, indeed, that the equilibrium had been destroyed, and the corner cleared only on two wheels.

"Drive on!" exclaimed Sir Philip Vining hoarsely. "Gallop!" And away sped the barouche for another mile along the unfrequented country road.

"Seen a carriage—Sir Philip's carriage and four?" shouted the coachman to a man driving a cart.

"Ah, raight on ahead, going full gallop," shouted the man in reply; and away once more sped the barouche, till white specks of foam began to appear upon the horses' glossy coats, to be succeeded by a lather wherever there was the play of rein or trace. Cart after cart was passed, and the same news was obtained of all, till, after a two-mile run without seeing any trace of vehicle or pedestrian of whom to inquire, a farmer's gig was overtaken.

"No, sir," was the reply; "I've seen no carriage but yours."

"Not one with four horses and postillions?" exclaimed Sir Philip.

"No, sir," said the fanner, "but you'd better not trust to me; I've not been long on this road."

"Drive on!" impatiently cried Sir Philip, who now became less agitated. Above four miles from Lexville, and no upset, there must have been time for the first heat of the excited beasts to cool down, and for the postillions to regain command over them; so that he was in momentary expectation of encountering the returning chariot; but still it did not appear.

"Should we be in time if we found him now?" exclaimed Sir Philip.

"What, to get back to the church?" said Mr Bray, nervously referring to his watch. "I fear not, I fear not."

"How unfortunate!" exclaimed Sir Philip; and then he relapsed into silence, save when at intervals he spoke to the coachman, who kept the well-bred pair of horses at a brisk gallop.

"Stop here," cried Sir Philip, as they neared a roadside inn, where a wagon and half a dozen labourers were standing, ready enough to stare at the rapidly-approaching vehicle.

"Carriage and four go by here a few minutes ago?" cried Sir Philip to the landlord, who now came bustling out.

"No, sir; not by here."

"Are you sure?" exclaimed Sir Philip, with a perplexed air.

"Sure, sir? O yes, sir, quite sure," said the landlord, "or must have seen it. We see everything that goes by here, sir.—Haven't seen a four-horse coach go by, have you, lads?" he continued, addressing the wagoners.

"No, no," cried Sir Philip. "A chariot with four horses and postillions— post-boys in bluejackets?"

"No, sir—no, sir—not come by here!" was chorused.

"We could not have passed them, upset in one of the ditches, could we?" hinted Mr Bray.

"Impossible!" cried Sir Philip. "But where could they have turned off?"

"Like to take the horses out and wait, sir? They may come soon," said the landlord.

"No, no, my man," hastily cried Sir Philip. "There is nowhere for a carriage to turn off from the high-road during these last two miles, is there?"

"Whoy yes, sur," said one of the wagoners, "there's Bogle's-lane as goes to Squire Lethbridge's fa-arm; and the low lane down by the beck."

"Ay, lad, and theer's ta by-ro-ad as goes to Bellby and La-a-anton."

"Laneton—Laneton?" Sir Philip exclaimed. "Here, my lads," he cried, and he threw two or three coins amongst the men. "To be sure! Turn back quick, William; they may have gone that way."

The coachman turned his panting horses, and they went back at a smart trot towards the by-lane mentioned, a good mile and a half back; while a flood of thought passed the while through Sir Philip's troubled brain.

"Laneton—Laneton! What could be the meaning of that? But absurd; the horses had taken fright and been turned up there. Of course, the lane would be very heavy at this time of the year, and it was done to tire out the horses. But then Mrs Brandon lived at Laneton. It was there that that interview took place with Miss Bedford. But absurd; Miss Bedford had left there for long enough, and no doubt they would find at the entrance of the lane that the carriage had turned down there, and now exhibited the back tracks. They had overshot the mark, and it was a great pity. It was unfortunate altogether, but one thing was evident: the wedding could not take place that day."

So mused Sir Philip, till, as they neared the narrow entrance that they had barely noticed, another troublous thought flashed upon his mind.

"Did you send a man on horseback from the church?" he asked eagerly of Mr Bray.

"Man on horseback?" said Mr Bray, looking confusedly up at where Sir Philip stood upon the front cushions.

"Yes, a messenger. Did you send one to the Court?"

"No," said Mr Bray decidedly.

"Did any one, then? do you know of one being sent?" exclaimed Sir Philip.

"No," said Mr Bray stoutly. "We sent no messenger."

What did it mean, then, that strange man on the panting horse, who had brought a message for his son? Something must, then, be wrong, and this was no accident.

"Gone down here, Sir Philip, after all," said the coachman, pointing with his whip, as he drew up at the entrance of the narrow lane.

"And come back again, have they not?" cried Sir Philip eagerly, peering down at the wheel-tracks in the hope of finding that in his own mind he had been raising up a bugbear of undefined shape and dread portent.

"No, Sir Philip, they ain't come back," said the coachman, turning his horses into the lane.

The carriage had to be driven here slowly through rut and hole, worn by the farmers' heavy wagons; but still at a good sharp trot where the road admitted, till a wagon blocked the way about a mile down, when a good deal of contriving had to be exercised for the two vehicles to pass.

"Did you see a carriage lower down?" asked Sir Philip of the wagoner.

"Ay, sur. A foine un it were, too: four bosses, and chaps in blue, and torsels in their caps. Passed me, ah, moren half an hour agoo."

"Were the horses running away asked?" Mr Bray, for Sir Philip was silent.

"Roonnin' awa-ay, sur? Noa, cos they had to wa-ait while I drawed up to ta hedgeside, for t' la-ane's narrerer lower deown."

"Go on, William!" said Sir Philip fiercely, for his suspicions were now assuming a bodily form; and it was with anger gathering in his breast that he sat there thinking—knowing, too, the goal to which to shape his course. But he said no word to Mr Bray, only sat down now, with his brow knit, as he felt the impossibility of overtaking the other carriage; but from time to time he started up impatiently, to urge the coachman to renewed efforts; so that whenever a plain hard piece of road presented itself, the horses appeared almost to fly.

Shame and disgrace seemed to Sir Philip to have marked him for their own; and he shrank from his companion, dreading, after awhile, to hear him speak; for his son's acts were as his own; nay, he felt that they would fall upon him more heavily. It was cruel, cruel, cruel; or was he mad? Impossible! But what could he do, what could he say?

"Wait awhile," he muttered at last; and then, starting up once more, he ordered the coachman to drive faster. And onward they tore, till the carriage jolted here and there, and the springs threatened to snap; but Sir Philip heeded nothing but his own thoughts, as his heart asked him where was his son. A question that he could have answered again and again, as his brow grew more deeply marked with the anger and shame that oppressed him; but he forbore.

"Quicker, William, quicker!" exclaimed Sir Philip at last; and the coachman lashed the horses into a gallop, but only to hasten the catastrophe that had been predicted for the chariot; for, as the horses sprang forward, and the barouche swayed again with the speed, there was a sharp crack, a swerve, a crash, and the handsome carriage was over, with the horses kicking madly, and the driver and occupants lying stunned and senseless in the muddy road.

Chapter Twelve
Going Back

As the old novelists used to say, in their courtly polished style, that makes us think that they must have written with a handsome bead-work presentation pen dipped in scented ink, and held by a delicate hand clothed in a white-kid glove, "Gentle reader, we must now return to our heroine."

In the plain English and more matter-of-fact way of the year of grace eighteen hundred and seventy, it is given to my hard steel broad-point to be dipped in the ordinary infusion of galls and copperas—rather bitty by the way, and given to turn mouldy—and then, when well-charged with the ink-rusting fluid to declare that we have a long arrear to fetch up relative to the proceedings of Ella Bedford, which could not well be told until the career of the two country families had reached the point recorded in the last chapter.

Ella's had been a weary life at Crescent Villas, and she had had much to contend with: the evil tempers of three spoiled children, who resented every word of correction, complained to their weak mother, and enlisted her sympathy; the pettish frivolous complaints of the lady herself; and the bitter knowledge that, according to all appearances, she was being made a screen for the foolish flirting attentions of Max Bray.

At one time she was under the impression that the attentions to Mrs Marter were an excuse for obtaining the entrée of the house; but the conduct of Max was so entirely different: he spoke to her so seldom, and then in so quiet and gentlemanly a tone, that, from being watchful and distant, Ella was at length completely thrown off her guard, though there seemed no occasion now for her to trouble herself respecting the visits paid to the house.

Vain to an excess, both Mr and Mrs Marter seemed to approve highly of the visits of so distinguished a leader of the fashion; but Mr Marter had his own ideas upon the subject, telling his lady that it would be a fine thing for Miss Bedford; whereupon the weak little woman nodded and smiled.

To use a very trite expression, there was not the slightest harm in Mrs Marter; but, all the same, she adored incense and the offerings of concert and opera tickets with an escort; when, had it not been for the said escort, she could not have gone, Mr Marter being a man without, so his lady said, a single taste; but all the same we must do Mrs Marter the credit of saying that she would not have stirred an inch to have seen the finest opera in the world without Ella Bedford was of the party; and hence it followed that, willing or no, Ella's visits to places of amusement were not very few.

But Ella was far from being at ease in her mind. She foresaw that the present state of things could not last; and during some capricious fit of Mrs Marter, when ill-temper, weakness, and petty annoyance were all employed to make her wretched, she would think that to stay out the year was a sheer impossibility. At such times, too, she would feel convinced that Max Bray was playing a part; so that, in spite of his distant respect, she became more cool and guarded in her behaviour; while, as to leaving, she determined to bear all, telling herself, with a feeling of something like despair, that, go where she would, she must be tracked. Then her thoughts turned on Charley Vining, whom she knew to have called; and, as she congratulated herself upon having escaped him—upon his having given up the quest in despair—the warm tears fell, and she knew in her heart of hearts that she was bitterly disappointed.

But it was quite right,—it was as matters should be, she thought; and she hastily dashed away the tears, little thinking that letter after letter had been sent to her, to be smiled over by Mrs Marter and Max, as the latter redirected them to the sender, telling Mrs Marter the while that she was doing an act of kindness and thoughtfulness towards the motherless girl looking to her for protection.

In fact, Max Bray most carefully flattered the self-esteem of Mrs Marter, till the foolish little woman felt herself to be a perfect paragon of matronly greatness and virtue. Mr Marter, too, was taken into their confidence upon this matter of Charley Vining's attentions to Ella.

"Of course, Mr and Mrs Marter, you can act as you please; for you see, bai Jove! it would ill become me to be offering advice upon such a matter; but for my part, I should never let him write to her, or see her for a moment. It's a great pity, bai Jove it is, that the young men of the present day have not better aspirations."

"Quite agree with you, Mr Bray—I do indeed!" said Mr Marter, while his lady smiled her approbation.

"You see, bai Jove! it hardly becomes me, as a near neighbour, to say anything against Vining: but I know as a fact that he worried the poor girl till she was obliged to leave Mrs Brandon's, the lady's, you know, where she went to last; and when a man has behaved, bai Jove! shabbily to another man's own sister, bai Jove! it's enough to make another man speak!"

"Very true, Mr Bray—very true. I quite agree with you," said Mr Marter, in a satisfied air.

"But, there, bai Jove! don't let me come hyar dictating to you. It's like my dooced confounded impudence to say a word. I'm only too grateful to find a welcome, and a little refined female society; for to a man situated as I am, London is a very dreary place. One can get amongst set after set of fellows, and into plenty of inane fashionable drawing-rooms; but, bai Jove! Mr Marter, that isn't the sort of thing, if I may be allowed to say so, that a man of soul thirsts after. He wants something to satisfy his brain—something that when he's spent an evening, he can go and lay his head down upon his pillow, bai Jove! and say to himself, 'Look here, bai Jove! old fellow: you've been out this evening; you've been in refined and improving society; and, bai Jove! here you are, just as you ought to be at the end of another day—a better man, bai Jove!'"

"Ah, Saint Clair," sighed Mrs Marter, "if you could only say that of a night!"

"To be sure," said Max, "mai dear fellow, you've no idea how much better you feel—you haven't indeed; but, bai Jove! we must change the conversation."

With all due modesty on his part, Max changed the conversation; for just then Ella, in obedience to orders, entered the room, playing pianoforte piece after piecer till the hour for Mr Bray's departure, when—was she deceived? or was that a quiet firm pressure of the hand he was bestowing upon her at parting?

The next minute he had gone, and Ella felt a strange shiver pass through her; for if there had been any mistake about the pressure of the hand, there could have been none concerning the look which followed.

"Bai Jove!" ejaculated Max, as he sought a cab on his departure, "how confoundedly slow! But it's nearly ripe at last!"

Then to make up for the slowness, Max Bray had himself driven to a highly genteel tavern in Saint James's, where the society was decidedly fast; so that, on returning about three to his apartments, and laying his head upon his pillow, the slow and the fast society must have balanced one another; for he snored very pleasantly, no doubt feeling a better man, bai Jove!

Chapter Thirteen
Rather Close

"Bai Jove, Mrs Marter, it does a man good to see you," said Max Bray, sauntering one afternoon into the Marter drawing-room, carefully dressed, as a matter of course, and with a choice Covent-garden exotic in his buttonhole. "I declare it makes one quite disgusted with the flowers one buys, it does, bai Jove!" and then showing his white teeth, he raised her hand, touched the extreme tips of her nails with his lips, and then resigned the hand, which fell gracefully upon the side of the couch. "Bai Jove, Marter, I envy you—I do, bai Jove! You're one of the lucky ones of this earth, only you don't know it: feast of reason, flow of soul, and all that sort of thing's blooming, if I may say so, upon your own premises."

"I'm sure," simpered Mrs Marter, "there ought to be a new official made at the palace—Court flatterer—and Mr Bray given the post."

"Wouldn't be amiss, if there was a good salary," said Mr Marter, looking up from his newspaper.

"Bai Jove, now, that's too bad—'tis indeed, bai Jove! There are some of you people get so hardened by contact with the world, that, bai Jove! you've no more faith in a fler's sincerity than if there wasn't such a thing to be found anywhere."

"O! but," simpered Mrs Marter, "do you think we can't tell when you are sincere?"

"Bai Jove, no!" said Max earnestly, and with a wonderful deal of truth. "But look here: I've got tickets for Her Majesty's to-night—three, you know—for *La Figlia*. You'll go, of course, Marter?"

"Go to an opera!" said Mr Marter, with a shake of the head. "I never go to operas—I only go to sleep."

"O, bai Jove! that's too bad!" cried Max. "You've never been with us anywhere yet; and I do think you ought to go for once in a way."

"No, I sha'n't go!" said Mr Marter; "and besides, I have promised to dine out. Take Miss Bedford."

"Bother Miss Bedford! Bai Jove, one can't stir without your governess. I say, Marter, do go!"

"Can't, I tell you; and, besides, I shouldn't go, if I had no engagement," said Mr Marter testily. "You three can go if you like."

Max Bray seemed rather put out by the refusal, and for a time it almost appeared as if he were about to throw the stall tickets behind the fire; but by degrees he cooled down, and after it had been decided that he was to call for the ladies about half-past seven, he rose to leave.

"But why not have an early dinner here?" said Mr Marter.

"No, bai Jove, no!" said Max. "I'm always here; and besides, I've some business to attend to. Till half-past seven, then—*au revoir*."

Max kissed the tips of his gloves to Mrs Marter as he left the room; and soon after he was being driven to his chambers, where he wrote a long letter to Laura, sent it by special messenger, and then sat impatiently waiting for an answer, gnawing his nails the while.

The reply came at last, very short and enigmatical, but it was sufficient to make him draw a long breath, as if of satisfaction, though the words were only—

"*Yes! No more; for we are going out.*"

Then Max Bray lit a cigar, and sat thinking over the events of the past few days, and of what he had done. He had been several times to the Marters'; he had run down, on the previous day, to Lexville; and a couple of days before that he had posted a letter, the reply to which he now anxiously awaited.

What time would it come? He kept referring to his watch, and then he went over and over again the arrangements for some project he evidently had in view, before sauntering off to his club and dining; when, to his great delight, upon his returning to dress for the evening's engagement, he found a couple of letters awaiting him, one of which he tore open, and then threw into the fire with an impatient "Pish!" the other he took up and examined carefully, reading the several postmarks, and then, smiling as he glanced at the round legal writing, placed it unopened in his breast-pocket.

There was a strange exultant look in Max Bray's eye as he drew on his white-kid gloves that evening, and started for the residence of Mrs Saint Clair Marter, where he found the ladies ready, and did not scruple to behave almost rudely to Ella as he prepared to take them down, hardly condescending to speak to her; but as the evening wore on, and they were seated in front of the orchestra, he condescended to make to her a few remarks, more than one of which drew forth a smile, from their satirical nature, as, evidently in a bitter spirit, he drew attention to the various eccentricities of dress in their neighbourhood.

Max Bray did not know, though, that within a few yards sat the man whom he had again and again maligned; neither did Ella Bedford divine that a pair of blood-shot eyes were gazing upon her almost fiercely, as she turned from time to time to respond to the remarks of Max, who talked on, till, towards the end of the opera, he stood up to direct his opera-glass here and there, for indulgence in that graceful, truly refined, nineteenth-century act, so much in vogue at the higher-class places of entertainment.

He had tried in three or four different directions; but, perhaps from being in a satirical mood, he did not see a single face to attract his attention, till, concluding with a grand sweep of the best tier, he suddenly stopped short, kept the glass tightly to his eyes, whisked round swiftly, and sat down; for the field of the glass had for the moment been filled by the figures of Mrs Bray and Sir Philip Vining.

"Bai Jove!" muttered Max to himself; and had Charley Vining and Laura been there all the evening, close behind him? They must have been, and be sitting now at the back of the private box. Bai Jove! what should he do? It was horrible to have gone so far—so near—and then to have all spoiled! What an ass he must have been! Laura had said that they were going out; but who would have thought that they were coming here?

Max sat rigidly still for the rest of the evening, encouraging Mrs Marter to stay through the ballet; and at last, cautiously peering round, he found, to his great satisfaction, that the private box occupied by the Brays was empty.

Ella had not seen who was so near, for she was calm and unmoved.

"Bai Jove, what an escape!" thought Max; and a cold chill ran through him—one that would have been more icy, had he known how close they had been to a *rencontre*. But there was still another peril—Charley Vining might be waiting yet, and she would see him!

They reached the fly, however, uninterrupted, and Max Bray's spirits rose; but, though he stayed to a late meal—half-tea, half-supper—at Crescent Villas, he was more distant than ever in his behaviour to Ella—so distant, indeed, that Mrs Marter was half-disposed to ask him if Miss Bedford had given him any offence.

It was past one when Max departed; and, hardly knowing why, Ella went to her bed that night tearful and sad, little thinking that it was a pillow she would never again press.

Chapter Fourteen
The Bearer of Tidings

Nine o'clock the next—or rather, by the way in which we calculate time, calling by the same title the hours of obscurity and those of sunshine, the same—morning, Mr and Mrs Marter were not down, nor likely to be for some time; but Ella was just rising from the schoolroom breakfast-table, where she had partaken of a pleasant meal of extremely weak tea, sweetened with moist sugar of a fine treacley odour, and thick bread, plastered with rank, tubby, salt butter. The meal had gone off more quietly than usual,—no one had upset any tea, neither had the youngest child turned her delicate hand and arm, as was much her custom, into a catapult, for the purpose of hurling bread-and-butter at her sisters. Certainly, this young lady had made one snatch at the butter, lying lumpy and yellow upon a plate, and had succeeded in grasping it, as was shown by the traces of her fingers; but when admonished therefor, and threatened with long tasks, she had only howled for five minutes, and had not, as was her wont, thrown herself upon her back upon the floor, and screamed until she was black in the face.

"Mr Bray wants to see you, miss," said a housemaid, entering the schoolroom, the footman not being dressed at so early an hour.

"To see me?" ejaculated Ella.

"Yes, miss; he says he wants to see *you* pertickler, and he's now waiting in the dining-room."

"Is Mrs Marter down yet?" said Ella, troubled at this unusual call, and at such a strange hour.

"No, miss; nor won't be for long enough."

"Ask Mr Bray if he would be kind enough to call again at twelve," said Ella, after a few moments' thought. "I am engaged now with the children."

"Yes, miss," said the girl; and she departed, to return at the end of five minutes, with a card bearing in pencil:

"If you value your peace of mind, come to me. I have a letter for you from the country. A case of life or death!"

"Mrs Brandon must be ill," thought Ella; and hurriedly leaving the room, she stood the next minute face to face with Max, who was very pale, as he respectfully held out his hand, which was, however, unnoticed.

"Miss Bedford," he said softly, "I fear that my visits have always been associated with that which was to you unpleasant, from the fact, though, that you did not know my real nature. This visit will, I fear, be only another that shall add to the dislike you entertain for me, but which of late you have so kindly disguised."

Ella did not speak, but stood watching him eagerly.

"You know I was late home last night. I found there this letter, delivered evidently by the late post, and you will guess my emotion when you read it. I came back here; but I could not get a cab, and it was half-past two when I reached the house. If I had roused you, nothing could have been done, while now a calm night's rest has made you better prepared. So I returned to lie down upon the sofa for a few hours' rest, meaning to be here as soon as the house was opened; but—I am almost ashamed to tell it—I slept heavily from the effects of my long walk, and did not wake till eight. Can you bear to read it?" he said gently.

"Yes, yes," cried Ella huskily; and she took a formal-looking letter, that had evidently been hurriedly torn open. She glanced at the address— to "Maximilian Bray, Esq., 109 Bury-street, Saint James's, London." The postmark, two days old, Penzance, while the London mark was of the day before. "Am I to read this?" she said, without raising her eyes.

"Yes," he said gently; and he turned away from her, but only to go to the mantelpiece and cover his eyes with his hands, where it was quite possible that he might have been able to see, by means of the mirror, every act of the trembling girl.

Ella drew out a folded letter from the envelope, when a smaller one fell to the ground, addressed to her in the same hand as that in which the larger letter was written.

The characters seemed to run together as she opened this second envelope, took out a little folded note in another hand, read it, and then for a few moments the room seemed to swim round. But by an effort she mastered her emotion, re-read the note, and then hastily perused the letter through and through before doubling both together, and standing white and trembling, clutching the papers tightly as she gazed straight before her at vacancy.

There was no cry, no display of wild excitement; nothing but those white quivering lips and the drawn despairing look, to show the agony suffered by that heart, till she started back, as it were, into life, when Max turned softly and stood before her.

"Miss Bedford," he said gently, "I will not trouble you with words of commiseration. I must go now to make preparations."

"Preparations?" she said, as if not understanding his remark.

"Yes; preparations. I telegraphed to Lexville as I came; and now I must go, for I shall run down by the express. There will be no time saved if I start earlier."

"You are going?" said Ella dreamily.

"Yes," he said almost angrily, "of course! Do you take me to be utterly devoid of feeling? But you will write, and I will be the bearer."

"Write!" said Ella, with a wild hysterical sob—"write!"

"Yes. Surely you will do that," he said anxiously.

"Heaven help me!" cried Ella. "I must go."

"You will go?" he said excitedly.

"Yes," she said, with a strange dreamy look; "it is my fate. I must go."

"Ella—Miss Bedford—will you trust me?" said Max in an earnest voice. "Leave matters to me, and I will arrange all. But Mrs Marter will object to your leaving."

"I must go," said Ella, who seemed to be speaking as if under some strange influence.

"You will go in spite of her wishes?" said Max.

"Yes, yes; I must go," said Ella huskily; and raising her hands to her face, she would have left the room.

Chapter Fifteen
Hovering round the Snare

"Stop, stop!" said Max hoarsely. "We must have no scene with that weak woman. I will be in waiting by the park entrance of the Colosseum with a cab at four. Meet me there. The train leaves Paddington at 4:50. But do you hear me?"

"Yes," she said, speaking as if in a dream.

"Do you understand? At the Colosseum at four, without fail."

"Yes," said Ella again abstractedly, as he held her cold hand in his, her face being turned towards the door.

"But mind this," he said, "this is no time for child's-play. If you are not there soon after the time named, I must catch the train, and I dare not wait. If you are not there, I go alone!"

"Do you think I could fail?" said Ella, turning upon him her sweet candid countenance. "I will be there."

Was Max Bray ashamed of his face, that he held it down as he hurried from the house? Perhaps not; but he was evidently much excited, for he muttered half aloud, as if running over certain plans that he had arranged for a particular end.

"Could it be right? Was it all true?" Ella asked herself, when alone in her bedroom, with the sense of a deep unutterable misery crushing her; and once more she read the letters she had retained.

"O yes, it was too true, too true! But what was she about to do? To accompany the man she mistrusted, the man she dreaded? He had been trusted, though, before now; and of late, too, his conduct had been so different—he had even seemed to dislike her. Still, under any other circumstances, she would not have gone; but at such a time, in answer to such an appeal, how could she stay?"

Her brain was in a whirl, and she could not reason quietly. She only knew now the depth of love she felt, and urged by that love, everything else seemed little and of no import.

Hours must have passed, when, after sending twice to Mrs Marter, she received that lady's gracious permission to wait upon her.

"I should have sent for you before long—as soon as I felt that I could bear it, Miss Bedford," said Mrs Marter—"to demand some explanation of your receiving visitors early in the morning without my consent. I understand that somewhere about seven o'clock—"

"I believe the clock had struck nine," said Ella quietly.

"Seven, or eight, or nine, or ten, it's all the same!" exclaimed Mrs Marter angrily. "Pray, Miss Bedford, what did Mr Bray want here this morning? Was it supposed that I should not know of the visit?"

"Mr Bray came to tell me of the illness of a very dear friend," said Ella pitifully; "and now I come to ask your consent to absent myself for a few days."

"Of course, I might have known that that was coming! Certainly not, Miss Bedford! And until I have communicated with Mrs Brandon, I desire you do not leave the house. What next, I wonder?"

"Mr Bray brought me letters. It is a matter of life and death!" said Ella earnestly. "Surely, madam, in such a case you will not refuse me?"

"And pray who is it that is ill?" said Mrs Marter sneeringly.

Ella was silent. She could not have spoken then, in spite of every effort, even to have saved her life.

"I can see through it all! I am not blind!" exclaimed Mrs Marter. "I shall certainly not give my consent, Miss Bedford. It is a planned affair, and I have been deceived. Now leave the room."

Ella would have spoken, but she felt that it would have been without avail; and hurrying out, she once more sought her own chamber.

What did Mrs Marter mean? What was planned? Impossible! She had the proof in those letters. And once more she read them with beating heart before asking herself whether she would be doing right or wrong.

What had she promised? To meet Max Bray at four—to trust herself to his guidance. What had she to fear? Surely scheming baseness could never go so low! But it was absurd! She had those letters, and did she not know the handwriting?

She examined her purse. The store was slender, but not so small as of old. Then she prepared a few necessaries in a small travelling-bag before referring again and again to the time, which seemed to lag slowly by, as she pictured scene after scene of misery and death, till she seated herself at a table, and rested her aching throbbing brow upon her hands.

About two o'clock a message came from Mrs Marter to know why she did not attend the young ladies' dinner; when, starting up, she descended, matters of the present having quite escaped her in the rush of terrible thoughts which swept through her brain.

She went through her duties mechanically, hurrying back as soon as she possibly could to her room, and dressed for a journey; when standing, bag in hand, ready, and waiting for the appointed hour, now very near at hand, a strange nervous dread began to oppress her—a cold shivering sense of evil, which made her hands feel damp and cold, and her lips hot, parched, and dry.

Twenty times over she was about to tear off her things and give up, but her hand seemed to go mechanically to her breast, when a touch of those letters strengthened her resolve. She felt then that she must go—something was drawing her that she could not resist. But again began the shrinking, and each time to be struggled with till the dread was beaten; and at last, waking from a wild, nervous, excited struggle between strength and indecision, Ella found that the hour was long past, and, bag in hand, she fled down the stairs.

"Miss Bedford—Miss Bedford!" screamed a passionate voice as she passed the drawing-room. But, with face pale and eyes fixed, Ella seemed to be walking in her sleep, or labouring under the stupor produced by some narcotic; for she passed on, heedless of the call—one hand holding the travelling-bag, the other clasping the letters, which acted as a talisman to nerve her in each sore time of shrinking.

The poison was working well. But in the passage she stayed for an instant, hesitating. What step was she taking? Where would this end?

A cold shudder passed through her; but once more she was drawn on against her will, her better sense, and the powers that should have withheld her.

Another moment and her hand was on the fastening of the door; and for the last time she paused, hung back for an instant, and would have returned, when her hand again pressed the letters. She uttered a feeble wailing cry as her lips formed a name, and then, opening the door, she stood upon the steps as if hesitating; but the portal swung to, and fastened itself with a loud snap; and fully feeling now that she had taken the step, she drew down her veil and hurried over the distance that lay between her and the Colosseum, suffering from a new dread.

The step taken, she felt now nerved for any contingency, and recalling Max Bray's words, she reproached herself for her delay.

What had he said? If she were not there, he would go alone!

She almost ran now over the pathway till she caught sight of a cab.

Was that the one, or had he gone? Was she too late?

Yes, she was too late, she told herself, for he was not there; but the next moment, giddy with excitement, she felt her hand seized, the bag taken from her, the banging of a cab-door; when, as a voice exclaimed, "At last!" there was a noise of wheels, and she felt that she was being hurried through the streets.

Chapter Sixteen
In the Gin of the Fowler

"I was afraid that you would not come, Miss Bedford," said Max respectfully. "You look pale and ill."

Ella could not answer, when, seeing her agitation, her companion forbore to speak, but kept on consulting his watch. Now he pulled down the front window to tell the driver to hasten; now he drew it up again, but only five minutes after, to tell the man to slacken his pace, till, apparently annoyed at the interruptions, the driver settled down into a quiet regular trot, out of which neither the threats nor exhortations of his fare could move him.

In one of his movements, Max dropped a note from his breast-pocket, as he knocked down Ella's reticule, which flew open; but gathering up the escaped contents, he replaced them for her, and with them his own letter, when closing the snap, he handed the reticule back to her, saying, "There is nothing lost, Miss Bedford."

He was quite right; but for Ella there was much gained.

"We shall lose the train!" now exclaimed Max excitedly. "Bai Jove, we shall! and when one had got so near too!"

Then he once more shouted at the driver to hasten; but in vain. At last, though, as they reached Paddington, Max referred again to his watch, his face flushing the while with excitement, as he exclaimed, "We shall be just right, after all!"

Then, in what seemed a dream of excited haste, Ella felt herself dragged from the cab—there was the loud ringing of a bell; the rattling of money; Max's voice adjuring the porter to hasten with their little luggage; and then, profoundly ignorant that Charley Vining was within a few yards, Ella felt herself half lifted into a first-class carriage, where she sank back amongst the cushions as the door banged; and, as if to increase her giddiness, the train glided past walls, empty carriages, signal-posts, engine-houses, and then over a maze of switches and points—farther and farther each moment, off and away with a wild scream down the main line.

"Hard fought for, but gained!" muttered Max Bray, as he stooped down to conceal the look of triumph which overspread his countenance; and in that attitude he remained for fully half an hour, when, carefully arranging rug and wrapper for his companion's comfort, he once more leaned back, drew forth a paper, and answering one or two attempts made by fellow-passengers to commence conversation with a bow of the head, he appeared to read.

And for Ella?

Giddiness and excitement, the rattle of the train, the flashing of the lights of stations they dashed by as night came on, and then a stoppage, and a voice called out, "Reading!" Then on again, giddiness and excitement and the rattle of the train seeming to form itself into one deep voice, the burden of whose song was always telling her to hasten onward, till in the dim light of the ill-lit carriage, she felt ready at times to start forward and ask if any one had called. Then it seemed in the darkness as if the train was rapidly going back, at a time when she was hungering to get to her journey's end.

Max sat back, silent and thoughtful, opposite to her, apparently without taking the slightest heed; but once or twice it seemed to her that she caught sight of a flashing eye.

There were two more passengers in the same compartment; but after the first attempt at conversation, they subsided into their corners, and not a word was spoken.

Another slackening of the swift express, after thundering along for another many miles' run, and still Ella feared no evil; but as Max roused himself and threw aside wrappers, she evinced her readiness to follow him.

"Swindon!" he said. "Just upon seven. We had better have a little refreshment here, for it is one of the best places we shall pass till we get to Exeter at 10:20. Take my arm, Miss Bedford?"

"Thank you," said Ella; "but I cannot I would rather not have any refreshment."

"It is absolutely necessary," he said firmly. "You have a very long journey before you, and unless you prepare for it, you will be totally unfit to get through it all. Let me draw this closer round your throat."

Quiet gentlemanly attentions, kind consideration, great respect. Was this the Max Bray of old? Ella was ready to ask herself, as she suffered him to draw her cloak more tightly round her; and then, taking advantage of the ten minutes' law allowed, he pressed upon her refreshments, every mouthful of which was as gall and ashes between her lips.

More giddiness and excitement, the clanging of a bell, and they were once more in their places. There was the guard's shrill whistle, the engine's shriek, and then again the rattle of the train forcing itself into adjuring words, bidding her "hasten on—hasten on!" or she would be too late; and then out once more in the darkness, rushing on with a wild thundering speed, away dashed the train, whirling up dust, dead leaf, or scrap of straw, and casting each fragment away, as the very earth quivered beneath the weight of the huge load. And still again came that strange sense of the engine now standing still, now reversing its action, so that they were hurrying once more back towards town.

"Hasten on—hasten on! Too late—too late!" The words kept repeating themselves to her excited imagination; and to relieve herself from the apprehensive feelings engendered, she tried to gaze out of the window; but all was darkness. She glanced round the compartment. The two passengers were evidently asleep, and for the first time now since they had started, a shiver of dread came over her, as her eyes rested for a moment on Max, who, leaning back, silent and reserved, was evidently watching her every movement.

But she drove away the fancy that troubled her, and sat trying to picture the scene she would soon be called upon to witness, and a sigh of misery and despair tore from her breast.

And still on and on, hour after hour, till, well on their journey, Exeter was reached. A five minutes' stay made, and then they glided out of the great station, and into the darkness once more. Half-past ten now, and nearly two more hours to travel before Plymouth would be reached—the extent of their journey for that night.

There were three other passengers in the train this time; but a movement upon the part of Max Bray now troubled her. It was a mere trifle, but the slightest act was likely to arouse her distrust; and, as he changed his seat from opposite to her side, she involuntarily shrank away, when he immediately returned, folded his arms, and sat watching her.

And now more than ever came upon her the thoughts of the extent of the step she had taken, oppressing her terribly, till, as if seeking relief, she began to repeat the words of the letter placed in her hands that day.

Chapter Seventeen
Aid Where Unexpected

"Hasten on—hasten on!" The rattle of the train still repeating those words, and Ella's heart sinking, as they sped through the darkness; for still, in spite of her struggle with reason, it would seem as if they were ever going back. Her brain seemed at times unable to support the stress placed upon it—the excitement more than she could bear.

She gazed out upon the black night, but only to see in the dim breath-blurred glass the interior of the carriage reproduced, with the dark-blue cloth padding, the silent passengers, the globe lamp, and Max Bray seated opposite, with his eyes glittering as if ready to spring at her each instant. She could at any moment have succumbed, become weak and helpless, and trembled at her forlorn condition; but the brave spirit held up, although incipient fever was claiming her for its own, and a strange unnatural throbbing in the pulses of her temple told where the peril lay.

Plymouth at last!—the train's resting-place for the night; and again quiet and thoughtful, Max engaged a fly, wrapper and luggage were placed therein, and, quiet and gentlemanlike, he talked to her till they reached one of the principal hotels, where Ella gladly sought her chamber, and tried to find in sleep the relief from the mental strain she so sadly needed.

But all through the early hours of that wintry morning came to torture her the endless repetition of those words: "Hasten on—hasten on!" while her burning head seemed chained to the pillow by links heated to redness.

Again and again she started up, to gaze round the dark room, thinking that a voice whose tones she so well remembered was calling her; but, with a sigh, she sank back once more, to doze and listen in her sleep to the endless warning, "Hasten on—hasten on!"

She descended to breakfast pale, restless, and excited. She could not eat, though pressed again and again by Max, who was gentle and attentive, asking with every show of consideration respecting her health.

"I have made all arrangements and inquiries," he said, "and been down to the station this morning. Our train leaves at ten."

"Not till ten?" she said in a disappointed tone.

He smiled as he drew forth his watch.

"It is half-past nine now," he said. "We have only time to get comfortably down to the station."

Ella rose and left the room, to return in a few minutes ready to continue the journey; but during her absence, Max had placed a letter in the waiter's hand, with an accompanying half-sovereign.

"To be posted in a week's time," were the instructions.

"More wrecks down in the bay," said Max, as Ella re-entered the room. "It has been a sad winter!"

"Let us—let us—hasten on," she said with an effort; and leading her out, they were soon in the station, and secured their seats in an empty compartment, where Ella took her place by the window, to gaze abstractedly out at the damp sodden landscape for quite an hour.

"Have we far to go now?" she asked of Max, who sat watching her.

"Not much farther," he said.

And again she asked that question at the end of an hour, and of another hour, but always to receive the same answer.

"Is it not less than a hundred miles from Plymouth to Penzance?" she at length asked uneasily.

"Yes," he said; "but you are travelling now upon a line of rail where stoppages are frequent and there is no speed. Bai Jove, though, they ought to be prosecuted for dawdling so."

Max smiled as he said those words, for his plan was nearly ripe; and that smile was not lost upon his companion. But she said nothing, only sat there pale, excited, and watchful till another hour had elapsed, during which time the well-fee'd guard had not intruded another passenger.

But this could not last for ever. One moment silent and watchful, the next moment with the full conviction of how she had been betrayed upon her, Ella Bedford sprang up and tried to open the door, the train dashing along at the rate of forty miles an hour.

There was a strong pair of hands upon her wrists, though, in an instant, and she was forced back into her seat.

"Silly child!" exclaimed Max, with an insolent laugh. "What are you going to do?"

"We are going back!" exclaimed Ella, struggling to free herself.

"Well, not exactly," he said, laughing, and now throwing off all disguise.

"Where are you taking me?" she exclaimed.

"O, only into North Wales, my trembling little dove," laughed Max, as he held his captive firmly in her place. "Now look here, little one: every dog has his day. It is mine now, and I mean to make use of it. You have braved and jilted me long enough, and it is my turn now. There, you need not struggle; it is of no use. Let's quietly look at the state of affairs. What have you done? Well, you've made an excuse to Mrs Marter, something about going to see a sick friend, and, bai Jove—not to put too fine a point on it—you have eloped with me, Maximilian Bray. I've no doubt our dear friend Mrs Marter has sent word of it to Mrs Brandon by this time. Mrs Brandon will tell the Brays of Lexville, when Mrs Bray will be shocked, and my beloved papa will no doubt leave me his curse; but, all the same, the Vinings will hear all about it. My plan took a long time hatching, but, now it is hatched, it cuts double-edged."

"Will you loose my wrists?" cried Ella faintly, "or am I to call for assistance?"

"O, call if you like, my love; bai Jove, as much as you like! only you may save yourself the trouble, for no one will hear you. What!" he cried, laughing, "can the little gentle dove turn savage, and ruffle her plumes and peck? Come, now, what is the use of being vicious? You have thrown away that delicate little gossamer dress that ladies call fame, so why not say pleasantly, 'My dear Maximilian, let us be married at once, and live happy ever after'? No, it's of no use; you are not going to jump out on to the line to be broken up, I value you too much; and as I told you before, it is of no use to scream. There's no dear Charley Vining to come to your help, for he is too busy with his *fiancée*, my sweet sister Laura. Now, come, sit still and listen. Are you going to be reasonable? It's of no use to be angry because I brought you off so cleverly; and bear in mind that I have been waiting months upon months, with the patience of half-a-dozen Jobs, to bring this plan from the most raw sourness to full ripening. Confound the girl! how strong she is! Bai Jove, Ella, you are a little Tartar!"

Max Bray had talked on, and part of what he had said was understood; but no explanation was needed. Ella Bedford knew one thing—that she had been cruelly betrayed, and that she was in the hands of a brutal heartless libertine, who, under the guise of a gentleman, possessed a nature blacker than that of the lowest rough in London.

He spoke on, holding her wrists pinioned as he did so; but despair and the fever fire in her blood gave her strength, and twice over it was only by a desperate struggle that he was able to prevent her from dashing herself through the open window.

She did not cry out, feeling that it would be useless; but her struggles to escape from his pinioning hands were frantic, till there came a warning shriek from the engine. The train drew up at a platform, and as Max started back into his seat, the carriage-door opened, and Ella Bedford fainted.

"Taken ill," said Max in explanation. "Half mad, bai Jove! Hard work to keep her from dashing out of the window. Most painful thing."

"Friend or stranger?" said the newcomer, suspiciously watching the countenance of Max.

"Friend or stranger!" said Max. "Bai Jove, that's cool. My wife—travelling for pleasure."

"I beg pardon, I'm sure," said the stranger; "but I should certainly alight at the next station. Your pleasure-travel is over, sir, and you must get all the medical aid you can, for your lady is in a high state of fever."

"Fever!" cried Max, involuntarily shrinking.

"Yes," said the other, with a look of contempt. "But you need not fear, sir; I should say it is the brain. The lady has evidently suffered from some severe mental strain."

"Bai Jove!" ejaculated Max; "are you a doctor?"

"No, sir; only an old Indian officer; but I have seen sufficient illness to know a case of fever when I see one."

"Bai Jove!" exclaimed Max again; and then he sat helpless and frowning, while the stranger laid back the poor girl's head that she might breathe more freely, and half supported her till they reached the next stopping station, where she was transferred to a fly, and conveyed, under the care of Max Bray, to the nearest hotel.

There is no difficulty in obtaining a doctor in a country town, and it was not long before one was by the sofa upon which Ella had been laid.

"Well," said Max, after five minutes' examination, "what's to be done?"

"Send for a nurse, and have Mrs—Mrs—I beg pardon, what name did you say?"

"Williams," said Max.

"To be sure—Williams," said the doctor; "and let Mrs Williams be at once conveyed to bed. She will have to be carefully tended and watched."

"Fit to travel again to-morrow, I suppose?" said Max. "Come, now, no professional dodging."

"To-morrow two months," said the doctor sharply, "perhaps;" and then he looked anything but pleasantly at Max.

"What!" exclaimed Max viciously. "Bai Jove, you don't mean that!"

"I mean, sir," said the doctor seriously, "that your lady is in a dangerous state, and I would not answer for her life if she were moved. I'll do my best, and we must be hopeful for what is to follow."

"Bai Jove!" ejaculated Max, as he left the room; and sympathising hands were soon busy with the insensible form.

"Mrs Williams, eh?" said the doctor to himself, as he superintended a portion of the arrangements; and then left to get some medicine made up. "Mrs Williams, eh? But, poor child, she does not travel in her wedding-ring!"

Chapter Eighteen
An Overtaxed Brain

"It was dooced unfortunate, bai Jove!" Max Bray said to himself, as he sat over his dinner at the snug little hotel at the end of the third day. He could not think what the foolish girl wanted to excite herself for to such an extent. It was absurd, "bai Jove, it was!" But his plan had answered all the same, and he'd wait till she got well, if it were a month first—he would, "bai Jove!" She'd come round then, with a little quiet talking to; and, after all, they were snug and out of sight in the little town, and nobody knew them, nor was likely to know them, that was the beauty of it. Certainly he could not get his letters; but that did not matter: they were sure to be all dunning affairs, and he'd not the slightest wish to have them. The only thing he regretted was not hearing from Laura.

One thing, he said, was very evident—Ella must have been ill when they started, or this attack would never have come on so suddenly.

And all this while, burning with fever, Ella Bedford lay delirious, and with a nurse at her bedside night and day. The doctor was unremitting in his attention, and was undoubtedly skilful; but he soon found that all he could do was to palliate, for the disease would run its course. The place they were in was fortunately kept by a quiet old couple, whose sympathies were aroused by the sufferings of the gentle girl; and though, as a rule, sick visitors are not welcomed very warmly at hotels, here Ella met with almost motherly treatment.

Doctor, nurse, landlady—all had their suspicions; but the ravings of a fever-stricken girl were not sufficient warranty for them to do more than patiently watch the progress of events, and at times they anticipated that the end would be one that they could not but deplore.

For Ella indeed seemed sick unto death, and lay tossing her fevered head on the pillow, or struggled to get away to give the help that she said was needed of her.

"Hasten on, hasten on!" Those words were always ringing in her ears, and troubling her; and then she would start up in bed, press her long glorious hair back from her burning temples, and listen as if called.

Then would come a change, and she would be talking to an imaginary flower, as she plucked its petals out one by one, calling each petal a hope or aspiration; whispering too, at times, in a voice so low that it was never heard by those who bent over her, what seemed to be a name, while a smile of ineffable joy swept over her lips as she spoke.

Once more, though, those words, "Hasten on, hasten on!" repeated incessantly as she struggled to free herself from the hands that held her to her bed.

"Let me go to him," she whispered softly once to her nurse. "He is dying, and he calls me. Let me see him once, only for a few minutes, that I may tell him how I loved him, before he goes. Please let me go!" she said pitifully, clasping her hands together; "just to see him once, and then I will go away—far away—and try to be at peace."

"My poor child, yes," sobbed the landlady. "I fear you will, and very soon too. But does she want him from downstairs? I'll go and fetch him up."

The landlady descended, to find Max, as usual, smoking, and told him of what had passed.

"Bai Jove, no! I won't come up, thanks. I'm nervous, and have a great dread of infection, and that sort of thing."

"But 'tisn't an infectious disorder, sir," said the landlady; "and I'm afraid, sir, that if you don't come now—"

"Eh, what? I say, bai Jove, you don't mean that it's serious!" exclaimed Max excitedly. "There's no danger of *that*, is there?"

The landlady smoothed down her apron with a solemn look in her face; then left the room, with genuine tears of sorrow stealing down her cheeks.

"Poor young creature!" she sighed. "Such a mere girl too!"

And then she hurried back to the sick-chamber, to find Ella lying back in a state of exhaustion.

Another day, another, and another, with life seeming to hang as by a thread; while Max, strictly avoiding the sick-chamber, waited anxiously for the result; for this was an accident upon which, with all his foresight, he had not calculated. But he could obtain no comfort from doctor or nurse. Their looks grew more and more ominous, and at last he began to calculate upon what would be his position, should the worst come to the worst. Certainly, he had by deception—a stratagem, he termed it—induced Ella Bedford to place herself under his protection, and if she died it would be in the doctor's hands. There would be no coroner's inquest, and the law could not touch

him. And besides, she had no relatives to call him to account, while surely —
he smiled gravely as he thought it — *his brother-in-law* would say nothing!

But all the same, in his heart of hearts Max Bray knew that, if Ella died,
he would be morally guilty of her murder.

That last was an ugly word, but it insisted upon being spoken, to
afterwards ring again and again in his ears as he restlessly moved in his
seat.

But now a change had taken place in Ella's state. From the soft appealing
prayer for leave to go and answer the calls she fancied that she heard, she
now became fiercely excited, moved by a dread of pursuit, and shrinking
from every one who approached her. She would even wildly inveigh against
the doctor, whom she accused of being in the pay of Max to drag her away.

No more soft appeals now, but frantic shrieks and fierce struggles for
freedom.

Again and again those who watched found that she had taken advantage
of a few minutes' absence to dress hurriedly, when it was only by a gentle
application of force that she could be overcome.

Then came the time when she seemed to have fallen into a weak and
helpless state, lying day after day apparently devoid of sense and feeling.

Max was asked again and again whether he would see her; but he
invariably refused with a coward's shiver of dread, to the great disgust of
all who had taken interest in the poor girl's state.

"I declare, it's scandalous!" said the landlady in confidence to her
husband. "He seems to neither know nor care how she is. No relatives are
sent to, he has no letters; and it's my belief there's more than we know
hanging to this."

"'Tisn't our business to interfere," said the landlord. "He pays like a
gentleman, if he isn't one; and if we get our living by visitors, it isn't for us
to be playing the spy upon them."

The landlady did not say anything, but she evidently thought a great
deal. The doctor, too, had his opinion upon the subject, but he was silent,
and tended his patient to the best of his ability, shaking his head when
questioned as to her recovery.

Chapter Nineteen
The Net Breaks

There is a boundary even to human patience; and now, after many days, Max Bray began to find his position very irksome. There was every probability of Ella's being a long and tedious illness, succeeded by a very slow return to convalescence; and he sat, at length, one day thinking matters over, for he was thoroughly tired out. There were no amusements in the place, and not wishing to attract curiosity, he had kept himself closely within doors. It was tiresome to a degree, and, besides, his stock of money would not last for ever. Come what might, he felt that he could put up with his position no longer. To a great extent his stratagem had been successful; but this unforeseen illness had made it now a failure, and he might as well give up and go to London. It had been expensive certainly; but though he was a loser, some one else would gain enormously; and he grinned again and again as he softly rubbed his white hands together, and thought of what a banker that some one would in the future prove. She would never be able to refuse him money, however extravagant he might be, and fortunately the Vinings were enormously wealthy. "But, bai Jove!" said Max Bray half aloud, "what a sweet thing is love between brother and sister!"

Then Mr Maximilian Bray began to make his plans for the future. He told himself that time enough had elapsed; that he need not certainly give up Ella, but arrange with the landlord that he should be informed directly she was getting better, and then he could come down again—that could be easily managed—and he really was tired out of this. He also made a few other plans; building, too, a few more castles in the air, ending with the determination of going up to town by the first train in the morning, and getting to know how Laura's affair was progressing.

"At all events, her way's clear," said Max, "and, bai Jove, she shall pay me for it by and by."

"*L'homme propose, mais Dieu dispose.*" Max Bray arranged all future matters to his entire satisfaction, but again there were contingencies that he could not foresee. Sitting there, rolling his cigar in his mouth and reckoning how long it would be to lunch, he had made up his mind to dine the next day at his club; but he did not; neither did other matters turn out quite so satisfactorily as he wished.

The sojourn was at a quiet little hotel in a Gloucestershire town that it is unnecessary to name; suffice it if we say that, save on the weekly market-day, the streets, with two exceptions, were silent and deserted; the two exceptions being the time when the children were set free from the National Schools. Hence, then, any little noise or excitement was unusual, and it was no wonder that Max Bray was startled by a scream above stairs, a cry for help, and the trampling of feet; sounds which his coward heart soon interpreted for him to mean an awful termination to his "stratagem," when, rising hurriedly to his feet, he stood there resting one hand upon the table, and the cold perspiration standing in great drops upon his pallid face.

There were people coming towards his room—they were coming to tell him. "What of it, then?" he cried savagely. "Could he help it? Had no doctor been obtained? It was her own mad excitement led to this termination."

"O, sir! O, sir!" exclaimed the landlady, bursting tearful-eyed into the room, "your poor, dear, sweet lady!"

"Dead?" asked Max in a harsh whisper, his knees shaking beneath him as he spoke.

"No, sir, not dead. I only left her for a few minutes, and when I came back—"

"Well, what? Speak, woman!" cried Max fiercely.

"She was gone, sir."

Max Bray stood for a minute as if stunned, and then leaping at the woman he shook her savagely, before he started off to make inquiries.

"Had anyone seen her?"

"No, not a soul." But her clothes that she had worn the day she was borne insensible to the hotel were gone, as was also her little leather reticule-bag.

"Where could she have gone?"

Only one place could strike Max Bray, as he thought of what she would do if sense had returned, and she had mastered her weakness sufficiently to enable her to steal from the house unobserved. There was only one place that she could seek with the intention of fleeing from him, and that was the railway station.

"Was their life to be bound up somehow with railways?" he asked himself as he started off in the direction of the station. "Bai Jove!" he seemed to have been always either meeting or inquiring about her at booking-offices; but why had she not been better watched?

Why indeed, unless it was that a chance might be given her for seeking freedom. But the landlady's few minutes had been a full hour, and, as if in her sleep, Ella had slowly risen, dressed for a journey, taken her reticule in her hand, her shawl over her arm, and then, drawing down her veil, walked—unseen, unchallenged—from the house, and, as if guided by instinct, gone straight to the station.

A train was nearly due—a fast train—and still in the same quiet way she applied for a through ticket to London, took her change and walked out on to the platform, to stand there perfectly motionless and fixed of eye.

No one heeded her of the few who were waiting, no one spoke; and at last came the faint and distant sound of the panting train, nearer, nearer, nearer.

Would she escape, or would she be stayed before she could take her place?

It might have been thought that she would feel, if not betray, some excitement; but no; she stood motionless, not even seeming to hear the coming train: it was as though she were moved by some power independent of her own will.

There was the ringing of the bell, the altering of a distance signal, and the train gliding up to the platform, as a farming-looking man drew the attention of another to a gentleman running swiftly a quarter of a mile down the road.

"He'll be too late, safe."

"Ah!" said the other. "And they won't wait for him; for they're very particular here since the row was made about the accident being through the bad time-keeping of the trains."

"Look at him, how he's waving his hat!" said the first speaker. "He's running too, and no mistake. Why, it's that dandy swell fellow that's staying at Linton's, where his wife's ill."

"Serve him right too," said the other. "Why wasn't he in better time? Those swells are always behindhand."

"Now then, all going on!" cried a voice; and the two men stepped into a second-class carriage, against the door of which, and looking towards the booking-office, Ella was already seated, cold, fixed, and apparently perfectly insensible to what was going on.

"Cold day, miss," said the man who took his seat opposite to her; but there was no reply, and the next moment the man's attention was caught by what took place at the booking-office door.

Max Bray dashed panting up as the guard sounded his whistle, but only to find the glass door fastened, when, evidently half wild with excitement, he beat at the panels, gesticulating furiously as he saw the train begin slowly to move, and Ella seated at one window.

She could have seen him too, for her face was turned towards him; she must have heard his cries for the door to be opened; but she did not start, she did not shrink back; and now, mad almost with rage and disappointment, Max Bray forgot all about telegraphs surpassing trains, everything, in the sight of his prize escaping from within his fingers; and for what? To expose his cruel duplicity.

It would be ruin, he felt, and he must reach her at all hazards.

Turning, then, from the door, he ran along by the station to where a wooden palisade bounded the platform, and as the train was slowly gliding by him, he climbed over to reach the ground before the carriage containing Ella had passed.

"Stop him!" shouted the station-master; and the guard, who had run and leaped into his van, stood pointing out the breaker of rules as he paused for a few moments upon his step.

"Here, hi! You're too late, sir!" roared a couple of porters running in pursuit; and as Max Bray leaped on to the door-step, and clung to the handle of the compartment with his face within a few inches of Ella's, a porter's hand was upon his arm; there was a shout, a curse, the words "Bai Jove!" half uttered, and then the speaker felt his hands snatched from their hold; the next moment it was as though a fearful blow was struck him, and he and the porter were rolling upon the platform. But again there was a jerk, a wild shriek that froze the bystanders' blood, and the form of one of the wrestlers was seen to be drawn down between the last carriage and the platform; the guard's break passed on, and Max Bray lay motionless upon the line.

Chapter Twenty
The Bird Flies

"Here, let-down the window! Open the door! Good heavens, there'll be some one killed! Let him be; we'll get him in. Those porters are so officious, and they cause accidents, instead of preventing 'em. Let him be, I tell you, and report him afterwards. There, I thought so! They'll be killed! Heaven help him—he's down under one of the carriages!"

So cried one of Ella's fellow-travellers as he witnessed the struggle from within, heedless, in his excitement, that not a word he uttered was heard by the actors in the thrilling scene. But as Max was caught by the carriage and dragged under the train, the man threw open the window and leaned out as far as he could, to draw his head back after a few moments, and impart his intelligence to the pale figure close beside him.

"I'm afraid he's killed, miss!"

Still no answer. Ella neither heard nor saw, for this part of her life—from the time when Max caught her wrists in his, and till long after—was a void that her memory could never again people.

"Deaf as a post, and a good thing too, poor lass!" muttered the man as he again leaned out.

And now there was shouting, signalling, and the stopping of the train for a few minutes, long enough for the passengers to see a motionless form lifted from the line and borne into one of the waiting-rooms, the passenger who had watched the proceedings having leaped out, but now coming panting back to reach his place as the signal for starting was once more given.

"Is he much hurt?" was eagerly asked by the other occupants of the carnage.

"I'm afraid so," said the passenger.

"Not killed?"

"No, I don't think he's killed. You see, he went down at the end of the platform just where it begins to slope. If it had been off the level, he must have been crushed to death in an instant. But I didn't have above a quarter of a minute to see him."

"It's very, very dangerous," observed one, "this trying to get into a train when it's started."

"Very," said another; "but they will do it. That gentleman, too, was so determined, climbing over the fence; and I suppose that made the railway folks determined too."

"He must have been anxious to get off, or he would not have acted as he did."

"Some particular appointment or another, I should think."

"Well, poor fellow, I hope he is not badly injured," was the charitable wish now uttered, when a dissertation upon the right or wrong action of porters in trying to stop people ensued, it being generally accorded that the by-laws upon which they acted ought to be rescinded, and that the guard ought to report all breaches of the regulations at the next station.

And all these comments were made within Ella's hearing, but without once diverting her steadfast stony gaze, as now, leaning back in her corner, she looked straight out at the flying landscape as mile after mile was passed.

Once or twice a remark was made to her, but she merely bent her head; and at last she was allowed to remain unquestioned, unnoticed, as the train sped on swiftly towards the great metropolis.

She changed carriages mechanically when requested, and again and again produced her ticket, but always in the same dreamy strange way. Passengers came, and passengers went, some speaking, others paying no heed to their closely veiled and silent companion; but not once did Ella speak or evince any knowledge of what was passing around.

How that journey was performed, she never knew, nor by what strange influence she was guided in her acts; but press on she did, and to the end.

Chapter Twenty One
The Copse-Hall Ghost

"I wonder what's become of Miss Bedford!" said the cook at Mrs Brandon's, as she sat with her fellow-servants enjoying the genial warmth of the fire before retiring to rest.

It was about half-past ten, and, probably to soften Edward the hard, the stewpan was in use, and steaming mugs of hot spiced liquid were being from time to time applied to lips.

"Married long before this, I should think," said the housemaid, tossing her head. "You don't suppose she's like some people I know, going on shilly-shallying year after year, as if they never meant to get married at all."

"Never you mind about that," said Edward gruffly; "perhaps we shall get married when it suits us, and perhaps we sha'n't. I don't see no fun in going away from a good home and a good missus, to hard lines and spending all your savings, like some people as ain't old enough to know better."

"Does missus ever talk about her, Mr Eddard?" said Cook persuasively.

"Not often," said Edward; "but I know one thing,—she ain't had a letter from her for ever so long, now."

"How do you know?" said the housemaid.

"How do I know?" exclaimed Mr Eddard contemptuously. "Why, don't I see all the envelopes, and can't I tell that way? But there's something wrong about her, I believe; for there came a letter about three weeks or a month ago, and it seemed to cut missus up a good deal, and I heard her say something out aloud."

"What did she say?" said Cook and Mary in a breath, for the recounter had stopped.

"Well, I didn't catch it all," said Edward, speaking in his mug; "but it was something like: 'Gone with Mr Bray? Impossible!'"

"But what made her say that?" exclaimed Cook.

"Why, from what she read in a letter from London, to be sure, stupid. Why else should she say it?"

"There, didn't I tell you so!" exclaimed Cook triumphantly.

"What are you up to now?" said Edward in a tone of gruff contempt. "What do you mean?"

"Why, I always thought she'd have Mr Bray, as was so wonderful attentive. Why, Mrs Pottles, down at the Seven Bells, has told me lots of times about how he used to come and put his horse up there, and then follow her about."

"Humph!" ejaculated Edward. "When did you see Mother Pottles last?"

"Yesterday," said Cook. "And she said she thought that Pottles would take the twenty pounds off the good-will, and—"

"Why didn't you tell me so before?" said Edward gruffly.

"Because she said Mr Pottles would come over and see you, and you do snub me so for interfering."

"Humph!" ejaculated Edward again.

"What, you are going to have the Seven Bells, then?" said the housemaid. "O, I am glad; it will be nice! And you're going to be married, after all."

"Don't you be in a hurry," growled Edward. "We ain't gone yet, and perhaps we shan't go at all; so now then. There goes the bell; now, then, clear off. Missus is going to bed."

"Did you fasten the side-door, Mr Ed-dard?" said the housemaid.

"Slipped the top bolt, that's all," said the footman, as he went to answer the bell.

"Let's lay them bits of lace out on the lawn, Cook, and leave 'em all night; the frost 'll bleach 'em beautiful," said the housemaid.

"Ah, so we might," said Cook; and taking some wet twisted-up scraps of lace from a basin, cook and housemaid tied their handkerchiefs round their necks, placed their aprons over their heads, and ran down a passage, unbolted the side-door, and went over the gravel drive to lay the lace upon the front lawn.

"I'll pop out and take them in when I light the breakfast-room fire," said the housemaid. "My, what a lovely night! it must be full moon."

"Scr-r-r-r-r-r-eech—screech—screech!" went the cook.

"Scre-e-e-e-e-ch-h-h-h!" went the housemaid, giving vent to a shrill cry that would have made an emulative locomotive burst in despair; and, still screaming, the two women clung together, and backed slowly to the house, ran down the passage to the kitchen, shrieking still, where the cook sank into a chair, which gave way beneath her, and she fell heavily on the floor.

"Are you mad, Mary—Cook? What is the matter?" exclaimed Mrs Brandon, running into the kitchen, chamber-candlestick in hand, closely followed by Edward.

"They *are* mad—both on 'em!" growled the footman.

"A ghost, a ghost!" panted Mary, shuddering, and pointing towards the passage.

"A ghost!" exclaimed Mrs Brandon contemptuously. "You foolish wicked woman! How dare you alarm the children with such ridiculous, such absurd old grandmothers' notions? You've been out, I suppose?"

"Yes, yes!" sobbed Mary, covering her blanched face with her hands.

"And you saw something white, I suppose, in the moonlight?"

"N-n-n-o, 'm! It was a black one, all but the horrid face with the moon on it."

"Edward," said Mrs Brandon, "some one has been trying to frighten them, and they have left the passage door open. You are not afraid?"

"How should I know till I see what it's like!" growled Edward. "Anyhow, I'll go and try."

"I'll go with you," said Mrs Brandon.

Edward led the way to where the moonlight was streaming in through the open door, when he started back against his mistress, forcing her into the kitchen.

"There *is* something, mum!" he said hoarsely, "and I think I am a little afraid. No, no, 'm, you sha'n't go. I'll go first: I can't stand that, if I am frighted."

He again made a step in advance, for Mrs Brandon was about to take the *pas*; but the next moment mistress and man drew involuntarily back, as, slowly, as if feeling its way through some thick darkness, hands stretched out, palms downward, to their fullest extent, head thrown back, wild eyes staring straight before it, and face unnaturally pale, came towards them a figure draped in black.

On and on, in a strange unearthly way, rigid as if of marble, came the figure across the great kitchen, and in spite of herself Mrs Brandon felt a strange thrill pass through her as she slowly gave way; but followed still by the figure through the open door into the hall, where, reason reasserting itself, she set down the candlestick upon the marble slab, and stood firm till the strange visitor came close up to her, and she took two cold stony hands in hers.

"Ella, my child!" she gasped.

It was as though those three words had dissolved a spell; for the staring eyes slowly closed, a faint dawning as of a smile relaxed the rigid features, and, as the white lips parted, there came forth a low sigh as of relief, and then the form sank slowly down till it was supported only by the grasp Mrs Brandon maintained upon the hands.

"Here! Quick! Help, Edward!" exclaimed Mrs Brandon, blushing for her excusable dread. "Good Heavens, what infamy has been practised, that this poor child should seek refuge here in such a plight? Edward!"

"I'm here, ma'am," cried the hard footman, smiting himself heavily upon the cheek. "That I should have been such a fool! But 'twas enough to startle—"

"Man—man, don't talk!" cried his mistress. "Run to Mr Tiddson, he is the nearest; and don't tell him to come, but bring him. Do you hear?—*bring him*!"

"That I just will," cried the man, giving one glance at the figure at his mistress's feet, and the next moment he was in the kitchen. "Here, rouse up!" he cried, "'tain't nothing sooper—"

Edward said "natural" as he ran out, hatless, into the frosty night to fetch the doctor, tying his handkerchief round his head as he sped on.

Meanwhile, Mrs Brandon lifted the wasted form in her arms, and bore it to a couch, where she strove ineffectually to restore animation. Everything she tried seemed useless; and at last, weeping bitterly, she sank upon her knees, and clasped the fragile figure to her heart, moaning as she did so:

"My poor stricken bird! my poor little dove! what does it mean—what does it mean?"

But the form she clasped might have been that from which the vital spark had just fled, save that the icy coldness began gradually to yield to the temperature of the room.

Chapter Twenty Two
Light!—and Darkness?

Dr Tiddson at last, panting and out of breath; for he had run the greater part of two miles, and upon hearing the few words Mrs Brandon had to utter, he cast aside all the pedantry of his profession to which he clung, and knelt down by the inanimate form.

"Every symptom of having passed through a state of fever," he said softly. "Slightly convulsed, even now," he muttered, as from the pulse his finger went to her face. "The candle a little nearer," he said, as he raised an eyelid. "Yes, I thought so! Lungs seem right. I'd stake my life she has but lately risen from a sick bed. Heaven bless the poor child, she's worn to a skeleton! Here, quick, Edward!"

"I'm here, sir," growled the hard footman.

"Take that to my house," he said, hurriedly writing some directions. "Run, my good man, please."

"I will, sir," said Edward huskily, as a great tear ran trickling down his nose; "but please tell me, sir—we all liked her very much—you—you don't think she'll die?"

"We'll hope not, Edward—we'll hope not," said the doctor solemnly. "Now go."

Edward gave a great coarse sigh as he ran out of the room; but it was genuine sympathy, and worth a host of fine words.

"There's something more than ordinary disease here, Mrs Brandon," said the doctor. "We'll watch by her to-night; and if there is no change by morning, I should like to share the responsibility, and have the counsel of some able practitioner."

They passed that night and many more by the wasted girl's bedside, during which time not once did she give sign of consciousness. Occasionally a faint fluttering of the pulse seemed to tell of returning power; but it was but a false hope held out.

An almost supernatural strength had enabled her to seek the refuge, where she had somehow, in the darkened state of her intellect, recalled that she would be welcome. Led almost by a subtle instinct, she had made her way by the different lines, and then exhausted her last powers in slowly walking over from Laneton, to sink inanimate at her protectress's feet.

It was long before her senses had thoroughly returned, so that she could recognise those around, and speak in the faintest whisper; but Mrs Brandon trembled, for she judged by what she saw in the doctor's looks that it was but the precursor of a deeper sleep.

Several times over there was a faint whisper breathed into Mrs Brandon's ear that the sufferer had much to say; but invariably Mrs Brandon closed those pale lips with a kiss.

"Wrong or right, my poor child," she said sadly, "rest in peace, for this is your home."

But there was an air of trouble and appeal in Ella's face that would not be gainsayed; and one night Mrs Brandon was seated by her side, when her lips parted to faintly whisper:

"If I am to go, let me know that you all believe in me."

As she spoke, her trembling little hand drew a large envelope from beneath her pillow—a crumpled and bruised envelope.

"Do you wish me to read this?" said Mrs Brandon tenderly.

Ella's lips formed the word "Yes."

Chapter Twenty Three
It Never Rains but it Pours

The first paper Mrs Brandon drew from the envelope was one in a bold lady's-hand, evidently written hastily, and contained but the following words:

> "Dear Max,—I will take him into the waiting-room, where there is a good view of the platform. I can keep him there, I think. But you must be quick. Recollect, a momentary glance will do. Run by, if you can, at the very last minute. But pray, pray be careful. *It is victory or ruin; for he would never forgive either. Laura.*

> "P.S. *Burn this*, and every note I send."

Mrs Brandon's face wore a troubled puzzled expression as she glanced at Ella, whose lips moved.

"I found that in my reticule since I have lain here," she whispered. "Read on, and you will understand."

Mrs Brandon took out from the envelope another paper, and read, in a round legal hand:

> "Cliff-terrace, Penzance,—18—

> "Sir,—I am requested by my patient, Mr Charles Vining, to enclose the note here contained, one which, at his wish, I have addressed as you see. He tells me that he is doubtful of its reaching the lady if sent by post, and desires me to implore you to be its bearer, delivering it yourself, and adding your persuasions if she should decline compliance. He would have written more, but the note enclosed was penned in my brief absence, and I sternly forbade farther exertion. By way of explanation, I may tell you that my patient came in here, with two more gentlemen, in a yacht, driven to the bay by stress of weather. The next night there was a fearful wreck close in shore, and Mr Vining and one of

his friends volunteered, and were out in the lifeboat. I regret to say that their gallant attempt only added to the long list of those gone to their account. Two of the lifeboat's crew were drowned, while your friend was cast upon the rocks fearfully injured.

"Let me assure you that he has had the best advice the town affords.—I am, sir, your obedient servant,

"Henry Penellyn, M.R.C.S.

"To Maximilian Bray, Esq.

"P.S. Mr Vining bids me tell you that the above is his last request.

"I do not read to him the following: Not a moment is to be lost, for internal haemorrhage has set in."

Mrs Brandon's breath came thick and fast, as dashing down this letter, she took up the next.

"My only love,—*Pray* come to me. I am half-killed.—Ever yours,

"Charles Vining."

"But that is—stop a minute," exclaimed Mrs Brandon, who was terribly agitated, and she rang the bell. "Bring my desk quickly," she said to the maid who answered. "Yes," she exclaimed, as she unlocked the desk and drew out a letter, and compared it carefully. "It is the same hand. It is his writing!"

"Yes," whispered Ella sadly.

"What does it all mean, then?" exclaimed Mrs Brandon confusedly.

"I cannot tell—I cannot understand," whispered Ella. "I was deceived and led away, and he must have seen me; but he would not have betrayed me thus."

"But how to explain it all!" cried Mrs Brandon excitedly. "He is to be married to Laura Bray—"

"Ah, me! What have I done, what have I said?" cried Mrs Brandon. "My poor child, I must have been mad to have let my foolish lips utter those words!" And she gently raised the fainting girl in her arms; for at those bitter words, Ella had uttered that faint sigh, her face had been contracted as by a violent spasm, and her eyes had closed.

"It is nothing," sighed Ella, reviving. "If he is only happy!"

"Happy!" cried Mrs Brandon, her breast heaving with passion. "It is some cruel conspiracy. But tell me—if you can bear to speak—tell me all."

It was a long recital; for it was told in a faint whisper, and spread over some time, Ella's strength seeming often to fail her. Twice over Mrs Brandon would have arrested her, but she begged to be allowed to proceed.

"It will make me happier," she whispered. And Mrs Brandon could only bend her head.

Three o'clock had struck by the pendule, whose slow beat seemed to be numbering off Ella's last minutes, when Mrs Brandon left her in the charge of the nurse she had summoned, sleeping now calmly, and as if relieved by confiding her sad little last month's history to another breast.

It was late; but Mrs Brandon had another duty to perform, one which she did, with her mind now confused, now seeming to see plainly the whole of the plot. But there was that letter—those lines in Charley Vining's hand. But for them, all would have been plain.

At times she was moved by a burning indignation; at others she weakly wept; but before returning to Ella's bedside, she took a large sheet of paper, secured to it the three missives she had brought from the bedside, and then wrote under them:

"Charles Vining,—The victim of a cruel plot—Ella Bedford — was enticed from the home I had found for her by Maximilian Bray, from whom she escaped, to crawl, *dying*, to my house, where she now lies, to breathe her last in peace. As an English gentleman, I ask you, Have you had any hand in this? If not, explain how a letter should be sent to her in your handwriting. I can see part; but the rest remains for you to clear. Emily Brandon."

This letter Mrs Brandon carefully sealed, with its contents, and then returned to watch by Ella's bedside.

Soon after eight that morning she dispatched the note by a trusty messenger, to be delivered into no other hands than Charley Vining's—little wotting the events to take place that day—and into Charley Vining's hands that letter was placed, as we have seen.

Sir Philip Vining's coachman was the first to recover himself and to go to his master's assistance, just as, half stunned and confused, Sir Philip was struggling to his feet.

"Not much hurt, I think!" said Sir Philip. "But where is Mr Bray?"

"There he lies, Sir Philip," said the coachman.

And together they went to raise the unfortunate companion of their ride, insensible now, and bleeding from a cut on the temple.

"Beg pardon, Sir Philip," said the coachman appealingly. "I've been with you fifteen years now; I hope you won't turn me off for this job. I was driving as carefully as I could."

"My good fellow, no; of course not. I was to blame. Thank Heaven there are some men coming!—Bray, my dear friend, how is it with you?"

Mr Bray looked up on being addressed, and, with a little assistance, rose to his feet; but he was weak and helpless, seating himself directly after.

In spite of the serious aspect of affairs, a little examination proved that, though cut about, and some of the harness injured, the horses were very little the worse; while, with the exception of the loss of some paint and a smashed panel, the carriage, on being placed in its normal position, was found to be quite capable of continuing its journey. Plenty of help had arrived, and the labourers had worked with a will; but upon Mr Bray being assisted to his seat, he seemed so ill and shaken, that Sir Philip gave orders for the carriage to make the best of its way home.

"But you will come too?" said Mr Bray feebly.

"No," said Sir Philip, frowning angrily; "I shall go forward."

And then, without another word, he strode off in the direction of Laneton.

Mr Bray was for following him; but the coachman shook his head.

"Master's as good and true-hearted a gentleman as ever breathed, sir. Here's fifty—ah, with the way them horses are marked, a hundred and fifty-pounds' worth of damage done in a moment. And does he do what ninety masters out of a hundred would have done—tell me to leave to-morrow? Not he, sir. He just claps me on the shoulder, and says it was his own fault—which it really was, sir, though lots wouldn't have owned to it. But no, sir; Sir Philip's orders was to take you home, and disobeying his orders means throwing away a good place."

So, as Sir Philip disappeared down the lane, the carriage was once more put in motion, and dragged heavily through the muddy rutty by-way back towards Lexville.

It was a long and dreary ride, performed in a slow and spiritless way, Mr Bray shrinking back in his seat as they reached and drove through the town; for, in addition to bodily pain, there was the mental suffering—the blow at his pride; for it seemed, though he could not penetrate the mystery, that there was something radically wrong, and that all prospect of the wedding taking place was at an end.

In spite of his shrinking back, he could not avoid seeing the curiosity-moved faces at door and window; and, in his heart, he fancied he could make out what was said respecting pride and its fall, for his family was not very popular at Lexville; while the state of horses, carriage, and coachman all tended to make people hurry out to gaze upon this sequel to the broken-off wedding, the theme now of every gossip in the place.

"It never rains but it pours," says the old saw; and so it seemed to be here; for upon Mr Bray alighting at the Elms, stiff and bruised and giddy, it was to find Laura—now that she was hidden from the public gaze, where she had held up so bravely, even to taking her place calmly in the waiting carriage—falling from one violent hysterical fit into another, shrieking and raving against Max, and crying out that what had befallen her was a judgment.

Mother, sister, friends, all listened in weeping amazement as they tried to soothe and minister to her, but in vain; and it was not until the coming of the family medical man, and a soothing draught had been administered, that Laura sank back, silent and overcome.

The doctor was still busy, when Sir Philip Vining's carriage drove up with a fresh patient, one who sadly needed his services; while, as Mr Bray was lying bandaged, and at length somewhat more at ease, a servant brought up a telegram.

"News, then, at last, from Charley Vining!" exclaimed Mrs Bray excitedly, breaking the official envelope.

But Mrs Bray was wrong. The telegram contained news, startling news—such as made the father forget his own sufferings, and rise again to prepare for a journey; and upon its being inadvertently conveyed to Laura some time after, she threw up her hands, shrieked aloud, and then seemed to shrink, trembling within herself, as if expecting momentarily that some great blow would fall crushingly upon her.

Chapter Twenty Four
Sleep or Death?

The telegram to the Bray family was from the little Gloucestershire town, telling what the hotel-keepers were at length able to impart, through a letter they had found in his portmanteau, after missing it in previous searches, that Max Bray was lying in a precarious state, the result of an accident upon the railway.

For Max had so far escaped with lifer but he had not yet awoke to consciousness, and to know that he was occupying the couch of her whom he had long marked down as his victim. As the railway passenger had remarked, Max had fallen where the platform sloped; but he was suffering from concussion of the brain; and one maimed limb had been removed by the surgeon's knife.

But we must leave him to his slow recovery, while the landlady declared in confidence to her husband every night, that she had always known that Williams was an assumed name, because there was a "B" on the gentleman's socks.

Sir Philip Vining reached Laneton at last, to see his chariot standing in the inn-yard; but he knew, without questioning the grooms, where Charley would be; and fierce now with the anger that burned within him, he made his way to Copse Hall, to be told that his son was by Miss Bedford's couch, where he had been since he arrived.

For, after a furious gallop, the chariot had dashed up to Copse Hall covered with mud, the horses in a foam and ready to drop, while, springing up more like, a madman than one in possession of his full senses, Charley had leaped out, and almost forced his way to Ella's side, to fall sobbing on his knees as he clasped her thin transparent hand, a faint smile welcoming his coming, as, with her soul seeming to leap from her longing eyes, she vainly strove to turn towards him.

Mrs Brandon stayed to ask no explanation then; for she was alarmed at the fierce rage that flashed from Charley's eyes at her first words, as he stood there in his wedding garments.

She left the explanation for some other time, and, trembling and excited, she left them alone, to find from the servants, upon descending, that this was to have been Charley Vining's wedding-morn.

But Ella must have heard some explanation; for when, nearly two hours after, Mrs Brandon went to the room to whisper to the son of the father's coming, that softly-shaded head was lying upon Charley's arm, and there was a sweet satisfied smile upon those pale lips. But as Ella's eyes opened, and she saw Mrs Brandon approach, they wore that old piteous appealing look, and she whispered, "For I love him!"

The words were meant for Mrs Brandon; but they went no farther than Charley's ear, to bring a wild convulsive sob from his breast, as in his despair he felt that it was too late.

"Let him come here!" cried Charley sternly, as Mrs Brandon whispered of his father's coming. "Let him come here!" And then, as, black and frowning, Sir Philip strode into the room, he turned towards him.

"Well!" exclaimed Charley, staying the flood of reproaches Sir Philip was about to heap upon his head; and, as he gazed upon the pale face, the father's aspect changed, his stride became a gentle step, and he gazed from one to the other. "Well," cried Charley, "have you come to look upon their work? Have you come to commune once more with the sweet gentle spirit before it passes away? I tell you they have murdered her—murdered my own darling who would have died for me; whilst I, poor, weak, pitiful idiot that I was, believed all I saw—walked blindly into their traps like a foolish child. Curse them—curse them!" he raged, as he ground his teeth together, and spoke in a low hoarse voice, that was awful in its deep suppressed hatred. "You want to know why I dashed off this morning. I tell you, it was to save myself from being a murderer. I tell you, father, that after what I learned on leaving you, if I had faced that cursed Jezebel, it would have been to strangle her. There—there, read those letters!" he cried, tearing the papers from his breast, and dashing them at Sir Philip. "Read how brother and sister could plot to delude this poor child—plot with a diabolical cunning that was nearly crowned with success; for they had a simple unworldly man to deal with; read how we were to be torn asunder by their cursed malice—how I was to be poisoned at heart by seeing her appear to flee with that scoundrel Max Bray; while I, like a simple sheep, was led by that false wretch to see it all. She played her cards well—to become Lady Vining, forsooth! And then read on how this poor angel was beguiled by lying forgeries to hurry away with Max to Cornwall, to see me—me—dying from injuries; while, to give force to his lies, the villain added to, and then sent, the note, that must have been lying in his desk above a year—the note

I sent to him, telling him to come to me, for I was half-killed, when I had my hunting fall. God!" he hissed forth in a fierce way, that made his hearers tremble, "God! that my right hand had withered away before it penned a line! But no, no!" he exclaimed, and his teeth grated, "I shall want this right hand yet; for the day of reckoning shall surely come!"

There was something fearful in the young man's aspect, as down there upon one knee by the bedside, his left arm beneath that fair golden-clustered head, he clenched his right hand, and, gazing before him at vacancy, he shook that clenched hand fiercely, and his mad rage was such that could he have grasped Max Bray then, he would have dashed him down, and crushed his heel upon his false cruel face, for he knew not of the retribution that had already fallen to the deceiver's lot.

But the next moment Charley Vining turned to look down upon the pale horror-stricken face at his side, when the rugged brow was smoothed, the clenched hand dropped, and a deep groan burst from the young man's breast.

"O, heaven forgive me! What am I saying? Father, father," he cried, in pitiful tones, "they've broken my heart!"

And then, the strong man humbled, he bowed down over the bedside till his agony-distorted face rested upon that fluttering breast; and weak now as the weakest, he wept like a child, his broad shoulders heaving from the convulsive sobs that burst forth with the wild hysterical violence of a woman's grief.

"Charley, my son," gasped Sir Philip at last, as he knelt by the young man's side, and laid his hand upon his head, "you do not think—you cannot think—that I knew of all this?"

"No—no—no!" groaned Charley. "I never thought it."

Chapter Twenty Five
Hope Rises

"It is cruel, monstrous!" exclaimed Sir Philip, after a long pause. "But, O my boy, what have I done? I thought to make you honoured and loved of all. My sole desire was to make you happy and content. But, my boy, you will forgive me. I humble myself to you. I was wrong."

"Hush, hush, father!" cried Charley sternly, as he raised one arm, and laid it upon his father's shoulder. "What have I to forgive in you?"

He turned again, gazing with a despairing, stunned expression upon Ella's face.

"But," cried Sir Philip hastily, "what has been done?—Mrs Brandon, what medical advice have you had?"

"The best that money can procure," said Mrs Brandon, in a choking voice. "We have done all that is possible."

There was a dead silence now reigning in that chamber, broken at last by Sir Philip, as, forgetful of all else but the fearful wrong that had been done the suffering girl before him, he bent over Ella to kiss her tenderly.

"O my child, my child!" he moaned, "my poor child! I came here angry and bitter to upbraid; but has it come to this? that you, so young, so pure, must leave us to go where all is love, to bear witness to my selfish pride and ambition? Heaven forgive me!" he sobbed, as his tears fell fast upon the little hand he held, "heaven forgive me! for, in my blindness, I have broken two loving hearts—sacrificed them to my insensate pride! Blind—blind—blind that I was, not to remember that the love of a pure true-hearted woman was a gem beyond price. Has it indeed come to this, that there is nothing to be done but for a poor, weak, blind old man to ask forgiveness for your wrongs?—Charley," he sobbed, turning to his son, "my boy—my pride, the hope of my old age, forgive me, for I can never forgive myself!"

"Father, for heaven's sake, hush!" cried Charley in his blank despair. "This is too much. I cannot bear it. I have nothing to forgive. It was our fate; but, O!" he said huskily, as he drew Ella nearer to his breast, "it is hard—hard—hard to bear!"

Here Mrs Brandon interposed; it was too much for the sufferer to encounter; and gently drawing the young man away, she bent over to whisper to Ella, but, in obedience to a whispered wish, she drew back, as Charley, weak now and trembling, gazed in his father's quivering face for a few moments, and then, as did the patriarch of old, he fell upon the loving old man's neck and kissed him, and wept sore.

The silence then in that sad chamber was painful; but at last, trembling in every limb, Sir Philip crept to the bedside, to take the place lately occupied by his son — to pass one arm beneath Ella's neck, and then, with all a father's gentle love, to raise her more and more, till her head, with all that glory of bright fair hair, rested upon his breast, and his old and wrinkled cheek touched the vein-mapped, transparent forehead.

"If I could die for you, my child," he murmured; "if my few poor useless days could be given, that you might live, I should be content. Heaven hear my prayer!" he cried piteously. "Poor sufferer! Has she not borne enough? Have we not all tried our best to make her way thorny and harsh? O my child, I loved you from the first, though my pride would not let me acknowledge it, and I left you that day moved almost beyond human power to bear; while, on my return, even the eyes of my wife's poor semblance seemed, from the canvas, almost to look — to look down upon me with reproach. But you must not leave us — surely our prayers must be heard — you, so young, so gentle! My poor blighted flower! But you will live to bless us both — to be my stay and comfort — to help a weak old man tenderly along his path to the grave — to be the hope and stay of my boy — to be my pride! I ask you — I ask you this — I, his father, ask you to live for us, to bless us both with your pure and gentle love! Charley my boy, here — quick — quick — My God, she is dying!"

A faint shudder had passed through Ella's frame as Sir Philip uttered that exclamation, and her pinched pale face looked more strange and unearthly than ever; but she had heard every word uttered by the old man; words which, feeble as she was, had made her heart leap with a strange joy, sending life and energy once more through every vein and nerve, but only with the effect of a few drops of oil upon an expiring flame: the light sprang up for a few moments, and then seemed to sink lower and lower, till, with a shiver of dread, Mrs Brandon softly approached.

She paused though, for at that moment Ella's eyes softly unclosed, to gaze trustingly at Sir Philip Vining. Then they were turned to Charley; and as they rested there, her pale lips parted, but no word came. A faint sad smile of content, though, flitted for an instant over her face, and those lips spoke in silence their wishes — wishes read by heartbroken Charley, who, resting one hand upon his father's shoulder, pressed upon that pale rosebud of a mouth a long, long kiss of love, one, though, to which there was no response. He did not even feel the soft fluttering breath, playing and hesitating, as it were, round her lips as her eyes slowly closed.

Was it in sleep or in death? The question was mentally asked again and again; but no one spoke, as all stood there watching—hardly daring to breathe.

Night had come, and still no movement, no trace by which hope could be for a moment illumined, and still they watched on; Lexville, the Brays, everything, being forgotten in this great sorrow. But with the night came again the doctor, with an old friend and physician; then followed a long consultation in the sick-chamber, and another in the drawing-room, while friend and lover waited tremblingly for the sentence to be pronounced.

"My friend thinks with me that there is a change," said Mr Tiddson; "and really, Mrs Brandon, in the whole course of my practice, nothing ever gave me greater pleasure."

The next day, and the lamp of life still burning, but the brain-symptoms had passed away, in spite of the great excitement. There was extreme weakness, but soon that was all; and until, joyful and exultant, Sir Philip avowed to himself that the danger was past, he did not return to Blandfield Court.

"Saved, my boy, saved! our prayers were heard!" he exclaimed then fervently; and from that day Sir Philip seemed to know no rest when he was away from the invalid chamber.

Scandal and wonders seldom last above their reputed nine days; and so it seemed here at Lexville. People talked tremendously, and commented upon the absence of the Vinings, and their treatment of their old friends, the Brays. But from the Bray family themselves came not one word of rebuke or complaint. They started for London the day but one after that appointed for the wedding, to take up, as it proved, their permanent residence in Harley street; and at the end of a month it was announced that The Elms was for sale; and, at a great price, the local auctioneer disposed of the whole of "Mr Onesimus Bray's well-known and carefully-selected live and dead farming stock," in spite of the old-fashioned farmers' head-shaking and nods and winks.

But, as time wore on, though the past was never again reverted to, pudgy quiet Mr Bray more than once had a snug *tête-à-tête* club dinner with his old friend Sir Philip Vining, and they parted in the best of fellowship.

And now we must ask our readers to follow us hastily through a few scenes, whose intent is to fill up voids in our narrative, and to bring it more quickly to a close.

Any one who knows the neighbourhood of Blandfield and Laneton will acknowledge that no more pleasant piece of rural undulating country can be found within a radius of fifty miles round London; and through those pleasant dales and glades, day after day of the bright spring-time, might one or other of Sir Philip Vining's carriages be seen with the old gentleman himself in constant attendance upon his chosen daughter. His love had long been withheld, but now it was showered down abundantly.

The slightest increase of pallor, a warm flush, anything, was sufficient to arouse the worthy old man's alarms. And they were not quite needless; for the struggle back to health was on Ella Bedford's part long and protracted.

Charley Vining used to declare that he was quite excluded, and that he did not get anything like a fair share of Ella's heart; but the warm glow of pleasure which suffused his face, as he saw the pride and affection Sir Philip had in his son's choice, was, as Mrs Brandon used to say, "a sight to make any one happy."

Often and often Mrs Brandon used to declare that the Vinings might just as well come and take up their residence altogether at Copse Hall, for she should never think of parting with Ella; while, as the summer came in, and with it strength and brightness of eye to the invalid, Sir Philip Vining's great pleasure was, just before leaving of an evening, just as it was growing dusk, to lead Ella to the piano, where, unasked, she would plaintively sing him the old ballad that had once drawn a tear from Charley Vining's eye, when he had told the singer that he was glad Sir Philip was not present.

And on those occasions, seated with his back to the light, and his forehead down upon his hand, the old man would be carried far back into the days of the past, when the wife he loved was with him; and as the sweet low notes rose and fell, now loud and clear, now soft and tremulous with pathos, Sir Philip's lip would tremble, and more than once, when he bade her good-night, Ella felt that his cheek was wet.

Chapter Twenty Six
At Last

The summer was drawing to an end; the ripe tints of the coming autumn were beginning to appear in many a rich clump of trees; but Sir Philip said, in his quiet courtly style, that Blandfield Court had never looked to greater advantage; for Mrs Brandon, her daughters, and Ella, had spent the day there.

And now, in the warm glow of a pleasant evening, just before dew-fall, Charley Vining was leading his fair betrothed along alley after alley, her light dress rustling from time to time among the first-fallen leaves. Hours upon hours they had spent alone together during her return to health; but never till this eve had Ella felt so great a tremor as that which now pervaded her frame. Was it that his eyes had spoken more eloquently than usual? She could not say; but now that he halted by the tree from which a rose had once been plucked, and led her to the garden-seat, there was no resistance, and she suffered him to draw her to his side closer, closer, closer still, till her fair hair mingled with his crisp curls, and her soft breath played upon his cheek.

"My own," he cried softly, but in tremulous tones, "six months have passed now since I made you a promise."

"Yes," she whispered, as her hands rested upon his shoulder; and she nestled closer to his broad breast, dove-like in the gentleness and aspect of seeking protection where she knew she would be safe.

"I have kept the promise," he said again. "Yes," she replied, "to forgive, as we hope to be forgiven."

There was silence then for a few moments before he spoke again.

"And now," he said, "I claim my reward. Ella dearest, my own, can you forgive my weakness, my doubts, my boyish folly?"

"Forgive?" she said; and as she gazed up in his face there was a look of proud joy before her eyes sank, and her head drooped, blushing before his loving glance.

"I was weak, I own, mad; but tell me, Ella dearest. I have been patient."

His voice was low as he pressed her still closer to his heart.

"Tell me," he said, "tell me when;" and his voice had sunk to a whisper.

"Charley—husband," she whispered, raising her eyes once more to his, "I am yours—when you will!"

Chapter Twenty Seven
The Reward of Merit—Bai Jove!

People will talk, and the more you try to regulate your life by their opinions, the worse you will fare. Vide "The Old Man and his Ass."

They said it was too bad that the heir to Blandfield Court should be married in London; but whether too bad or no, in the course of the autumn Charles Vining and his lady were announced as having departed for the Continent after a particular ceremony at Saint George's, Hanover-square; a church where the wedding-fees must amount to something tolerably respectable in the course of the year; while, if at any time it should be announced that the clerk, beadle, and pew-opener all have country houses at Sydenham, Teddington, or some other pleasant spot a few miles from Babel smoke, and give champagne dinners, the writer, for one, will feel no surprise; though a feeling of envy may spring up in his breast the next time he encounters the gorgeous beadle sunning himself upon the broad steps of the sacred fane.

But the wedding trip was short on account of Sir Philip, who, though he did not complain, showed by his letters how eagerly he was looking forward to their return, which soon followed; and for them life glided on in a pleasant round of social enjoyment, either at Blandfield or the house Sir Philip had secured in Westbournia.

Two years had glided by, when, so as to do as others do in the season, Charley Vining was escorting his bonnie wife through the exhibition of the Royal Academy, though, truth to say, Charley had more than once been guilty of yawning as he stood before a grand specimen of Turneresque painting, for he said that he liked to see that sort of thing in a state of nature.

They were passing from one room to another, when suddenly there fell upon Charley Vining's ears a strange sound—not loud, in fact it was very faint, but it was peculiar, and being somewhat bored and tired by the pictures, any little thing sufficed to attract his attention.

"Squea-eek, squea-eek, squea-eek!" went the noise, as of some mechanism slightly in want of oil; when, as Charley turned, his face suddenly became suffused, his broad chest swelled, his teeth were set, and his fists clenched, as, with flashing eyes, he looked like some refined and polished lion about to make a spring upon an enemy.

Ella saw what had attracted his attention at the same moment, and trembling like an aspen, the blood fled from her face, and her hands closed on her husband's arm as she tried to draw him away.

But she might as well have tried to move an oak, as the stalwart frowning Hercules who stood there gazing over his shoulder at a most carefully-dressed man, walking with a peculiar limp—a halt which told of a cork leg, without the wheezing squeak it gave at every mincingly-taken step.

Apparently familiarised to the noise himself, the dandy did not perceive that it attracted the attention of others as he moved along, catalogue in one hand, in the other the thin red-leather cord attached to a vixenish-looking toy terrier—an uncomfortable-looking little beast, that kept running between his legs or over the sweeping train of the elderly vinegary-featured lady by his side, winding the leather thong round the sound or else the cork leg, and once, in a rapid *pas*, securely binding the two; so that, what with his eyeglass, his catalogue, and the dog, the gentleman seemed to have his hands completely filled.

"What picture is that, Maximilian?" suddenly exclaimed the lady, in a tone that was as acid as her looks; and she stopped short, with her back to Charley and Ella, and by the help of a gold eyeglass inspected a painting.

There was no response; for the dog, the cork leg, and the thong, were in a state of tangle.

"Maximilian, I asked you the name of that picture!" cried the lady more shrilly.

"Bai Jove, there, don't be in such a hurry; don't you see what a confounded mess I'm in? There, now, hold Finette, while I look at the catalogue. Let me see, ah! yaas! Number 369. 'Dandy of the days of Charles II.' Bai Jove, ah! very fair indeed. Pity that style of dress don't come in again."

"Squea-eek, squea-eek, squea-eek" went the leg, as the admirers of the cavalier passed slowly on; while, as they mingled with the throng, a long pent-up breath escaped from Charley Vining's breast, and apparently greatly relieved, he exclaimed aloud:

"Poor devil!"

"Pray take me out, Charley," whispered Ella; and for the first time he noticed her pallor.

"Take you out? to be sure!" he cried, as he tenderly drew her hand farther through his arm. "Really, though, for a moment or two, I felt as if I could have wrung his neck."

"Charley, dear husband!" whispered Ella; for at that moment there was again the sound of the leg, and Charley's breast began to swell and his eyes to flash.

"All right, little one, take me away," he said, smiling; "for I feel like a big dog scenting a rat. But there, my own, I'm frightening you; come along."

He drew her rapidly away towards the entrance, her breath coming more freely at every step; but not so fast but that they caught another glimpse of the lady and gentleman, standing in rapt attention before a fresh picture, and at the same moment heard, in tones that seemed as if they were expressive of profound admiration:

"Bai Jove!"

But that was the last time they ever saw Max Bray.

Chapter Twenty Eight
Home

A week after, Charley and Ella were in the hall, and about to leave their house, when there was a summons at the door, and they retreated to the drawing-room.

"Mr and Mrs Hugh Lingon," announced the butler the next minute; and a fair fat young man entered, with a tall handsome lady, who threw back her mantle, and rushed at Ella, to clasp her in her arms, kissing and sobbing over her for a minute, before darting away, rushing at Charley Vining, throwing her arms round his neck, and kissing him with a loud smack.

"There! I forgot!" she exclaimed the next moment, half laughing, half crying; "but you won't mind, dear Hugh, it's only old Charley Vining, whom I've loved ever since I was a tiny girl. But my own dear, dear, darling Miss Bedford—for I can't ever call you anything else—I am so, so, so glad to see you again. And we were only married yesterday, and I wouldn't go anywhere else till Hugh brought me to see you both. And you will love me still, won't you?"

As she spoke she threw herself on the carpet at Ella's feet, clasping her round the waist, and nestling closely to her, and in spite of every effort, insisting upon staying there till they left.

There was no going out that day; for London ceremony had to be set aside for country hospitality, and it was late when the Lingons left, to start the next morning for Paris; as quaint, but as amiable and happy a couple as ever the sun shone upon.

But before leaving, heedless of his dark-veiled brow, Nelly Lingon told Charley that Max was married to "such an old screw-cum—a rich old dowager; while Laura"—and she spoke now sadly—"Laura ran off with a French count, when we were all at Baden; and I'm afraid he's a brute to her. But I'm sorry for Laura, Charley," said Nelly; "for, after her fashion, I think she loved you!"

How the years glide by! Blandfield again, with Charley Vining more portly and noble-looking than ever. It is a glorious sunshiny day, and in his broad hat and velvet coat he looks free, happy, and hearty, as he leads a little gem of an Exmoor pony in either hand, on one of which is a sturdy-looking curly-headed boy, shouting with glee, and drumming the pony's sides with his little heels; on the other, a sweet-faced girl a couple of years older, whose fair hair hangs down to the waist of her tiny riding-habit.

But we have not done. Standing by a chair, placed upon the lawn, her hand held by Sir Philip Vining, not looking a day older, but watching with a grandfather's fondness the children led round and round, is Ella—the same sweet-faced gentle Ella as of old, with the same glorious clusters and braids looped back from her pure white forehead. There is a glow, too, upon her countenance—it may be from pride, or merely that from the sun, as she holds a shade above her shapely head.

And there we leave her in her home of peace, rich in the love of her husband, her children, and that of her new parent, whose great delight upon one occasion it was to superintend the placing of Ella's portrait in the library, side by side with the picture upon which he loved to gaze.

"How well they match, Charley!" Sir Philip said. "It is like making my room complete—her face is so soft and gentle. It is a splendid likeness. God bless her! she makes glad my old age; and," he added, with a glance of his old pride, "she is by birth a lady!—"